MW00849124

Blind Date with a Book Nerd

The Bookish Romance Series

Book Two

by

Erica Dansereau
& Britt Howard

Copyright © 2024 by Erica Dansereau & Britt Howard

All rights reserved. No part of this publication may be reproduced, stored in a retrieval system, or transmitted in any form or by any means, including photocopying, recording, or other electronic or mechanical methods, including artificial intelligence or automated processes, without the prior written permission of the publisher, except for brief quotations in printed reviews.

Identifiers:
Library of Congress Control Number: 2024917055
ISBN: 979-8-9912652-0-1 (paperback)
ISBN: 979-8-9858237-9-0 (ebook)

This is a work of fiction. Any references to historical events, real people, real publications, or real places are used fictitiously. Other names, dialogue, characters, and events are products of the author's imagination. Any resemblance to actual persons, living or dead, is purely coincidental.

Cover design by Britt Howard

"Therefore if any man be in Christ, he is a new creature: old things are passed away; behold, all things are become new."
2 Corinthians 5:17

Authors' Note

Dear Reader,

In these pages we hope you find encouragement, are reminded of your worth, and that the messages of faith give you peace in your identity in Christ. As a warning, we'd like you to know that dysfunctional family relationships, divorce, and gaslighting are present in this book.

Love,
Britt and Erica

1

Ava

"Ava, didn't I already make myself clear? What are you doing over there?"

The stern voice snaps my attention away from the email thread displayed on my cell phone screen. Shock waves of guilt and embarrassment ricochet through my stomach. I stare with wide eyes at the woman who just walked through the doorway on the other side of the room. She is frowning at me with her hands perched on her hips. My brain blanks as I scramble for a reply.

I blurt out the first sentence that breaks through my foggy brain. "Definitely not doing anything but getting ready to celebrate you."

Charlie's frown cracks. A smile spreads across her lips, filling me with instant relief as she walks forward and peeks at the phone in my hand. "You're supposed to be relaxing this weekend, my friend," she says pointedly, one eyebrow arching, "not answering yet another of Kristi's frantic emails."

I've been caught. With a bashful blush, I tuck the phone away into the small silk purse on my wrist, mumbling a reply. "James Wolfe . . . manuscript . . . always wanting to change something . . ."

My ramble doesn't make any sense, but Charlie's melodic laugh echoes in the bridal suite. She leans toward the full-length mirror on the wall to swipe a rich plum shade over her lips. I catch the eye roll and the little shake of her head.

"Authors. Am I right?"

Despite my lingering embarrassment, this draws a chuckle out of me. Charlie Blaire is an author herself—a globally acclaimed one—and one of my dearest friends. We're getting ready to celebrate her rehearsal dinner before she marries one of my other best friends, Andrew Ketner, who also happens to be the co-owner of CityLight Press where I work.

I try to shake the stress off my shoulders as she flashes me a saucy wink. This is supposed to be a fun weekend, after all. I haven't taken a weekend off work in ages. "Authors," I repeat. "What a finicky bunch."

What I don't say is that my boss is also breathing down my neck, pressuring me to find a way to make James Wolfe happy or . . . I don't want to find out what will happen if Gary Ketner decides he is disappointed in my performance. My promotion to senior editor is still new, and I don't want to let my company down. But it's not in anyone's best interest to relay my concerns to Charlie at this moment, though, since this is her special weekend, *and* Gary is her future father-in-law.

She points the lipstick tube in my direction. Her long, dark hair drapes over one shoulder. "You know I appreciate your editing expertise more than anyone, but you aren't supposed to do anything work-related this weekend, Little-Miss-Always-Editing. One weekend off. Bride's orders."

Lora, a friend of Charlie's who flew in from Vermont today, peeks at the mirror and fluffs her fingers through her mahogany pixie cut. "That's a good point. What the bride says goes, Ava. It's her weekend after all. There was a delivery fiasco at my bookshop back home in Pleasant Hollow. This lady wouldn't even let me take the call." She drapes her arm affectionately around Charlie's shoulders and gives her a squeeze.

"Hey," Charlie protests, a hand on her hip again. "That's what assistants are for. You need to give yours the chance to handle Bluebird Books while you are gone. It's time for her to spread her business wings while you spread your vacation ones. Both of you."

She sends me a pointed look before slipping a fresh, soft pink rose behind her ear.

Piper, Charlie's cousin, swoops in from the en suite. "Ugh. Is work addiction a side effect of adulthood? You ladies do *not* make a girl look forward to graduating college. The last thing I want to do is live and breathe for a career." She flicks her curled, dark hair over her shoulder.

A slight frown crosses my face. "Some of us just really love what we do, and it makes the long hours and late nights a little easier."

I catch sight of Piper's exaggerated grimace in my direction. Charlie laughs at her younger cousin. The first time I met Piper, it was obvious the two were related. They both have the same fiery brown eyes, smooth, coffee-infused hair, short stature, and spunky personalities. A far cry from my five-ten frame, blonde locks that never want to be tamed, blue eyes, and (even I can admit) far too much of a workaholic demeanor.

With an inward sigh, I watch them banter with each other, wishing—not for the first time—that I didn't feel the weight of the world quite so strongly. Carefree, spontaneous, a youthful sparkle . . . Oh, to feel that way again . . . or ever.

"You know that saying about doing what you love and never having to work a day in your life?" I muse aloud again, attempting in vain to alleviate the knot in my stomach.

"You sure must love it a lot then. Enough to work when you're not even working. That or you don't know how to have a life outside of the office anymore." Piper smacks her bright red lips together and smiles at herself in the mirror, apparently not registering the subtle dig in her statement.

"Hey, I still know how to have fun," I protest.

"I can personally attest to this. Give this girl a mic on karaoke night, and she'll tear down the roof." Charlie nudges me with her elbow.

Piper looks me up and down. "Still, she's about three years away from becoming a crazy cat lady. I can tell."

Charlie catches my eye and winces. She smiles apologetically. "Bluntness runs in the family. She comes by it honestly."

I laugh lightly, trying not to dwell on Piper's words, and survey myself in the mirror one last time. Secretly, my fingers itch for my phone. The discomfort returns, worry that I'm leaving my assistant hanging warring with guilt for not

I catch Charlie's eye without meaning to and think of the many times she's encouraged me to put myself out there and give someone a chance. "Nope."

"Why not?" Piper demands.

"Guess I'm too busy being a boring adult." I give Piper a wink and follow Charlie toward the door.

We walk along the corridor together and head toward the grand staircase that descends to the foyer. The wedding coordinator has instructed us to meet the rest of the wedding party at the entrance. From there, we'll all proceed to the rehearsal site to run through the itinerary for tomorrow. The group of us are a noisy bunch, stilettos clicking obnoxiously against the hardwood floors of the historic estate which now serves as the most elegant and dreamy wedding venue I've ever seen.

Charlie lingers until I catch up. Her hand slips into mine, her voice only for my ears. "I wish you had someone here to keep you company this weekend."

I fold my free hand over hers and whisper, "I'm okay. I promise." Seven years. It's been this long. I'll make it through one more wedding. "This weekend is about you and Andrew."

She casts a thoughtful glance up at me. "Someday, it's going to be about you. I promise, Ava."

"Who are we all walking with again?" Lora asks, a few steps ahead of us. "Two bridesmaids have to double up with one groomsman, right? Because there's an odd number?"

"Yeah, Parker had to drop out last minute. Family emergency," Piper answers quickly before Charlie can speak, putting air quotes around the final two words.

"Peacefully welcoming one's first child into the world

hardly constitutes a family emergency," Charlie huffs, biting back a laugh at her cousin. "We're very happy for Parker. Fortunately, Andrew was able to fill that spot after all, so none of you have to double up walking down the aisle."

"Ouch, a second-string groomsman," Piper giggles. "Who's the fill-in?"

We reach the landing of the stairs and turn toward the foyer.

"An old friend of Andrew's," Charlie replies.

"Andrew has more than three friends?" I joke.

At the base of the staircase, the man himself waits, his face alight with the biggest, goofiest grin I've ever seen him wear. A few other people are milling about the foyer, but I can't take my eyes off the soon-to-be-newlyweds.

When we reach the bottom step, Charlie strides away from us, tucking herself into her groom's side, the two greeting each other with smiles full of love. The sight sparks something deep within the farthest recesses of my heart. It's a faint hope that maybe my love story will be written one day, too, despite everything I've convinced myself about love . . . or more so about my ability to be loved. But the usual doubts creep in quickly to crush the feeling.

After all, as I remind myself often, I edit love stories. I don't live them.

Feeling a familiar jolt of disappointment in my chest, I tear my eyes away from the bride and groom to gather my composure.

The fresh balminess of the warm spring evening drifts into the foyer. The glitter and hum of voices filter through the house. The massive, wooden front doors of the mansion are flung open. Gorgeous pots of white hydrangeas bloom fragrantly on either side of the doorway. I catch a whiff of their sweet honey perfume and want to melt. This weekend is going to be perfect.

A few people move about on the lawn just outside. Most of the guests will arrive tomorrow for the ceremony, but of the guests who were specially invited to attend the rehearsal, I see that everyone is dressed in their finest cocktail dresses and elegant suits.

This wedding is black tie only. It's obvious no expenses were spared. With Andrew's family coming from old money, I'm not surprised. His maternal grandfather was a terrifically wealthy man who went on to found CityLight Press.

I smooth down the skirt of my floor-length, dark green silk dress and feel myself slip into a familiar dysphoria as thoughts of my own family's ruin edge in.

It's been years since my family's fall from the upper echelons of East Coast society. Thanks to my job, I've done well for myself, but it's hard not to feel less than even after so much time.

Instinctively, I straighten my posture as the self-deprecating thoughts swirl in my stomach. Turning back toward the bride and groom to see if we are ready to head outside, I see they have moved away from the staircase and are talking to a man standing with his back to me.

Andrew is facing me, the grin still playing across his face. He glances away from the man and catches my eye. I smile, but his grin falters, uncertainty coming into his expression.

I've known Andrew for so long that I can read him like a book. Thinking he must be stuck talking to someone he'd rather not be, I take a few steps in his direction to rescue him, my stilettos clicking against the flooring. I study the trio.

Something suddenly nags at the back of my mind as the stranger's profile comes into view. Seeing Andrew's distracted gaze, the man turns in my direction, his face slowly revealing itself.

I'd love to blame the buckling of my knees and my subsequent hurtle toward the floor on an uneven patch in the hand-hewn wooden planks. I trip, and my pride hits the ground miles before my body. Someone's quick reflexes keep me from biffing it completely, grabbing my arm before I can land on the floor in the middle of the grand entrance. Looking up, I see the kindly face of my boss and Andrew's father, Gary Ketner. He pulls me upright and pats my forearm.

A hot flush crawls across my skin.

"I've got you, dear," he says in a fatherly tone. Like a mortified, fumbling-to-find-my-footing idiot, I clutch onto his arm.

Charlie rushes toward me, and I'm acutely aware of the men following in her wake.

"And I thought I was the klutz," Charlie calls out teasingly.

I try to smile and tug at the bodice of my dress, which suddenly feels far too tight and far too revealing as the warm evening air brushes across my skin. "Don't worry," I reply with a breeziness I do not feel, "you still are."

"Are you alright, Ava?" Andrew's voice is laced with concern, but I don't think it's because of my near tumble.

I stare at him, purposely avoiding any eye contact with the man now lingering just behind him.

An unspoken apology covers Andrew's face. My heart clutches because I know what he is thinking. I want to tell him he has no reason to feel bad for inviting whoever he wants to his wedding.

Instead of sinking into the floor in a puddle of humiliation, I plaster a smile onto my face and say cheerfully, "Of course. Your dad is a lifesaver."

I pat Gary's arm, and he releases me.

Andrew awkwardly steps to the side and gestures to his guest. I don't have to be told that this is the mysterious fill-in groomsman. "Um, you remember . . ."

"Hi, Ava." The man speaks for the first time. His hazel eyes lock with mine, the smoldering intensity of his gaze unmistakable behind the sophisticated frames of the glasses he has always worn.

Dawson Hayes.

My breath hitches at the sound of his voice wrapped around my name.

Suddenly, Piper is at my side. Leave it to her to zero in on a potentially juicy moment. "Wait, do you two already know each other?"

She looks between us and brightens as though this is the best possible news. Little does she know, my world is crashing down around me.

I tune out Piper's chattering and force myself to meet Dawson's questioning gaze without faltering. His soft, dark curls are tame compared to how I remember them looking. He has styled them tonight in a swoopy, old Hollywood sort of way. Freshly shaven, the spicy tobacco scent of his aftershave drifts to me in the soft breeze, more intense and potent than any blooms in the flower-filled foyer. The muscles across his shoulders and chest look firm, filling out the expensive suit he is wearing. Since he is only an inch or so taller than me, we're at eye level as we face off in a silent conversation while the rest of the wedding party chatters around us.

I finally find my voice. "Hi . . . Dawson." The greeting comes out in a tremble, but it's all I can muster without spontaneously combusting.

When I speak, he takes a step closer and opens his mouth, but just then, the wedding coordinator claps her hands and commands us into a line. I force myself to turn away and listen to her. We follow her instructions as she leads us through the historic Halloway Estate toward the gardens at the back of the mansion. Halloway Estate is a countryside manor perched on acres of sprawling grass and hills in upstate New York. The property's owners converted the estate into a golf course and event venue some years ago. Since Charlie is from a small town in Vermont, the woodsy but elegant venue was her choice.

I force myself to put one foot in front of the other, refusing to lose my footing again. We emerge on the sprawling terrace and follow the coordinator down the brick steps to the main lawn where tomorrow's ceremony will take place. She promptly puts us all into position, a clipboard and pen in her hand.

"Lora?" she asks.

Lora holds up a hand and steps forward.

"You're walking down with"—she checks the clipboard—"Dawson."

Immediate relief washes over me, even as my heart twinges painfully. I watch Dawson and Lora meet in the middle. This twist in events churns over and over in my mind as they take their position.

I'd be lying if I didn't admit the thought that he might attend the wedding crossed my mind the instant Charlie and Andrew announced their engagement. I assumed Andrew and Dawson have kept in touch over the years. After all, our group was close friends during college.

But the last I knew of his whereabouts, Dawson was still living in London. When Charlie showed me the wedding guest RSVP list a couple of months ago, he wasn't there. I know that for a fact because I triple-checked just to be sure. Did he fly all this way to be here tonight on a day's notice?

The question floats suspended in my brain. *Why is he here? Why is he here?*

Lucinda, the coordinator, chirps orders, directing everyone to where she wants them to stand. I can't help but steal glances at Andrew, hoping to capture his attention long enough for an explanation so I can take a deep breath again. But his focus is fixed on Lucinda. The only time he looks away is to sneak a glance at his beaming bride.

"Ava and Justin, you're next," Lucinda calls.

I step into place beside Andrew's cousin, trying to smile. Justin has been at several Ketner family get-togethers over the last few years.

He grins back at me. His blond, cropped hair catches the light. Charlie confided once that Justin has a crush on me, so I'm cautious as I return his smile, thinking it is no doubt why they've paired us together for the wedding. Andrew has hinted several times at trying to set me up with him.

I've had to remind them time and time again: Ava Fox doesn't date.

My willingly single status seems to confuse the blissfully in-love couple.

Justin leans over me, his voice husky and low. "You look lovely tonight, Ava. Love the hair."

With the briefest flicker, my eyes dart to the broad pair of shoulders just a few steps ahead. It might be my imagination, but it seems as if his head is turned slightly in our direction.

Did Dawson overhear Justin's compliment? Does he even care if a man flirts with me?

My heart kicks in my chest. *Do . . . I?*

"Thank you," I say in response to Justin and absentmindedly run a hand over the ponytail braid that swings behind me.

"I can't wait to dance with you tomorrow at the reception." Justin isn't finished.

Rather than reply, I pull my shoulders back, attempting to look more confident than I feel, and focus intently on Lucinda's instructions.

Piper, as Charlie's maid of honor, lines up behind me. She is paired with Bryant, another of Andrew's cousins and his best man. Once we're all lined up, Lucinda gives us a rundown of how the ceremony is projected to go. She gives us individual directions so we stay on cue. Most of the rehearsal goes without a hitch. Immediately after completing a couple of practice runs, our group is led from the lawn back into the mansion's opulent dining hall for dinner.

If Dawson looks my way, he does it discreetly.

Just before we enter the house, Andrew catches me by the arm and holds me back. Charlie, glued to his side, gives him a curious look. I stare up at him, hoping my discomfort isn't written across my face.

Andrew is apologetic. "I realize now I probably should

have warned you that Dawson was stepping in for Parker. It was so last minute. I know this is probably really awkward for you."

"Oh. It's . . . it's okay." I wave him off, mortified at the thought of ruining his and Charlie's special night. "Don't be concerned about me. It's your wedding party. I think it's great he came back home to support you this weekend."

Charlie's eyes widen. Gently, she lays her hand on Andrew's forearm and leans closer to me with a conspiratorial look in her bright eyes. "Wait, is there something between you and Dawson?"

My throat feels thick, and I have to choke out the words. "Um . . . he and I dated in college. It was a long time ago."

Charlie's eyes widen. "You and Dawson used to date? Why didn't I know this?" Her hiss is directed toward Andrew. "I thought he was just the nerdy overseas friend you play video games with and randomly FaceTime."

My mind goes into overdrive. So then, he does still live in London.

Andrew sighs, rubbing the bridge of his nose. "I invited Dawson to the wedding when our invitations first went out. Truthfully, he wasn't sure he'd even be able to attend, so he didn't send the RSVP. He has been based out of London for years and travels a lot in Europe for the software development firm he works for. But he just became a partner and . . ." Andrew opens his eyes and looks at me. "Recently, he moved back to The City permanently. When Cassie had her baby and Parker couldn't make it, it was an easy choice to call him and ask him to step in as a groomsman." He sighs. "So that's why he's . . ."

"Here." Finally, I manage to get my throat to swallow.

"I promise I wasn't trying to ambush you, Ava," Andrew reassures me.

I'm waving him away as though the thought didn't even cross my mind when someone clinks a fork against a glass in the dining hall. We walk into the mansion.

"I just wanted to check on you," Andrew's voice lowers. "I didn't know what terms you two were on these days." At the end, his voice lifts as if asking me to fill him in so he doesn't have to ask the uncomfortable questions outright.

My smile is tight.

"When was the last time you spoke?" Charlie whispers as we enter the dining hall together.

My eyes dart briefly to her, then back to Andrew before I answer. "Right before I broke his heart."

2

Dawson

I honored her request for privacy all these years, but tonight, I'll allow myself just one hour to catch up on the life of Ava Fox. Though sorely tempted, I refrained from keeping tabs on her social media after our breakup. She said it would be too weird to know I was watching, so I didn't.

I stare at the screen of my brightly lit cell phone. One tap and her profile is displayed before me. Her follower count is impressive, well into the triple digits. It's obvious that her love of books still runs deep, as they are the main feature of her page, which makes sense since the other focus of the page is her role as an editor for CityLight Press.

It would seem Ava Fox has done very well for herself.

And she is just as beautiful as the last day I saw her seven years ago. Memories flood into my brain, feelings that have never really gone away resurfacing quickly as each moment of the night plays over and over.

I came back to my room only a few minutes ago. Standing on the balcony that overlooks the green lawn where, tomorrow, Andrew and Charlie will exchange vows to unite their lives forever, I study the photos and videos on Ava's page, scrolling through each one by one.

With my skills, it would have been easy for me to follow every detail of her life online, but this is the first time I've let myself search for her. I kept my word to myself. I let her go, at least externally, even if I could never quite get her out of my head or my heart.

Not to pretend I haven't been tempted to quickly scan her social media or check the internet to see if her name pops up anywhere. London is far, but not far enough away that I could forget her. I know she isn't married—Andrew would have told me. I just want to know . . . Is she happy? Does she wish we'd made different choices?

Well, her choices, really—not mine.

I loosen the tie knotted around my neck and shrug off my jacket, tossing it on a nearby chair. Though I wish I could have avoided getting involved in this wedding, I'm happy for Andrew. We've stayed close throughout the years despite the distance.

When the invitation to his wedding arrived, I was torn. I was still living in London then, so sending my regrets wasn't a big deal. Moving back to my home state of New York wasn't planned. But the opportunity to take over the stateside offices of the software and app development firm I'm now a junior partner in was too good to pass up.

In the States again, there wasn't much reason to avoid my college roommate's wedding. I planned to skip the reception and only attend the ceremony. I was going to slip in late and get lost in the crowd. There was far less chance of Ava spotting me if I could fade into the scenery.

But when Andrew called me just a day ago, hoping I could stand in for the groomsman whose wife was delivering their baby a couple of weeks early, I couldn't refuse. We've been friends for far too long for me to let him down on a day like this.

So now, here I am, at this luxurious upstate venue, both dreading tomorrow and wishing it was already here. For the first time since our breakup, Ava and I are under the same roof. The bridesmaids are all in the east wing, the groomsmen in the west. I don't know how I'm going to hold it together when she refuses to look at me again tomorrow.

I snuck glances at her all night and never caught her looking in my direction.

My phone is still clenched in my hand as the moon hangs in the balmy night sky. I study the selfie she posted four hours ago. The dark green silk of her dress shimmered as she took Justin's arm for the rehearsal ceremony tonight. At least they didn't pair me up to walk down the aisle with her. That would have added insult to injury for both of us. I couldn't do that to Ava.

When she first saw me tonight, my presence caught her off guard, and she'd almost stumbled before Gary Ketner caught her. I saw her tremble, and then she pulled herself together in that characteristic, picture-perfect, unphased-by-anything, Ava-Fox-way she always had.

Later, her blonde braid had swished over her shoulder when she turned away from me, gold and diamond earrings sparkling on her pretty ears. On the soft evening breeze, I'd caught the scent of that floral perfume she always used to wear.

Occasionally, it used to be hard to get a read on what she was thinking, even when life was easy and our relationship lighthearted. Some things never change.

Andrew's cousin, Justin, had the nerve to flirt with her the entire rehearsal. I just had to stand by and listen.

I push my glasses back up on my nose and run my hand through my hair. It's already reverting to its usual messy look now that I'm alone in the room for the night.

As I continue to scroll through Ava's social media, I'm fascinated by the depiction of her life on a screen. I can see why she has earned so many followers. Her photos and videos are bright and carefree, full of picturesque city scenes and quaint coffee shops and flowers and art museums and books. Always books. Her love for them runs deep and strong, something we had in common, though our taste in books couldn't have been more different. But books were her life and still seem to be.

I want her to be happy so badly it hurts.

I've wondered if she was happy so many times.

She's living what looks like the perfect life. The sight of it makes a spot deep in my chest ache.

Frustrated, I turn away from the moonlit sky and head back into the empty room. Moonlight is for people in love. I may only be a tech nerd whose record for finding love is crash-and-burn, but I'm romantic enough to know that.

I'm also pushing thirty-two and still single. Women always talk about the urge to settle down, but men experience it too. No one wants to come home to a lonely apartment night after night, wake in an empty bed, and drink coffee in deafening silence morning after morning.

Why can't I experience even a fraction of the good

fortune of my old buddy, Andrew Ketner? Everyone is buzzing about his and Charlie's love story—apparently, Andrew had discovered her talented writing abilities when a novel she submitted to CityLight Press, his family's publishing house, landed on his radar. There was some mix-up about a pen name and a television interview that went viral, but I am hazy about the rest of the story.

All I know is that the woman I once planned to marry is sleeping peacefully under this roof, and I can't do a single thing to make her mine. The only thing that would bring us together again is a miracle from heaven itself.

For the past seven years, I've wondered if we would ever have a second chance. Year after year, that hope died a little more.

I returned to New York a different man. Moving overseas for the better part of a decade changed me. I'm not the awkward, quiet, computer programming nerd I was when I left. London was good for me. Physically, mentally, spiritually, and financially. As the firm's youngest partner, I'm no longer the poor college kid on a scholarship to Columbia University. Hours in the gym have made me lean and toned. A year or so ago, I hired a personal stylist, and I've banished my preferred faded jeans and old t-shirts to the back of the closet in favor of polos and expensive button-downs. Style over comfort these days. However, despite the changes, I couldn't give up my signature glasses for contacts.

Though I may now look like I belong on the Upper East Side, my self-doubt always wonders if it will ever be enough.

"I'm frustrated, Lord," I mutter into the quiet room, my warring emotions pushing me to prayer. "I don't want to get caught up in these memories. I've tried to forget her, but somehow . . . she's stuck in my heart. Help me to get her out, or give her . . ."

My finger hits the phone screen at random, and I freeze. I stare at my phone in horror as the tiny heart on Ava's latest post displays a sudden brilliant red.

"No, no, no! Don't do this to me now."

With frantic urgency, I hastily unlike the post and cringe. All I can hope is that she isn't online at this exact moment to see my embarrassing misstep. Thoroughly done with technology for the night, I walk toward the nightstand, intending to put my phone away before I can humiliate myself further.

But the phone vibrates in my hand with an incoming call before I can set it down. The number belongs to a programmer who is helping me to write code for a software project.

I hold it to my ear. "You're calling late."

"Sorry to interrupt your weekend away, boss. Do you have a minute to go over the app revisions?" Cole replies.

I picture him sitting in front of the trio of screens on his desk with thousands of lines of computer code displayed across them. I know what his setup looks like because mine back home looks the same. Cole is one of the leads on the team I manage at my software firm, but tonight, he is freelancing on a personal project for me. I told him not to hesitate to call if he ran into any snags.

I stride over to the vintage walnut rollup desk in the corner of the room, where my laptop sits open. It comes to life when I touch the mousepad.

"Hold on. Give me a second to get logged in." I tap the speaker function and set the phone on the desk as I pull up the chair. My fingers fly across the keys, and a shared project workspace appears on the screen. My mind calms as I focus on the familiar lines of code, their language unfurling clearly before me. Once we get started, I know it will be a late night, but that doesn't bother me. This is my world, and I'm more comfortable analyzing the programming language spoken here than being anywhere else.

The project we're working on is near and dear to me. It's one I've been dreaming up for a half dozen years. With my promotion, I finally have the funding to see it to fruition, and it's set to launch within the next few months.

"Okay. I'm in. Walk me through it."

—

I descend the grand staircase and walk across the foyer toward the breakfast room. It's still early morning. The estate is noticeably quiet, only the staff moving about, the sunlight soft and muted. Cole and I worked until the wee hours of the morning, touching up various lines of code on the app I am getting ready to launch, but I didn't allow myself to sleep in.

Instead, I was up with the dawn, sneakers on and out the door for a run before anyone else stirred. Running is a habit I picked up in London when I felt homesick and stir-crazy. I've jogged or hit the gym almost every day since.

Now, the scent of coffee and bacon pulls me toward the breakfast room. I plan to grab my meal and get the heck out of Dodge before the bridesmaids descend. Or, more specifically, one bridesmaid. I'd welcome the chance to catch up with Andrew and get to know Charlie better.

Today will go one of two ways, and neither is an outcome I would pick if I had a choice. My only hope for the day is to cause as little awkwardness as possible. I'm a systems guy.

Surely, I can figure out how to enjoy my friend's wedding without traumatizing Ava unnecessarily.

I can either avoid Ava today and give her space or try to act as if she is just any other member of the wedding party by striking up a casual conversation. Nothing too intense. No pressure. Just, *"Hey, Ava. How are you? You're looking well. Care to stop avoiding me and acting like I'm Frankenstein's monster?"*

Light conversation.

Considering how she avoided eye contact with me last night at the rehearsal dinner, I suspect she'd prefer the first option.

I felt guilty for sitting with the wedding party at all. Ava didn't have to say how she felt. Her posture stayed rigid and taut, and every time she could, she moved to mingle on the other side of the room and kept herself out of my line of access for the rest of the night.

Now, I wonder if I should have reached out before this weekend. Should I have disclosed that I moved back to NYC four weeks ago?

My steps are light and nearly silent as I enter the bright and spacious breakfast room, lost in thought. I turn the corner and, too late, notice a cascading waterfall of wavy blonde hair in front of me.

Sensing my entrance, Ava swings away from the fruit trays spread across the buffet, her movements sharp and clumsy. The bowl in her hand tilts toward the floor. Her shoulders cave in, and she seems to shrink a little. I freeze as our eyes connect.

Even across the room, her crystalline blue irises take my breath away. In the soft light of morning, I marvel at her.

Seven years has done nothing to diminish her beauty. Creamy skin, fluffy hair that begs to be touched, and features at once soft and memorable. She's dressed in athletic wear, and the faint sheen of sweat on her skin suggests she just came up from the gym on the lower levels of the mansion. I try to look away but can't.

"I'm sorry." I finally manage to croak out a few words. "I didn't realize anyone would be in here this early. I'll go and leave you alone to finish your meal."

Her posture straightens immediately, and she rights the tilting bowl. Her voice is smooth and serene as she gestures grandly around the room. "Absolutely not. You have just as much right to be here as I do. I'll be out of your hair in a moment."

I stare at her shapely shoulders as she turns away and picks up a piece of pineapple from a tray. We may have dated for two years in graduate school, but parts of Ava were always a mystery to me. Maybe that's because she experienced a very different upbringing than me. Her dad is a wealthy businessman, and she enjoyed all the luxuries life could offer a young woman growing up on the upper crust of New York City society: private school, a master's at Columbia, a brownstone on the Upper West Side.

Once, we became best friends, though now that years apart stretch between us, I can see that she kept aspects of herself hidden from me.

I study her for a moment. Her persona is simultaneously troubled and unbothered, lost and sophisticated at the same time. She's as cool as a cucumber, yet there's something more I can sense in this mature version of her. Something . . . wounded.

Trying to pretend this isn't the most awkward moment in the history of all moments, I amble to the buffet and grab a plate. "Fruit and yogurt for breakfast still, huh?"

She casts a glance in my direction. "Old habits die hard, I guess."

It's hard to suppress the urge to strike up a conversation with her. We used to tell each other everything. Or, at least, I thought we did. Obviously, there must have been some things she never shared, like why she broke up with me. It's been years, but when I sneak a look at her now as she sprinkles a spoonful of granola over her bowl, it feels like we just parted ways yesterday.

Despite the years between us, there is a comforting familiarity in the way she walks, talks, and moves. I have to remind myself that Ava is essentially a stranger now.

She drizzles a spoonful of honey over the mixture in her bowl and turns to leave. With a clatter, I throw the plate back on the stack, desperate to get my apology out there. Taking a big sidestep toward her, I reach for her, the tips of my fingers barely brushing the sleeve of her shirt. She spins around and stares at me.

She's so beautiful that my heart aches.

Everything I want to say flies out of my head. I force my vocal cords to hum out something that sounds like words. "Um, Ava—" I begin.

"Let's not do this, Dawson," she interrupts. Her palm rises, facing out in a signal for me to stop. "We don't have to pretend . . ."

I shake my head, wondering what she thought I was about to say. "I just want to say I'm sorry. I should have warned you before I just showed up this weekend."

The reflection in her eyes is sad, but the smile painted across her full lips is polite. "You don't owe me anything. Andrew is your friend, and I'm a big girl. I don't need you to try to protect me from a little awkwardness."

It feels like a lot of awkwardness, but that's just me.

"I don't want things to be strained between us, though." I clear my throat.

"And why should they be?" she replies with a shake of her wavy hair. "We're adults. I intend to have a perfectly lovely weekend, and I hope you do the same. Let's set aside the past."

Her tone and her words say she is being both generous and gracious, but I'm not satisfied.

I lean toward her as if we are conspiring together. "So, we agree to not act standoffish and stiff around each other?" I pause, fixing my gaze on her. "Like you're acting now."

The apples of her cheeks flush ever so slightly. I've called her out. "Of course." She waves her empty hand. "We'll just act like a couple of old friends reunited for the weekend to celebrate the happy couple. That's the least we can do for Charlie and Andrew."

"So, friends, then?" I extend my hand toward her.

Her gaze shifts. She hesitates for a moment, staring at me with a crease between her eyebrows. Finally, she extends her free hand. The touch of her soft, delicate palm connecting with mine after so many years startles me, but I quickly recover. We shake, and she drops my hand immediately.

"Friends," she says sweetly. She moves away and disappears through the doorway before I can get out another word.

3

Ava

If only I could sink into my thoughts and find a quiet moment to dissect every detail of my encounter with Dawson this morning.

The chatter of the bridal party pulls me in and out of my rumination as I try to stay present and enjoy Charlie's special moment.

I figured I'd be alone when I went down to breakfast so early. I overheard the groomsmen talking about sleeping in and hitting the course for a nine-hole round of golf mid-morning. The girls had to wake up early for hair and makeup before the photographer arrived, but I was up before anyone else, planning to get in a workout and catch up on emails before the festivities began. Or I thought I would be the first. Of course, as fate would have it, my solitude in the dining room was interrupted by the man already responsible for derailing my entire heart this weekend.

It seems that Dawson has only gotten better in the last handful of years. I can't help but wonder if that's because he has been away from me.

He looks incredible, muscular, and fit, with maturity filling out his frame. His dark locks are still curly and doing that thing where an unruly piece swoops down over his glasses, and he has to keep pushing his hand through his hair to fix it. And those glasses. They always made my heart skip a beat before, and the sight of his eyes studying me from behind their frames made my nerves flutter yesterday too.

Adorkable.

The man is positively adorkable. There's no other way to describe his special brand of handsome. For my own sake, I hope he wears contacts for the rest of the day because the sight of Dawson in those frames again could make my heart burst.

His presence is like a hug that might kill me with its overpowering warmth. It gives me a peaceful thrill of coming home and is a reminder of my biggest regret all at once.

Because I do regret breaking up with him. I regretted it the second I mailed the letter, but at the time, I was just coming to terms with my parents' fresh divorce and the extra weight of responsibility for Mom that subsequently fell on me. Her mood swings and emotional manipulation were crushing me. I didn't think there was another option. I wish I'd left all this behind and flown to London that summer.

I'm the first bridesmaid to finish makeup and hair. The stylist has swept my hair into a chic updo. Curls frame my face. Careful not to mess it up, I wriggle into the olive-green dress Charlie chose for us. I'll keep my heels off until it is time to walk out the door.

With the other ladies still occupied, I slip barefoot down the hall and onto a balcony, hoping the fresh air and time alone will steady my thoughts and prepare my heart for the rest of the night. The grounds below are set up perfectly for the impending ceremony, pampas grass swaying at the end of each row of seats in the ever-so-soft spring breeze. White chairs are set up and adorned with dusty pink ribbons across the back, and a hand-carved wooden arbor wrapped in flowers is set up at the altar overlooking the woodsy view.

My heart longs for a quiet place to pray as frustration and guilt war within my chest. I haven't been able to get our conversation out of my mind since this morning. I don't think I handled the encounter with the grace I wish I'd been able to muster. I never apologized for the way I ended things between us. The guilt has gnawed at me every day since, but after our private conversation, my regret has intensified tenfold. The look in Dawson's eyes as I hurried away has haunted me all day.

"Lord," I begin. My whisper gets lost in the breeze, and I close my eyes. "I'm sorry for the way I hurt Dawson in the past. Please help him to forgive me. I know I lost the right to his goodwill a long time ago, but seeing him again is stirring up feelings I know I can't have. I don't want to get hung up on him again, Lord."

My voice falters. "And please help me to focus on making this day special for Charlie and Andrew. I want to glorify You and the beauty of their connection. Not think about all the reasons a relationship and marriage aren't right for me."

The prayer hurts to say out loud. I feel my heart prick

instructs us to descend the grand staircase to the foyer.

The groomsmen are already congregated downstairs. Like a moth drawn to a flame, my eyes find Dawson immediately. He is still wearing those irresistible glasses, and I see that he is looking toward me with an unreadable expression on his face. I have to force my gaze away so it doesn't seem like I'm staring. A flush heats my skin.

Gary Ketner comes forward and extends his arm to his soon-to-be daughter-in-law.

"Careful, Mr. Ketner. She's blazing hot, and you might get burned," Piper quips as she waltzes ahead, taking no time to find the best man and claim Bryant's arm for herself.

Gary only laughs and floods Charlie with well-deserved compliments. Justin's heavy gaze sears my skin like a beacon from across the room. I pretend not to notice his approach, my heels carrying me hastily (though carefully, so I don't trip again) away toward the nearby French doors that look over the lawn. The chairs are full, the final few guests finding their spots.

I catch sight of Andrew standing at the altar, patiently waiting alongside our pastor.

Grinning, I look over my shoulder and catch Charlie's attention. "He's ready for you."

She squeals and rushes to join me. Her eyes find her groom, their depths gleaming with joy. I grab one of her shaking hands and give it a squeeze.

"Are you nervous?"

Her laugh is airy and light. "Nervous about walking down the aisle in front of all those people? Yes. Marrying Andrew? Not one bit."

"You hear that?" I say to Gary, who lingers a few feet

away. "Make sure to keep her upright."

"Not to worry," he replies with a laugh. "Andrew has already warned me of as much."

Charlie's mouth falls open. "Did he really?"

"He said something about a fountain and *The Little Mermaid*. I didn't quite understand." He waves his hand through the air as though the details are unimportant.

Lucinda barks at us to line up. She disappears to check on another ceremony detail. I feel a tap on my shoulder. My stomach leaps with hope and dread as I turn. Hopefully, the disappointment on my face isn't evident when I see Justin offering me his arm.

"My lady," he says in his best British accent.

Not your lady, I think to myself, cheeks burning. I take his arm, involuntarily glancing up and catching Dawson's eye.

He peers at me curiously from behind those infuriatingly cute glasses.

Stop it with the attraction, Ava. You had your chance, and it was a very long time ago.

Feeling a rush of emotion come over me, I offer him a smile. It's a peace treaty of sorts, an *I'm-sorry-this-is-awkward-and-I-broke-your-heart-and-you're-so-cute-right-now-I-could-cry* sort of smile. To my relief, Dawson sends me a tight-lipped one in return before offering his arm to Lora and turning away.

My gut sinks. It's all I can do not to stare at the back of his head as Justin and I line up behind them. Piper begins humming the bridal entrance song behind me, and, for once, I appreciate the distraction. It gives me something to be annoyed at rather than staring in hopeless regret at the handsome backside of Dawson's head as we proceed down the aisle.

Andrew and Charlie's ceremony is the most beautiful ceremony I've ever witnessed. Watching them pledge their love to each other is equal parts inspiring and painful. I don't think I've ever known two people who love each other more.

Emotion clutches my throat. The truth is, while I may long for what they have, I don't see such a love story in my own future. Some people are too broken and dysfunctional for love, and I am self-aware enough to recognize my own weaknesses.

After our pastor declares them husband and wife and the bride and groom share the sweetest kiss, the entire wedding party is directed aside for photographs with the family as the guests make their way toward the reception tent. It's a beautiful evening, and a sprawling white tent has been set up on the lawn. It sparkles, strung with twinkling lights, a dance floor set up in the middle.

I try to focus on enjoying the moment and smiling prettily for the camera rather than on Dawson's presence as we all pose together.

By the time we finish taking photographs, my feet are aching, and my stomach is growling. Leaving the bride and groom behind to finish the photo shoot, everyone else heads for the tent.

I trail behind Dawson and Bryant, my heels already off and in my hand. The soft grass is cool and soothing under my feet. We walk under a few trees. A minute later, I glance up and, to my horror, notice a spider the size of a nickel crawling slowly across Dawson's back. My stomach tightens.

The Dawson I used to know was a talented and funny

individual. One thing he was not: comfortable with eight-legged creatures. Spider wrangler was definitely not a skill on his resume. I've never met a man more afraid of spiders.

A mix of alarm and amusement rises in my belly. My mind darts through all the possible scenarios. Do I tell him it's there? No. That would only make it worse. He might burn the whole property to the ground.

Eyeing the heels in my hands, I know what I have to do. I clear my throat loud enough to get their attention. Dawson and Bryant slow their pace and glance over their shoulders.

"Uh, Dawson, can you hold on a second?"

He turns to face me, and my heart clenches at the eager expression that instantly crosses his face.

"I think someone must have gotten a little dirt across your back." I grab him by the shoulders and spin him away from me, spotting the little menace running quickly toward his shoulder now. Just as I raise a heel to squash it, Dawson freaks out.

"Is it a spider?" He shimmies away from me, twisting his body and arching to look backward over his shoulder, a mix of half-yells and grunts escaping his mouth as he flails the tails of his tuxedo jacket in the air.

I do my best to remain calm. "If you'll hold still, I'll—"

But it's too late. The jacket is off, tossed on the grass, and he's officially wigging out. I pick it up and give it a firm shake. The spider drops on the lawn and scurries away.

"It's gone!" I call, keeping my voice steady and cheerful.

Dawson is still doing the arachnophobia body roll. A few guests notice and rise from their seats at the tables scattered under the tent. A few others come to the edges and watch us.

"Daws!" I shout. "It's gone!"

He freezes in the middle of an arm shake. His brow lifts suspiciously. "Are you sure?"

"Yes, I promise."

"You're not just saying that to make me feel better?" he demands.

"If it will stop whatever *that* was, then lie, Ava, lie," Bryant sputters through a laugh. "You're that afraid of spiders, bro?"

I throw him a dirty look. Dawson grimaces. Bryant only shakes his head and continues alone toward the tent. Dawson turns back to look at me, his eyebrows still raised in question.

"Triple prom," I reassure him.

It's only when I replay my words back in my head that I realize what I've just said. His face dissolves instantly into a real smile. I should retract it and apologize for using the silly little phrase we used to say to each other back when we were in love, but his grin keeps me from doing so.

"Here," I say, holding out his jacket. "Spider free."

"Thanks," he says and drapes it over his arm. He rakes a hand through his hair, messy from his freak-out session, and exhales sharply.

"Some things never change, huh?" I can't help saying it.

He laughs and winces. "Sorry for embarrassing you. It appears you're still foolishly unafraid of creepy beasts."

My eyebrows shoot up, and I prepare to protest, but suddenly, I feel someone appear beside me.

Justin.

Speaking of creepy beasts. I shake the thought away and scold myself inwardly for being rude, even if it is only in my own head. Justin isn't creepy. That isn't fair at all to think. In fact, he's a nice, solid guy. But he's just . . . not Dawson.

No one has ever come close to replicating the unique charm of Dawson Hayes.

At Justin's appearance, Dawson turns away and heads for the tent, calling over his shoulder, "Thanks again for your irrational ease with arachnids."

"Anytime," I murmur. I fall into step with Justin.

He tries to start a conversation, but I'm only vaguely aware of it, my mind racing a mile a minute. Did I really just use mine and Dawson's old promise? *Triple prom.* The words thunder in my head. I haven't thought of that silly phrase in years, and yet it slipped out so easily . . .

Justin and I step into the tent. Well-dressed guests mill about, drinks or appetizers in hand. The band is playing a lively dance tune in the corner. I hear the man beside me ask, "So, what do you say?"

I glance back at him. "I'm sorry. What do I say about what?"

He swallows, his Adam's apple bobbing up and down. "I was just thinking that maybe I could take you out next weekend if you aren't too busy." His blue eyes are pleading and earnest.

I offer a smile. "That's really sweet, but—"

"I know, I know," he interrupts. "Ava Fox doesn't date. I've heard the spiel. But surely, one date couldn't hurt that much?"

Dawson hasn't made it that far into the tent. He lingers at a nearby table, and I'm acutely aware of his proximity. I see him lift a flute of champagne to his lips. He has left his jacket off. The white shirt underneath is unbuttoned slightly, and his bowtie is undone. My cheeks flush as I try to think of an excuse for Justin's question.

Someone nudges me in the ribs. "If you don't say yes, then I will for you."

Piper appears next to me. The urge to hug her for interrupting this awkward moment is overwhelming. I grip her tanned arm and grin.

"Justin, you know my good, gorgeous, *single* friend, Piper, don't you?"

She giggles, and Justin looks pained, but I whisk myself away from the pair and make a beeline for Lora, who is standing at the refreshment table.

4

Dawson

"Triple prom."

The words from long ago echo in the air, sparking an emotion I can't quite name.

When Justin approaches Ava, I see the eager expression on his face. I walk away so I don't make more of a fool of myself than I already have. Jumping around like a maniac just because a spider was in my vicinity was not the impression I hoped to make tonight.

It only took having a mild panic attack, and Ava was right by my side.

"At least she's talking to me now," I mutter as I walk toward the glittering reception tent. Music drifts out merrily onto the lawn. The creep of phantom spider legs across my neck makes me reach up again to dash the sensation away. "Ava to the rescue. Smooth move, Daws."

Daws. Her nickname for me echoes painfully in the air. I need some refreshment and a few deep breaths to center my irritated emotions. I weave through the gathered wedding guests, guessing that everyone is having a better time than me as I dodge groups of laughing, well-dressed people who snack enthusiastically on the hors d'oeuvres carried around on trays by the waitstaff.

My appetite hasn't quite recovered since my breakfast encounter with Ava, but a cold drink is much needed at the moment.

The worst part of the last five minutes wasn't the spider. It was Justin swooping in yet again to steal away my girl.

Except, she's not your girl. My ever-present sense of logic cruelly reminds me of this fact. *She didn't want you seven years ago. You can't just ride into town and think she's going to fall into your arms the first time she sees you again.*

I tell myself that I have got to stop thinking this wedding is my second chance with her. It never was. I'm a stand-in for a groomsman who couldn't make it. The look of pity in Ava's eyes as I flailed like a madman to rid myself of a tiny eight-legged creature is going to be burned into my brain for a long time.

The only reason I'm here is to celebrate my friend's marriage to his bride. I have to admit, it was a beautiful ceremony. I've seen a lot of marriages begin and fail. This one—as I listened to the words the bride and groom exchanged in the presence of all their witnesses—felt founded on something more than physical attraction alone.

Love. Trust. Commitment. Sacrifice.

Easy to claim. Hard to find.

I make a beeline for the refreshment table and accept a chilled glass from the young woman behind it. A smile flashes across her face as my fingertips momentarily brush hers.

"Bride or groom?" she asks.

"Huh?" I'm lost in thought and don't comprehend her question at first. "What's that?"

"Are you here for the bride or the groom?" she repeats.

Her eyes dance, and I realize how pretty she is all at once. Instantly, the bowtie at my neck feels like it's about to strangle me. I reach up and tug it loose.

"Oh. Old friend of the groom's from way, way, *way* back." The third way slips out unintentionally.

"So, you've known each other for a long time then, huh?" she teases. "You barely look old enough to have a way, way, *way* back. Maybe it's the glasses. They give you that Clark Kent vibe. Who is he really? Mild-mannered office worker or the hero who saves us all?"

Her flirtation is innocent, but my discomfort is growing. I tug at my collar again, unbuttoning the top button of my shirt to breathe a little easier. Flirting has never been my strong suit.

"I don't know. I think Clark Kent is a little more . . . will you excuse me, please?" I turn away and speed walk in any direction that takes me away from the awkward moment unfolding just then.

Out of the corner of my eye, I catch sight of Ava and Justin entering the tent together. *Together.*

Is it wrong to feel jealous that he gets to talk to her so freely?

They are walking toward me. Ava's eyes are turned to the grass underneath her feet as Justin talks in her ear. Without meaning to, I'm drawn in their direction. But the music in the tent and the conversations happening around me are too loud to hear what he is saying.

I lean over a table, pretending to look for my assigned

seat so I don't appear like I'm eavesdropping.

The feeling of eyes upon me compels me to look up.

The cornflower-blue shade of her gaze is so intense that it hits me like a wave. My hand trembles as I lift my glass to my lips, our eye contact across the tent eliciting a visceral reaction in my core.

Justin bends over her. He's tall, and his fingers brush the upper part of her arm. She breaks our gaze to turn to him again. Her face lifts with a smile, causing my heart to constrict painfully in my chest.

I move to another table. I can't watch. It's enough of a challenge to force down the envy spiking in my chest.

Why, Lord? We could have been so different.

"Dawson, your seat is at the wedding party's table." The voice at my elbow is soft and familiar.

Startled, I look up to see Ava gesturing toward the head of the tent. A long table stretches in front of the dance floor. She continues walking in its direction. The bridesmaid's dress that complements her skin and hair so perfectly swishes around her ankles. I decide olive green is my favorite color now.

Her steps veer toward the pretty, pixie-haired bridesmaid named Lora, who walked on my arm at the ceremony. She was sweet and candid. I'd gathered as much during the brief exchanges Lora and I shared.

Before I can follow Ava, Piper comes bounding up to me, a grin across her face. From what I've seen of Charlie so far, she carries herself with a sophisticated yet decidedly down-to-earth air. Her cousin, Piper, is the opposite. I've already realized that wherever Piper is, laughter is soon to follow. I eye her skeptically, wondering what she has up her sleeve.

"I hope you are prepared to dance your heart out tonight," she exclaims, grabbing my arm and dragging me toward the table at the head of the tent. "We're going to shut this reception down."

———

I've been listening to speeches and toasts for the bride and groom for the past twenty minutes, and I still have no idea what to say. The moment I need to stand up and say a few words is rapidly approaching, and I wish I could sink into the floor. Giving speeches was never my favorite activity, and the years haven't changed my mind. I'm a partner in my software firm and developing my own app, yet I'll happily let someone else do the talking.

Perhaps I can lead with, *"Hey, Andrew, could you put in a good word for me with our old college friend who subsequently broke up with me without giving any reason so that maybe someday I won't feel like such a loveless loser? Thanks."*

It would be a memorable speech, that's for sure. A bit dramatic, though. I'll have to think of something more neutral.

Andrew's dad hands the microphone to the DJ's assistant, who extends it toward the crowd with raised eyebrows. I raise my hand, and he walks to me. It's now or never. I stand and turn toward the bride and groom.

"H-h-ey, everyone. Most of you are probably wondering how this weird-looking bloke with a slight British accent got a seat at the best table in the house."

There's some tittering from the crowd, and I let it die down, trying not to let my attention shift toward Ava, who is seated on the other side of Charlie.

"The accent is fake. The friendship is real. I didn't

prepare a proper speech because I'm only fortunate enough to be in this spot because some guy's wife had a baby. A round of applause for birthdays, people."

This gets a laugh. I continue, "I've known Andrew for over a decade now, and I'm happy to report this is the happiest I've ever seen him. Whatever you are doing, Charlie, keep it up."

She smiles, her blushing face turning up to Andrew's. He draws her closer.

I lift my glass. "Even from the little I've gotten to see of you two this weekend, your love story is truly enviable. May we all be fortunate enough to find what you have someday."

With a superhuman effort, I keep my eyes turned away from Ava as the crowd claps. I sink back into my seat at the long table, trying to stay focused on the moments to come and not letting myself overthink it. Andrew sweeps Charlie onto the floor for the bride and groom's first dance.

The first dance ends. Andrew twirls Charlie one last time, then dips her backward in a dramatic finish as the guests erupt in exuberant cheers. The ring bearer runs forward, dragging a chair behind him. He slides it onto the dance floor as Andrew leads Charlie to it. She sinks into the seat, confusion on her face. He leans in for a kiss and then slides backward across the floor in a move I have to admit is stylish for a guy who struggled to master Gangnam style for our entire first year in college.

Not that I'm much better of a dancer.

Andrew's next move is my signal. Bryant, Justin, and I jump up from our seats and run around to join the groom on the dance floor as the DJ announces our presence loudly. The nerves that have lingered in my stomach all day start to pound.

"And now, ladies and gentlemen, may I present to you, straight from CityLight Studios, your next Manhattan dance crew: Andrew, Bryant, Justin, and *Dawson*." He draws out my name and flips a switch. Colored strobe lights appear above our heads.

"DJ, drop that beat," calls Andrew. "And four, three, two, one . . ."

My Girl sounds through the speakers. It's an easy one, with dance moves that are second nature. The four of us sway and step to the beat of the classic song as Andrew pretends to sing the words to his bride. She's clapping and laughing, her face beaming from ear to ear.

Each bridesmaid jumps up from her seat and runs toward the dance floor, pulling her phone out to record.

When Andrew drew me aside late last night to tell me that he and the groomsmen had been practicing for weeks to learn a choreographed dance to surprise Charlie with at the reception, I had a moment of panic as my takeover duties now came with an unexpected challenge. Dancing wasn't the issue. It was dancing in front of a crowd of strangers that kept a stranglehold on my throat all day.

And if I were truthful, dancing in front of *her* felt impossible.

Guess I'm going to look like a fool, was my first thought.

The intrusive thoughts lingered all day. Telling myself that all eyes will be on the bride and groom is the only thing keeping me from tripping over my own feet.

The DJ shifts the music into a fresh beat, and the opening lyrics of *I Want It That Way* drop. I let myself risk a glance in Ava's direction. Now, these moves I know.

And she knows them too.

We've danced to this song before, laughing and giggling, doing our best to outdo the other on dance moves. But her face isn't lit up like the rest of the crowd as the guys and I do our best nineties boy band impression on the dance floor. To my relief, I haven't dropped a step or missed a move yet. Our dress shoes clatter as the song comes to an end.

Charlie claps and whistles. She calls out an enthusiastic, "Come on, girls! Let's show these boys how it's done," and jumps up, followed immediately by Lora and Piper.

Ava trails behind them. Since the other women got there first, Ava's only choice is to stand across from me. Immediately, I notice the beet-red flush across her skin. Her face is drawn, even though a smile is plastered across her mouth.

The music shifts. A new song plays by the Bee Gees. Charlie leads the pack, dancing up to Andrew with glee. None of it is coordinated, but the joy on her face gives away how much fun she is having.

Andrew calls to us, "Looks like it's time for a dance-off, boys."

Suddenly, we're in a freestyle dance battle I never expected. Instead of a group effort, it's become a one-on-one, bridesmaid-against-groomsman throwdown. After a couple of rounds against Lora and Piper (who can officially out-dance anyone), I find myself face-to-face with Ava.

Every dance move I've ever learned flies out of my head.

She stares at me, that polite smile still on her face, but her eyes say she feels otherwise. My glasses fog up, temporarily blinding me. I'm sweating under my dress shirt, and it isn't because of the cardio.

"Get it, Dawson," Andrew cheers.

I realize I've frozen on the dance floor, lost in staring at Ava, who is staring at me. This is the one scenario where dancing like a fool is the less awkward option.

Naturally, I pull out the only move I can remember at the moment and start a very exaggerated, very bad rendition of the chicken dance. It's absurd and ridiculous, and I'm going to cringe if I ever see it on social media, but the wedding guests go wild. They don't hold back any longer. Rushing the dance floor, everyone begins to do the chicken dance, which must be a universal dance language.

Everyone is dancing. Except for Ava, who is staring at me with a stricken look, as if all she wants to do is fall through a hole in the floor.

I freeze again.

Am I embarrassing her?

All the feelings I had when she broke up with me flood back. I remember all the days and nights I spent despising myself for losing her and all the changes I made from that point onward.

She grew up wealthy, so I worked night and day to become a partner at the firm.

She was used to smooth, sophisticated men, so I changed everything about myself to become that man.

She valued innovation and creativity, so I developed my own app, and when she someday learns of what I've done, maybe she'll be proud of the man she once knew.

Someone pushes me forward. I find my hand attached to Ava's as we swing in and out of the circle. The tips of her fingers are icy. I wish I could pull her to me as the music shifts into a slow dance. I just want to talk to her. If I could plead my case, maybe we can salvage the time we lost.

Seven years without her. My heart aches.

I'll be anything . . . anyone she wants. I know without a shadow of a doubt that I don't care how long we've been apart. I want her back.

Is it too late for us?

Ava keeps her head down and doesn't meet my gaze. She drops my hand as soon as she can and lets the crowd of dancers carry her away from me. The next I see her, she is at the outer edge of the tent, tendrils of her updo coming loose and trailing down her back as she flees into the night.

5

Ava

Three Weeks Later

The keys on my laptop *clack, clack, clack* beneath my flying fingertips. Soothing brown noise churns in my earbuds, drowning out the ambient drone of The Drip, my favorite coffee shop just down the street from my office at CityLight.

Charlie is due to arrive any minute for our coffee date, so I'm rushing to reply to the email James Wolfe's agent sent me just as I walked out of the office. James is CityLight's hotshot thriller author who is bound and determined to give us a run for our money with his upcoming release. Just a few more words . . .

With a sigh of relief, I hit send and shut my laptop. I'll get to the rest of my to-do list later tonight. At the moment, I'm way behind on social media post prep, and if I hope to stick to my streak of posting every day, I need to get to work. Tucking my earbuds away, I push my tortoiseshell reading glasses to the top of my head and pull out several books from the bag on the bench beside me.

There is something about the first days of summer in New York City. The sun filters through the tall row of windows lining the front wall of the shop. My heart cheers for the happiness-inducing weather.

Why do sunshine and coffee shops make me so ridiculously happy?

Over the past few years, I've become what is called a bookish influencer, though the term throws me off. I never intended to be an influencer but only to share my love of books with the world. I'm convinced that if more people knew of the transformative powers of reading, the world would be a better place.

As my follower count has grown, I've taken to sharing my insight into the world of publishing as an editor, hoping to help aspiring authors land that publishing deal. I also take pleasure in offering thoughtful and engaging book reviews. The result of my efforts has been a steady stream of books sent to the PO Box I keep for that exact purpose, books sent to me by independent authors and fellow publishing houses for review.

I take each one of them seriously. Each book represents the dreams of someone I know only through the pages. Sharing and promoting their work feels like a full-time job sometimes, especially since I am very particular about the aesthetic of my profile.

Carefully, I set up the books on the small marble table, styling them just so. I arrange myself in the photo, too, making sure that my outfit of the day peeps into the frame just enough to contribute to the ambiance. I take several dozen photos of the scene, then spend a few minutes giving it my signature edit. Normally, I have posts scheduled well in advance, but work has had me scrambling to keep up lately.

Pasting the caption I wrote last night, I upload the photo to my social media accounts. Only a few sips remain of the iced lavender latte I ordered. I finish what's left and absently twirl the straw around in the glass, the melting ice clinking in a satisfying way, and a sense of relief finally allowing me to relax as I wait for my friend to arrive.

Charlie and Andrew's wedding was beautiful, but seeing Dawson rattled my heart. I'm ashamed to admit that I was glad when the festivities were over and I could dive back into all things editing and publishing at CityLight. Work is my safe haven, a way to keep my mind occupied and pressing onward at all times. Because heaven knows if I stay idle too long, I'll start looking into the past.

Just the thought of Dawson makes my hands shake. I tell myself it's probably just the caffeine. My phone *dings*. I look down, expecting it to be a message from Charlie telling me she is on her way.

MOM: I wish you had time for me like you do coffee shops.

With a snap, my eyes close, and I think of the photo I just uploaded. A wave of nausea sends my stomach roiling. Shaking, I shove my phone back into my bag. The guilt forces me to extract it not long after.

As I type a quick reply, the familiar and desperate urge to explain and exonerate myself of wrongdoing rumbles through me like a freight train. My fingers shake as I type. Even at thirty-one years old, I slip with troubling ease into feeling like a naughty child.

ME: Just taking a little break from work at the coffee shop down the street. I've been working on my laptop most of the time I've been here.

MOM: You could spend your break calling me. You know how bored I get, sitting at home with nothing to do and no one to care for. Your sister calls me on her work breaks.

My eyes sting. I will *not* cry in The Drip. It should infuriate me that she has such control over my emotions, even from several train stops away. A single text from her often ruins my whole day. Mostly, I'm just weary of trying to anticipate her needs to prevent her displeasure from descending on me.

ME: Sorry I'm not more like Natasha.

I know the response is flippant, but I can't help it.

MOM: At least one of my kids loves me.

At that, I shove the phone away. *More like she chooses to suffer your abuse.*

Mom hasn't been the same since Dad left. While she wasn't exactly a joy to be around growing up—her expectations always high and her tongue always sharp—I'm well aware of everything she lost when their marriage failed amidst Dad's financial crisis. It doesn't help that in the years since their divorce, Dad has moved on, reestablished his fortune, and is living the high life in California, while Mom continues to struggle with the meager finances she has left. I've been picking up the pieces for ages. As the oldest sister, the brunt of Mom's care fell to me, including meekly taking the full force of her bitterness. When she uses me as her punching bag, I tell myself that I should cut ties and walk away completely, but love, guilt, or sorrow for my mom's situation keeps me locked in place. I feel responsible for her happiness, and it is forever at the cost of my own.

When she begs me for grandchildren, all I can think of is how guilty I would feel for bringing any child around her toxicity . . . or any man I loved for that matter.

At least I had the courage to move out finally, so it's not a daily battle to survive anymore . . .

"Ava!" Charlie squeals. Her cheerful voice interrupts my dismal thoughts and rattles me out of my dark headspace. The light emanating from her makes me brighten in response. I smile, glad to have my friend's company again. I'm so grateful she's back in the city with me. I stand and wrap her in a hug.

"Look how tan you are!" I place my arm next to hers. It pales in comparison. "I can't wait to hear everything! Well, not *everything* . . ."

She smacks my arm and laughs before heading to order a coffee. Back at the table and between sips of her double espresso, Charlie prattles about conch fritters, snorkeling adventures, ruins explorations, and almost capsizing on a boat. Her warmth is everything I need to thaw the coldness constricting my heart.

"So," she finally lets out a long sigh, "I've talked myself breathless. Your turn."

"My turn? Nothing new. Nothing exciting. Oh! I finally binged those Korean dramas you told me about."

"About time! What else?"

I smile and rack my brain for something exciting to tell her. "Elaine at church had her baby," I offer.

"Okay, but what about *you?*"

"What about me?" My nails scratch at the marble tabletop.

"You know I wasn't asking about Elaine."

"Oh." I shrug, suddenly feeling my mask slip back into place. The warmth recedes. I don't want to be exposed. "I'm fine. Good. To be honest—" I stop, already regretting the words, unprepared to crack that door open. "Never mind."

Charlie leans forward, bringing her head closer to mine. "Oh no, you don't. Come on. Spill it."

I groan. I know she won't relent. "I don't know. It's been three weeks, but I'm feeling all woozy and rattled about seeing Dawson."

She winces. "I'm sorry. I can only imagine how hard it was to see him at the wedding."

"No, no—I had a fantastic time. It was such a beautiful weekend. I just . . . seeing him is awkward, you know? The way it ended . . ."

Charlie eyes me, curiosity blatant on her face. "Do you think you two—"

"No." I shake my head. "After the way we left things, I don't think he wants to see me again. I feel so guilty. I know it's my fault. I don't blame him in the slightest."

She takes a sip of her espresso, her dark eyes studying me. "You said you broke his heart."

I get the feeling that Charlie would love to hear the full story, but I don't have the strength to tell her. "I did," I simply say.

"Is he the reason why 'Ava Fox doesn't date'?"

My stomach twists into a knot. There's no easy way to answer her question without splitting my heart wide open. Thankfully, she doesn't wait too long for a reply before asking her next question.

"Ava, do you *want* to fall in love again? Get married one day?"

The shift in subject startles me. *Do I want those things?* I ponder her question for a moment, but the truth hides reluctantly in the shadows. When my parents went through their divorce and Dad moved away, leaving Mom here to cope with the loss of her entire life, I realized what a toxic environment I'd grown up in. The idea of falling in love, getting married, and trying to build a life with someone that doesn't end in pain seems unrealistic to me now.

I reply as honestly as I can. "I love my job too much. No, marriage is not in the books for someone like me."

"What about Andrew and me? We love our work *and* each other."

I look at her. "The two of you are an exception. You both are amazing people."

She shakes her head. "You are an amazing person, too, Ava. I feel like you're making excuses for why you don't deserve love."

The knot in my stomach twists tighter. She is exposing me. Panic churns in my chest. "It's complicated, Charlie."

"Well, cutting yourself off from romance and love is so sad. You deserve more."

Do I, though? Perhaps I deserved it long ago . . . but after breaking Dawson's heart so unfairly, I'm not sure anymore. And I just can't imagine it fair to any man to bring him into the toxic soup that is my family life if I'm not even able to protect myself from my mother's ire. The dream of writing my own love story faded years ago. It's easier to avoid dating completely now rather than let love get too close and end up hurting me.

"I think you should give someone a chance to get to know you." Her voice is gentle and probing. "What about Justin? He really likes you."

I smile politely and twirl my straw in the puddle of nearly melted ice at the bottom of my glass, avoiding her gaze. "He's nice and all, and I know he's Andrew's cousin, but we don't have anything in common. He doesn't even read!" I cry as if a love of reading is the meter by which I judge all men. And maybe it is.

"Who *is* the right fit?" Without giving me a chance to respond, Charlie lights up. "Wait a second!" She pulls my laptop across the table toward her. "Can I use this?"

I give her a bewildered look. "I guess?"

Charlie opens the laptop, and I type in my password for her. She clicks the internet browser and types something in while I watch her in confusion. There is a decided giddiness in her movements.

"What are you doing?" When she swings the laptop screen toward me, I peer at it and read the header on the website she has pulled up. "Blind Date with a Book Nerd? What is this?"

She grins. "While we were on our honeymoon, Andrew told me about this new dating site designed to match book lovers with their perfect fit based on their literary preferences. It just opened up for a few guinea pigs to try it out and see how it works."

I eye her skeptically. "So, you're calling me a guinea pig?"

She rolls her eyes and jabs at the screen with a laugh. "Look at this and tell me it doesn't have *you* written all over it!"

Slipping on my glasses, I scroll down the home page, reading the text aloud, "Have you ever been on a blind date with a book? Wrapped in innocuous brown paper packaging with only a few words of description to give you a clue to the identity of the literary masterpiece inside, the mystery of it all allows a reader to be whisked away on a grand adventure. There's no judging a book by its cover here. There are no preconceived notions to get in the way of discovering what could be your new literary favorite.

"Let's put a twist on that. What if dating was like going on a blind date with a book? What if our literary preferences could help us discover romantic connections for a change? Be one of the first to . . ."

I pause and look at Charlie, my eyebrows arching. "Charlie, this is . . . Look, I don't date, remember?"

Charlie stifles a laugh at my noticeable discomfort but otherwise ignores me, her fingers already flying across the keys. To my horror, she is signing me up to test the site. "I'm just going to use your 'Foxy Book Lady' handle from your social media accounts, okay?"

Before I can protest, she exclaims, "There are bookish quizzes!"

"Quizzes?" I lean in, trying not to show my intrigue. Quizzes *are* fun, especially when they relate to books.

"Once you've filled out our detailed questionnaire, let our advanced algorithm sort through your responses to find a book lover in your area who might be a good match for you," Charlie reads. "If you are intrigued by the profiles you are matched with, strike up a conversation or request a blind date with a book nerd. You never know what you'll find beneath that brown paper packaging. Happy reading, book nerds!"

"Hm," I reply, still skeptical but curious. I have to admit that the idea of pairing people up based on their bookish compatibility is a clever one.

Before I know it, we're sucked into page after page of hilarious book-themed quizzes and personality tests, all designed to determine your unique literary personality. I can't help but admit I'm charmed by the idea and curious to see my results. Once we've completed them all, I can't help but hit the "Match Me with a Book Lover" button just to see what will happen. A tiny spinning book appears on the screen. It makes a full rotation, then the pages open and flutter before it closes and spins again. A flock of butterflies stirs in my stomach. Finally, the results are in.

"You have five local matches," Charlie reads the message off the screen. "Would you like to view your matches now?" She peeks up at me, her eyes dancing. "I mean, how could you not after all that?"

I grin back. "Okay, I'll admit I want to know how close they got it. Let's see the results."

With a squeal of delight, Charlie requests the matches, and a new screen loads.

Five faceless profiles appear. I'm disappointed before I realize that is the whole point of the site—not judging a book by its cover or judging a man by his appearance in this case.

In place of profile pictures, each user is paired with a book that matches their unique bookish style. I was paired up with *The Great Gatsby*, which impresses me because it has been my favorite book since I read it in high school. The 1920s glitz and glamour, the Art Deco architecture and design, the clothes—I adore everything about the period.

I scan the list of book titles that represent my blind date

matches, making commentary as I read them aloud. "*Little Women*: Love it. *Lord of the Rings*: Adore it. *Till We Have Faces*: Oh, a scholarly gentleman. *Crime and Punishment*: No, thank you. Next."

My heart catches in my chest, skipping a beat. I stare at the screen. Charlie leans in too.

"Honestly, I'm impressed," I admit, staring at the last profile on the bottom of the page. "It's matched me with another user who also seems to have earned *The Great Gatsby* identity."

"See!" Charlie says, her face beaming with joy. "Your literary hero is out there. He's waiting for you!"

"It's a ninety-five percent match," I mutter.

"Wow," Charlie replies. "That's pretty high."

"It's too good to be true. That's what it is." But still, I click on the match and skim the profile of the man I've matched with. There are no pictures, of course, because this *is* a blind date dating site, after all. But as I peruse—I check the profile name and see "Lord of the Book Nerds"—all the books we have in common and all the points in which our bookish personalities match up, I can see that, at least by the evidence on the screen, the algorithm has done a pretty good job.

"He sounds promising," Charlie says, practically bouncing off her seat. "Book him."

I sigh, shaking my head at her, and read the instructions. "Do you want to *book* your blind date with this book nerd? There are two options: 'Book This Nerd or Browse New Nerds.'" I laugh. "I would be annoyed with you for showing me this site if it wasn't so stinking cute. How do I know this blind date isn't going to lead me to some serial killer, though?"

Charlie squints at the screen. "His 'Most Likely Literary Character Match' is Jay Gatsby, and his 'Least Likely' is Dr. Jekyll. I think you're probably safe. Besides, look at this chart. True crime is one of his least favorite genres."

"Any good serial killer would say that," I groan.

"Come on, Ava," Charlie presses. "How can you pass this up? Aren't you a little curious? I mean, this *is* the most clever dating site I've ever seen. Do it for me. Pretty please!"

I eye her, a hopelessly tragic expression painted across my face. "If I do this and go on one date—*one date*—will you let me become a crazy cat lady in peace?"

"You have my word."

I sigh. "Okay, then."

When I click the option to "Book This Nerd," a new webpage appears. A mockup of a book loads on the screen, *Dewey Belong Together?* as its title. The book flips open, its pages ruffling before transforming into a chat box with directions. "Type your message to 'Lord of the Book Nerds' here," I read aloud.

A quill pen appears, and as I type into the chat box, it scrawls across the parchment-inspired page in exquisite handwriting. "Fancy. Feels very *Pride and Prejudice*," I murmur, entirely amused. "I could see this turning into a fun pastime.

Charlie peers into my face. "Ava, you are not going to live out some weird Regency fantasy on this site. You are securing a *date*, remember?"

I wave her off and type away. "Yeah, yeah. You wanted this, remember?"

"You're in your very own modern-day Austen novel in your head right now, aren't you?"

I grin. "Absolutely." When I finish typing, I sit back so Charlie can see my message, which reads:

My Dearest Lord of the Book Nerds,

The fortitude which has carried me through life has been revealed to me an utter and somber lie, as today, the twenty-fourth of June, I am brought to my knees, suddenly aware of my own suffering as the knowledge of your very existence has now delighted my eyes. I must beg of you to give me the pleasure of meeting in person.

Ardently Yours,
Foxy Book Lady

Charlie's mouth falls open. "No. Nope. Uh-uh. Rewrite it."

"I beg your pardon!" I scoff and slide my laptop closer to myself protectively.

She purses her lips together and steeples her fingers. "It's not that it isn't good. It's that it's . . . really, really terrible. Who's going to take you seriously?"

I roll my eyes. "Who's taking any of this seriously?"

"Ava . . ."

I groan. "Okay, fine." I delete the message and rewrite it as casually and basically as possible. "How's this? 'Hi, Lord of the Book Nerds. Fun to match with you here. It seems we have a lot in common. Any interest in booking a blind date?'"

"Better than whatever that nineteenth-century trainwreck was back there."

After sending the message, a popup appears on the screen:

Local events found near you! Worried about meeting someone for the first time? Blind dates can be nerve-racking, not to mention awkward. Our team is here to help! We've found a few local and public events you may be interested in to ease those first-date nerves.

I skim the list of this week's upcoming events.

June 27th. 5:30 p.m. Book reading at Strand Bookstore.
June 29th. 7:00 p.m. Come for famous pour-over coffee and open mic poetry at Ink Bean.
June 30th. 1:00 p.m. Shakespeare in Central Park.

Simply click to RSVP. An invite will automatically be sent to your Book Nerd match. Hint: Send a message to your Book Nerd with a signal on how to find you at the event. Perhaps you'll be the one smoking a pipe like Sherlock Holmes or carrying a special book. Or maybe you're playing it cool and dressing like the best character of all—yourself—wearing your favorite plaid jumper.

"Favorite jumper? Are we in Great Britain?" I eye Charlie suspiciously. "Are you sure about this?"

"Tell me that you aren't intrigued by your *ninety-five percent* match." She crosses her arms, knowing that this site is, in fact, adorable.

The book nerd in me forges onward. "Alright. A deal is a deal." I click to RSVP to the event at Ink Bean. "My one condition is that you have to be on standby to rescue me in case it goes downhill. Promise?"

"Absolutely. I already planned to secretly spy on you now that I know the date and time of the event." She grins.

"Hey, you could tag along. I'm sure they'd be thrilled to have a global bestselling author in the shop."

"This isn't about me, missy. Now, let's figure out what your signal is going to be."

I scan the coffee shop and think for a moment before typing my decision into the chat box. I catch sight of my reflection on my laptop screen.

Despite a nagging feeling that all of this is going to go terribly wrong, a tiny smile tugs at my lips. I have to admit I'm strangely curious and . . . hopeful. Maybe someday— despite all my mistakes in the past and my fear of bringing a husband into the chaotic mix of my family dynamic— something will change, and I can open a new chapter on love for the first time in what feels like forever.

6

Dawson

I told her we were never meant to be, and the words have haunted me since they left my mouth three weeks ago. Everywhere I go, something happens to serve as a reminder of the way Ava and I left things the night of Andrew and Charlie's reception. I know I should stop torturing myself with regret, but the feeling that I could have handled our conversations so much better lingers.

When I walk into my new apartment on the Upper West Side—though, I suppose I should stop calling it new since I moved in almost two months ago—I proceed immediately to the refrigerator. Pulling it open, I stare at the contents inside, which are arguably little since I keep forgetting to visit the market down the street on my way home from the office. None of the sparse options look appealing tonight, so with a sigh, I toss my backpack onto the table in the small dining room that serves as both an eating space and an office and put on a kettle of water to boil instead.

Moving through the one-bedroom unit, I change out of the button-down, suit jacket, and trousers I usually wear to the office and into comfortable athletic wear. I brew a pot of strong Assam tea when I return to the living space. The astringent tea is a habit I picked up during my sojourn in foggy England. I sink into my computer chair and look around the apartment as the trio of screens on the desk in the corner comes to life.

When I moved back to the city, the apartment I chose declared "young professional who made his fortune overseas and is going places" quite loudly. Too expensive and cold and modern, in my opinion, but it's strategically located in the city with Central Park only a couple of blocks away and, most importantly, is notably affluent.

I laugh aloud in the quiet space at myself. Years ago, I convinced myself that a place like this would impress Ava. Not that impressing her is my mission in life anymore.

Fat chance of that happening anyway after we ended things so badly the night of the wedding. I can't get the way her face looked in the moonlight out of my head.

When I watched Ava sneak off the dance floor that night, something compelled me to follow. I needed the answer to one question, the same question that has badgered my thoughts for the past seven years. The same question that has made it impossible for me to move on.

Why did she break up with me?

And is there any way to fix what broke between us?

The breakup happened a month after I moved to London for a programming internship after graduating from

Columbia. She was supposed to visit that summer and stay with one of her friends. The two of us were planning to explore the city together. Instead of having the chance to hold her in my arms when she stepped off the plane, I received a letter ending it all. She said she couldn't be with me, and that was that.

The years have passed, but I'm still looking for closure.

My fingers move across the keyboard in front of me, but my mind is replaying every detail of the reception and what transpired when I followed Ava into the night.

Three weeks, and the vividness of the memory hasn't yet faded.

I watch her slim frame retreat from the tent down the pathway toward the gardens, her hand lifting to her face as if wiping away tears. My shoes crunch across the pea gravel, but every other sound is drowned out by the music slipping across the moonlit night.

When she disappears behind the hedges, I can't see her anymore, but I hear sniffles up ahead. My heart falls. She clearly came out there to be alone, but I can't hear Ava crying without going to comfort her.

It's a gamble picking my way through the gardens in the dark. Fortunately, each garden path leads to a gazebo standing in the middle of the space. Navigating the dark maze, I reach the center just in time to see Ava sink onto a bench in the rounded, wooden structure. The moon casts a silver glow over the scene, though the gazebo's interior is mostly in shadow.

Ava spots my approach and turns away, her fingers still wiping her eyes.

Within seconds, I drop to one knee at her side, reaching for her hands and saying with a sudden gruffness that denies the ache in my chest. *"I didn't mean to make you cry."*

"It isn't you." Her voice shakes.

That doesn't ease my tension. *"Then why do you cringe and turn away every time our eyes meet?"*

It is unfair considering she rescued me from a spider attack tonight, and the question earns me a scathing stare. *"I do not do any such thing! Why would you think that?"*

Rising, I pace across the gazebo, my limbs too long and awkward and out of place in Ava's graceful presence. I feel like a gawky schoolboy in front of her. Finally, I have the chance to talk to her face-to-face, and my words freeze in my throat.

"But you do. Do you hate me that much?" *The words are abrupt and choppy, but at least they are honest.*

"I don't hate you. I could never hate you, Dawson."

"You couldn't love me either, it seems."

I hear her sharp intake of breath, and I am immediately sorry for the words that fell out before I could stop them. *"I'm sorry, Ava. I'm just frustrated. I knew we'd see each other at this event, but I didn't expect it to be so . . ."*

"Awkward?" *She fills in the rest.*

Painful, I think.

Instead, I say, *"Can't we at least be friends? Like we agreed upon this morning?"*

She sighs. Around us, echoes of the reception travel through the grounds, a reminder of the fun we could be having if only many years and a letter didn't stand between us. The night shifts, whispering of the lost futures we used to dream of.

The brush of her fingers startles me. She rises from the bench, the fabric of her dress swaying around our legs.

Her voice is a whisper. *"I wish we could. But what's between us . . . I can't change the past."*

"You mean you don't want to change it?"

"I mean, I can't. There are things you don't . . ."

Her words grip my throat cruelly, a vise constricting my lungs. "What things? Was it me? I'm different now. I'm a partner at my firm. I've got money and stability. I'm even about to launch my own . . ."

She moves away, visibly startled, her eyes wide orbs lit by the moon peeking into the gazebo.

I take a step backward too. "I get that I'm a total nerd. I'll never be the Wall Street type. I only got into Columbia on a scholarship, and my family isn't rich, but . . . I just didn't think that mattered so much to you."

The wall of ice between us grows higher. I've always understood the real reason she ended things with me. She didn't have to say it. I wasn't good enough for her. How could I ever be? I should be thanking her because her rejection made me the man I am today. I worked tirelessly to prove her wrong, becoming the successful man she is worthy of. But the sting has never lessened.

Ava draws herself up to her full height. Her voice cracks. "That's not . . ."

My palm slaps the gazebo's post in frustration. Catching myself, I pause and take a deep breath, willing my heart rate to descend. "I'm sorry, Ava." My voice and apology are sincere. "I guess the truth is that we never were meant to be. But I just want you to know that if you ever need a friend, I'm just a phone call away."

I leave before she can break my heart again with her answer.

—

The dating app designed for book lovers came to me in a flash of inspiration. When the fog cleared after Ava broke up with me, I needed something to throw my concentration into, something that didn't have fluffy, blonde hair and blue eyes that looked like the sky after a spring rainstorm.

Blind Date with a Book Nerd was born of memories that were too painful to process in any way other than the meticulous creation of algorithms and lines of code. We used to joke about being complete opposites in almost every way. But I've always been a reader, and Ava was already pursuing her graduate degree in English, preparing for her career in the publishing world.

I'm a science fiction guy. The classic novels Ava devoured never were my cup of tea. She didn't know that, though. For her, I would read anything—if only to have an excuse to talk it over with her and watch her eyes light up as she discussed the brilliance of her favorites. I learned to enjoy the works of Austen, Brontë, and the like. Ava never quite managed to get into science fiction.

The Great Gatsby was her favorite book from the beginning.

We used to joke that the only thing that brought us together was God and our love of reading. If only people could find their perfect match based on their bookish compatibility, maybe love would be easier to find, we said, laughing as if we'd discovered the secret to a happy relationship.

There must have come a day when the books weren't enough.

As the breakup settled in, I couldn't help but wonder if our theory was true, so I put it to the test, hoping and praying that, one day, she'd know I did it for her.

A sudden *pinging* on the computer screen jolts me out of the memory. I blink and lean forward, my eyes tired with overuse behind my glasses. It's late, and I've been working for hours. A few slices of pizza are growing cold in the box beside me.

The icon of a book jumps onto the screen. I'm testing some glitches reported by a few beta members of my site, one of which is long delays in receiving messages and whole conversations deleted out of nowhere. I'm using my personal account to make the adjustments. The site only soft-launched a couple of weeks ago, and I'm quickly realizing the task of maintaining the software and marketing the app is going to become a full-time job before I know it.

The pages of the book on the screen open to reveal a new message: *Hi, Lord of the Book Nerds. Fun to match with you here. It seems we have a lot in common. Any interest in booking a blind date?*

I stare at the screen. The familiar username, "Foxy Book Lady," stares back at me. It's the handle Ava has used for all her bookish social media accounts for years. My heart is going to thunder completely out of my chest and land on the floor. There is no way this is real.

I'm about to throw up and run a mile all at once.

Swinging to the screen on my right, my fingertips thunder across the keys. I don't dare touch the message on the center screen until I've made sure. Clicking wildly through the backend of the dating app, I find the newest signup, who signed up as a new member earlier this evening. Due to the app glitch, the notification has just reached me.

My eyes scan the information available. It's all there, spelled out before me in black and white. I lean back and run my hand over my face, unable to believe what I see.

How did she find me? Or rather, how did she stumble

81

across my app so soon? It isn't even officially launched yet. The preliminary marketing plan only launched within the past month. The home page of the website displays an announcement that free memberships are currently being offered for the beta testing phase to work out the final kinks, but only a couple hundred people have signed up.

Dewey Belong Together? A notification flashes on the center screen. The prompt pushes me to decline or accept her invitation to a blind date in three days at Ink Bean.

"Lord, is this possible? Do I get a second chance with her?" I speak out loud to the only One who knows the endless nights and years of sacrifice to make this moment happen.

My finger hovers over the mouse. I can't think, can't process, can't do anything but stare at her message. Everything around me fades until those words are the only thing I see.

With a hasty tap, I confirm the date, my heart rate erratic. *Your Blind Date with a Book Nerd is confirmed."*

By whatever means, Ava just stumbled back into my life. If I can just show her what I'm made of, maybe I'll have one more chance to make things right.

7

Ava

"It's one date." I take a slow breath and pick up a bobby pin. My hands shake, and I struggle to slip the pin into place among my wavy hair. "Just one date."

I almost called the whole thing off.

The memories of my parents' endless bickering and the trauma of their divorce have haunted me ever since the moment I let Charlie convince me to invite "Lord of the Book Nerds" on a blind date.

I never want memories like those to become part of my own life story. I'd rather stay single forever than risk the devastation my parents left in their wake. In addition, Mom has never been able to cope with the realities of life after my dad left, and her resulting codependence on me has left me too emotionally drained to even consider what a healthy relationship could look like.

Who cares that the site's matchmaking software found us

to be a 95 percent match? How could a computer possibly determine someone's compatibility based on literary characteristics and preferences?

Impossible.

There is another part of me, though, a curious side that wonders how close the algorithm got. Which is why, instead of canceling the date as I should, I get dressed, my hands trembling and my nerves as jumpy as if I just drank an entire pot of the obscenely strong coffee Andrew brews at the office.

I have five minutes left to change my mind, but instead, I stand in front of the mirror and inspect my outfit.

The front sides of my hair are braided away from my face. Behind my ear, I slip a white daisy, clipped fresh from a bouquet I bought at the farmers' market this morning. The rest of my hair, lightly misted with a salty spray, drapes over my shoulders. I've donned a gauzy peach-colored skirt, loose and airy enough for the early summer evening's warmth. It's paired with a white tank top and a cute floral-embellished vest.

Charlie stopped by earlier—no doubt to convince me to stick to the date—and called me a "bohemian wonder" as she slipped a stack of bangles from my jewelry drawer onto my wrist. Her praise was welcome, but as I analyze myself in the mirror before I leave my apartment, I can't help but feel an uncomfortable insecurity gurgling in the pit of my stomach. It's been years since I've gone on a date, and even though I requested this one on a whim just for fun and to appease Charlie's insistence, the very thought of trying to connect with a stranger is disquieting.

"It's just a date. It means nothing," I tell myself with a resolute nod in the mirror.

For a moment, when I step outside and turn toward Ink Bean, the evening too beautiful to do anything other than walk, the hopeless romantic in me is swept away on the breeze, traveling on a ribbon of whimsy across the city. I'm a fairy-tale princess, free to fall helplessly in love without a care. The fairy-tale version of me has well and truly found *the one whom her soul loveth*, the man I've secretly dreamed God has set aside specially for me.

As I stand just outside the entrance of my apartment building, my phone rings. I blink out of the daydream and exhale. Instant worry gnaws at my stomach. Sliding the screen to answer the call, I can't shake the feeling that I'm in trouble for something. Again.

"Hi, Mom."

"What are you doing?" The question is more of an accusation than a greeting.

Suddenly, I'm at a fork in the road. A choice needs to be made. Do I tell the truth and invite her in, or lie? My throat moves in a painful swallow. I've never been one to take lying lightly.

"Actually,"—I hate how shaky my voice sounds—"I'm about to go on a date."

I can feel her practically beaming through the phone. "Oh, that's incredible, sweetie!"

Relief courses through me. I said the right thing. I'm in her good graces . . . for now.

"Thanks," I reply as brightly as I can.

"I was beginning to think your sister was my only hope for grandbabies. You've made me wait way too long. It's about time you get yourself out there."

As her words reach my ears, I turn to stone, my protective

walls quickly rebuilding. A small part of me wants to engage, to retort, to defend my choices. There was a time I thought my mom had it in her to change, but I know it's no use to hold out hope.

This is one reason I don't want to date. What man wants to be brought into an already toxic environment that just keeps getting worse every year.

"Yeah . . . we'll see how it goes. But I have to run. I'm a little late."

Tensing, I wait for her reply, the blare of a horn somewhere up the street making me hold the phone closer to my ear. Did I offend her?

To forestall her response, I add quickly, "But what were you calling about? Everything okay?"

The wound in her voice is evident. "Yeah, it's fine. I'm fine." Her clipped tone tells a different story. Guilt seeps into my bones. "Have fun on your date," she continues. "And remember, you need to establish your place in the relationship right off the bat. Scare him a little. He'll learn to do what you want and never cross you."

My mouth falls open as my entire body cringes. My blood boils. I think of my dad, who moved to California years ago, putting as much distance between them as possible. Even though I wish he had fought for what they once had, sometimes, I don't blame him. Blinking away an angry tear, I give her as civil a goodbye as I can.

My phone vibrates with an incoming text—not even a minute later.

MOM: I don't have a good feeling about this. You should stay home tonight.

I ignore the text, my steps brisk as I walk toward

Midtown, knowing I'll be under fire for my lack of response later. Instead, I send a quick text to Charlie.

ME: Heading to Ink Bean now! Pray for me . . .*nervous emoji*

CHARLIE: Andrew and I will be just down the street having dinner if you need us! God has you! Just have fun. You love poetry, coffee, and at least the idea of love.

ME: Ha. Yes. The idea of it, for sure.

CHARLIE: Worst case, you're only a few hours away from me letting you become the crazy cat lady of your dreams. Try to enjoy it a little.

Enjoy it a little? Can I do that?

The starry-eyed princess is gone, and in her place is the scullion I usually am, the character in my life left to sweep up the mess left behind by the hopeless romantic in me who keeps popping her head up without warning.

I know deep down that inviting someone into my life isn't fair, not with everything he'd inherit with me. The family drama and toxicity are too much, my resulting insecurities and baggage too heavy.

I sigh, pulling my shoulders straight. I refuse to give the fairy-tale princess cause for hope. For where there is hope, there is also opportunity for failure. If I refuse to give wings to my hope for a future love, I can't fail. No one has to discover my ugly secrets at all.

The air is balmy and invigorating as I head for Ink Bean. The city is alive and well, bustling with its usual sense of business and life. I scan the pedestrians on the street, checking each man for the sight of a book tucked under his arm. My date is nowhere in sight, not that I would recognize him anyway. I just need to keep my eye open for a man carrying a copy of *The Great Gatsby*, which is the signal we arranged when he replied to my request for a date. I reach up to make sure the daisy in my hair is still in place.

Ink Bean's door is propped open when I walk up to the entrance. I almost trip as I step over the threshold. Despite everything, I peer around the space with more eagerness than I'd like to admit. Most of the tables are full. It's a bit dark inside, and the atmosphere reminds me of my college days when literary creativity was everything. A rush of fond memories and a warm feeling soothe my stomach temporarily.

On the stage at the front of the room, a woman recites slam poetry as listeners snap occasionally. Her voice is driving and deep, with a marred undertone in it. Yet there is also a sense of hope as she concludes the verses and steps from under the spotlight to leave the small stage.

Politely, I clap along with the rest of the crowd, my eyes scanning the tables, still looking for anyone whose vibe says "Lord of the Book Nerds," but I have no idea who I'm looking for. I'm still standing just inside the doorway, blocking traffic to and from the shop while simultaneously blocking the line to order. It's starting to feel awkward, and I wonder if I should just find an empty table to wait.

Maybe he decided not to show up? I muse, wondering if that would be the better outcome after all.

I'm about to go to the counter and order a coffee anyway—I'm managing several new releases in addition to James Wolfe's upcoming book and brought home a pile of work from the office to review, so I'll be up late regardless—when someone taps me politely on the shoulder.

Immediately, I jump out of the way, realizing all over

again that I'm hindering the passage of a whole line of people by loitering in the doorway. My cheeks flush. Pasting a regretful smile on my face, I swing around to make my apologies. I freeze.

A pair of familiar hazel eyes stare curiously at me behind sophisticated rims. His devastatingly handsome face and that floppy, curly hair fills my vision. Even as my pulse picks up its pace, my chest swells with embarrassment, joy, hope . . . I can't identify the emotion. I feel a tremble in my knees as butterflies stir in my stomach, and I wonder at the intensity of my reaction to the sight of him.

For the space of three-point-five seconds, all I need to know is that Dawson Hayes is standing in front of me, and his sweet lips are stretched in a smile that goes almost ear to ear, and that smile is directed at me. After the way we left things at the reception, I didn't realize how much I'd hoped to have a chance to apologize for everything I'd done wrong the weekend of the wedding.

"You're here," I exclaim, almost bursting into a sudden fit of laughter at this funnily timed, must-be-orchestrated-by-fate coincidence. "Do you live in this neighborhood?"

"Actually, I, uh . . ."

All at once, the intensity of his gaze overwhelms me. My eyes drop, and my breath catches. Dawson's right hand is clutching none other than a vintage copy of *The Great Gatsby.*

I feel myself stiffen. The wheels in my brain begin to spin wildly. Cocking my head, I give him a puzzled stare.

What is happening? Why is Dawson here tonight, at this exact time, with that exact book? With a superhuman effort, I regain my composure and point to the book in his hand.

"Are you doing some light summer reading?" Pursing

my lips, I peer at him again and ignore the nagging feeling in my gut.

How is this possible?

A pause stretches on awkwardly between us. Dawson glances briefly toward the man now reading a poem on the stage. When his gaze returns to mine, his eyes are smoldering with an intensity that makes goosebumps run up and down my arms. He leans closer until it's just the two of us in the corner, the rest of the coffee shop flitting away to another planet.

His voice is raspy and hesitant when he speaks. It sends a shiver down my spine. "I wasn't sure it was possible. But by that daisy in your hair, I take it you really are 'Foxy Book Lady'?"

The lower part of my jaw feels like it hits the concrete flooring. Someone scoots around us, muttering something rude. I realize we're still taking up the entryway.

Gesturing outside wordlessly, I let Dawson lead me through the doorway to a bistro table and chairs on the patio. I tuck my skirt carefully under me as I sit on one of the chairs. Resting an elbow on the table, I let my forehead fall into my palm.

I stare at him. "Dawson, how on earth is this happening? How are you here right now?"

"I'm probably the last person you expected to see."

The angle of his smile seems more sad than happy. I take in his earthy brown summer button-down, linen shorts, and casual blue sneakers. His dark brown hair is in perfect disarray.

I can't help but laugh at the irony. "I hate to say it, but you're right. How are we . . . I don't understand what is happening right now."

With a flash, I realize this must be as painful for him as it is for me. "Before you explain this insane coincidence, I owe you an apology. I was overwhelmed at the wedding and let my emotions get the best of me. Seeing you in the garden in my moment of . . . for lack of a better word, collapse . . . was . . . embarrassing."

I sigh and place my palms flat on the table. "You caught me off guard." I'm trying to be as authentic as possible. I owe him that much *now*, even if I couldn't give him that honesty *then*. "I'm sorry for everything," I conclude, hoping it is enough to repair the wrong I've done but knowing it isn't.

Dawson sets the book on the table between us. I resist the urge to see which edition he brought. It's a bit of an addiction to collect different editions of my favorite book. Seeing my curiosity, he nudges it toward me.

"Go ahead. I know you want to look inside."

His words make me blush. It's easy to forget that at one point in my life, the man before me knew me better than anyone else. Pulling the book closer, I admire the cover and spine, letting the pages fall open as I do.

"The dust jacket is quite beaten up, but—" he begins.

"This is a Scribner first edition," I gasp, inspecting the copyright page. My jaw falls again, and my eyes widen with disbelief. "You're casually walking around the streets of New York with this . . . this . . . *treasure?*" I lower my voice to a whisper. "Do you know what this is worth?"

The value of a first edition *The Great Gatsby* is in the upper tens of thousands. Dawson either sold a kidney to afford the book, or he is no longer the poor college student subsisting on Top Ramen and peanut butter sandwiches. I eye him in confusion and admiration.

He shrugs, but his eyes dance. "Just a little something I picked up while I lived in London. I saw it posted for sale and couldn't resist. I know how much you always loved it."

"And you couldn't stand the book." I carefully (and begrudgingly) set it on the table. I'm almost afraid some random passerby will make a mad dash to grab it and take off.

He grins. "Things change. Though, I suppose, if you were to ask the bleak pessimist, F. Scott Fitzgerald, he'd say they don't."

"'So we beat on, boats against the current . . .'"

"'Borne back ceaselessly into the past.'" Dawson finishes the quote and scrubs a hand over his face. "Talk about a downer."

"I thought you loved *Gatsby* now."

"I can't say I *love* the thing, but maybe you loving it made me hate it a little less over the years."

"So, I've influenced your literary tastes for the better, then?" I can't help but slip into a teasing tone. "Or are you still hung up on *Doom*?"

Dawson barks out a laugh. "If you're referring to the literary masterpiece that is *Dune*, then yes, I am still hung up on it."

"Ha! I knew it! You're still the funny sci-fi boy. Borne back ceaselessly . . ." I say and cross my arms in triumph, suddenly riddled with goosebumps.

"Pardon me for enjoying something so lowbrow as a mere novel filled with political intrigue, impeccable characters, immaculate world-building, and a deep message about the fallacies of an all-powerful leadership."

I roll my eyes. The moment feels like déjà vu, my

memory taking me back to a time when life didn't feel quite so heavy. The silence reminds me of why I'm here.

I lean forward, ready for answers. "I'm baffled as to how we matched because I know none of my quiz answers included your old sci-fi favorites. The algorithm did us both dirty."

"Ava, I told you things have changed." The way he says my name leaves traces of nostalgia in the air, and tension grips my stomach. "And there is something you need to know."

"What?"

"It's . . . it's my site."

I blink in confusion. "Your site? What do you mean?"

He pushes those glasses higher on the bridge of his nose. "The dating app. Blind Date with a Book Nerd. I . . . I created it."

My eyebrows shoot toward my hairline. "I beg your pardon?"

Confusion swirls in my brain, along with something else. Suddenly, this chance matchup feels . . . calculated? As if I'm the butt end of a joke. I stare at him accusingly. "You . . . Wait. Did you . . . arrange all of this?"

His eyebrows scrunch behind his frames. Both of his hands lift in protest. "Yes and no. Do you remember that time we joked about a mutual love of books being the ideal way to create meaningful connections between people? It stuck with me, and after we broke up, I started wondering if maybe people could find a relationship based on certain literary traits in common."

I'm listening, my breath frozen.

"I've been working on it off and on for years. It soft

launched recently and will be fully up and running soon. I never expected you to see it."

"That's still not explaining why you and I matched up the second I opened an account." My teeth are clenched as I say the words.

He shakes his head, chagrin painted across his expression. "I'm so sorry. I needed a way to test the algorithm, so I created a profile for myself that was designed to match the answers I thought you would give to all the questionnaires and quizzes. I'd set that up years ago when I . . ." He winces. "Still had hope for us."

I level him with a glare. "And you didn't think to change that, why?"

"It was a great way to train my algorithm. The parameters allowed me to predict the outcome. I never thought you'd join the site. When I saw that my account had matched with a name I immediately recognized as yours the other day, I wasn't even sure it was you at first. The good news is: My software design works." He gives me a hopeful, lopsided grin.

"So, you showed up tonight to see if it was really me?" I am equally shocked, annoyed, and impressed at his genius. "Why launch it now?"

I'm afraid to hear his answer. Does Dawson secretly still hope there is a chance to win me back?

"I promise this timing—as bad as it looks—is all just coincidence. I'm a partner at my software development firm now, so it felt like it was finally time to launch my own project. The site is only open for testing. We aren't even really in business yet."

"It's your site. Why didn't you pull the data and see

from the backend that it was me?" I demand, realizing that I don't fully believe him. Surely, he would have a way of checking, right? But then again, when has Dawson ever lied to me?

He hangs his head. "To be perfectly honest, I did. But standing you up seemed . . . wrong." He shrugs.

Inside Ink Bean, the echo of applause reaches our ears as another poet finishes a set. I'm faced with a lot of questions that I don't have the answers to. What did I expect from this night? Did I expect to meet the love of my life and be swept away? Nope. Definitely not. I agreed to this blind date specifically to humor Charlie.

Why is it, then, that I feel so disappointed as it sinks in that Dawson probably designed this whole site to find his *own* perfect match?

"So you're dating then?" I blurt out.

His gaze meets mine in a challenge. "As are you, I assume?"

I can't help but laugh. The absurdity of the whole scenario is hitting me. "Not exactly. I agreed to do this so Charlie would get off my case."

"You're . . . off the market, then?"

"Like the out-of-print edition that I am."

He rolls his eyes. "You know that's not what I meant."

"No." I shake my head. Of course, the spark of hope I let myself feel earlier was only a momentary lapse of reason. I'm back to my usual levelheaded self now. "I'm not in a relationship, nor am I seeking to be. Does that answer your question?"

Dawson drums his nails against the cover of the book. "It's a shame." His eyes shift into a teasing glint as they watch me. "This software I've designed could find you a real classic book hero to sweep you off your feet."

"You mean the algorithm you rigged to pair us up?"

He throws back his head and laughs. "Okay, I deserve that, but I'm hopeful this algorithm is going to do its job. Honestly, it might end up being just a good idea in theory. It's been hard to market it enough to get people to actually want to sign up as test subjects. I'm hoping to fully launch in a couple of months, but at the rate I'm going . . ."

An idea hits that takes my breath away. "Let me help you."

Dawson looks confused. "Help me with what?"

"Launch your dating app. It's the least I can do." I lean forward, my brain racing.

"How can you do that?" His head tilts sideways. A curious gleam enters his eyes.

"My social media accounts," I begin, waving my hands around my head as the idea takes hold. "I can collaborate with you and advertise it on my pages. My followers would eat this up. What book lover doesn't want to date someone who also loves books?" I lean forward and hope he senses my sincere wish to help. "Your site is brilliant, Dawson. It really is. You may have single-handedly solved the literature lover's dating crisis."

My eyes light up. "And since I've gone on my first official date, I can probably give you some feedback on how the site works."

He squints and studies me for a second. "Why would you do this?"

Sweat forms at the nape of my neck. I scramble silently. What am I supposed to say? That I feel bad for breaking his heart? That I want him to find someone to grow old with because he deserves love? Even though I secretly wish it could be . . .

"Because I care," I finally reply.

"You care, huh?"

I let my gaze linger on him steadily, not flinching under his curious inspection. "I do care, Daws. Triple prom."

And I mean it. Dawson Hayes is a good man, and if my social media influence can get his clever app in front of more people, I owe him that much.

He purses his lips. His cheek dimples, and it's adorable. "What's in it for you? Is this a ploy to get my rare and extremely valuable copy of *Gatsby*?"

I glare at him and resist glancing at the treasured book on the table. "Must I remind you which of us is the calculating mastermind here? Hm?"

There's a flicker of something in his eyes. I can practically see the wheels spinning in his mind. Something about the way he gazes at me now causes another uptick in my pulse. It's all I can do to maintain my composure around Dawson in general. If he keeps looking at me like that . . .

"You really want to help me?" he asks with a glint in his eyes.

I nod. *Is he up to something?* "Of course."

"How about this," he says slowly, as though his idea needs a few extra seconds to percolate. "I saw you had five initial matches on the site. I want you to go on five dates—"

"I told you, I don't date," I protest.

He lifts his palm. "But you're the only person I can trust to give me unbiased feedback. It's even better that you aren't interested in dating. You won't get caught up emotionally. I want you to give me feedback on how well the matches fit and brainstorm how I can improve the matchmaking side of things. That's the only way I'm going to let you help me. Deal?"

Despite every bit of self-preservation yelling at me that this is a bad idea, I hold out my hand to seal the deal. "I offered my help. If five dates is what it takes, you've got it."

8

Dawson

I hold my breath as she contemplates my proposal.

It was a bold move. Suggesting that she act as a guinea pig, going on blind dates in order to provide me with unbiased feedback about my dating app, was a spontaneous request. I'm well aware of how much it could backfire. If she agrees, she might go on one of these five dates and end up finding someone she wants to spend the rest of her life with.

Someone who is not me.

But what other idea will give me a chance to see her again? How else can I spend time with her? It's a business proposal, but my heart tells me it's so much more. I thought I'd successfully resigned all dreams of a future with her, but that was before Andrew's wedding. Seeing her again . . . it sparked something inside of me.

My heart pounds. This rekindled hope could very well leave me burned and scarred worse than before, but I can't help but reach for the fragment.

When she extends her hand toward me across the table, I release a heavy exhale. Her slim fingers are soft and warm in mine.

"I offered my help. If five dates is what it takes, you've got it." There is a look on her face that I can't quite read, a combination of amusement, curiosity, and trepidation.

"My second condition," I reply, "is that if you are going to act as my ambassador and use your influence to grow my business, I'm going to pay you."

"Dawson, no," she protests immediately. "That's not necessary."

When she tries to pull her hand away, I tighten my grip just enough that she can't escape my grasp yet. I look at her earnestly. "It's only right. I insist." I release her hand.

She shakes her head, her face bright, her eyes dancing with glee. "Dawson Hayes doesn't change. You were always an honorable man and a good friend."

My gaze doesn't relent as I study her expression, searching her eyes for the truth. "Are we friends?"

Her hesitation is telling. "Of course. Always."

Silence falls over our table. The sonorous tones of a man reciting a very impassioned piece of slam poetry echoes out over the speakers. Ava straightens her shoulders. "But if you're going to insist on paying me, I'm going to insist on treating this as I would any other collaboration. I want to interview you about the dating app for my vlog. Would you be willing to do that?"

I contemplate the idea. So far, I've remained in the shadows of my burgeoning business venture, staying as anonymous as possible while developing the app. Most startups like mine have a whole team behind them, with investors and advisors to lean on when things get tough. I'm not cut out for the public eye, nor do I have any interest in gaining attention. I just want my dating app to make some people happy.

I've bootstrapped most of the business myself, bringing in other software developers and graphic designers only when I really needed them, and staying firmly in the background while I work through the app's soft launch. I'm well aware of how much my position as a partner in my software firm could influence the direction of the app's success. Yet, I'd rather my creation stands solidly on its own merits.

But that doesn't mean I'll turn down help when it's offered. Especially from Ava.

"Okay," I reply to her. "Let's get it scheduled."

"I'll figure out the logistics and reach out to you," she grins. "This is going to be fun. My audience is going to eat this up."

Her bright eyes are soft and hopeful. The sweetness of her smile makes my heart constrict. She's trying so hard to help me make my dream come to life. Can we work together without the awkwardness of our past interfering with the present? The harder to answer question is: Can I work with Ava without fanning this tiny flame of hope into a raging wildfire? I think I can, and she is worth it to me to try. At the very least, I'd love the chance for us to salvage some of our friendship.

She runs her index finger across the cover of the book that acts like a bridge on the table between us. "So . . ." she begins, "now that you're a hotshot software developer who just launched his own dating app, I bet you've been on lots of dates with book girlies looking for love."

I grimace. "No. I'm not interested in using the site for my own dating life."

"But your dating app, the whole project, what's it all for if not to find love?"

I shrug, wondering if honesty is really the way to go here. But I know that my authenticity now can glorify God. "It was supposed to be to impress you." At the sudden alarm in her eyes, I lift my palms. "*Was* being the operative word. I thought you would like the idea of people connecting on a level beyond their physical attraction to each other and focus on all the other pieces of ourselves that build our character and personalities. But along the way, I felt as if the rough patches I've gone through could be turned into something good."

I don't expound on my belief that God directs not only our lives but our love stories, too, if we let Him, yet Ava seems to pick up on the unspoken words.

"You haven't lost faith that God has designed the perfect match for each of us, have you?" she asks.

"Not for a second," I reply simply, then break into a laugh. "As if I could ever forget after you drilled the idea into my head back in college? Do you remember Mr. Bodner's 'The Bible for Lonely Singles' class? Now, that was an experience."

To my relief, her laugh sparkles into the warm night air, her wavy hair flowing around her shoulders as they shake. "How could I ever forget that Bible study? I mostly remember definitely not being single by the end of that semester." She sobers and levels her gaze at me again.

I'm not sure what compels my sudden honesty. "I always thought you were the one God made for me."

She averts her gaze and stares down at her lap. Her hair spills over her shoulders, shielding her face from my view. I'm annoyed with myself. Why did I have to ruin the moment?

Finally, she lifts her head again "Daws, I'm not the perfect match for you. Someone is out there who is so much better than *me*. Someone who can offer you the pure and unadulterated love you deserve."

A hollow feeling opens in my stomach. I feel that renewed spark of hope fighting to stay lit. "What if I believe you're wrong?"

She shakes her head. The sadness of her smile makes my heart crack. "I'm not looking for a relationship. Let me ask you this: Are you holding on so tightly to our past because you are afraid to let go and see what happens with your surrender?"

Her words hit me like a ton of bricks. She's not wrong, and I see my stubbornness in a sudden flash of clarity. Before I can speak, her soft voice carries across the table again.

"What if I suggest something crazy?"

Gathering what's left of my dignity, I lift my head. "Something crazier than you and Andrew putting me up to crashing the French final when I'd never taken a day of French in my life?" Despite the ache in my heart, the memory makes me smile.

Her smile and laugh are my reward. "Even crazier." She leans forward. "I've agreed to your terms. Now, I dare you to use your dating app for real and go on five blind dates."

"You want me to go on dates?"

She nods. "Yes. I want to be friends and help you with your business, Dawson, but the only way I'll feel comfortable with this arrangement is if I know we are in the same boat. You have to promise me you'll put your future in God's hands and stop clinging to the past."

I contemplate the idea, trying not to get sidetracked by the fact that she just said she wants to be my friend. Is it enough for me? Can I be friends again with the woman who broke my heart and never told me why? My heart says no, while my head says yes.

She stares at me, biting her lower lip. Her face is flushed. "Can you do this for me, Dawson? I want to make up for all the years I hurt you by helping you find your perfect person."

When I can't find the words to reply, her voice turns pleading. She seems to shrink into herself. "Did I upset you?" she asks quietly. "I'm sorry. Me and my big mouth and crazy ideas."

"No!" I hurry to reassure her, seeing her blaming herself for my silence. "Let's do it. Five matches, five blind dates each. But I want to use this to make the app better. After each date, we have to give each other honest feedback about how well my matchmaking algorithm did. Agreed?" I stretch my hand across the table toward her once more.

She reaches for it without hesitation, sliding her smooth, soft palm against mine. "Deal. But no funny business. No cheating, no orchestrating matches, no checking the data to find out someone's name . . ." She levels a pointed look at me. "And if you make a connection with someone special, you can't reject her because you're hoping things will work out with me."

"And what about you? Will you still want to be my friend

when you match with the perfect guy, and you realize how easy it would be to fall in love?" The challenge in my tone is clear. The thought of Ava falling for some other guy because of my dating app fills me with so much dread I almost call the whole thing off here and now.

Her head swivels away as she tracks the progression of an older couple holding hands as they walk down the crowded sidewalk. When she turns back, her expression is bright, her smile wide, but she can't hide the sadness behind her eyes from me no matter how hard she tries.

"Now that I have you back in my life, I'll always want to be your friend, Dawson. But to be honest, you have nothing to worry about anyway. I'm planning to adopt a bunch of cats."

Nothing has changed. Her charm and gentle spirit still take my breath away. This is a woman who will allow herself to be uncomfortable just to help a friend. I've lost so much time with her already. For some reason I don't quite understand, Ava is opening a door and allowing me back into her life. If she doesn't want to be with anyone, so be it. I'll be there for her anyway. She doesn't understand what she always meant to me and always will. As her lilting voice prattles on teasingly about naming a fat, orange, fluffy cat, Chester the Pester, and selling t-shirts featuring his grumpy face, I silently promise myself that whatever comes, I'll make sure Ava ends up happy.

—

"I can't let her go, man."

Andrew picked up on the third ring. It's late. Ava and I parted ways at Ink Bean and went to our respective homes. Or, at least, she went home. Night fell over the city an hour ago. I've been pacing the streets ever since, walking up and down block after block, trying to erase her face from my mind.

It isn't working.

"Whoa, whoa, whoa, slow down." On the other end of the line, I hear what sounds like a soft, feminine voice asking a question and his muffled reply. There's a *whoosh*, and I know he has stepped outside as the sounds of the city at night fill the phone.

"I'm sorry. I didn't know who else to call," I reply.

It's true because I left most of my friends back in London, and it's after two o'clock in the morning over there.

"It was her, wasn't it? At the blind date tonight?" Andrew doesn't even need an explanation. I wonder if Ava has already shared the events of tonight with Charlie.

"Yeah." I'm embarrassed to admit my scheming out loud now. "When I started building Blind Date with a Book Nerd, I set up the matchmaking algorithm with answers I thought Ava would give to see if it worked. I never really thought she would create an account, but I think part of me hoped that someday, she would find out what I'd created and realize that God meant us for each other all along. But I think it had the opposite effect." I bark out a harsh laugh in disbelief at my own foolishness.

"She wants us to date other people. Or rather, she wants me to give dating a try," I continue with a calmness I don't feel. A restaurant door opens onto the street. A large group spills out, couples splitting off, and everyone calling goodnight to each other as they flag down a cab. I wait as they spill around me, then continue walking. The city hasn't slowed its pace despite the hour. It hums and pulses with an energy that feels stressful to me.

I turn toward my neighborhood block. It's quieter there, and I'll be able to think better.

"She says there's someone out there for me; it's just not her. Why can't I let her go, Drew? I want her to be happy. If she's happier without me, why can't I accept that?"

He exhales heavily on the other end of the line. "Have you talked to God about this?"

"A thousand times."

"Then, it's going to come down to trust. Have you prayed over the future God has planned for Ava or just the one you want?"

My breath leaves me with the gut punch of his words. Unlike Ava and I, who have always had our faith in common, Andrew struggled to connect the dots between the truth in the Bible and his own lived experience. When I moved back to NYC, he shared his testimony and the story of finding the strength to renew his broken faith after his mom passed away when Charlie came into his life. For a guy who is still new to a relationship with God, he's hit the nail on the head with one try.

I swallow painfully, my throat dry and hoarse. My street looms ahead, the shadows of the trees lining the sidewalk casting themselves eerily over the concrete. "I don't know if I can do that."

"You've got to find the faith to surrender it all to Him." Andrew's voice is earnest. "I thought I had messed up so badly that I'd never be worthy of love, let alone marry the most incredible woman in the world. But God, through His never-ending mercy, gave me a second chance because He had a different plan than I thought my weaknesses allowed.

Your second chance might come from somewhere you don't expect."

He continues without giving me a chance to respond. "Why don't you come to church with us tomorrow? Charlie and I have been meaning to invite you."

I find myself saying "yes" before I can come up with any excuses. I need to get myself connected to a new church, to a community. Since leaving London, I've been putting it off. I'm grateful for the invitation. We sign off for the night, and I ponder the advice in his words as I climb the steep staircase and unlock the door to my dark and lonely apartment.

9

Ava

My phone buzzes softly in my purse. Tearing my gaze from our pastor at the front of the church—who is passionately walking us through the book of Philippians—I discreetly unclasp my purse and feel around to find the side buttons of the phone to silence the call entirely.

The phone buzzes again almost instantly. My cheeks flush. I silence it once more without looking at the screen. The buzzing barely pauses.

A wave of panic rises in the pit of my stomach. I lift the phone from my purse and glance at the screen. Three missed calls from my mom. I sigh, wondering if it's really an emergency this time or if I can wait to return the call after church.

The anxious feeling won't let me rest until I shoot a quick text to appease her.

ME: Sorry, I can't answer. I'm in church. I'll call you

when it's over.

MOM: You never told me how your date went last night.

She sends a series of question marks next.

Lifting my eyes away from her aggravating messages, I seek a momentary distraction. Charlie sits just to my right, and I glance at her discreetly.

Last night, her reaction was one of utter shock when I FaceTimed her to report that, in a twist I never could have predicted, the app she convinced me to sign up for matched me with the one person I could never date even if I were willing to give someone a chance. When I asked her, she admitted to knowing, but only vaguely, that Dawson created the app since Andrew had casually mentioned it on their honeymoon. She declared that she only withheld that information because she didn't want it to negatively impact my interest in the concept. She promised she wasn't scheming or trying to matchmake, and I believe her.

Glancing farther down the row, I see Dawson sitting just on the other side of Andrew. It was quite a surprise to see him join us this morning. By the expression on his face, I don't think he had realized I attend church with Andrew and Charlie as well. He's leaning forward now, both elbows resting on his knees, his eyes trained ahead on the pastor.

Suddenly, my brain snaps to attention long enough to hear the pastor's words. He recites Scripture, "'Forgetting those things which are behind, and reaching forth unto those things which are before.'" He pauses for emphasis before repeating the verse and continuing his message on spiritual growth.

Deep down, I know the Word of God isn't meant to be cherry-picked. Taking verses out of context can be disastrous, but I can't help but wonder at the timing as I use my peripheral vision to peek at Dawson. The verse feels as if it applies to our current situation. Can we forget the past and focus instead on the path God has called us to walk? I meant it last night when I convinced him to join me on our little five-date dare. More than anything, I want Dawson to be happy.

Why, then, does the thought of him dating make my jaw clench? Taking a slow breath, I smooth my now-sweaty palm on the marigold voile fabric of my skirt. My phone buzzes in my other hand again.

MOM: Why aren't you answering me?

I feel guilty for texting in church. My fingers fly as fast as they can as I type out a quick reply.

ME: Sorry, like I said, I'm in church. It went fine, but he's not the one for me.

MOM: Of course he's not.

I frown. What is that supposed to mean? But I know better than to ask. There's no need to open up an opportunity to be belittled.

Seeing my distraction, Charlie nudges me gently. When I glance over at her, she smiles, her sweet brown eyes glancing at my phone. "Everything okay?" she mouths.

I nod and move to tuck my phone away, but it vibrates again, and it's a habit to glance down at the screen.

MOM: I found this online for twenty dollars. It's perfect for your apartment.

MOM: You'll have to come pick it up.

A photo appears featuring a shabby-looking armchair. I don't even want to know where it came from.

ME: Did you already buy it?

MOM: Yes! People pay big money for chairs like this. The guy gave me a really good deal.

My fingers twitch. I don't need a chair. I don't want a chair. Especially not *this* chair. Did she ever pause to think about *asking* me first before meeting an internet stranger and making the purchase?

ME: Thanks, Mom. I don't really have room in my place for it, though. Maybe Tashi can use it?

I probably shouldn't shove it off on my sister, but Natasha can do no wrong in my mother's eyes, so I'm surprised she didn't offer it to her first. Then again, Mom would probably have bought something expensive and new for her prized youngest daughter.

Mom's reply takes a few minutes to come in.

MOM: I was only trying to help.

Immediately, a surge of guilt rushes into my chest. She probably just thought she was doing something nice for me. I feel myself cracking.

ME: Okay. I'll take it. Thank you.

I cringe as I type the words. Why do I always feel like I have to give in?

MOM: Forget it.

At her short reply, I shove my phone back into my purse, knowing it doesn't matter what I say. The silent treatment has now begun. I've disappointed her, and Mom won't be sending any more texts or making any more calls to me for now. At least I'll get a break from the pressure of being Mom's perfect daughter for the week. I didn't respond the way she wanted, and now, I must suffer.

The sermon continues, but I'm so distracted and perturbed that I can't pay attention.

Help me capture these thoughts, Lord . . .

When church concludes, I rise alongside Charlie. She doesn't seem to notice the lack of peace I feel. Instead, she smiles at me. "That was a beautiful message today. I feel so renewed!"

I nod my head in what I hope seems like agreement. We shuffle down the row of seats and into the aisle, where we bump elbows with the flow of churchgoers who spill toward the wide, open doors leading to the sidewalk. Dawson swings in and out of my view up ahead. By the time I step into the sunlight, I've lost track of him entirely.

Charlie and Andrew stop to speak with another couple, and I step to the side, leaning into a sliver of shade cast by the stone building. We often go to brunch together after church, and even though my heart is heavy, I don't want to excuse myself and go home to be alone with my thoughts. Besides, if I don't find some way to distract myself this afternoon, I'll probably end up on the train to go out to check on Mom. If she isn't happy to see me, the results could be worse than the silent treatment.

When Dad announced he was leaving Mom, things went from uncomfortable to bad to worse. Time has not lessened her bitterness or softened her expectations. It didn't help that Dad made some bad business investments and lost most of the money that would have kept Mom in the comfortable luxury she was accustomed to throughout their marriage.

Instead of continuing to live in the spacious condo in Carnegie Hill—Mom was so proud of that condo—she was forced to move into a charming townhome in New Rochelle, which I secretly thought had the potential to be a warmer and more welcoming home if she had just embraced the change. Natasha and I debated for a month on who should move in with her, and eventually, I gave into the pressure, moving in right out of college to make sure Mom made the transition to single life with as little stress as possible.

Since I already had an introductory internship at CityLight that eventually turned into being hired as a copy editor, I made the commute every day. It wasn't until the past couple of years that I finally found the courage to move out and get my own tiny apartment in the heart of the city. It took her a few months to start talking to me again after my move, so hopefully, this time won't be quite as long.

Almost everyone lingers on the sidewalk after church, exchanging greetings and enjoying the beautiful, warm day. I hang out in the shadows of the building until the pedestrians eventually dwindle, and I spot Dawson on the sidewalk alone.

He's dressed simply, in a pair of dark jeans and a tan t-shirt. I wonder if the color brings out the brown flecks in his eyes. He was never one for fashion statements, preferring to put his energy into the computer projects he threw himself into enthusiastically. I loved that about him, the what-you-see-is-what-you-get quality a comfort in the fake-polite-obsessed-with-materialism world I grew up in. And even though I can tell that the quality of his outfits has improved exponentially, the fabric and tailoring of his clothing speaking of a man with deep pockets, they still read true to Dawson Hayes.

He's still here. The thought brings a ray of sunshine into the dark, troubled rumblings of my mind.

His hands are shoved into his front pockets, his shoulders slouched ever so slightly. The high sun reaches down into the city, glinting off his glasses. *Is he mumbling to himself?* My feet turn in his direction, and I'm walking toward him before I even realize it, feeling as though a magnetic pull is overpowering my sense of logic.

When he sees me approaching, my heart skips a beat as his lips part into a hesitant grin.

"Is creating a comic book version of the Bible a terrible idea?"

The unexpected statement brings laughter bubbling up from my chest. "It's not the worst idea you've ever had." Teasingly, I nudge him with my elbow, slipping back into the same sense of comfortable ease we used to have around each other. "But I feel like that's something that has probably already been done."

"Oh, not with my cartoonist skills, it hasn't."

I laugh again. "You mean the ones that won you an award in, like, sixth grade or something?"

"It was seventh grade, thank you." He straightens his shoulders and pulls himself up to his full height. "I'm touched you remember, though."

When it comes to Dawson, I'm not lacking in the random facts department. We were together for two years, after all. And despite the time and distance and all that has happened since that time, all the sweet and silly stories he told me about his life remain safe and tucked away for what I'm afraid is going to be forever.

I shake off the memories, speaking brightly instead. "Well, if you ever create a comic book Bible, I know people in the publishing industry."

He smiles, and I love-hate the way his lips always curl into a shy, upward tilt. If I don't change the subject quickly, that smile might just unravel me.

My tone is brisk and matter-of-fact. "So, how is your end of our bargain going? Have you found your bookish match and scheduled a date yet?" I pull my sunglasses from my purse and slip them on to shield my eyes.

The abrupt change in subject seems to throw him off. He blinks and blows out a puff of air. "I gave you my word, didn't I? I'll schedule it."

The news creates an uncomfortable disruption inside my stomach. I don't like it, but I smile at him, nonetheless. "Great!" Even I know the word ejects from my mouth with far too much excitement.

"Did you . . .?" I expected the reciprocal question. Dawson lets it hang, and I wonder if he truly wants the answer.

I nod. "I have a date on Friday night. Any man who matches with me based on *Little Women* deserves a chance. Is he a professor? Or a writer, or an artist, or a musician? So many possibilities. I'm curious to find out why your algorithm thought we were a good match."

I'm teasing, but Dawson is not as good at hiding his emotions as I am. He grimaces. His characteristic bluntness was always something I admired and adored. Never having to mask what you're feeling? Never feeling the necessity to bend awkwardly backward in order to please people? Yes, please. Sign me up.

Not that I could ever break free of the doormat habit that defines at least half of my social interactions, I think ruefully.

Ava Fox is not bold enough for that.

"So . . ." Dawson begins. He glances behind us and lifts his hand in a quick wave. Turning to look back over my shoulder, I see Andrew waving at us from the top of the steps leading into the church. The man has the audacity to wink at me and make a kissy pouting face.

Immediately, heat rushes to my cheeks. Lowering my sunglasses, I glare at him properly. I can't wait for work to begin tomorrow. His teasing is going to be *so much fun*. I roll my eyes and turn back to Dawson.

"So . . . what?"

He clears his throat. "So, I'll set up a date this week."

"And I'm going on mine this Friday."

"Then how about we meet up Saturday morning for our Super-Blind-Date-With-A-Book-Nerd-Improvement-Team-Sesh?"

"That's . . ." I falter, my lower jaw dropping. "We need to come up with a new improvement team name."

He lifts both of his palms in surrender. "Hey, you know I'm open to suggestions."

"Well, what other ideas do you have?"

"Mega-Matchmakers'-Meeting? Book-Lovers'-Brainstorm?" His eyes squint in jest behind those sophisticated frames. "A One-On-One-Occasion-For-Finding-Our-One-And-Only?"

The last one makes me burst into uncontained laughter. "How can you be so good at creating clever software programs and yet be so incredibly terrible at naming a simple meeting?"

"I take it you have a better idea, then?" His challenge is playful.

I narrow my eyes, thinking intently. I snap my fingers and lift my head. "Not yet, but when I come up with one, I can assure you it won't be full of ridiculous alliterations."

He gasps in pretend shock. "Tut-tut. Alliterations are

117

amazingly amusing, Ava."

I raise my brow to double down on my opinion of the grammatical technique.

He presses an offended hand to his chest. "I take back everything I said the other day. Perhaps we aren't meant to be after all."

"And all it took was smack talking alliterations, huh?" My smile couldn't stretch wider, but my heart thumps painfully, sparked by his teasing. Resisting the charm that is Dawson when he's playful was always an impossible task, and it seems nothing has changed, or at least I haven't. At least we are conversing with something of our old camaraderie. Friendship with Dawson was always easy and lighthearted, and I welcome its return. I ignore the nagging notion that this feeling can't, won't, and shouldn't last. But I don't want to lose him again because, even after all this time, if home were a person, he'd be it.

He sets his fists on his hips and shakes his head with a theatrical flair, those dark curls trembling, his hazel eyes flashing with amusement. "I do have to draw the line somewhere, Ava."

"Fair enough." I pretend to wave off his statement. "So, Saturday morning, then?"

"It's a date." He winks at me, and before I can protest his choice of words, he asks, "Do you still have the same number?"

"If I'm anything, I'm consistent," I reply with a nod.

For a moment, Dawson looks like he wants to say something, but he holds it back. Instead, he only says, "Cool. I'll text you, and we'll figure out plans for our Super-Blind-Date-With-A-Book-Nerd-Improvement-Team-Sesh."

I groan, mumbling, "Well, at least you picked the one without all the alliterations."

The buzzing of our phones begins at the same moment. Dawson pulls his from the pocket of his jeans while I reach for mine at the bottom of my purse. Instead of reading the text, I watch him scan the message he just received. He looks up, his eyebrows pulled together.

"I have to go." I think I catch a hint of regret in his tone. "My family is expecting me for dinner, and it's a long drive."

I want to ask how they are, but instead, I say, "Tell them hi for me."

Back when Dawson and I were a couple, I met the Hayes several times. They were a warm and welcoming family, and I've missed them many times over the years. The thought of them meeting my dysfunctional family still makes me shiver, though, so I'm glad they were spared the trauma of that scenario before it was too late.

He smiles, his face lighting up. "I will. You probably wouldn't recognize any of them. My siblings are so grown up that I feel old whenever I'm around them."

"The passage of time will do that to you," I admit.

He leans forward, closing some of the distance between us, his voice low. "I'll see you Saturday."

Despite wondering for the thousandth time in less than twenty-four hours if I made a colossal mistake by volunteering to help Dawson promote his business, I give a resolute nod. "I'll see you then."

Before I can move away, he reaches for me, and I find myself folded into a gentle hug. It's for only the briefest of moments, but when he mumbles a goodbye and walks away, there's a tingle running across my skin from head to toe that feels like stepping into the sunlight after a rainstorm.

I want to cling to it, but the pleasant feeling disappears instantly when I glance down at my phone, remembering the message still waiting for me there.

NATASHA: What did you do to get Mom so worked up?

10

Dawson

As I walk up the front porch steps of my childhood home, I can hear the sound of chaos inside.

The door isn't locked. In the still-tiny college town of Aurora, New York, it hardly ever is, so I click the latch without knocking and enter. Tonight is Sunday family dinner night, and I'm running late. It's a nearly five-hour journey between the city and Aurora. Since I moved back to the city, I've been trying to make it up every couple of weeks for a visit.

Without pause, I walk past the staircase and down the hall to the kitchen at the back of the house, where the sounds of enthusiastic conversation carry. The house is a sprawling Victorian, and most of the living space looks over the back gardens. Our family dinners usually spill outdoors, the French doors just off the kitchen thrown wide open and a pack of children running through while the adults hang out.

The Hayes household is never quiet. It's always chaotic and wild, with everyone talking and laughing at once. As the oldest of five, I can hardly remember a day without the chatter of my siblings filling every corner of the house.

"Just the way I like it," Mom always says with a smile and a wink.

"D Dog!" Grayson's shout of greeting alerts the family to my presence as I enter the kitchen. Four pairs of heads lift, and four pairs of eyes light up at my entrance. Within seconds, I'm surrounded by clinging arms and patting hands as my three younger siblings rush to my side. It's the same scene every time I visit. Enthusiastic hugs and voices all clamoring over each other to be the one to fill me in on the latest news first.

I wouldn't change it for the world, and it's hard not to kick myself for staying in London for so long. I made it back for visits several times a year, but I still missed out on so much time with them.

"D Dog, wanna head outside and shoot some hoops? I've got a wild new dunk to show you," Grayson's deep voice carries over the chaos. My brother is only sixteen, but he already stands two or three inches taller than me and is on his way to being the star of his high school basketball team.

I flash him a thumbs-up as eight-year-old Lucy attempts to drag me by my shoulders to her level.

"After dinner, if that's okay?" I call out to Grayson. "Mom's probably going to have my hide for being late." *And missing dinner for three weeks in a row.*

I wink in my mother's direction. Apron spattered with what looks like spaghetti sauce, she waits patiently in line for her hug. I raise one arm to draw her in.

"I'm sure there are plenty of other things I could have your hide for, Dawson Hayes." Mom's amused tone doesn't match her words. "Now that you're finally here, I'll dish up." With a quick swat on my arm, she releases me and goes back to the stove, where several fragrant, bubbling pots sit.

"We almost left cold noodles at the bottom of the pot for you," Josephine teases as I reach for my father's hand. He has just entered the kitchen, his glasses slipping down his nose, a laptop tucked under one arm.

"Mom wouldn't do that to me, JoJo," I counter as Dad approaches. Not content with the handshake, he pulls me in for a hug. His hands slap my back enthusiastically. "We all know I'm her favorite. How are you, Dad?"

"Good, son, and you?" he replies.

"You left Mom for London," Josephine laughs. She is thirteen and just as full of jokes as Grayson. "I'm her favorite now."

"No, I'm her favorite," Lucy shouts.

"As her star basketball player, I'm clearly the favorite," Grayson whoops, dashing across the kitchen and pretending to dribble a basketball before he steps back and mimes a jump shot at an invisible hoop above the doorway.

"You're all wrong," a lighthearted, pleasant voice calls out.

Anne enters the room from the back hallway, a book tucked under her arm. "Her firstborn daughter will always be her favorite, of course. You, Dawson, were merely a test run. They obviously got it right when I came along."

She approaches me with a grin, laughing and protesting when I pretend to rub my knuckles across her mahogany hair. "Is that right, Anne with an E?"

"You are all my favorite," Mom declares across the kitchen. She looks at Anne. "Darling, did you finish that application?"

"Most of it, Mom. Thanks for handling dinner so I could finish up." Anne moves gracefully toward the table, immediately directing JoJo and Lucy to help her finish setting it for the meal. At twenty-two, she just graduated with a Bachelor's in English at the local Wells College, and I know she's in the thick of looking for an internship or job to launch the next phase of her life.

Dad hovers over the laptop, which is propped on the counter. He has been a professor of computer sciences at Wells for most of my life, teaching a few online classes for another university as well. Every year, he takes on a few summer school classes to supplement their income. I peek over his shoulder to read the project he's analyzing on the screen.

"Jim, can you take a break for dinner now that Dawson is here?" Mom walks over and leans her head on his shoulder. Her arms wrap around him, waiting patiently.

Ellie and Jim Hayes. A power couple if I ever saw one. Married for thirty-six years and counting. They met on their first day in college and have been together ever since. I came along four years after their wedding day. An English major herself, Mom has a romantic streak and gave her three daughters all names from classic literature.

Mom and Dad often say that if God blesses them with sixty-plus years together, it won't nearly be enough. It isn't lost on me that, by the time they were my age, they had already been married for nearly a decade. The years they spent building a family and a home are already behind me, and yet the scene before me feels very far away. That reality hits me hard as I walk toward the table.

My face must reflect my inner tension because Lucy grabs my hand on the way to the table and asks, "Why the long face, Daws?" Her lisp makes my name whistle between her teeth.

"Where were you last week?" Grayson interjects. "I could have used your help on my math homework."

I help Lucy fold napkins, placing them next to the plates. "I had some bugs that needed squashing," I reply in a teasing tone.

She wrinkles up her nose. "Disgusting. Did you really miss out on Mom's cooking to squash bugs?"

"Don't worry. They were on the app I just designed. I discovered some bugs in the code that needed to be worked out."

"That backend still giving you trouble?" Dad peers over his glasses at me as he comes to take a seat at the head of the table.

"Yeah. Maybe you can take a look at it with me before I leave?"

Mom sets a large serving dish piled with spaghetti, homemade meatballs, and a fragrant marinara in the center of the table. The girls carry over a crisp salad and a fresh loaf of bread.

"Your app is looking gorgeous, darling," Mom adds. "Did you add that quiz I was telling you about?"

I snap my fingers. "It's still on my list, Mom, but I'll get to it. I've been extra busy this week."

Conversations pause for a moment as the group joins hands, and Dad leads us in giving thanks for the meal. "And thank you for guiding us in the choices and decisions that bring you glory, Heavenly Father. Amen," he concludes.

Mom resumes her line of questioning as the food begins to make its way around the table. "Anything in particular keeping you extra busy?"

I know she'll find a way to uncover the truth one way or another. "Work, but also . . . uh, I went on a date."

The way her eyes light up across the table from me crushes my heart. "A date! 'Mr.-I-Don't-Date-Dawson' suddenly has a love interest? Do tell."

I bark out a short laugh. "It isn't what you're thinking. I created a profile on Blind Date with a Book Nerd to use as a test dummy for the soft launch of the app. I was only supposed to connect with this person if she gave a very specific set of answers to the questionnaires and quizzes I designed. Turns out, the algorithm worked just as I set it up to. She requested a date with me."

"We're on pins and needles. What is the lucky lady's name?" Anne says in a snarky tone.

I cast her a knowing look in return as Mom exclaims disapprovingly, "Dawson, that's the complete opposite of the purpose of your dating app. The whole point is to match people who might enjoy each other's company based on mutual interests and literary enjoyment rather than looks. How could you possibly design it to match you with a single person?"

Dad grunts over his plate. "Chalk that up to the magic of software programming, honey."

I knew she wouldn't approve. "It was an accident, Mom. I never really expected her to stumble across it, let alone sign up only a few weeks after our soft launch. We're only open for beta testers, anyway. But a mutual friend convinced her to try the app, and she had no idea it was my creation until I showed up to the blind date." I grimace, tearing at a piece of bread. "Suffice it to say, it was more than awkward."

A puzzled look spreads across Mom's face. "So, this was someone you knew already? Oh, Dawson, no." Realization dawns on her face. "You didn't!"

The bread has been reduced to bits over my plate. "I know. You don't even have to say it. It was a boneheaded move, to begin with. But hey, she's actually talking to me again, so it kind of worked."

"Um, who are we talking about here, and how does Mom already know her?" Anne quips.

Mom leans over, her voice quiet. "You remember Ava Fox?"

Understanding dawns on my sister's face. "Oh!" She looks at me with sudden sympathy. "Yikes. Didn't she break up with you in a letter or something?"

"Who would break up with Daws?" JoJo interjects.

"Annie," Dad's voice is stern but amused, "show your brother a little grace."

"That's harsh!" Grayson says. "I feel you, bro. There's this girl at school I've been kind of talking to. She just up and ghosted me last week. Who would wanna ghost this?" He lifts an arm and flexes his bicep, eliciting a chuckle from most of the table.

"I hope you apologized to her for your foolishness." Mom brings the conversation back to the matter at hand.

When I finally look up, her eyes are worried and brimming with emotion. Of all people, she knows what the breakup with Ava did to me years ago. Through countless phone calls, she and Dad walked me through the healing process as I tried to understand the questions to which there were no answers.

I hasten to set her mind at rest. "I explained everything, and we parted as friends. In fact, she asked to help me with marketing the app. She runs some pretty popular social media accounts for book lovers, and we're going to collaborate to get the app some notoriety." I flash a grin at Mom, but she only stares back at me knowingly.

I don't bring up the fact that I've promised Ava I'll go on a series of blind dates too. That'll just get everyone in the family more worked up than they already are. Besides, I only agreed to that plan because Ava asked me to do it. Dating for real is not in my plans anytime soon.

A pair of bright blue eyes and wavy golden hair flashes across my brain, distracting my focus away from our family dinner. Eventually, the conversation moves to topics other than my dating life, but it lingers in my mind as I make the drive back to the city the next morning.

The problem isn't that I don't want to pursue a love story like my parents. But for the last seven years, I couldn't imagine a future with anyone that looked remotely like the future I thought I was going to have with Ava. We didn't have that much in common besides our love for God and books, but that is what I thought made us tick. She was the rich girl; I was the kid raised on a professor's salary. She is confident and classy; I'm a shy techie who nerds out over software and science fiction. Ava is breathtaking, but it was her whip-smart mind and her kind heart that drew me to her in Bible study all those years ago.

Time showed that it wasn't enough for us to last. The irony that I've designed a dating app based solely around a compatibility defined by literary interests isn't lost on me.

Some of the marketing slogans I wrote play through my mind as I work through traffic.

Don't judge a book (or your future love story) by its cover.

Were your favorite literary characters the best matchmakers all along?

Find love between the pages. (Charlie suggested that line to me with a twinkle in her eye.)

Tired of swiping right only to meet someone who doesn't match their profile picture? Your favorite books might be the key to love.

I think people are tired of looks, social status, and wealth being the first (let's face it, the most noticeable) things to base attraction on. Rather than be part of the problem, I want to be part of the solution, bringing a different form of connection to the forefront.

I've poured out every spare minute fortifying and strengthening my app with every trick up my sleeve. I've pulled in developers from my software teams at work, as well as friends in the industry, to double-check my interface and make sure I'm not missing anything important as beta testing has progressed. So far, the response from new members has been enthusiastic.

I designed a plugin to keep track of the matches made through the app. Currently, it reads: *Fifty-nine blind dates with a book nerd made.*

A stab of guilt pierces the center of my chest as the day lengthens. Ava's request and my promise to test my own app for real knocks at my brain every five minutes. The brightness of her face as she happily informed me of her upcoming blind date at church yesterday stabs me again, but this time in the pit of my stomach.

If Ava finds love because of the app I originally designed to impress her, that'll be the irony of all ironies.

And where will that leave me?

I tell myself I just wanted to make things less awkward between us, but I won't pretend that it's going to be easy to keep my feelings toward her in check.

At the very least, you'll be friends again. Don't you want Ava to be happy?

The question hits me from a place deep inside, whispered by a familiar voice. Immediately, I know the answer, but I want to shove it away.

Please, God, don't ask me to let her go.

Can you trust me with her happiness? I sense, rather than hear, a calm voice whispering the reply in my heart.

The question lingers over me all day, even when I'm at the office sitting in project development meetings, staying with me even when I walk through the door of my dark, empty apartment. It's only then that I manage to gather the courage to reply.

"Of course, I want Ava to be happy," I grumble aloud. The only response is the glare of the blue backlighting of the three computers set up in the corner of the dining room. I answer their call and sit down, opening my website.

I stare at the screens, my eyes fuzzy and unfocused behind my glasses.

Ava was always above me, but from the first day we met, she felt like more than just an acquaintance, despite the differences in our upbringing. She comes from a well-to-do family and was raised in privilege and wealth. The last I knew, her father was a high-profile investor, and her mother was a socialite enjoying his success. I haven't thought of the Fox family in years, mostly because I never met Ava's parents.

Maybe that should have been a sign we wouldn't last.

Ava walked into the small Bible study class that met on our college campus with none of the snobbishness I'd experienced from other rich young women in New York City. She said she didn't want to be anything like her parents, instead making it her mission to be down-to-earth, genuine, kind, and real.

I fell for her hard. My family grew up on a rural college professor's salary; there was little extra, but we were happy. Ava's world of ease and luxury was foreign to me until I landed my current six-figure job in software development. Maybe her upbringing imparted an elegance to her, but there was always an otherworldly grace in Ava's beauty that came directly from her soul. She was a delicate flower in my awkward, tech-nerd world. I knew how easily she could bruise, so I never expected her to be the one to sucker punch my heart.

But I don't blame her for wanting more than I could offer her.

Since I've been back in the city, nothing about my return is what I expected it to be. Running into Ava wasn't part of the plan. Yet now that life has thrown us together several times, I sense a wound in her that wasn't there before I left for my internship in London.

There is a haunted look in her eyes. The confidence she used to carry is dimmed, and an air of insecurity has wrapped itself around her like layers of fabric. I wonder if I'm the only one who sees the difference.

My eyes come back into focus, and I find myself staring at my administrative profile. If I'm going to fulfill my promise to Ava, the person matching with fellow book lovers has to represent the most authentic parts of me. That's the whole point of the idea behind the dating app. I begin the process of changing every aspect of my "Lord of the Book Nerds" profile to reflect my most honest self, rather than working the answers to portray the kind of man I suspect Ava is most likely to want. I should have done this long ago, instead of clinging to my foolish, past fantasies of reuniting with her. Since I committed to this experiment, it's essential that I do this now. I don't want to lie to her and pretend I'm fulfilling my end of the bargain while holding parts of myself back. Not when she has allowed me back into her life by offering to help launch my business.

I lean forward, fingers descending on familiar keys, answering questions and filling out quizzes that are as familiar to me as my own hand because I designed them. Except this time, I'm determined to make my answers as honest as possible.

"If it takes going out on a few dates to make Ava happy, then so be it."

When I'm finished, I look over my profile and am struck with nervous dread. Will my algorithm fulfill its duty now that I've changed so many of my profile parameters? Since I've already gone on my first blind date, it's possible the bias I built into it to match me with Ava will linger and influence every other matchup, tainting the experiment.

When I hit the "Match Me with a Book Lover" button, a

message appears on the screen: *Congratulations, Lord of the Book Nerds. You've been matched with Shelly from the Bronx. Would you like to request a blind date?*

There's only one way to test the algorithm's capabilities for sure. Just like I created a profile to match me with any accounts with Ava's very specific parameters, I can use the same principle to check the accounts I match with from here on out. I log out and create a brand-new, secondary profile, using identical properties to my first account.

Welcome, Classic Book Hero Guy.

For the second time, I hit the "Match Me with a Book Lover" button and wait for my matches to load.

To my relief, though there are a few discrepancies, for the most part, the algorithm is working as predicted.

An hour later, I'm making some late-night scrambled eggs when the app alert *pings.* "Shelly from the Bronx" has accepted my blind date request. I grab my phone and open a new text thread, typing in a number I still know by heart.

ME: First blind date booked.

Her reply comes through shortly.

AVA: Who is this?

AVA: Kidding! Daws, that's great! I hope she knocks your socks off. Promise me that you'll enjoy yourself and give it your best shot.

I start to type a reply. My fingers hesitate over the keys, eventually backspacing and starting again.

ME: Thanks. Breakfast on Saturday to discuss our findings? That bagel place you liked on the Lower East Side is still open, I think?

She types for a full minute, bouncing dots floating across my screen. I wait.

AVA: I'm surprised you remember that place. Nine o'clock. Be there or be square!

My eggs almost burn as I stand in the kitchen and stare at the screen, wondering if I'm making the best or worst decision of my life.

11

Ava

Glancing to my immediate left, I catch Connor watching me instead of the movie playing on the giant projector screen up ahead.

My official blind date number one, AKA "Books Be Dope 27," is cute, with perfectly floppy hair, puppy dog eyes, and muscles that say, "I spend a lot of time flexing in gym mirrors." I wish he hadn't caught me looking in his direction, though, because now, I'm afraid he's mistaken the simple act as a flirtatious one. First, he winks, then smirks, the perfectly placed beauty mark above his upper lip like a period declaring his attractiveness. He knows he's handsome . . . and I loathe it.

Give me a pair of reading glasses and a guy who knows more about obscure movie classics than weightlifting and bulking.

Looking away, I try to immerse myself in the world of

the March sisters. Connor and I met up for the "Summer Movie Nights in the Park" program. Tonight's showing is the 1994 adaptation of *Little Women*, a serendipitous coincidence since Connor and I matched on Blind Date with a Book Nerd over that very same book.

It could have been a perfect match.

I should have known this night would be a bust when I agreed to go on a date with someone who picked the username "Books Be Dope 27." The first red flag. But alas, here we are, cool grass beneath me, a darkening sky above me, and an obnoxious man beside me who had the audacity to ask if *Little Women* was really about small people.

Second red flag.

Discreetly, I reach for my phone. I glance at the screen, noting the time. For once, my notifications list isn't inundated with frantic texts and missed calls from one junior editor or another. I suspect Andrew is the culprit, but it seems that everyone at the office knows I'm on my first real date in years tonight. Is it wrong for me to hope for a colossal emergency to drag me away unexpectedly?

What if I secretly wish for a text to come through at this moment from a certain someone, checking up on me to see if I actually showed up to the date? Is that wrong?

It's taken all the strength I have in me, but I've managed to resist texting Dawson all week. I found out through Andrew that his first date was Tuesday, which means he has had three extra days to ruminate over his match. To be quite honest, it's torturing me a bit to wonder how well his date went. Who wouldn't love Dawson Hayes?

Where did they go? What did they do? Did it go so well that they're out for a second date right now? If Dawson takes my advice and falls in love, will he still want to be my friend?

I tuck my phone back into my purse and glue my eyes to the movie screen, but though I love this adaptation, it can't hold my attention tonight. My anxious hands need something to do, so I pick at the grass. Sensing movement beside me, I refuse to give Connor any satisfaction by glancing in his direction again. It's not that he's done anything to truly offend me. But something is just off when a man's biceps are bigger than my thighs, and he keeps flexing them in my direction with a not-so-subtle look on his face.

It doesn't take long to discover what he's up to now. His arm snakes around my waist in one sudden, suave move as he pulls me toward him, scooting me across the blanket until there are only a couple of inches between us.

Third red flag.

I freeze. The people-pleaser in me doesn't want to offend him. Have I put out a vibe that taking this liberty is okay? Gently, I shift away from him and push his arm back as I wave toward a nearby concessions vendor.

The young man walks over, and I request a soda and popcorn. To be polite, I ask Connor if he'd like some too. Maybe if his hands are occupied by snacks, he won't think to reach for me again. But he shakes his head, declining on the grounds that he is currently on a cut and needs to save his calories for his next protein boost. I pay the vendor with cash and scoot away from Connor in what I pray is an obvious move to indicate my need for personal space.

The first bite of salty, buttery popcorn is bliss to my taste buds. I'm happy for the distraction, almost ignoring the movement to my left as Connor scoots closer. I tense, eyes glaring wide at the screen ahead, hoping if I can freeze still enough, maybe he won't remember I'm here.

It's not me he wants this time, though. His hand dives right into my bag of popcorn instead. With pursed lips, I watch him paw around in my bag until he pulls out a handful of the popcorn he didn't want.

All I can hear in my head is a voice shouting, *"Joey doesn't share food!"*

By the time intermission arrives, my popcorn is gone. It has been eaten exclusively by Connor, save for the one handful I managed to nab. The crowd around us stands to stretch, some people ambling off in search of refreshments. It takes every ounce of goodwill in me to turn to Connor and ask with a cheerful smile, "So, how did you hear about Blind Date with a Book Nerd?"

At least I can use this time to gain some intel to help Dawson.

Connor furrows his eyebrows and eyes me curiously. "What?"

"The dating site?" I remind him. Seeing his confusion, I add, "The one we matched on, the one where I asked you on a blind date."

Connor grabs my soda from the grass and slurps what's left of it through the straw. I visibly cringe. He doesn't know me, yet he's suddenly okay sharing a straw with me? *Gross.* At least I was finished with it.

"Oh, which one again?" he asks.

I'm starting to lose track of how many red flags there are with this guy.

"How many dating sites are you on?" I dare to ask the question, slightly afraid of the answer.

He shrugs and violently slurps up whatever dregs are left in the drink. "I mean, I've tried out a few. You know how it is. This one popped up somewhere, so I signed up on a whim."

"Gotcha." I'm sure this is the exact user Dawson had in mind for his site because epic love stories are built off wishes and whims, after all. Sighing heavily, I resolve to continue trying to gain insight. "So you wouldn't consider yourself a book nerd then?"

"I mean, I've been known to enjoy a good book here and there."

I perk up, his answer giving me a renewed sense of hope until he continues, "But truthfully," he says. "I kind of have a thing for bookish girlies."

My stomach churns. "I'm sorry. 'Bookish girlies'?"

Conner flashes a cocky smile my way. "You know . . . that mysterious, alluring, librarian type."

Lifting his hand, he flicks at the tortoiseshell reading glasses I forgot were perched on my head. They slip over my forehead and fall to my nose. My cheeks burn. Fire rises in my core. *Who does he think he—*

Connor reaches out to place his hand on my knee. Instantly, I pull away. Anger flashes in my eyes.

For some insane reason, he laughs. "Come on. You're not really that into books, are you? Surely, you don't need to put on the librarian act to get a date." The look in his eyes reveals everything he is thinking.

"That's kind of the whole point of the dating site," I reply with venom in my voice. "Or did you not catch that when you were filling out your profile and answering literature-related questionnaires."

"Ella . . ."

My laugh is loud and full of sarcasm. He doesn't even remember my name. "So let me get this straight. You signed up for a dating site that is focused on creating connections that are not based on looks, yet you've made it clear the only interest you have in me is for my looks. Did I get that right?"

"Yeah, yeah. Blind date. No photos. It's a mystery, a shot in the dark, like dating roulette. Come on. What's the big deal? We're both young and attractive. Let's just have fun and see where the night goes." Connor reaches over and brushes his fingertips across my forearm. I jerk away again.

"Have you ever fallen for a woman based on what's between her ears rather than her external features?" I ask, unable to let go of my disbelief that someone could be so shallow.

"I've dated a few nurses." The oblivious sincerity in his tone almost makes me puke.

"That's all I need to know." I'm seething. Standing, I grab my purse and walk away.

"Intermission is only ten more minutes!" He calls after me as though he's sure I'm going to return.

As I weave through the Park, carefully sidestepping around blankets, legs, and random belongings thrown on the grass, I bring out my phone to call Charlie, but then I remember that she and Andrew are on their way to Vermont for the weekend. Frustrated, I dial my sister instead. I need to talk to someone right now, or else I might explode.

"Hey, Tashi."

"Are you okay?" she asks. "You sound out of breath."

"Oh, I'm just fleeing a horrible date." I step over a bag of spilled popcorn and see the Park's exit ahead.

"Mom told me you were dating again. Weird timing because right after she said that I saw some pigs flying."

"Hardy har har." I hope she can hear my eyes roll through the phone. "I don't know why you two are so preoccupied with my love life. It's not like you're settled down with anyone."

"Didn't you hear? Bryan and I are back together." Triumph rings out in her voice.

"Oh, yeah? For how long this time?"

Natasha and Bryan have been on and off every few months for nearly two years now. Their romance is a true soap opera.

She snorts. "Well, he told my friend, Amara, he went ring shopping last week."

My jaw drops, more out of horror than happiness for my sister. "You're thinking of marriage?"

"Yeah, he said something about how he knows he needs to change and be the man I deserve, which, hello! That's what I've been saying this whole time."

My parents' marriage, fraught with petty arguments and dissatisfaction, flashes across my memory. Tashi was younger, oblivious, and immature when Mom and Dad separated, but surely, she observed how troubling a poorly grounded marriage could be.

"But you guys break up and get back together more often than I finish a new book. Do you think it's safe to go into a marriage with that tumultuous a history? How do you know things will be different this time for both of you?"

I try to pay attention to my surroundings as I cross the intersection and speed walk toward home. The streets are well-lit, but I'm not so keen on being out after dark alone. I pace in the direction of my apartment, my steps fast and sure.

"I don't know. Gotta have faith it'll work out, right? He says he doesn't want to lose me."

"That's what he said every other time too."

Natasha blows out a frustrated breath. "Is this therapy? When you are in a steady, healthy relationship, let me know, and then I'll listen to your advice."

"Tashi, I'm just looking out for you."

"You've never even given him a chance, Ava. Mom's the only one who—"

"Is not in touch with reality? Or healthy relationships whatsoever?" I finish her sentence.

I know my sister sees what I see, but on the flip of a dime, Tashi will go to bat for our mother, always the golden child keeping up her position as Mom's favorite. This time doesn't prove any different.

"You always side with Dad," she snaps. "News flash: He's the one who left." Her voice is sharp and pointed.

"Never mind that she practically pushed him out the door," I retort. I don't want to rehash the circumstances of our parents' divorce, but in my agitated state, I can't seem to stop myself. The back of my neck prickles with heat.

"Look, I've gotta run. My *boyfriend* and I have plans tonight," Tashi says. "Love you."

At least she ended with that. As often as my sister and I have disagreements, we have never pushed each other away to the point of not speaking.

I barely have time to squeeze out an "I love you too" before she ends the call. Tears prick my eyes. My sandals slap against the sidewalk as I push myself into a jog to make it home sooner. I want to call Dawson to tell him everything that just happened. But I can't go there. Leaning on him would be leading him on. He doesn't need or deserve the drama and baggage that defines my life.

My cozy apartment building welcomes me. I take the stairs to expend more of my angry energy. Just as I'm shoving the key into the lock, my phone rings. I scramble for it. My heart skips a beat. Could it be—

It's Mom.

"Hi, M—"

She doesn't wait for my greeting, diving right in and ripping me limb from limb with her words.

"How dare you talk to your sister that way! It's like you don't want anyone to be happy. Just because you can't find love doesn't mean she can't!"

Betrayal stabs my heart. I remind myself how easily this situation could be twisted and manipulated. Maybe Tashi did call Mom and complain about me. Or maybe Mom happened to call her, and some offhand comment from Tashi became this blown-out-of-proportion beratement I'm on the receiving end of now. Both tend to overdramatize their problems, gossip, and flat-out lie at times. It's hard to know what is up and what is down with them.

I finish unlocking the door, put the call on speaker, and place the phone face up on the coffee table when I walk inside. My mother's verbal abuse reverberates off the walls of my apartment, emphasizing how lonely and stuffy it feels. While she continues her scolding, I open a window, water a plant, and grab my laptop, prepared to settle in for a night of editing. When she viciously asks if I'm still on the line, I answer like a good, dutiful daughter, "Yes, I'm still here."

I despise myself for the way I let her treat me.

And I despise her for how small she makes me feel.

Finally, we hang up with no resolution, and I'm more deflated than ever. I open my laptop. Time to make use of my late afternoon caffeine fix. I can use the distraction of getting lost in another world with characters who have far greater problems than me for the next few hours. Before opening a manuscript to review, I check my email and find an awaiting message from James Wolfe. I sigh. *Another one?* He may be a pain to work with as an author, but his military thrillers are well-written and suspenseful. When I see he has sent yet another new draft of his upcoming release—the one that has already been sent into production—I almost hurl my laptop across the room.

I click out of my email and look at my phone instead. Something pulls me back into the Blind Date with a Book Nerd app. I'm fascinated by the creativity and ingenuity Dawson's genius has displayed through every detail of the site.

I feel as if I'm almost snooping as I peruse the app, but I'm not worried about him being able to follow my movements. A few days ago, I created a secondary account and made sure none of it would trigger his algorithm. My goal was to observe how the site worked without bias so I would be better informed when I share it with my followers. But I have to admit, it feels a little like getting a sneak peek into Dawson's world.

His forum is popping. I left a few comments on it the other day. When I open the app now, I notice a notification waiting for me.

You have one new message on Blind Date with a Book Nerd, the notification reads.

My heart softens as I stare at the screen. Now, whoever sent this message doesn't seem like Connor at all. The message is in direct response to a question I asked on the forum's discussion board. It is . . . thoughtful, sincere, and charming. I consider for a moment if I should respond at all—tonight made me think Dawson's matchmaking algorithm needs some work—but something pulls at me to reply. I type out a quick reply and send it off before turning my attention back to editing.

The pages welcome me into their escape, but my heart continues wishing in secret, as it did earlier tonight, that a certain someone would call or text.

But he never does.

12

Dawson

Did everyone and their mother decide to go out for a bagel this morning? Is this what summers in New York City have come to? Bagel wars?

Usually, I try to keep a lid on my natural sarcasm, but as I weave toward the line of people gathered in front of the vintage brick storefront of Ava's favorite bagel place, I can't help but let the annoyance I've felt all week slide into my brain. The crowd wears urgent expressions on their somber faces—most directed straight into their phones—but the few who do glance my way seem to stiffen as if I'm going to rush over and shove them out of line so I can be the first to eat a double chocolate chunk bagel and sweet cream cheese this morning.

I attach a nonthreatening grin to my face, trying to see over the heads blocking my view of the tables forming a patio on the sidewalk. I'll be surprised if she's here before me. I deliberately arrived early to secure a spot in line.

At this rate, there won't be any bagels left, I grumble internally.

I'm self-aware enough to know my sour mood isn't on account of the grumpy, early-morning bagel-seekers currently blocking my path to the front door. My plan for this morning is twofold: I want to get Ava's honest feedback about her first real blind date from Blind Date with a Book Nerd. I'm both hopeful and nervous about the quality of the matchup because it will impact the experience other future members have. On the one hand, if she felt a connection with the guy, that's great for my business. On the other hand, the thought of her laughing and making memories with some random guy makes me want to pound the pavement and take my tension out on a long run through the city.

My second purpose this morning is to feed her the best bagels in the city. If anything gets in the way of that mission, I'll have some strong words for the bagel people.

Not really. I'm a lover, not a fighter. But still, today feels like something—whether it's good or bad, I can't tell—is about to happen.

Ava and I walked here together on quite a few early Saturday morning bagel runs to fuel long study sessions during grad school. Ava was on a serious bagel kick for approximately fifteen months and twenty-three days. Every month during that timeframe, she would obsess over a different bagel flavor, her eyes lighting up with glee as soon as she saw the glass display cases. She always did a quirky little dance when the bagel attendant handed her the heavy brown bag, her feet shuffling as if her joy couldn't contain itself.

I'd like to see that look of glee light up her face again and know I'm the one who put it there.

She's not interested in you, Dawson, my brain reminds me cruelly, which it seems to do at inopportune moments, just when I'm starting to feel good about things.

"Hey, hey, anyone know where to buy a decent bagel in this town?" A sweet voice trills behind me, and my heart flips over.

I'm still putting it back into place when I feel a tap-tap-tap on my shoulder. I swing around. Ava grins at me. To my surprise, she reaches toward me, slipping her arm around my waist for a quick side hug. It feels like I just got an embrace from the sun.

How is she this gorgeous at nine a.m. on a Saturday morning?

I try to stop myself from staring at her admiringly. Instead of the casual weekend outfit that I expected her to be in, she is dressed as if it is vintage day at the office, with brown trouser pants and a crisp, sleeveless silk blouse. Brown flats peek out at me from the bottom of her pant legs. Her sunny hair is gathered over her shoulder in a loose braid. She looks like a movie star from the thirties. Ava could model for a fashion magazine, but that's nothing new.

I realize what a bad idea it was to walk here in joggers, a t-shirt, and sneakers, looking like I just stepped out of the gym. My bad. I try to straighten my shoulders and look like my casual outfit was intentional.

She seems to notice my subtle inspection. "I know what you're thinking," she sighs. "I look ridiculously stuffy for this early on the weekend. One of our authors asked for a meeting today, so I have to go into the office after this."

My heart lifts. She grins.

"Duty calls." I grin back. "At least you'll be well-fed before you face the lions." I motion toward the other waiting customers as we walk to the end of the line. "We must have had the right idea."

"Or the wrong idea," she laughs. "I don't remember this place being so popular when we used to come here."

We're moving closer to the bagel shop, standing in line behind a guy wearing headphones. His hands hold open a book, which he appears to be completely immersed in. The guy clearly came prepared for a long wait. I look at the title. It's a self-help book by a motivational speaker I vaguely recognize.

"Wait." I pause as we shuffle a few feet toward the entrance. "Don't tell me you haven't been here since grad school. How is possible that Ava-the-bagel-girl resisted their siren call for years on end?" I pin a look of mock horror on my face. "Don't tell me you've been cheating with another bagel place?"

She laughs again. A few heads turn to look over their shoulders at the sound, and I don't blame them. If wildflowers could laugh, that's what they would sound like. "As if I could ever. No, I just never felt like coming back after . . ."

Abruptly, the flow of her words stops. She looks down at her hands and rubs at a spot between her knuckles. When she looks up again and our eyes lock, I know we are both aware of everything she didn't say.

I watch her deliberately brighten her face, the shadow disappearing from her bold blue eyes as if it hadn't existed. "Anyway, this was a great suggestion. I already feel the bagel obsession coming back."

We share an awkward grin. Silence falls for a few minutes as we regain our composure.

The line moves slowly but steadily forward. Fortunately, it seems the bagel shop isn't running out of products because I haven't seen hordes of angry bagel-seekers exiting with empty hands and frowns on their faces yet. Though it's unlikely anyone is listening, I'm aware of the many sets of ears all around, so I keep our conversation light as we wait.

It feels good to banter with her again. Ava seems content to stand in the hazy morning sunlight, gracefully moving a few steps forward every few minutes. I'm shocked at how natural it feels to casually step back into conversation with her as if years of silence don't stretch between us. It's hard not to keep my eyes on her all the time. Every curve and feature of her face is mesmerizing to me. There is a sense of maturity and wisdom in her features that is fascinating. Though, at the same time, she has barely aged a day, and the moments we stand in line together feel like déjà vu, as if we've stepped back in time to those mornings long ago. I have to force myself to look away now and then, suppressing the longing that won't stop creeping into the pit of my stomach.

A few times, when I turn back toward her, I catch Ava's gaze trained intently on me. She quickly looks away each time. There's a glint in her eye that I don't know how to interpret. She is guarded, and it pains me to think that no matter how easily we fall into conversation again and how natural it feels to be together, that feeling only matters to me.

"Oh," she speaks brightly, "I've been meaning to ask about your family. Did you have a good visit with them last week?"

Her face turns up to mine. She's only a couple of inches

shorter than me, so I allow myself a moment to look at her appreciatively before I answer. The longer I look, the deeper the flush gets on her cheeks.

"It was a great visit. Every time I go up there, I'm reminded of how far the drive is and how much I wish I could see them every day."

"I'm sure it's hard to be away," Ava replies. "I miss them." A hint of sadness creeps into her tone. She seems to fall into a thoughtful reflection.

I miss you is my involuntary and silent reply. I clear my throat, and our conversation stops as we finally get the chance to enter the bagel shop. When we exit a few minutes later with paper bags of bagels and Styrofoam cups of coffee in hand, I use my elbow to nudge Ava's arm.

With a jolt, she seems to startle out of the reverie she's stuck in.

"Thanks for not picking the garlic bagel this time," I say lightly. "I'm no vampire—despite what everyone will tell you about the late hours we tech nerds like to keep—but the sheer amount of garlic on that thing is enough to make anyone vanish."

My joke makes her laugh. "I had mercy on you this time. An entire month's obsession was enough garlic bagels to last a lifetime. I'm a cinnamon raisin girl now." Playfully, she shakes the bag at my face.

"It could be argued that putting raisins in anything is a sacrilege," I reply somberly.

"At least I venture out. You are still ordering the double chocolate chunk bagel, I see," she teases.

"I'm nothing if not a loyal guy. You should know that about me."

151

I'm surprised to see the flush deepen on her cheeks again in response to my words. We find an empty bench. She waits until we are seated, bagels in hand, before turning expectantly to me.

"So . . . you've kept me in suspense long enough." Her stare pins me down with its intensity. "Will I be meeting the future Mrs. Hayes soon?" Her fingers tear at the bagel, creating little pieces I notice she doesn't eat.

That's right. We're here to talk about our first blind dates.

A dry chunk of chocolate chokes me a little. I rush to take a gulp of hot coffee to wash it down, which only succeeds in scalding my throat. A small hand begins to pat furiously between my shoulder blades. Ava leans forward and stares at me with concern in her eyes. I lift my hand to let her know I'm okay even while I continue to sputter.

"Uh, it was . . . let's just say an experience," I begin after recovering from my coughing fit.

She waits quietly for me to continue so I don't pause. "My date turned out to be an extremely sweet, fifty-six-year-old librarian with pink hair named Shelly. She's from the Bronx, has three grandchildren, and plans to retire to Montana in ten years. We decided I was a little too old for her, and it was best to just remain friends. She invited me to her rom-com book club, and I think I'm going to accept."

Ava sets the bagel in its wrapper on her lap. Her mouth drops open. A burst of laughter rings out into the morning. I grin as she gasps for air.

Finally, she manages to get some words out. "Okay, the first note for today's meeting: Add age preference parameters to your questionnaire. Age is just a number, but still, going on a blind date with someone your mother's age could be a surprise. I won't lie, though. The rom-com book club sounds amazing. Get me an invite, will you?"

I laugh at her when she pulls a small moleskin notebook from her pocket and begins to write in it, her head bent low in concentration.

"I can see how a parameter like that would be helpful. It might be too soon to bring another woman around Shelly, though," I reply in a monotone voice. She lifts her head and flashes me a grin. The feeling of amusement passes. A ball of dread abruptly begins to roil in my stomach. "Now, your turn. How was your date last night?"

"Well, Connor—or 'Books Be Dope 27'—was not quite as much of a delight as your Shelly," she begins ruefully.

My heart drops. "I don't like the sound of that. Was there a problem?"

She lifts both hands. "No problem . . . or it wasn't a problem exactly. He has a thing for 'bookish girlies" and thought *Little Women* was a movie about literal little women. He's also clearly a serial dating app opportunist who doesn't understand physical boundaries."

My fingers curl into tight fists. "Well, he's officially banned from the app today." In my head, I'm already writing a scathing message, informing him exactly why I am revoking his privileges.

She shakes her head and shrugs. "That's not necessary. We were in public, so he didn't try anything too crazy. Honestly, it was worse when he ate my entire bag of popcorn." The corners of her lips turn down as she laments the theft of her snack.

"Uh oh." I lean back on the bench in shock. "Joey doesn't share food." Ava is generous to a fault, except when it comes to food. I like to think that the adorable flaw was God's way of proving to us mere mortals that she is, in fact, human too.

"Right?" she wails. "Anyway, I don't think Connor would be able to tell a classic from a space opera. His definition of a graphic novel would be a steamy romance. He was good-looking, though. He gave me his number to hire him as a cover model for CityLight."

I roll my eyes. Being part of the marketing team goes hand in hand with the duties of her job. Still, I don't want this guy near her again, let alone working with her.

Ava continues, not noticing my annoyance. "I got the distinct impression that he signed up for your app because he assumed it was going to be filled with a bunch of stereotypical 'She takes off her glasses and pulls down her hair, and suddenly, she turns into Rachel Weisz' types."

I gesture to her little notebook. "We'd better make a note to add a question requiring new users to explain their intentions in seeking a date from the bookish community. We don't want a bunch of scuzzballs using it just because they think it'll be a quick way to get a date. That's not what my app is about."

Ava nods and bends over her notebook again. As her precise handwriting scribbles across the page, I sneak another look at her. Tendrils of hair have come loose from her braid, creating a halo around her face and shining like soft gold in the mid-morning sun. The silk collar of her blouse rubs against the skin of her neck.

When she looks up and catches me staring, I quickly look away.

"Yes, I think setting up the user's dating intentions is essential. Are they looking for a free download to speed-read—and have just a short-term fling—or are they looking for a beautifully bound hardcover to display on their bookshelf forever—the long-term commitment?" she says thoughtfully.

I smirk at her. "That's beautiful, Ava. Want to ditch CityLight and come work for me full-time? You can write my copy and design all our quizzes and questionnaires."

She wiggles her pen at my face. "You couldn't afford me," she teases. "Besides, I still haven't seen that paycheck you promised me."

I lift my now empty take-out bag. "Hey, it's coming. In the meantime, I pay generously in bagels and coffee."

Her lips suddenly press together in a smirk. She stares at my face.

"What?" I ask. "Do I have something on my face?"

"Uh, yeah," she replies. "Looks like someone wants to take their bagel home for later."

With a hot wave of embarrassment, I swipe the back of my hand across my mouth. "Did I get it?"

She laughs. "No, but the rest of your face is about to be covered in chocolate and cream cheese. Here—" Without hesitation, she raises her hand and uses the edge of a thin paper napkin to dab at the corner of my lips.

When her eyebrows furrow in concentration, and she keeps dabbing away, I reach up and capture her hand in my own. I tug it down. "Okay, okay, I think you got it."

Her laugh breaks out merrily. "I wondered how long you were going to let me keep doing that."

Her cornflower blue eyes lock with mine, and I take the chance to let a wave of admiration pass across my face. Her lashes are dark. They flutter over the tops of her cheekbones, but not before I see a self-conscious look appear in her eyes.

"Dawson," she says, "can I have my hand back now?"

With a start, I realize I still have her hand gripped between my fingers. Unconsciously, I've begun to make slow, lazy circles across her palm. Dropping it like a hot potato, I mutter a sheepish, "Sorry."

She grabs the notebook and pen and starts to scribble again. "Now, where were we? Oh, what do you think about setting up a way to rate your date? One star means it was awful. Five stars mean it was amazing, and you want to go out again. If a star rating appears next to a profile, it could help users weed through blind date matches who show up with less-than-noble intentions like Connor and motivate other people to be on their best behavior."

I struggle to pull myself back into business mode. "That sounds great. I'll work on adding that."

The rest of the hour we spend together on the bench is spent discussing the vlog-style interview she wants to conduct with me and the collaborative marketing campaign she has been designing.

"So anytime you want me to start posting these, I can. I think it's really going to get your app in front of its perfect target audience," she concludes, snapping the moleskin notebook shut and tucking it back into her pocket.

We rise from the bench together, throw away our empty wrappers and coffee cups, and linger at the edge of the sidewalk, chatting about what feels like everything and nothing. When we part ways, she'll go one way, and I'll go the other, and I'm not quite ready to let her go just yet.

"Do you have time for a stroll in the park?" I motion in its direction.

With a grimace, she glances down at the watch on her wrist. "Unfortunately, I have my meeting with that author. I should introduce you two; I think you'd like him. He writes all the stuff you probably read."

"Science fiction?"

"No, military thrillers," she replies. Her eyes peer up at me with a merry but curious glint. "I thought you weren't on the sci-fi kick anymore?"

I shrug and put on a mournful expression. "What can I say? Sci-fi is my go-to garlic bagel. A little weird to some people but oh-how-satisfying."

She takes a step backward, her face full of laughter, her hands raised in front of her, index fingers crossed in an X pattern. Suddenly, she resembles a librarian of artifacts on an epic quest for mummified treasure, and I wonder what her hair would look like spilling over her shoulders right now.

"Okay, garlic breath. Thanks for the breakfast," she says.

I match her step but move toward her and not away. People skirt around us on the sidewalk, and I'm sure we're getting some looks.

"When will I see you again?"

Her head tilts to the side, her expression playful. "Um . . . well, I may schedule a blind date this week. I'm thinking that matching with someone who loves *Lord of the Rings* has got to be a winner, right?"

"I guess we'll see." I'm standing right in front of her now, my fingertips lingering at her elbows, wishing I could pull her into my arms for a hug before she goes.

"I'll let you know when we should schedule our next Super-Blind-Date-With-A-Book-Nerd-Improvement-Team-

Sesh," she murmurs so softly I almost can't hear her over the noise of the city.

I lean closer to catch the words. "Okay," I whisper in reply. The tips of my fingers brush her bare forearms.

"Okay." She pulls away just before I wrap my arms around her waist, stepping backward and turning to walk away, calling over her shoulder as she does. "And you'd better schedule your second date for this week too! You'll have to get over Shelly someday."

13

Ava

"No problem, Mr. Ketner. I'll see to it as soon as I'm back in the office. I stepped out for lunch today."

"Don't make me regret your promotion, Ava."

My boss's warning sends thunder through my heart. I try to swallow, but my mouth is suddenly dry. I know he is just as stressed as I am and doesn't mean his words so harshly. But if I don't handle this James Wolfe fiasco correctly, will I even have a job anymore? My career is my entire identity . . .

The early afternoon sun feels brutal, beating down relentlessly, its heat radiating up from the sidewalks and pavement. The air is a stagnant blend of exhaust and humidity, and despite the brilliant blue sky, I want to hole up indoors in the safety of my perfectly air-conditioned office.

I wish I hadn't scheduled this date today.

But it's for Dawson, I remind myself as Gary Ketner

continues his spiel into my ear. I step past an alleyway, glancing over and making accidental eye contact with a sketchy-looking man standing with his back pressed against the building's shadows. He squints before I can avert my gaze and spits in my direction. I rush forward, grateful to be out in broad daylight for this date, attempting to remember everything my boss is saying.

By the time I reach the address my blind date insisted we meet at for lunch, I'm off the phone and am a tangle of nerves. For this date, for what I'll face back at the office afterward, for my actual future . . .

I crane my neck and stare up at a sign above the door that reads: "Uncle Tug's: Best Taste of Texas in NYC."

Is this . . . BBQ? Cringing, I take a deep breath. I should have looked this place up before agreeing to it.

Saddle up, sister. You can do this. For Dawson. He deserves every bit of help I can give him to make the launch of his app a success.

Steeling my courage, I step inside. The theme is red and cowhide. It appears to cover every square inch of the establishment. I do a quick once-over around the room. The only clue my date gave me as to his identity is that he would be dressed as an unmistakable character from the finest book in history. Based on his dining choice, perhaps he's a fan of Westerns in addition to *Lord of the Rings?*

"How many?"

I turn at the question and lock eyes with the hostess. She's wearing the world's smallest cowboy hat—the only blue object in sight. I smile at her. She doesn't smile back.

So much for Southern hospitality.

"How many?" she repeats impatiently, arching one

160

eyebrow impressively high. She drums her long, fake nails on the plastic menus.

"Two, but I don't know if my, uh, friend is here yet."

"Nobody has come in sayin' they're meetin' anyone." She grabs two menus and motions for me to follow. Leading me to a table for two by a window, she slaps the menus down on the tabletop, then walks away without another word.

Well, this place already seems promising.

I pick up a menu and peruse the food list. Without a doubt, my stomach will not fare well this evening. Everything is deep-fried, double-fried, or, as the menu literally states, "sticky." The few experiences with barbecued food I've had have never gone well. I'm getting the sense that today will be no different.

I can't compel myself to be excited about anything on the menu, so I turn my attention to the window, its view blocked by a noisy, chaotic construction site across the street.

Will my date even show? I wonder as I watch a large metal beam be lifted by a crane in fascination. As I stare across the street, something in the window catches my peripheral vision. Shifting my eyes, I suddenly realize what I'm seeing is a reflection, and as my eyes focus on the figure, I can't help but emit a shocked scream.

Whipping back to the restaurant, I take in a grotesque character standing at my table. The face is one of nightmares. Literal nightmares.

"Oh," the creature says, its manly and slightly worried voice not at all matching the costume. He pulls the creepy mask from his face and smiles. The man's blond hair is standing on end from a combination of the urgency with which he removed the mask and what I assume is sweat. He motions to the costume. "Sorry about this. Too much?"

My blind date drops into the seat across from me and tosses the mask onto the table. Its distorted face stares at the cowhide-strewn ceiling, and I shiver. Sweat glistens along the man's hairline. He wipes it away with the back of his hand. My face is permanently frozen in horror.

Slowly, he points his index finger in my direction. "You *are* my date, aren't you? 'Foxy Book Lady'?" The man looks pained and scrubs a hand over his face. "Sorry again. This is embarrassing. I just assumed it was you since there was no one else here waiting for their lunch party to arrive. I'm so sorry." Scooting out of the booth, he stands, and to my own surprise, I stop him.

Dawson is counting on me.

"Wait!"

The man pauses. My tongue is thick in my throat. I could get out of this easily right now by pretending I have no idea what he is talking about and hightailing it out of here immediately. Of all people, I know Dawson would understand.

Despite the man's terrifying first impression, I find myself asking, "Are you supposed to be . . . Gollum?"

"Why, yes. I am." He lights up and drops back onto the booth. "Well, I'm more of a Smeagol at the moment, if you know what I mean. So, you *are* my blind date, then?"

I'm still having trouble formulating words. This man couldn't have known that Gollum was the face of my nightmares for weeks on end after binging the entire *Lord of the Rings* movie series in college after Dawson found out I'd never seen them, only read the books. I literally called Dawson every night after waking up in a cold sweat with

Gollum's horrible face leering at me in my dreams. Still, the memory of watching them together is a fond one, and after I'd recovered from my initial horror, both the movies and books are among my favorites.

Before I can answer properly, a waitress stops at our table to take our drink order. I'm grateful for the extra time to process but panic when she finally walks away. I still have no idea what to say to the man in front of me.

He is still apologetic, but I detect a hint of pride as he motions to his disturbingly lifelike costume. "I normally wouldn't dress like this for a first date, but there is this incredible fantasy cosplay event happening in town today. Couldn't miss it. Do you like cosplay?"

Did he forget about his question? What is more likely is that he has made the reasonable assumption that no woman in her right mind would stick through lunch plans with a random grown man in a Gollum costume if she hadn't already planned for it. Thus, by the process of deduction, I must be, in fact, his date.

"A costume party can be fun," I reply. "But I can't say I've ever done a cosplay event. It's not exactly my thing."

With a snap of his fingers, he says, "Ah, that's because you haven't tried it. You should come with me. They will still be going by the time we're through with lunch. I'm sure we can scrape together a costume for you."

I don't even try to hold back my visible shudder. "I'm afraid I have to get back to work right after lunch, so that won't work out."

His sudden, distressed moan sets me on edge. "I was really hoping you'd agree. I kind of told a few of my buddies I was going on a date, and they thought I was lying. I said I'd convince you to come back with me. We bet twenty bucks on it . . . You see where this is going, right?"

"I do." My lips pull into a tight smile. "Unfortunately, I do."

He dives into all the reasons I should reconsider, and as I tune him out, I realize I don't even know this man's name. Even when the waitress returns with our drinks, he continues his case for cosplay, pausing only long enough to order lunch specials on behalf of both of us. His monologue continues even after we're served our food and only ends when I discover a bug floating in the swirling ocean of barbecue sauce on my plate. When I flag down the waitress and point it out to her, she tells me it makes the dish that much more authentic. I can't tell if she's joking or being serious.

Meanwhile, my date—whom I've now learned somewhere along the way is named Jeremiah—wolfs down his food like his life depends on it. Seeing my plate untouched, he then begins clearing my plate as well. At least he has the decency, unlike Connor, to *ask* to share my food first.

As Jeremiah seems to take his task of eating every scrap of food at the table very seriously, it turns out that he is also carrying the whole conversation. An uncomfortable silence hangs between us.

Think of something to say, anything to make this less awkward, I scold myself.

"You have such a realistic costume." The meager compliment is the only thing I can think of. I risk a glance at the creepy mask on the table. Its lifeless, gray face sends a shiver down my spine again.

"State of the art." He is clearly proud of the authenticity of his costume. "Wanna try it on? I bet you're the only one who could make Gollum look cute."

Turning up my palms, I shake my head. "No, no. That's . . . I couldn't." I stare at a spot that has suddenly appeared on his chest. "Oh. Uh, looks like you dropped a little sauce on your . . ." I gesture to the blemish.

His gaze drops instantly, and with a dramatic groan, he throws his head back. An ugly curse slips through his lips. "This suit had better not be ruined! Dry cleaning is so expensive these days."

He dabs at it with a napkin, which doesn't seem to help the situation at all. Whatever the suit is made of is readily absorbing the sticky, dark liquid. "If you'll excuse me," he grumbles, "I'm going to try scrubbing this out with soap in the restroom."

The thought of waiting here alone for him to rejoin me makes me queasy, and I'm sure my empty stomach is not to blame. "Actually," I interject, "I have to go. My boss needs me back at the office as soon as possible."

Jeremiah's face falls. "Oh. You won't be here when I get back, then?"

I almost feel bad for the guy. "Depending on how long your costume-scrubbing takes compared to the waitress bringing my bill, possibly not."

He waves a hand at me. "I've got the tab. I ate your entire portion anyway."

"Are you sure? I mean, I cost you earning an extra twenty bucks, remember?"

Jeremiah groans, his feet doing a funny little jig. "Ah, I already feel this seeping through. I've gotta go wash it off. Sorry."

With that, he makes a mad dash for the restroom, and it

takes me a few seconds to process the last half hour.

Rising from the table, I snap a photo of the creepy Gollum mask and text it to Dawson as I step outside and head briskly back to the office.

ME: If I get nightmares again, I blame you.

DAWSON: Do I even want to know?

ME: Blind date BBQ with Gollum.

DAWSON: My precious!

ME: THERE IS NOTHING PRECIOUS ABOUT THIS! I blame your matchmaking algorithm.

DAWSON: That is a terrible date on all fronts. BBQ and Gollum? I am so sorry.

Back at the office, I find myself slammed immediately with a rush of emails, phone calls, and James Wolfe damage control without even a spare second to think about my rumbling stomach. CityLight's biggest author is raising a ruckus over a self-induced fiasco with his latest release. Thankfully, he hasn't descended on the office just yet, but I expect his burly frame to pop through the door any minute.

Just when I think I might get a moment to steal away for a snack (and take a deep breath), a knock echoes at my office door.

"Come in," I call out, rummaging through one of my desk drawers for a granola bar, a beef jerky stick, literally anything to quiet the gnawing in my belly. My candy dispenser was wiped clean by a certain fellow editor this morning.

The door creaks open. I glance up and jump a little in surprise, not expecting to see Dawson standing in the doorway with a white bag of Chinese takeout in his hands.

"Did someone order the *Lord of the Rings* special with

Gollum sauce on the side?" His grin splits his face from ear to ear.

"You did not." A grin tugs on my own lips. My chest swells.

"It's the least I can do after you suffered through that terrible date to help me." He sets the bag on my desk, and the mouthwatering scent of sweet and sour sauce hits me. "BBQ and Gollum?" he whispers, shaking his head with confusion. "Of all the combinations."

"Believe me, it's so much worse than it sounds." I dig into the bag and pull out cartons of rice, sweet and sour chicken, and chow mein. "Two pairs of chopsticks?" I look up at Dawson in surprise.

"Hey, I haven't eaten lunch yet either." He takes one set from me.

"For you, I'll share my food," I reply, opening the container of chicken. I pop a satisfying bite into my mouth. "You are such a lifesaver. Thank you, Daws. This is so thoughtful."

Dawson pulls an extra chair closer to my desk and starts on the chow mein. In no time at all, we both lean back in our chairs, feet propped on my desk, empty cartons of Chinese food balancing on our full bellies, laughing about how poorly my date went today. In hindsight, I can see the humor, and I pour out all the details to Dawson, who takes notes on how to refine a member's matchmaking suggestions to reflect their interests even more.

It's a moment I wish I could freeze. For a few minutes, it feels as if Dawson and I never lost any time, as if we've been friends forever and a day. If only life was as simple as it is at this moment.

"Hey, Ava. I was wonder—" Andrew's voice cuts off our laughter. My friend stops short in the doorway, his head swinging from me to Dawson and back again. A knowing smile creeps onto his face. "You know what? I'll come back later. Sorry to interrupt." Backing away, Andrew disappears.

The disruption interrupts our lighthearted camaraderie. I pick at the leftover sweet and sour chicken with my chopsticks. Not even thirty seconds pass before my phone dings with a text.

CHARLIE: You're having lunch with Dawson in your office?

Immediately, my cheeks flush, heat blazing across my entire face and neck. I try to hide my phone but see Dawson flashing his in my direction.

"Did you just get a text from Charlie too?" he asks. I notice that his normally tan cheeks have reddened just a touch as well.

"Yep." As I avert my gaze from his, a sudden giddiness in my core sends a wave of panic through my veins. Trying not to let my hands shake, I busy myself with the lid of one of the food cartons, taking extra care to secure the flaps.

Breathe, Ava.

I clear my throat. "So anyway, maybe you can add a filter for users who are afraid of fictional characters, who aren't into cosplay, or who like their favorite fictional characters to be handsome and not terrifying. More Aragorns and fewer Gollums, thanks."

Dawson laughs, and I watch him stand, brushing fortune cookie crumbs from his lap. "I just can't believe he showed up like that. Of all the possible literary characters to dress as." He shakes his head in disbelief and gazes down at me. I resist the urge to squirm under his intense hazel eyes. "You have my number if Gollum haunts your dreams."

I smirk and try not to show how much his generosity means to me. It doesn't surprise me. Dawson has always been kind and thoughtful. "You might regret that at three a.m."

"It wouldn't be the first time."

Instantly, I see the longing in his eyes, which can't hide behind the amused look on his face. I know Dawson wouldn't care if I woke him up five times a night if it meant he was the one I chose to call. He wouldn't regret the disruption in sleep, and if I asked him to come over to keep me company through the darkest hours, he would be at my door in a heartbeat and stay on the phone with me until he arrived. This is the man who would lose sleep over me and for me any day of the week (and has).

Just the thought makes me feel like crying. I lift the cardigan draped across my chair and tug it over my shoulders, feeling as if I need a physical shield to hide my vulnerability right now.

Because Dawson Hayes feels like home, and how sad that home feels like such a dangerous place to be.

14

Dawson

Am I upset about having to postpone my second blind date tonight?

If Ava or my mom asks, yes, I'm devastated. She could have been the one.

The truth, though? I'll admit that "Let Me Be Your Romantasy" sounds like a hoot if her in-person conversation is anything like the slightly unhinged messages she's been sending me since my algorithm matched our accounts. Messages about half-fae, full-fae, some court, and asking me half a dozen times if I happen to have blue-black hair. It took gathering a lot of courage just to message her to suggest that we connect, but at this point, I'm beginning to wonder if my matchmaking software encountered a glitch.

Not that I doubt my programming abilities.

I just doubt my ability to ever find a woman who even comes close to matching the way Ava shines.

The expression on her face the other day when I brought a late lunch to her office hasn't left my mind. I made her tell me all about her obnoxious date while plying her with fragrant chow mein and fortune cookies. Nothing like comfort food and conversation to release some tension. Talking about it seemed to help her see the humor of the situation. Her merry laugh crawled into my soul and has echoed there for days.

Pushing my glasses farther up the bridge of my nose, I lean in for a better look at the screen to my right. The reason I canceled the date is spread out on the triple set of screens in front of me: A full systems crash on one of our overseas clients that locked out thousands of users. One of the senior partners dropped the fiasco in my lap at ten-fifteen on Saturday morning and told me to get it handled by the beginning of the week.

Immediately, I pulled in a few other programmers and settled in for a long day and night in front of my screens. And probably a long weekend, since it'll most likely take the team that long to track down the source of the crash and fix all the messes it left along the way. Rather than go into the office, I chose to work with my team from home. It is the weekend, after all, and I have a dating app to get ready for its official launch in between fixing the problems at my day job.

"Yeah, Mom. I'm still here." I pull the phone closer to me across the desk and prop it against the base of one of the screens. My mom's face appears on FaceTime. "Sorry, just chasing down a bug."

"Don't work too hard," she quips, although she knows that she and Dad taught me that hard work pays off. Maybe it won't be in financial reward but in character and satisfaction instead. "Are you planning to come up this Sunday after church?" she continues, her voice slightly drowned out by the clatter of my fingers across my keyboard.

I dash off a quick instant message to one of the other programmers with a link I want him to run a check on for me before answering her. "That was my plan. We'll see if I'm able to make it now that I'm dealing with this site crash."

"I'll be praying that whatever it is gets resolved quickly," she replies immediately. She's always been the prayer warrior of our family, and I know she'll follow through on her word.

There's no hint of letdown in her tone, but I know how disappointed the whole family will be if I miss another Sunday dinner. Ever since I moved back to New York, our biweekly family feasts, movie nights, and sleepovers are something we all look forward to. I missed each of them so much. It's hard not to let the guilt of missing years of their lives while I built my career overseas affect my thoughts.

"Don't dwell on the past. Move forward and onward. That's all anyone can do," Dad always says.

"Thanks, Mom. Your prayers are appreciated."

"Oh! I had some more ideas about your Blind-Date-with-a-Book-Nerd-meets-*The-Great-Gatsby* mashup launch party."

I asked Mom to be in charge of planning the launch party for the site. I told her I didn't just want any party. I want a celebration that plays off the themes of our site's mission and creates a memory that no one on the invite list is soon to forget. Part mixer, part masquerade party is what I'm thinking. It's bold. It's fun. And it just might make a certain someone stand up and take notice of everything the app is accomplishing.

Even though the app isn't fully up and running, it's been

interesting to see how connections are already developing on it. Ava's first collaborative post launched on her social media accounts a few days ago. She urged her followers to be part of the growing movement of people seeking love not based solely on looks but on mutual interests and hobbies. It's clear her followers listen to her recommendations. I was astonished at the outpouring of responses and the number of people clamoring for an invitation to be one of the final beta testers of the design. Even more signed up after she hosted a live interview with me a day later.

Mom continues to rattle off ideas for the party, but I'm distracted by a message that *pings* through on one of my screens. It's open to the Blind Date with a Book Nerd dashboard. The message lands in my second account, "Classic Book Hero Guy," the one I set up to test my algorithm after realizing my original account could still be skewed with a programming bias. For now, I'm using my "Lord of the Book Nerd" profile to set up the blind dates I promised Ava I would go on and checking the algorithm against the matches on my secondary account. I'm not active on it beyond that, though I have joined a few forum discussions on my "Classic Book Hero Guy" account.

The forum has exploded in the past few days. It seems that I hit a nerve with the bookish community, and many are eager to connect more easily with someone who shares their deep love for books. I've made it a point to browse the topics, taking notes on the social and romantic issues being discussed already.

There's also a growing discussion forum exclusively related to books, and I'm already finding the conversations invigorating.

One of the newest members started a thread asking for recommendations regarding favorite science fiction books that could also be considered classic novels, and, of course, I had to weigh in on the conversation under my "Classic Book Hero" account.

The new message in my inbox is from the original poster of the thread, an account named "Never Met a Classic I Didn't Like." The poster writes:

You were right. Journey to the Center of the Earth *is a perfect balance of science fiction and classic novel. I can't believe I've never read it before! Thanks for the recommendation. – @NeverMetAClassicIDidn'tLike*

As a book lover, I'm pleased that someone trusted my recommendation. I pull my attention away from work to type out a quick reply: *I know my stuff. Now give* 20,000 Leagues Under the Sea *a go. It'll take you on a "voyage" you'll never forget – @ClassicBookHeroGuy*

The message sent, I turn away, dividing my attention between Mom and the software crisis unfolding in front of me. A few minutes later, I realize a reply is already waiting:

I'm on it. But if the "voyage" gets too tempestuous, I'm blaming you – @NeverMetAClassicIDidn'tLike

"I was planning to send you home with a couple of casseroles that you could warm up through the week. And one of those gooseberry pies you've always liked. But if you're not going to be able to make it . . ."

I realize Mom has shifted back to talking about whether I'll be able to make it up for Sunday dinner this week or if this work crisis will prevent me from driving up. I pull an exaggerated frown across my mouth. "Gooseberry pie? Now you're just rubbing salt in the wound."

She laughs, her eyes crinkling up with merriment. "More for the girls and me, I suppose." Her face becomes serious again. "Truly though, son, you're looking a little thin. Are you sure you're taking care of yourself?"

I shake my head. "You worry too much. I'm fine. Just a lot on my plate between moving countries, managing my project load, launching the app, and reconnecting with . . . everyone."

Her expression says she is reading between the lines, but she doesn't make any comments. We sign off shortly after. It isn't until an hour has passed that I remember the unanswered message in my inbox. I type out a quick reply:

If you run into any trouble, just signal, and I'll send reinforcements – @ClassicBookHeroGuy

I hit send. A few minutes later, I'm immersed in repairing a corrupted line of code, and the next time I glance back over at the screen, "Never Met a Classic I Didn't Like" has logged off without reply.

—

Five hours later, I'm eyeballs deep in a line-by-line code repair. The *Lord of the Rings* soundtrack has been playing on repeat for the last hour, and I almost don't hear the sound of my phone *pinging* on the desk with an incoming text message.

AVA: I hope tonight goes well. Here's to hoping she's an Arwen and not a Shelob.

Laughing, I reply quickly.

ME: Only you would remember the name of the spider in *Lord of the Rings*. Unfortunately, I had to cancel the date.

AVA: Reneging on our agreement already, Daws? Or do you miss Shelly?

ME: A work emergency came up. Stuck being the hero of the story all weekend. *sigh*

AVA: Bringing that main character energy, huh?

ME: Always.

The screen bounces for a few seconds with dots, but her reply doesn't come through until a couple of minutes later.

AVA: If I didn't already say it, thanks for bringing food to my office the other day. If you hadn't come to the rescue, hangry Ava was about to bring out the claws on my poor assistants. Not even the demands of bestselling authors stand a chance between a girl and her hunger.

AVA: Look! There you go, being the hero of the story again.

While I have to admit it's nice to find myself in an easy text conversation with Ava again, I wish I could take the sweet and flirtatious nature of her messages to heart. Ava always was a witty texter, and I know she's just trying to thank me for my act of kindness without getting too awkward about it. The lighthearted vibe of her messages is the result. I pause briefly before typing a reply.

ME: Just doing my duty, protecting the people of NYC from hangry Ava. Quick! Get her a bagel and hide!

She quickly sends back a bagel emoji. The dots bounce again.

AVA: I'll have to repay the favor. You're a good friend, Daws.

ME: What can I say? My mama raised me right. Sadly, she also raised me to be a hard worker, so back to the trenches I go.

Friend. The word lingers, stinging more than it should. *I don't want to just be your friend,* my heart whispers. Knowing it won't do me any good to think about it, I resolutely turn my attention back to my work. Getting distracted by Ava is the last thing I need if I hope to have any free time this weekend.

By the time the afternoon shifts into the evening, my team and I are still hard at work fixing the issues our client's site is experiencing. We've run a few tests, and while it isn't completely fixed, I think we're on the right track.

A few times, I look longingly toward my kitchen, wishing I could take the time to make a quick meal or grab a snack, but I don't want to take a break when the repairs are finally making progress. I'm in the zone, and there's no stopping me. Telling myself I can order a pizza for delivery later, I push away my hunger. Another hour flies by without me noticing.

My phone goes off a couple more times, but I ignore it.

I'm so immersed in the screens in front of me that I jump when a sudden sharp and insistent rapping sounds at my door. "Did I black out and order that pizza after all?" I mutter.

I've been sitting so long that I'm a little stiff as I push myself out of the chair and walk to the small entryway.

When I swing the door open, I'm taken aback at the sight on the other side. My stomach jumps, and I flounder for words. Bright eyes peer up at me. Smooth, full lips part in a wide smile that shows her pretty teeth. She's dressed in colorful workout attire and wearing sneakers on her feet.

"What are you doing here?" I blurt out.

Ava steps over my threshold, holding up a pair of paper take-out bags. "Repaying the favor, as I said. You know I don't like owing my friends any favors. I figured you probably wouldn't feed yourself today with your project tunnel vision. I take a Pilates class on Saturdays not far away, so I brought you lasagna and cacio e pepe from my favorite Italian place. The carbs will fuel your brain."

"How in the world do you know where I live?" I eye her with pretend skepticism. I lean in and whisper, "Did you follow me home after I brought you food the other day?"

She just purses her lips and shakes her head. Her lower lip catches between her teeth, her gaze examining me critically before she replies. "I asked Andrew for your address. Knowing you two, he probably already warned you I was headed over, but you didn't get the message because you are too busy being a computer whiz." Her free hand plants itself on her hip. "You're looking like you're in need of nourishment and sleep, Dawson. Burning the candle at both ends these days?"

Without waiting for a reply, she pushes past me, heading into my apartment with no hesitation.

I realize I'm still gripping the door handle like I'm trying to squeeze the metal flat. I release it and shut the door, following her toward my kitchen. I'm still having a hard time understanding the circumstances that have transpired to result in *the* Ava Fox walking into *my* kitchen at this exact moment.

"You sound just like my mother," I mutter as I trail behind her.

She throws me a pointed look over her shoulder. Her ponytail sways. "I take that as a compliment. Your mother is a pretty cool lady." She places both take-out bags on the counter and immediately starts rooting around in my cupboards. I lean against the wall and watch her.

"Of course I'm burning the candle at both ends," I continue in protest. "I've just designed an entire app and founded a startup while working full-time and maintaining family, social, and church obligations. Now, you've got me running around on all these dates I don't even want to go on."

She freezes and points a plastic fork in my direction. "Those dates are for your own good." She swings away and starts opening the cupboard doors again.

"Are you looking for plates?" I say, a slight hint of exasperation in my tone.

My emotions are rioting under the surface, as they typically are whenever Ava is around, and the effect is amplified by the sight of her in my home. I've suppressed what I feel for her for so long that it's like a basalt crust topping a hot lava pit. On the one hand, I'm thrilled to see her. She might say that showing up with bags full of delicious-smelling food is just to repay me, but bringing me dinner is an act of friendship that isn't lost on me after all the years we spent not speaking. This version of my friendship with Ava is different and new. I'd like to say I'm fully content with it, but that wouldn't be true. At least the awkwardness that tainted our first interactions slowly seems to be dissipating.

On the other hand, watching her move around my kitchen as if she has been here a hundred times before is a slow form of torture that should be illegal.

"Of course!" she replies to my question. "Where do you keep stuff in this kitchen?"

I take a long step forward at the same second she swings back around to face me. Suddenly, her face smacks against my shoulder as we collide in the small space.

"Ow!" She steps back as I reach out to steady her, her hand flying up to her face.

My hands land on her elbows. I cup them gently, stopping her from swaying backward from the surprise of our collision, a panicked feeling ricocheting in the pit of my stomach. "I'm so sorry, Ava. Are you hurt?"

I lean over her, trying to peer into her face, worried that I just broke her nose. The thought of hurting Ava nearly sends me into a frenzy. My heart slams in my chest. Her eyes are closed, and she's holding one hand over her face. An agonizing second ticks by as I scan the parts of her face I can see through her fingers, waiting for blood or bruising to appear.

"No," she finally replies, lowering her hand. She frowns in the direction of my arm. "But why is your shoulder made of stone?" There's a small red spot on her cheek, but no bruising yet. My racing heart finally slows. Ava reaches up with her free hand and pats my deltoid as if to check if I've added a layer of cement under my shirt. When she lifts her chin, I register an expression of surprise in the blush across her cheeks.

A flush warms my own face. It fogs my glasses briefly. "I've been working out a little extra," I admit sheepishly.

"I can see that." Quickly, she drops her hand from my shoulder and turns away from me back to the cupboard. I can't see her face anymore. "Those plates?"

Carefully, trying not to hurt her again, I lean in behind her and tap the one cupboard door she hasn't thrown open. "They are in here."

She tosses her head back and peers up at me. "You do realize this is the weirdest cupboard for plates, right?"

Instantly, she freezes as she registers the fact that her movement has brought our faces only inches apart. Her lips part, her gaze dropping swiftly, then darting back up again.

Barely breathing, I stare down at her. I'm afraid to make a sudden movement and spook her. "Are you some kind of kitchen arrangement snob?" I finally manage to retort, but the words come out in a raspy whisper.

Her chest rises and falls. She tries to rally her sass. "I suppose you'll tell me next that you keep the silverware in the cheese drawer?"

"Of course. Quick access when I need a snack."

That draws a little laugh from her. Her gaze drops again, pausing for the briefest of seconds on the lower part of my face, suspiciously close to my mouth. I bend toward her a fraction of an inch, feeling the warmth of her sharp exhale brush across the stubble on my jaw. The urge to kiss her overwhelms me. I could lean forward another inch and claim those soft lips as mine until she becomes a melting puddle in my arms. Surely, kissing her would erase the years and give us a reason to remember how deeply we once were in love? My fingertips linger at the small of her back, her warmth spreading up my veins.

I clear my throat, and when I try to speak, my own voice surprises me. "Ava . . .?"

Her long, dark eyelashes flutter, hiding her crystalline eyes from me. When they reappear, an undertone of shock and uncertainty plays at the edges of her face. "Daws . . ." she whispers.

Just as I've convinced myself that it wouldn't have a detrimental effect on our friendship if I leaned the rest of the way down and kissed her pretty lips right now, a cacophony of raucous banging erupts at my front door. It sounds as if a tribe of gorillas has arrived to smash their fists against the wood all at once. I jump backward, swinging away from Ava, unease rushing in to fill the space between us. She looks as startled as I feel.

"Let me just—I'm going to see who that is." I bolt down the hall toward the entrance, silently hoping I'm about to encounter a persistent salesperson with a lengthy spiel to sell me on their goods and services so I can hide out at the front door for the next hundred years. Or at least until I regain my composure enough to be able to face the woman in my kitchen again.

I swing the door open without looking and am immediately accosted by a pair of small arms thrown around my neck.

"Surprise!" Lucy grins and squeezes me with as much force as she can muster.

Instinctively, my arms go around her to return the hug as I look up in astonishment. Anne, Grayson, Josephine, Mom, and Dad press in at the door, their faces filled with glee at catching me off guard. Everyone's arms are filled with what looks like casserole dishes and pie pans.

"Well, aren't you going to invite us in?" Anne quips.

"What are you all doing here?" I ask, shaking my head in disbelief and stepping out of the doorway to give them room to enter. They tumble into the small space, which is suddenly crowded and loud as their voices echo.

"Since you decided to ditch us tomorrow, we thought we'd bring the party to you," Anne's smooth tones inform me serenely.

"Time to grub," Grayson shouts.

"Mom made pie," JoJo says.

My mother's arms wrap around me in a soft, warm hug. "Hi, son. Sorry to descend on you like this, but we thought it would be a fun surprise to bring you dinner and those casseroles I mentioned. We started driving about an hour after I talked to you. I hope we aren't going to disrupt you, but they wanted to surprise you so badly."

I hug her back. "Not a disruption at all."

Dad claps me on the shoulder as we start moving en masse down the short hallway to the kitchen.

"There's a girl here." JoJo's surprised voice triggers my memory all at once.

"Ava!" Mom exclaims.

The two women step forward simultaneously. Ava bends gracefully, her tall form stooping to wrap her arms around my mother's shorter frame. Their embrace is heartfelt. My mother glances over her shoulder at me with surprise in her face.

"It's so good to see you, Mrs. Hayes," Ava says. "And you, Mr. Hayes." She smiles toward Dad.

"Ellie and Jim, dear," Mom replies.

"Did we interrupt something?" Anne remarks with an exaggerated lift of her eyebrows.

Ava laughs and shakes her head. "It looks like we had the same idea. I brought Dawson dinner as a thank you for bringing me lunch the other day. I'm going to head out, though, so you all can enjoy some time with him."

If Mom wonders about this revelation, she doesn't miss a beat. Instead, she sets her lips firmly. "Absolutely not. Let's pile all the food up and eat together. Dawson, you can take a break for a few minutes, can't you? Will you stay, Ava?"

With a startled glance over at me, Ava looks at my mother. "I . . . I don't . . . want to interrupt your family time. I really just came by to drop off this takeout."

"Nonsense. Dawson," Mom calls over her shoulder.

Looking at Ava apologetically, I raise my shoulders in a shrug. "Mom says you're staying."

Her eyes blink rapidly, and a flush works across the delicate features of her face as Mom bustles away and everyone disperses toward the living room.

"Plates, Dawson?" Mom calls out.

"Here they are, Mrs. Hayes . . . sorry, Ellie." Ava steps forward, pulling open the cupboard I showed her earlier. "I have no clue where he keeps the silverware, though."

15

Ava

The sound of family reverberates off the walls of Dawson's apartment after dinner. I sit and take it all in.

Conversation punctuated by frequent laughter sweeps me back in time to our carefree early twenties and spontaneous trips upstate to visit his family. The last time I saw the Hayes family, Lucy was an infant, Josephine was only a little girl getting used to her new glasses, Grayson was a rough-and-tumble kid, and Anne was a brace-faced teenager with her nose stuck in a book. I glance around the room, astounded at how much and how little has changed.

It was always the most magical feeling to walk through the door of the Hayes' family home. Visitors were greeted with genuine love and care. I could feel their love then, just as I feel it tonight as his family showers me with questions about how I've been and what I've been up to. It isn't a question of whether my answers matter or if my thoughts are met with authentic interest. I know that whatever I say is important.

The difference between speaking with people who approach others with such high regard is in stark contrast to what I'm used to. Often, in conversations with my own family, it's an instant dissection of my flaws, always a rebuttal ready to prove that I've somehow answered a subjective question incorrectly.

I never had the opportunity to introduce Dawson to my family. However, the truth is, I avoided the ordeal entirely and broke up with him before he could discover the true state of disrepair and dysfunction that permeates the Fox family.

How could I have expected Dawson to understand the dynamics of my stiff and calloused home when his family was always so warm and welcoming? How could I have invited him into the petty deception, snobbery, and drama when I knew that all he wanted out of life was a rendition of the successful love story his parents share?

There was never going to be a way I could give that to him, not when I was playing peacekeeper in my own family, trying to hold together my parents' doomed marriage, and being a scapegoat for everything that went wrong at the hands of the selfish adults who should have known better. Nothing has ever felt within my control when it comes to my family. I never expected him to deal with it all.

I have never been able to protect myself from them. But I could protect Dawson, and so I did. I knew what I was saving him from. He deserves to walk into his future wife's family home feeling welcomed and cared for, not manipulated and emotionally battered.

Tonight, the pain of what I lost hits my heart afresh as I realize that I never even gave him the chance to try.

A squeal distracts me from my pensive thoughts. Lucy swings onto Dawson's back and leverages herself up to his shoulders, managing to knock his glasses half off his face in the process. She screeches as he turns in a circle to her glee. The sight pulls my lips into a grin.

Without warning, something zips past my face, and I turn in time to watch a small object land in the sink full of soapy dishwater.

"Grayson Miles!" Ellie hollers from the kitchen. She extracts a soggy pair of wadded-up socks out of the water.

"Sorry!" Grayson tears into the kitchen, regret on his face. "Sorry, Mom!"

His mother wrings out the socks and hands them over. "What have I told you about throwing things in the house? And why aren't these on your feet?" She looks down and grimaces. "No sockball in the house."

"It's an apartment, not a house," Grayson quips over his shoulder as he jogs out of the small kitchen, wet socks in hand.

Ellie gives an exasperated sigh and glances in my direction. "Teenage boys, let me tell ya." She blows a stray gray hair from her face and sinks her hands back into the dishwater.

Lucy whines in the living room as Dawson sets her down. He plops into the chair at his desk, his voice apologetic. "Sorry, sis. I have to send a quick message. People are waiting for me to help with something at work."

I feel sorry for Dawson tonight, torn between needing to work and hosting this giant mess of people. But their presence seems good for him. Even I noticed the bags forming under his eyes. It's obvious the man has been staring at a screen all day.

Lucy watches curiously over his shoulder, then turns her attention to the multiple screens set up on the desk. "You have a message!" She leans forward and reads excitedly, pointing to one screen. "Look at the cute little pen guy."

Shifting, Dawson quickly clicks out of the open tab, but I would recognize the little pen guy anywhere. It's a cute, new messaging feature on the Blind Date with a Book Nerd site.

Dawson is chatting with someone tonight?

Big deal, I think. *That's great.* The sudden pit in my stomach says otherwise. *Shouldn't I be happy for him? That's the whole reason I made him agree to use his own site—so he could have a chance to find the love of his life.*

"Ava, you're an editor for the publishing house where Andrew Ketner works, right?" Ellie disrupts my wandering thoughts.

I swallow the lump in my throat and smile. "Yes, I've been there a handful of years now and absolutely love it."

"Andrew was always such a fun kid. Dawson told me he got married?"

"Yes, Charlie is a wonderful woman. She's a good friend of mine now and an author at CityLight Press. It's a funny story. He should tell it to you someday. And their wedding is where Dawson and I, uh"—what am I saying again?—"reconnected."

"Mm-hmm," she replies slowly, scrubbing a casserole dish. "It's been a few years for you two, hasn't it?"

My skin prickles. While I know Ellie doesn't mean her question to come off with an inflection of guilt, I still feel it deep in my bones. "Yeah. Too many years," I hear myself reply and realize I mean it.

Before she can respond, a sock flies into the kitchen a second time. Ellie's dripping hands go straight to her hips without even an attempt at drying them as she stalks out of the kitchen. Grayson is in for it now. I turn to watch the scene unfold and catch Anne inspecting me from her seat at the dining table. I offer a friendly wave, ignoring the pull to watch Ellie dole out Grayson's punishment instead.

The Anne I remember had a serious, albeit mostly friendly, demeanor. Her greenish-hazel eyes resemble the color of Dawson's, and they don't hesitate to pierce right through the subject of their inspection. Right now, under her scrutinizing gaze, I feel like I'm on trial. Of all the Hayes children, she's the one who would remember me the most.

I stand and move closer as she pushes away the book sitting closed in front of her.

"Reading anything good?" I peek at the thick book.

"Just getting a jumpstart on the reading for my graduate program," she says with an air of exhaustion. "I'm trying to get an internship in the city while working on my master's degree this coming year."

"A master's while interning, huh? You're an ambitious young lady."

Anne shrugs. There's a slightly bored look in her eye. My stomach tightens as I wonder if she hates me for breaking her brother's heart. "I like school. And I like being busy," she answers as if that should explain it.

"Good for you. You're an English major?"

"With a minor in creative writing, yes."

My lips lift into a smile at the familiar subjects. "Any

interest in editing in the future?"

To my relief, a light turns on in her eyes. "Yes, actually. Do you like your job?"

"I do, though it can be a grueling job. There are long hours, high expectations, and industry politics, plus all the interpersonal things you'd find within any career, I suppose. But I'm quite fortunate to work for the company I do. They've been really good and fair to me. Not every publishing house is as great."

Suddenly, Anne comes alive. I take a seat at the table, and she picks my brain for the next twenty minutes until Josephine interrupts to set up a game of Scrabble. In the corner of the dining room, I hear Dawson's fingers clicking across his keyboard. For a moment, I envision myself going over to him, leaning over his shoulders, and wrapping him in a hug from behind.

The vision is so clear, and it's crazy that I already know how natural it would feel.

Instead, I walk over and stand a foot away, eyeing the gibberish on the screen. "This makes sense to you?"

His lips twitch into a smile, and he finishes his task before swiveling in the chair to face me. "If it made sense, I would have finished mopping up the mess by now."

"In all fairness, your work night got hijacked."

"It's alright. It was good to be forced to eat. I'm going to be up all night working, most likely." The tone of his voice sounds discouraged.

"That stinks," I commiserate, the memory of many all-nighters working through a manuscript in my head as well. "Well, hey, at least I won't wake you when I call you in tears from a Gollum dream, right?"

A small laugh escapes him. "True. I guess it all works out then."

"Game time!" Josephine announces from the dining table.

As the Hayes family gathers to play, I call out over the noise, "I actually should head out."

Dawson's disappointment is written on his face. And based on the frown that I'm not sure he even knows he is making, I know leaving now is the right decision. No matter how much I want to stay, I've already toed the line tonight. I'm not doing either of us any favors by being here.

The warm touch of his hand on my arm makes me flinch.

"Are you alright?" He is standing now, his voice low in my ear. "Are you sure you need to go?"

I nod resolutely, not letting myself break. "Yeah. Thanks for the nice evening. I'm just going to turn in early and rest for the night. Don't stay up too late, Daws."

I bid a too quick but heartfelt goodbye to his family. Dawson walks me to the door, where we linger for a moment.

"Are you okay to get home? I don't mind calling you a cab and waiting with you downstairs."

"No, you have your family here. Enjoy your time with them."

His eyes flicker back and forth like he's searching for something in my face. Perhaps, like me, he is looking for the courage to say what's on his mind. Fear bubbles in my core, and before I can allow him to take this any further, I blurt out, "Just because you're busy with work doesn't mean you can slither out of our deal. Make sure to reschedule your date. I'm already one ahead of you, and I don't want to lap you."

Dawson attempts a smile of sorts, but it doesn't even come close to reaching his eyes. "Goodnight, Ava. Thanks for being such a good friend."

It's the same line I said to him earlier, the same line used for millennia to remind another person of their place. I hate the sound of it and hate the very idea that Dawson might be finally accepting my place as just his friend despite the palpable tension between us earlier tonight. If he had kissed me, I don't know if I would have had the strength to tear myself away.

A horrifying thought enters my mind. My mouth goes dry. Can Dawson and I ever truly be just friends?

"Goodnight," I say.

My feet are like lead as I turn away and leave his apartment with my stomach in tangles. It's almost more torturous to be just friends with him than to ban him from my life entirely.

What happens after these five blind dates? We can't possibly keep going forward, seeing each other weekly like this. It's not like we're going to continue hanging out. Is our friendship going to die out and fade away like it never existed at all?

I shudder at a sudden vision of bumping into him and his fictional future girlfriend at the farmers' market at Union Square. I envision them walking hand in hand, giggly and gushy, entirely smitten with one another. It's the future I want for him. I want him to have someone who is everything he needs. And yet, the thought of it becoming a reality crushes me too.

Three more dates to go, and I can set him free.

And then I realize . . . it's only three more dates.

My mouth goes dry. Three more dates, and I have to let go of Dawson forever.

It feels like I've just gotten him back, at least a piece of him, anyway. And in just a short time, I'm going to force myself to let him go all over again. Once, he was my best friend. Once, when we were falling in love and falling hard, I thought I could never live without him.

But if you love them, let them go . . . to find something better with someone who isn't carrying so much hidden emotional baggage.

I remind myself that I also never thought my dad would leave, my mom would spiral, and my heart would become afraid of the very thing that made it whole . . . But here we are.

When I return to my apartment, I look at the work waiting for me on my laptop and turn away to take a warm bath and listen to an audiobook to relax instead. Just as the bubbles are beginning to dissipate, a text alert comes through on my phone.

DAWSON: Is CityLight in search of a custodian by chance?

ME: The problem is that bad, huh?

DAWSON: My brain is officially fried.

ME: Maybe you should get some rest. A good night's sleep often solves the worst problems.

DAWSON: Tell that to my boss.

DAWSON: By the way, Lucy asked me to tell you that she wishes you'd be her best friend. In her words, she thinks you're pretty cool. Don't ask me why . . .

His words are so sweet, but the text brings tears to my eyes. I try to type a reply that matches my usual level of wit and humor, but an uncomfortable pressure builds in my chest. My brain won't form any words, and I let the phone slip to the bathroom floor as the first tear slides slowly down my cheek without waiting for permission to fall.

It splashes into the tub, and I'm suddenly ugly crying in the bath. The sobs are deep and soul-baring, a lament for the things that feel unobtainable for me, for the hopelessness I feel inside, for the old me who feels so far from reach.

I cry because I used to feel whole. I cry for how distant I often feel from God and for how guilty I feel for my preoccupation with my problems when, in reality, things could be worse. Guarded as I've been for so long, the onslaught of emotions surprises me, slipping out with a rawness I couldn't separate myself from if I tried.

As the water cools, my lips utter a shaky prayer for help, the sound coming out more guttural than intelligible. As messily imperfect as my heart is, I know the only one who can understand my cry is the One I don't need to speak to with words.

Instead, I let the tears create ripples in the water and do the talking for me until I'm utterly spent.

16

Dawson

"Lord of the Book Nerds?"

When several women, each dressed in varying shades of pastel athletic wear, all look up at me with curious expressions on their faces, I finally remember that I'm "Lord of the Book Nerds," and the pleasant, feminine voice is addressing me. I turn around to scan the group for its owner.

"Here," I reply.

It's early morning. The sun only peeked over the horizon twenty minutes ago, and Central Park is still dim in the shady spots. A short, slim woman steps forward from the group of runners who have just gathered under a sprawling tree. I arrived less than sixty seconds ago and am still trying to orient myself in the group.

"Lord of the Book Nerds?" the short woman asks again.

Quickly losing interest, the other women turn away as they realize that I am not, in fact, standing in the middle of a women's running group searching for a workout buddy.

"That's me. Are you 'Let Me Be Your Romantasy'?" I move to greet my date, and she extends her hand toward me. Her grip is firm as we shake.

"Megan," she affirms. "It's nice to meet you."

"Dawson," I reply. "Thanks for being flexible on rescheduling our date."

"No problem," she quips in a cheery tone. I watch as she lifts her foot behind her, grabs her sock-covered ankle, and stretches her quad. I warmed up before I arrived at the Park, so I stand off to the side, feeling awkward and like I suddenly have way too many limbs taking up space.

Megan eyeballs me as she stretches, her dark brown eyes assessing me with a fearlessness that would be admirable if it wasn't so unnerving. Her medium-length, brunette hair swings across her shoulders. She's pretty, with strong features and olive skin. Cute freckles dance across her nose and cheeks. I try to look comfortable and confident under her scrutinizing gaze.

"You're cute and basically what I was expecting from your profile name," she finally breaks the silence. She casts a doubtful glance at me. "I mean, you do look like the lord of the book nerds if you know what I mean."

I catch a few discreet looks from the other women in the group as heat spreads across my face. My stomach drops.

"Do you always wear glasses?" she continues.

"Uh, yeah, I have since I was a kid."

I struggle not to let the mortification instantly get to me. I've never considered myself the best-looking guy in the room, but I thought I got by. At the very least, I hoped I offered enough between looks, brains, and humor to get a woman's attention despite the admittedly computer nerd glasses I've never seen any reason to switch out for contacts. Plus, I revamped my personal style several years ago, and I work out regularly. Am I still that far off the mark?

Megan steps closer and peers up at my face. "Take the glasses off for me for a second," she instructs with a brusque, matter-of-fact tone. I just met this woman, and something tells me that she is used to getting what she asks for, so I don't protest.

I oblige her request, dragging the glasses down my face. Her face instantly goes blurry and washed out in the backdrop of greenery around us. I try not to squint to bring her expression back into focus. I catch the corner of her mouth lifted in a smirk when I slip the glasses back over the bridge of my nose a few seconds later.

"Well, you're no Superman," she says with a satisfied nod. "I'm usually into the classic novel, tortured hero, dark and stormy type, but like I said, you're pretty cute."

"Uh, thanks," I reply, hoping that at least a few of the other women around us have somehow missed this conversation. Then, realizing I'm also supposed to be getting to know my blind date, I add, "Heathcliff's your type, huh?"

"More of a Rhysand girl, honestly," she replies, fluttering her eyelashes.

As I lengthen my stride to keep up with her brisk steps, I refrain from asking what her definition of a classic novel is. Together, we follow the group of runners to the trail. An older woman, whom I assume is the group's leader, steps to the front of the line, doling out details about today's route in tones that could rival a loudspeaker. Her eyes scan the group, then flash toward me skeptically. I'm prepared to be kicked out, but she doesn't say anything.

We set off at a steady pace, and for the next ten minutes, I focus on regulating my breathing and not tripping over the shorter steps of the runners in front of me.

After taking a rain check on my blind date last weekend, "Let Me Be Your Romantasy"—Megan—reached out to ask if I'd like to join her running group for an early morning workout. *Two birds, one stone. I like to be efficient,* she wrote.

With some reluctance, I agreed. At the very least, I won't have to go for my usual run later today. At the very best, I'll be able to check another date off my list and have an excuse to set up a meeting with Ava to review our findings to improve my dating app.

Less than a week has passed since Ava brought dinner to my apartment and ended up hanging out with my family when they surprised me for the evening. That night, I thought she was having a good time, but I haven't heard from her since, so I'm beginning to doubt it. I haven't even received a quick text from her to tease me into setting up another date.

I can't help but worry that the moment of tension we seemed to share in the kitchen ruined whatever rapport I have succeeded in building with Ava since we've been back in each other's lives. I don't know when it happened, but things don't seem as awkward between us anymore. However, I'll admit for every step forward, we also seem to take two steps back.

Despite her confusing silence, it does feel as if slowly but surely, we are becoming friends again. I'll do anything to protect the fragile rebuilding of our shattered relationship.

Even if it means getting up at the crack of dawn to go on

a blind date with a stranger I have no intention of dating.

A stranger who is also currently outpacing me on the trail. I lengthen my strides to keep up with Megan. Her silky hair, which she pulled up into a ponytail as we began, bounces with each step. She looks over and flashes me a grin, which I do my best to return.

"Having trouble keeping up? Is the trail too long for you?" she says in a teasing and slightly out-of-breath tone.

I work to keep my voice even. "'Only those who will risk going too far can possibly find out how far one can go,'" I reply in the wisest tone I can muster.

She grins again. "A man who quotes T.S. Eliot by heart? I can work with that."

The fact that she recognizes the random quote I pulled out of a hazy memory of literature class in undergrad is impressive. It invigorates me enough to lengthen my stride. I'm breathless by the time we hit the two-mile mark, but the fresh morning air and nature-rich setting revitalize me after the hours I've spent indoors glued to a computer screen.

As I remind myself to ensure my work doesn't interfere with my running as often as it has lately, I sneak a glance at Megan. She seems like she has a fun personality, despite how much her direct comments about my looks threw me off earlier. When the run ends after a cool down and a stretch thirty minutes later, I turn to her.

"May I buy you a cup of coffee?"

Megan shakes off the last of her stretching routine and smiles up at me. "I have to be at work soon, but make it a post-workout smoothie, and you have yourself a deal."

I'm surprised by how easily we fall into conversation as we walk toward the Park's entrance and emerge onto the street. It's only surface-level small talk, but I learn that she works as a research scientist in the biology department at Columbia. Working for my own alma mater is impressive. I find myself growing more intrigued by her as we order smoothies from a shop just down the street that already has a line out the door.

By some stroke of good fortune, we snag a table on the shop's tiny patio and settle in with our post-workout drinks.

"So, why did you sign up for my . . . for Blind Date with a Book Nerd?" I ask her, settling into the uncomfortable wicker chair. I take a drink of the smoothie, which tastes more like chalky protein powder and kale than the chocolate delight I was promised by the colorful hand-lettered menu over the register.

Megan sips her smoothie through a yellow straw. She pulls her dark hair out of the band and sets it free to bounce around her shoulders. "Believe it or not, the dating scene for a research scientist who basically lives at the lab is dismally small. Even less when you're a bookworm and spend all your free time reading. I love being a total book nerd, but even I know it can be a solitary activity." She smiles ruefully, her teeth even and white. "Getting out to run with my group is the extent of my social time for most of the week. Isn't that sad?"

I can't help but grin. "I hear you on the sad lack of a social life. Any free time I have, I spend upstate with my family. Oh, and I go to a local church every week."

She eyes me under long, fluffy lashes, the straw captured between her teeth now. "So you're a church boy, huh?"

"Consistently, for most of my life. Even though I don't think church is a requirement for faith, I find it to be a great source of encouragement, learning, and community," I reply.

"I bet you sing in the choir every Sunday," she teases.

"Well, if I did, I'm not sure anyone would be left in church to hear Pastor's message," I laugh, and she joins me. When it fades, something presses on my heart, so I continue without pause, "My faith is really important to me. Jesus is the foundation for every decision I make. He got me through some dark times in my life."

She doesn't hide her wince. "I take it you're looking for a woman who can join you on that journey?" she asks, pressing her lips together.

I nod. "I am."

"My grandma made me go to church with her every Sunday when I was a kid. I haven't been back since and don't have any intentions of it. I don't exactly believe in a higher power." She looks away, studying the pedestrians hurrying down the sidewalk. Her response catches me off guard, even though I appreciate her honesty. Before I can ask a follow-up question, she changes the subject. "What did you say you do for work again?"

It's still hard to talk about the brainchild that is Blind Date with a Book Nerd. My natural introversion lends a self-conscious disadvantage to the subject. But I know it's the right time to disclose my ownership of the app. I begin slowly. "I'm in software and app development. I'm a partner at my firm, but I also just built and launched my own dating app." Lifting my eyes, I peek up to gauge her reaction.

Megan's eyes widen. "Wait, don't tell me you . . . you're the creator of the app?" A grin breaks across her face. "Dawson, you're brilliant. It's a genius idea." Her head shakes a little. "All those algorithms and codes, though. It's all Greek to me."

I feel self-consciousness taking hold at her praise, but I try to maintain my composure. "Thank you. Now, after meeting me today, do you think my matchmaking algorithm did a good job of pairing us up?" On the one hand, I am looking for usable feedback from her, but I'm also curious.

Megan twists her lips, her eyes narrowing thoughtfully. "I don't know you very well yet, but I see some classical book hero traits in you, Dawson. I think the algorithm knew what it was doing to match two science geeks who both love Eliot's poetry, though I don't know if our other values quite align. I appreciate that your app isn't about appearances or flashy selfies. Connection should be deeper than physical attraction alone, anyway."

She glances at the fitness watch band on her wrist and startles, holding her hand up to stop my reply. "I have to go. I'm going to be late. I'm so sorry to cut this short." She rises, and I stand with her. "Thanks for the date. And the delicious smoothie."

Delicious is debatable.

She pauses, and I sense an expectant question in the brief silence. My mind races. Megan seems kind, and we have a few things in common, but our obvious differences in faith indicate that we aren't a great match. I make a mental note to bring up the idea of adding a spiritual compatibility filter to the app's questionnaire the next time Ava and I have a troubleshooting meeting.

Megan's brown eyes look me up and down. Whatever it seems she is going to say passes. "See ya around."

I hail a cab for her. When she's gone, I turn and throw

the smoothie into the nearest trash can. For a blind date, I can't find much to complain about. Something nags at me, though, and I can't put my finger on what bothered me about our interaction.

My heart lifts a prayer to heaven, the words a whisper under my breath. "Lord, I don't know if I'm ever supposed to see that woman again, but one thing I do know. I fully believe You matched me with her so I could share even a little bit of the Gospel with her. I don't know her history with You, but I lift her up in prayer right now. Please reveal Yourself to her and show her that You left the ninety-nine to bring her home."

Though my apartment is a few blocks away, I decide that a walk in the fresh air will give me a chance to clear my brain, which feels as cloudy and stormy as the morning sky above the city. As if to match my mood, it looks like a summer rainstorm is blowing in.

Halfway home, I pull my phone from my pocket. I type out a quick text and send it.

ME: Just worked out and drank a smoothie that tasted like a garden. In need of a donut before I start growing a kale patch in my stomach. Do you want to grab one with me before you go to the office?

I walk two more blocks before the phone buzzes. Glancing down, I scan the text quickly.

AVA: Sorry. Can't. Some family stuff came up this morning that I have to deal with, and I won't be at the office until later.

I try to read between the lines, but I can't, so I attempt a different approach.

ME: So you need a serotonin boost for sure, then? Text

me your location, and I'll bring donuts for everyone. I could use an excuse to delay starting work today.

Her reply only takes a few seconds.

AVA: Don't worry about us. I'm not in the city. I need to focus on this, but thanks anyway, Daws.

I guess I need to learn to take a hint.

Disappointed, I slip the phone back into the pocket of my joggers and yank open the door to the gourmet donut shop down the street from my apartment with so much force the bells clank wildly against the glass. Wincing my apology, I step inside. I'm almost at the counter when I feel a buzz against my thigh.

AVA: Isn't tonight your first book club meeting? Want some company? I could use a night of talking books.

As I order a salted chocolate bar and a coffee to go, the grin spreading across my face from ear to ear has nothing to do with the treats and everything to do with a certain blue-eyed beauty who is now only a few hours away.

17

Ava

Her messages come through at the crack of dawn. Bleary-eyed, I grab my phone and skim the flurry of texts, unsure what to think about my mom's sudden announcement of serious medical concerns. Pushing myself upright, I wipe the sleep from my eyes and immediately tap the screen to call her.

No answer.

My next resort is to type out a quick text. When I send it, my heart is pounding. My mother hasn't prioritized her health since the divorce, though I sometimes wonder if it's as much mental as physical at this point. She didn't handle my father leaving well and, in my opinion, has never fully recovered from the shocking blow.

ME: Mom, are you okay? I'm heading out there. Call me when you can, please. I'm worried.

I shoot a text to my sister as well, then stumble out of bed, rushing around and feeling frantic as I try to hope for the best but plan for the worst. It doesn't help that my brain feels foggy and disoriented this morning. The aftermath of staying up too late binge-watching episodes of reality TV, I'm sure. After whipping my hair into a ponytail, I yank on a pair of leggings, a lightly wrinkled t-shirt, and a jacket. I grab a snack for the road and slip my laptop into my bag. I might be dealing with a personal crisis today, but the train ride up to New Rochelle will provide me with a bit of time to work so I don't get too behind at the office.

Once seated on the train, I don't touch my laptop the entire journey. My stomach churns, knotted from worry, disrupted sleep, and the lack of a proper breakfast. The tiny bag of trail mix I grabbed on the way out didn't quite cut it. Opting out of work for the day isn't helping either. The guilt of missing meetings and author conference calls nibbles at my belly too. When I send a text to Gary to let him know about the situation, he seems understanding enough. He knows I'll make the work up later, so I let myself sit and watch the city go by.

I called New Rochelle home for over five years and often took the train to commute into the city. My phone *dings* as the scene zipping past my window becomes more familiar. Almost there.

NATASHA: Sorry, I just woke up. What's going on?

ME: Heading home to check on Mom. Have you heard from her?

NATASHA: Not today. Everything okay?

ME: I don't know. She sent me a bunch of messages about some health concerns that are apparently going on. Then she ghosted me as soon as I tried to call her.

NATASHA: She probably fell asleep. She hasn't told me

about anything. I think she had a doctor's appointment the other day, though.

Her nonchalance does nothing to placate me or steady the pounding of my heart. I sigh, a heaviness pressing onto my chest. Suddenly, the train feels stuffy and overcrowded. I have to remind myself to breathe.

We're almost there. Almost off this thing. Don't panic.

My phone *dings* again, and my eyes shoot down to the screen, expecting to see another message from my sister. Instead, Dawson is inviting me to grab donuts before work.

My heart sinks. Of all mornings.

Quickly, I send a reply, evading his inevitable offers and questions as much as possible. When Shelly's book club pops into my head, I send an impulsive message inviting myself to tag along. I need something to look forward to as I anticipate the stress of the day. As I wait for his reply, time slows down for a moment, and my heartbeat becomes erratic. When he replies with an enthusiastic yes, just the thought of seeing him tonight gives me a momentary sense of calm. I hope I can get back to the city in time to make it. The possibility of letting him down only brings my anxiety flooding back. Perhaps I shouldn't have said anything at all until I made sure Mom was okay. I do hope she's alright, though a part of me begrudgingly wonders if this is all a game.

I shake the thought away, scolding myself inwardly for even having it.

I try texting her again (for the umpteenth time now) right before we arrive at the station. The line to exit is painstakingly slow. Keeping my composure as the passengers shuffle out of the station takes every ounce of strength I have. Once off the train, I find the Uber I reserved during the ride and begin the last leg of my journey to my mom's house.

Every time I make this journey, I'm reminded of how much I miss my car. But after moving back to the city, having a car doesn't make sense when I can walk practically anywhere. Neither did paying to store it somewhere. Eventually, I sold it.

When the driver drops me off and I'm standing outside Mom's townhome, the dread in my stomach intensifies. Mom moved into it when Dad moved to California, shortly after she foreclosed on my childhood home in the city that she'd insisted on keeping. It was inevitable that she lost the grand condo of my youth after Dad's poor investments, and one day, all my childhood memories, good or bad, were auctioned to the highest bidder. Mom downsized to a small, humble townhome on the outskirts of New Rochelle.

I think her new home has more charm than any of the swanky city penthouses she coveted during her post-foreclosure home search. Mom disagrees, no matter how affordable it is. I swallow my nerves and take the porch steps two at a time. In case she is asleep like Tashi suggested, I unlock the door with my key and quietly slip inside.

Immediately, I trip over an empty box in the entryway and smack my knee when I land on the tiled floor. Looking around, I realize multiple unopened boxes have been stacked in the small space. Mom has always liked to shop online, but why haven't any of these been opened?

Despite how long she has lived here, there is no sense of life in the house. The walls here are empty and still, the air stagnant, like the house itself is waiting with hot, bated breath for something to happen.

"Ava? Is that you?"

Relief washes over me when I hear her voice. I follow it to the living room. She's on the couch, blanket over her lap, phone in her hand, the morning news muted on the television.

I rush forward. "What's going on, Mom? Are you okay?"

She doesn't respond. Her eyebrows furrow as she stares at her phone. She still hasn't bothered to even glance up at me. My eyes narrow as I zero in on her scrolling through social media.

"I tried to call and sent a few texts," I say and pause, allowing a moment for her to reply. When she doesn't, I continue, "I've been worried."

Finally, she sets her phone down with a sigh and looks at me. "You look terrible today, Ava. Please tell me you aren't planning on going in public like that."

My jaw clenches, but before I can say anything, Mom looks back at her phone and says, "You heard about that explosion overseas, didn't you?"

My limbs buzz like a mouse who knows it is caught. *This is a game,* says a small voice inside again. I don't want to believe it, though. I never do. I sit on the end of the couch and shake my head.

"You haven't? Oh, it's catastrophic. Here." She unmutes the TV and increases the volume to an uncomfortable level.

"Mom, are—"

"Shh!" She points to the TV as if I've committed a grave offense. "I'm trying to hear."

I hold in a sigh and turn my attention back to the news anchor who is covering the horrible accident. When it cuts to a commercial, I try again. "Mom, what's going on? Are you . . . okay?"

She mutes the TV again. A silence hangs in the air that feels purposeful and oppressive. She folds her hands in her lap and purses her lips. "I think I'm dying."

I go completely still. "Why? What's going on?"

"I can't explain it. I just feel it in my gut. Something bad is going to happen to me, and the worst part is no one is going to care." There's a flare of emotion at the end of her sentence.

My nerves heighten. "Of course we'll all care. I mean, I took the day off work to rush over and check on you."

"Oh, big deal!" She dramatically rolls her eyes. "Miss Big-City-Girl-Ava took the day off work, and all it took was her dying mother!"

Hostility courses through the room like a heat wave. The tiny voice in my brain that tried telling me this was a trap finally gains strength and screams.

"Have you been to a doctor?" It's a struggle to keep my voice direct and level.

Mom's cheeks are hollow for a moment like she's biting the insides. "I go to the doctor when I need to, Ava."

That doesn't exactly answer my question. I try again. "Have you seen a doctor for whatever is making you think you're dying?"

She scoffs and tilts her head back with a sneering laugh. "I knew you would do this. You never believe me when I say that something is wrong."

My cheeks burn, and I feel the heat of stress traveling along my skin. "A lot of times," I say in a gentle voice, "what seems so bad turns out fine." I want to point out all the times that her "gut feeling" has been wrong. However, I can't seem to find the strength. I know that nothing I say will help her to see reality any clearer at this moment.

"So you don't trust me."

"That's not what I said at all, Mom. Please don't put words in my mouth. All I'm trying to do is reassure you that, most likely, everything is fine. Why don't we take you in to get checked out? I'll drive. Where are your keys?"

Mom tosses the blanket from her lap and points a finger at me. "Don't come in here and think you're going to just toss me into some hospital. I don't need you telling me what to do!"

I feel myself growing smaller by the second. "I'm just trying to help. I don't understand what's going on."

She turns her face from me and sets her lips into a frown. "Just forget it. I'll call your sister."

Blindsided, I'm afraid to move or even breathe. What am I supposed to do or say? How can anyone ever reason with her?

"What are your symptoms?"

But Mom is too far gone. I haven't performed to her standards or given her whatever she is looking for today. My phone *dings* twice in my pocket, but the room feels too oppressive to dare disrupt the fragile silence by checking it. When it starts ringing, she snaps.

"Aren't you going to get that?"

I silence it without even checking to see who is calling.

"I want to help you—"

"I don't want your help," she says with pointed venom. "In fact, just leave. I don't even want to look at you right now. I don't recognize you anymore, Ava."

It's not the first time she has said something like that to me—and I'm sure it won't be the last—but every time feels like a slap in the face. The only move I can make now is the wrong one. If I insist on staying, I'll be deemed disobedient and unwanted. If I leave as she's insisting, I'll be labeled as uncaring and cold.

No matter what I do, it's not good enough.

It's no wonder Dad left.

"Do *you* need a doctor? Can you hear me? I said to leave."

The blood drains from my face when she locks eyes with me. Her unwarranted fury is enough to make me look away. She's succeeded in making me feel like a failure. At least she'll get that boost to help her through the day, I suppose. I try looking at her again and am overwhelmed with sadness. How can she live in such a disjointed reality? Why does she want to be this angry and bitter all the time?

I wish I could save her from this. I take a brave breath.

"Mom, I . . . I don't think you're dying. I think with everything that's happened in the last few years and with the doom-and-gloom news that you're always consuming, maybe you're—"

"Get out," she screams. "If you're going to accuse me of something, just get out. I try to tell my own daughter how I feel, and this is how I'm treated? You'll regret it once I'm cold in my grave."

I'm speechless and disappointed. Maybe some things aren't ever meant to change.

I clap my hands together and stand to leave. "Let me know when the funeral is, I guess." I regret the words after they leave my mouth because even though I mean them as a joke, my snark only fuels the fire and gives her more ammunition to prove how uncaring and cold I am.

Mom erupts, and this time, she's screaming at me not to

walk out that door. But I know that she only wants someone to unleash her fury at. For so long, I didn't have the option or courage to leave, but somehow, today my two feet carry me out the front door despite the tears rolling down my face.

My phone buzzes in my pocket. I know it's Mom, ready to continue the fight. I almost don't even check the caller ID. But at the last moment, I yank it out of my purse and see Dawson's name flashing across my screen.

"Hey, Daws," I answer, my voice shaking. "It's really good to hear your voice right now."

18

Dawson

As soon as Ava steps out of the concourse and moves toward the staircase, I catch sight of her immediately. My heart gives a painful thump as I watch her slowly progress through the crowd.

Her slim figure is almost lost in the sea of passengers who have just disembarked from the latest influx of trains. Her shoulders are slumped, her head bowed, that usually perky ponytail limp. Defeat pulses off her like a wave that hits me even from the distance. And it breaks me. I can't bear the sight of Ava like this.

If someone hurt her, so help me . . .

I am waiting next to the clock in the main concourse of Grand Central Station. I curb my impatience and hold still as she works through the crowd. The terminal is characteristically loud, with clanging voices and sharp footsteps echoing off the marble and granite of the ornate space. A musician plays a violin in the corner, the notes sweet and alluring as they reach me under all the noise. In the twenty minutes I've been waiting here, only a few people have stopped to give him attention. I walked over a few minutes ago to place a tip in the small jar at his feet. He thanked me by way of a friendly nod and a smile, a renewed energy in his bow as it danced across the strings.

Everyone else in the train station is in their own world, unaware of the countless stories happening in the continuous flood of activity around them. I'm no different. My attention is focused only on Ava as I track her movement across the concourse. The defeat grows heavier on her with each step.

Breaking my concentration for a moment, my eyes lift to the star-studded ceiling. I mutter under my breath, praying for the wisdom to know how to handle whatever I'm about to discover. As many times as I've prayed for a future with Ava, I'd give up everything I've ever hoped for if I could just see a radiant smile break across her face and know that the joy she feels is real and here to stay.

My resolve strengthens as she approaches. I don't know what happened this morning to put that traumatized expression on her face, but with me, Ava will always find a safe place for her spirit to mend.

When she finally lifts her head, I wave. My movement catches her attention, and she lifts her hand in greeting. The crowd is thick this time of day, and it is with slow steps that she progresses down the marble staircase to the heart of the station.

When Ava approaches, her state of dishevelment startles me. I've never seen her like this. In all the times I've seen her since Andrew and Charlie's wedding, her sense of fashion has never wavered. Her clothes are expertly tailored, her hair and makeup are always perfectly done, and even her athleisure wear is tasteful and color-coordinated. Everything about Ava says that the impression she gives to the world is important to her.

As a man who used to throw on the first pair of basketball shorts and wrinkled t-shirt he could pull out of the clean laundry basket, the care and effort she puts into the persona she presents to the world isn't lost on me. Ava's grace and elegance prompted my own style changes years ago when I told myself I needed to upgrade my lifestyle if I ever hoped to have a second chance with her.

But that hasn't stopped me from wishing she would let her guard down just once as proof that she trusts me.

This morning, her black leggings are dotted with stray fuzz; her t-shirt and loose jacket are wrinkled. A messy ponytail hangs over one shoulder, and her makeup-free face is splotchy and red from what appears to be recent tears.

When she reaches me, my arms automatically slide around her back for a brief hug. As if by mutual muscle memory, we've slipped back into the habit the last couple of times we've seen each other, and I am most certainly not complaining.

I never expect anything more than the briefest chance to hug her, though, so it startles me when Ava wraps her arms around my waist and presses her face into my shoulder. I can feel her breath hitching as she struggles to control herself. Carefully—afraid to startle her—I tighten my hold around her waist, pulling her into me until she's safe in my embrace. I don't care one bit about the looks we're getting from passengers pouring through the station.

We breathe in sync for a long minute, words unnecessary as the world moves on without us. Boldly, I bury my face in her hair and use my thumb to rub small circles on her back, the sweet scent of her floral perfume intoxicating my senses. It's hard to think with her in my arms, but for a brief moment, I feel her tension slip away.

Finally, she pulls back, wiping fresh tears from her eyes, a polite smile pasted across her face. "Thanks," she says with a sheepish air. "I really needed a hug today, and when you called . . . I've got to look like such a mess right now." Her laugh is nervous, those cornflower blue eyes flashing up to mine as if to beg me not to judge her need for comfort.

I feel a heady rush in my brain, the unshed tears in her eyes making them too bright, the sight of her suppressed emotion making me want to pull her into my arms and hold her so tightly that the pain has no room to exist. I almost don't register her nervous chatter.

"I didn't have time to get dressed or do my makeup this morning. I know I'm a mess . . . my face, my hair . . . I'd normally never go out in public like—"

She jumps when my hands slide down her arms until I'm cradling her delicate fingers in my palms.

"Ava, stop . . ."

So many questions are ricocheting through my brain, but none of them matter right now. What matters is that Ava is hurting, and I will do anything to bring joy to her eyes again.

Her face drops. "I'm so sorry to ask you to meet me here out of the blue like this. I'm sure you're busy with work, and I've probably made you late to the office. I just felt bad that I couldn't meet you for donuts this morning . . ."

I want to tell her to stop apologizing. She has nothing to apologize for, especially to me. Instead, I hear myself blurting out the name "Nancy Meyers."

Startled, Ava freezes. Her chin lifts, her eyes widening with alarm. "I'm sorry. What does—"

"Years ago, I remember you saying once that peak happiness would be to spend a day pretending to be a character in a Nancy Meyers' movie. Do you remember that? Well, today is that day."

Her pink, full lips part as confusion washes over her face. I watch her thoughts work overtime. "How could you possibly remember . . .?" She shakes her head, and her words spill out. "Dawson, I have to get to the office. I'm sure you do too. I don't even know why I asked you to meet me here. I just felt like I needed one of your hugs . . . And what would a Nancy Meyers' day even look like?"

Her sentence ends with a little laugh, and I hear an edge of delight and curiosity slipping into her tone.

Tilting my head, I twist my lips and give her a goofy, exaggerated look. "Don't you know? A Nancy Meyers' day is full of aesthetically pleasing scenery, lots of complementary color tones, and cheery, uplifting music that plays while the characters dance through their messy lives that are still somehow charming, down-to-earth, and yet simultaneously enviable."

She rolls her eyes at me, but her face is bright. "Don't you mean it's full of a soothing yet iconic style, idyllic days, and characters who work with grace and humor through their troublesome situations?"

I smirk. "Isn't that what I said?"

Her laugh makes my head feel light. "Okay, Mr.-Has-All-the-Answers-Today-Hayes. What could we possibly do to pretend we are in a Nancy Meyers' movie?"

My reply is prompt and entirely off the cuff. "Afternoon tea at the Plaza Hotel. But first, a stroll through the Flower District in Chelsea. And tonight, you—the leading lady—will accompany me—your handsome costar—to the Ladies of the Library evening book club."

Ava pulls her lower lip through her teeth, staring up at me with an expression of shock and disbelief. A battle between sheer delight and trepidation flashes across her face.

"You certainly have some wild ideas," she exhales with a breathy *whoosh*. "I don't think I have the time—"

I interrupt her, squeezing her hands. "When is the last time you, Ava Fox, took even part of a day just for yourself? Tell me you haven't put everything above yourself and been a workaholic for months." I lean closer to her, letting my voice drop into a whisper. "You forget, I follow you on social media now."

She shakes her head. "Dawson, I . . . I . . . well, I can't go into the Plaza Hotel looking like this." Pulling her hands away, she flings them about wildly, motioning to her outfit.

The serious expression on her face is replaced by her soft smile, which breaks out like a beam of light, filling the space between us. My heart might be literally walking on a cloud.

Suddenly, I see her as I imagine her Creator must see her, and the realization takes my breath away. Ava's beauty has always been ethereal. She is almost angelic, and the silent years between us haven't diminished an ounce of my attraction to her. But what I feel for her is more than just physical. Despite our differences, I've always felt connected to her on a deeper level. I used to understand what touched her heart, and even though an entire ocean once separated us, my instincts still seem to hit the right notes.

I want to take a photo of the expression on her face right now and bring it out to show her when that light in her eyes dims. It's a struggle to get out the words stuck in my throat.

I snap my fingers. "Okay, then. First stop, the dress shop."

Her eyes sparkle with unrestrained delight. "Oh, so I'm just going to find the perfect dress at some idyllic, charming shop, try it on, and walk out of there wearing it?"

She's teasing, but I reply with solemn intensity. "Yes, Ava. That's how it works in a Nancy Meyers' world."

She laughs.

Leaning over her a little in a mock bow, I extend my arm. "Shall we?"

Ava hesitates, studying me. When she finally reaches up and slips her fingers through the crook of my arm, her hand is warm, its pressure light. A smile plays across her lips.

"I'm going along with this because I've had a very bad morning, and I'd like life to look a little more like a movie sometimes. Everything always works out in the movies."

Fortunately, we're both wearing tennis shoes, so it's easy to wander along Park Avenue, peeking into window displays and taking in the constant hustle and bustle of the city as if we're tourists visiting Manhattan for the first time. We don't discuss a path but simply wander until our feet take us onto Madison Avenue, where the storefronts of iconic fashion designers call out to passersby. Ava peers into the extravagant window displays with an eagerness I can feel radiating off her. Despite her earlier protests, her enthusiasm seems to be growing as the minutes pass.

To my surprise, she bypasses the most notable fashion

houses, continuing to peruse the storefronts until we happen past a more modest shop display. The tiny boutique is tucked away in a quiet corner.

Ava pauses, peeking into the windows. "Maybe I can find a dress here."

When we enter the shop, a bell rings over the door. A pleasant-looking older woman greets us, welcoming us kindly. While Ava browses the colorful racks of clothes, I linger near the entrance, using the downtime to check my emails and reschedule a few team meetings scheduled for later in the afternoon. *The perks of making partner,* I tell myself with satisfaction. I make my own schedule now.

"What do you think?"

I look up just in time to see Ava stepping out of a dressing room. My breath catches at the sight of her. A white cotton dress drapes over her willowy form. The hem flows down to her ankles, allowing only a glimpse of creamy skin. The loose sleeves flow across her arms, see-through lace stitched into the fabric. All I can think is that my mother would call them "Anne Shirley sleeves," whatever that means.

The dress only amplifies her ethereal beauty. I don't bother to hide my admiration as I walk forward and stare at her. "It's perfect," I reply.

Suddenly, a nervous look passes over her features. With a hasty movement, she grabs her ponytail and pulls the band out of her hair, allowing her natural waves to spill over her shoulders. They fall over her cheeks, temporarily hiding her face from me.

"I'll take it." She turns to the clerk, pulling her wallet out of her bag. "I don't know what I'm going to do about shoes, though."

The clerk peeps down at her feet.

"I think what you have on is just darling with this dress," she croons.

I step forward, drawing my wallet out of my back pocket. Ava sees me and realizes what I'm doing. Her hands lift in protest. I shake my head, handing my card to the saleswoman. "I invited you out for a Nancy Meyers' day, so a new dress is my treat."

The clerk's face breaks into a smile as she completes the transaction. "What a delightful outing! I hope you lovebirds have the best date together today."

"Oh, that's not—"

"Oh, we're not—"

The heat in Ava's face is mirrored by the fire in my own. When our sentences break off awkwardly, the clerk's smile only intensifies as she glances back and forth between the two of us.

When we step onto the street again, I turn to Ava and offer her my arm. "For our next destination, what's more idyllic? A taxi, the subway, or walking?"

She taps her lips with one elegant finger. "It's such a beautiful summer day. Let's walk and pretend we're new to the city."

I try to memorize the exact shape of her fingers and palm as they press into the crook of my arm.

The Flower District isn't far from Madison Avenue. We take our time, wandering toward 29th Street, peeking with interest at the food in the boutique cafés, taverns, and upscale eateries we pass. Even the taciturn New York City pedestrians seem to come alive as the radiant sun shines upon the streets. I look around with fresh eyes, feeling how deeply the city is an interplay of old and new, modern and vintage, all of it meeting in a convergence that represents the best of the city I fell in love with.

My heart warms with fondness for this place, for the people who work and live and love in this city. The place that brought me to this moment. It's not a city without faults, but it's mine. Seven years away was far too long.

The Flower District is upon us suddenly, a hidden gem in the concrete jungle. We step into a passageway of green, leafy tropical leaves hiding us from the warmth of the sun. Open doorways beckon us inside, riotous washes of color and the sweet fragrance of blooms overwhelming our senses.

"It's like I've stepped into *The Secret Garden*." Ava peers up at me and grins. When I laugh, her long eyelashes flutter coyly over her cheeks. "Classic book lover things. I couldn't help it."

"You know your classics," I reply with a wink.

Blooms spill out and around the base of a shop doorway. We step over the threshold, marveling at the chaos of beauty surrounding us. Flowers of every variety and color are stacked in crates. Entering the building is an experience, an immediate immersion in a land made of blooms. To enhance the effect, large, gold-rimmed mirrors have been hung from the ceiling, their reflection multiplying the rows of color until it's all the eye can see. "Make your own bouquet" is written on wooden placards that dot the space.

I pluck a large, white daisy—its golden-yellow center like an exclamation mark—from a nearby bucket. With a grand flourish, I extend the stem to Ava.

"M'lady," I say, "shall we assemble a fine bouquet from this plethora of sumptuous offerings and seize the day?

Though, I have my doubts that any flower in this place can rival your exquisite beauty."

Her cheeks flush to a shade that nearly matches the pinkest of the pink flowers in the shop. She takes the daisy from my hand, the tips of our fingertips brushing with a brief flash of heat that singes my very soul. Lifting it to her nose, she inhales its herbal scent. Briefly, her eyes flutter closed, hiding their blue from my searching gaze.

Her voice carries a distinctive rhythm when her eyes open, and she finally speaks. "Good sir, methinks you are a veritable coffer of brilliant ideas." In response to my visible wince at her attempted British accent, she throws her head back and laughs. "Did I go too full pirate on you there?"

I hold up my thumb and index finger, not more than a centimeter separating them. "Just a little."

Gracefully, she moves through the rows of flower crates. I follow, watching the sway of her fluffy hair spilling over the cotton dress in golden waves down her back. When her arms are overflowing with blooms, she glances over her shoulder at me. "My eyes may have been bigger than my ability to hold all these."

A decorative mirror is hanging just beside me, and as Ava turns all the way around, I see the instant her eyes catch sight of herself in its reflection. She starts, pulling back, a hot flash of red blooming across her cheeks. Looking away quickly, her gaze darts nervously in my direction.

"Oh, goodness gracious, I look like a fright. I should have stopped to throw on some makeup before we left the boutique."

The weight of her self-doubt is so strong it nearly crushes my heart. This woman stands before me, harshly criticizing herself, and all I can think of is how beautiful and wonderful she is. The contrast between this halting, self-deprecating Ava and the Ava who was full of hope and zest for life when I left for my internship in London after graduation hits me like a sledgehammer. I don't know what transpired between now and then to destroy her self-confidence, and I'm unsure if it's my place to ask. All I know is that something in her life (or someone) has hurt her.

Not for the first time since I've been in her life again, I promise myself that, with me, she'll never have a reason to doubt her worth.

Stooping, I break off a dainty daisy bud from the pile of flowers in her arms, its soft white petals reaching out like tiny rays of sunshine. Lifting it, I slide the stem over her ear and tuck it into her golden hair. I allow my fingertips to trail along the space between her ear and jawline, unable to resist the call of her smooth skin. Letting the full weight of my attraction for her flash across my face, I gaze down at her.

I think both of us are barely breathing.

"That's all the adornment you could ever need." My voice comes out raspy, emotion thickening my vocal cords.

Her breath catches audibly, those full, pink lips parting, and what almost looks like a frown crosses her face. A soft sheen of unshed tears washes over her eyes, instantly causing my heart to constrict with the fear that, despite my intentions, I've said and done the wrong thing. Why is it that I seem to keep driving her away, even though my hope is to draw her closer? Just when I think some of the distance between us is finally shrinking, something I do shoves it wider again.

Ava's fingers reach out to grasp my wrist, and their

pressure is gentle and warm. She leans in so that her voice is only a whisper in my ear. "Thank you, Dawson," she breathes, "for everything. I . . ."

Whatever else she is going to say gets choked out by the blaring of a horn somewhere down the street. The sound disrupts the moment, and startled, our gazes drop away. The tension of the moment is broken as we laugh.

She raises the wild bouquet in her arms. "Well, now that I've collected enough blooms to start a flower shop of my own, I owe you an afternoon tea at the Plaza. I'm parched."

19

Ava

Dawson swings open the main door of the New York Public Library and flashes me a grin as I duck under his arm. Today has been one for the books. What started as one of my worst days in a long time somehow morphed into an afternoon of unadulterated delight.

"I think Shelly said they gather in a reading room on the second floor." He gestures toward the magnificent marble staircase. "I hope they don't mind us crashing the party a few minutes late."

Earlier today, when Dawson called me, all the pain and disappointment of the past seven years nearly spilled out of my mouth. Instead, I choked it back and told him I was on my way to the train station and back to the city. When he said he would meet me at Grand Central, my brain didn't do the normal panic-and-avoid thing it likes to do when I'm in stressful situations. Contrary to my usual tendencies, I didn't want to run away and hide in a dark cave until I somehow gathered the strength to emerge.

For some odd reason, I murmured a simple "Okay." I'm a wreck today, a bona fide wreck. But I didn't care. All I could think was how comforting one of his hugs would feel. Dawson has always given the most epic hugs.

However, I *did* tell him my train was arriving fifteen minutes later than it was scheduled. I thought I could buy myself enough time to sneak into the bathroom and apply a touch of makeup to cover the telltale signs of tears on my face. I could have done my makeup on the train. I always carry concealer, powder, mascara, and a mirror in my bag, but I was too drained—too numb. Besides, I never actually managed to slow the drip of occasional tears on the ride back into the city.

But Dawson arrived early, or rather, on time with my train. To my surprise, the fact that he saw me looking like such a mess didn't make me fall apart the way I thought I might.

"Did you actually read the book?" I whisper to him now. Our footsteps thud on the marble as we walk upstairs.

He scoffs. "Of course I did. I'd be too embarrassed to show up to a book club meeting having not read the book." His eyebrows draw together into a frown, his gaze landing on me as if a sudden thought just struck him. "I'm sorry. I had no idea you'd be joining me tonight, or I would have sent you the title so you could read it too."

I can't help but laugh at the distress on his face. "Quick, give me a run down so I don't make a fool out of myself. What's the title?"

"It's called *Just in Time* by Doranna . . . Shields, I think is her name? It's a new release."

A sudden flush burns my cheeks as I work valiantly to suppress my grin. "Hm . . . interesting title . . . And what is it about?"

"Well," Dawson clears his throat and nods toward the opulent reading room that looms ahead of us, "it was, uh, a hockey romance."

"Really?" I start to laugh but immediately pivot the sound into a gasp. "What was the premise?"

Dawson slows our pace. "The main character is this hotshot hockey player who ends up falling in love with the Zamboni driver's daughter, only to find out she's a petty thief. One thing leads to another, and they're framed for a big crime they didn't commit and go on the run together to clear their names. It was Shelly's turn to pick the book for the club this month."

My face twists. It's almost impossible to contain my laughter. Managing to gasp for a breath, I reply, "Thanks for the heads-up. That's quite the storyline."

With the utmost seriousness, he nods. We walk into the reading room together. Instantly, a woman I can only assume is Shelly herself hops up from a chair, her pink hair blazing a trail through the room as she heads straight for Dawson. When she reaches us, the older woman wraps him in a sweet hug.

"Look, everyone!" she announces. "My sugar daddy came!"

To my amusement, Dawson flushes visibly, but his voice reflects his characteristic humor. "Shelly, darling, I thought we agreed on candy companion instead?"

Shelly laughs so hard she cackles. "Or was it fructose friend?"

"We vetoed that one," Dawson says as Shelly's eyes finally fall on me.

"So this is what I was competing against?" she quips, her bright eyes inspecting me curiously. "No wonder you said we probably wouldn't work out. I'll admit that I never had a chance."

The flush on Dawson's face deepens, but I know it's nothing compared to mine. For the second time today, someone has mistaken us for a couple, and both times, the assumption has completely thrown me for a loop.

"We're not . . . I'm just here for . . ." *Where are my words?* "I'm just a really big book lover, that's all. Daws told me about your book club, and I couldn't stay away. What can I say?"

Shelly reaches for me, and I'm wrapped in a hug equally as sweet as the one she gave Dawson. "You're in the right place, then. What's your name?"

"Ava."

"Come on and sit, you two. We're just getting started."

A small group of wooden chairs has been drawn together. The only two open seats are separate from each other, and none of the ladies offer to move so that Dawson and I—who are supposedly a couple—can sit next to each other. With a subtle shrug, he smirks at me and goes to take the open seat next to Shelly. I take the last chair next to a gray-haired woman, the *clack* of knitting needles coming from her lap as her hands fly through the stitches.

"Alright, ladies." A woman stands and swings her hips with gusto. She pauses when she looks at Dawson and adds, "And sugar daddies." Her wink is full of amusement.

"Candy companion," Shelly corrects with a snicker.

The woman laughs. "Everyone finished *Just in Time*, right?"

Murmurs of agreeance fill the room. A woman to my right makes the joke that they'd all finished the book "just in time."

"Great," the woman, whom I am guessing is the group leader, continues, "initial thoughts? Anyone?"

Boldly, I raise my hand. Dawson's eyes widen at me across the circle. "I'm sure we'll discuss this at some point during the evening, but I especially treasured the way Gillian's character arc wasn't so much about reconciling her grievances against her controlling father as it was about finding her place in a very chaotic and confusing world."

Dawson's mouth drops open, and I resist looking at him as long as I can. When I finally break and peek in his direction, there's a twinkle in his eye. I wink. He thought he'd gotten me with that baloney spiel about the plot of *Just in Time* he gave me on the way into the library. Little did he know, I already knew this book *extremely* well.

"Oh, Ava. I never even caught that!" Shelly exclaims as she slaps her book on her knee.

The book club discussion continues, and without showing off too much, I put Dawson further in his place by giving the wittiest and most insightful answers to the group's questions that I can manage. Afterward, when the meeting comes to an end and we say our goodbyes to the Ladies of the Library, Dawson and I linger on the sidewalk. Rather than part ways, almost by silent but mutual agreement, we hail a cab and let it drive us uptown.

The sun grew hazy while we lingered on the library steps, a patch of clouds softening its brightness. The cab is filled with a golden glow that is both cozy and romantic, and I feel a wave of gratitude for the direction this day took. My heart nearly threatens to burst inside my chest, and I hate how vulnerable it makes me feel.

We sit quietly in the cab together, saying nothing, yet it feels like everything. Dawson takes off his glasses and gently cleans them with a small cloth he pulls from his pocket. Glancing over, I notice the soft indentation they've left on the bridge of his nose, and I'm thankful for the brief flicker of time to look at his face with nothing in the way. I'll always adore his glasses—he is a man made for frames—but seeing him without them is a reminder of his own vulnerability. We're just two people who used to be in love, and I know how easily I could break his heart. The realization only heightens the threat of emotion in my chest.

Replacing his glasses, Dawson finally turns to me. "Alright, so I guess I owe you an apology."

Playfully, I reach across and smack his arm. "Finally! Yes, you do. Trying to pull that old joke on me. You brat."

"Well, it worked in one literature class. I figured it might work now too." His lips pull into a smile, and the sight of it makes my head feel light.

"I don't read an assigned book *one* time, and you take full advantage of me forever? For shame, Dawson Hayes. Bet you didn't expect me to pull that out of my hat today, did you?"

"I should have known you'd already read it. You read everything."

"While that's not a false statement, you forget I'm also an editor for a living."

"You worked on this book?"

My attempt at containing my giggles fails miserably.

"And you only chose to reveal this *now*?" Dawson shakes his head, his jaw slack, the grin still planted firmly on his face. "Well played, Ava Fox. I didn't know you were so duplicitous."

"I prefer the term 'mysterious,' and it's not like you have room to talk, Mr. Candy Companion." A tear of laughter slips from the corner of my eye.

Dawson purses his lips and sobers his face immediately. "I'm sorry you had to find out about Shelly and me this way."

Rolling my eyes, I reach out to smack his arm again, but the cab driver suddenly makes a sharp turn, throwing me across the open middle seat. I have to grab hold of Dawson's arm instead to steady myself. His skin is warm, the sinuous muscle of his arm an instant comfort I didn't know I needed. A subtle hint of his cologne hits me, the woodsy spice faint after a full day but dizzying, nonetheless. He places his free hand over my arm.

"You alright, there?"

My mouth feels as if it has been glued shut. I can only nod and right myself, begrudgingly removing my hand from his arm. When I catch his gaze a moment later, there's a flicker of uncertainty in his eyes.

"Hey, Ava?" he asks. The sudden shift in the tone of his voice from playful to serious makes my stomach drop. "Do you want to talk about what happened this morning?"

"Oh." The word slips softly from my lips. Averting my gaze from his, I stare out the window for a few moments, the only sounds in the cab coming from the radio playing softly in the front seat. I turn back to Dawson with a brilliant smile pasted across my face. "A much better idea would be to talk about anything but that. What shall we do tonight?"

"I just . . . I want you to know I'm here if you need someone to confide in." Despite me putting him off, he looks at me hopefully, as though maybe the stonewalling Ava he has come to know might suddenly morph into the woman who used to tell him everything. Well, almost everything.

Knowing I'm going to disappoint him, I reply with a cheerful tone anyway, "Thanks, Daws."

"Ava."

I pretend not to hear him. "By the way, is my Nancy Meyers' day over yet? If it's not, we should do something really fun and spontaneous and not at all depressing right now."

Dawson sighs and studies me through his lenses. Frustration pulses off him in waves. Why wouldn't he be frustrated? He saw me at my worst today, and now, I'm refusing to let him in and refusing any sort of explanation. He glances through the window for a few moments, then suddenly tells the driver to let us out up ahead.

On the sidewalk, Dawson grabs me by the hand and leads me toward a charming restaurant down the street. It's dimly lit and moody inside, with the vibe of a speakeasy from the twenties. It's easy to imagine Jay Gatsby and Daisy Buchanan first locking eyes across the space.

"Do you still enjoy the occasional glass of chardonnay and charcuterie?" Dawson leans over and whispers to me after we take two open seats at the gleaming mahogany bar.

"Why do you ask?"

"There's always wine in Nancy Meyers' movies." He shrugs.

I grin. "Oh, then the answer is yes."

We order a glass each, plus a charcuterie board to share.

As we wait, Dawson tries the same question he had in the cab.

"Want to play a guessing game?" he asks, wiggling his eyebrows playfully.

The spontaneity makes me giddy. "Yes!"

"Okay, I'm going to guess what was wrong this morning, and if I get it right, you have to tell me."

The degree to which he cares touches me deeply. The pleading look in his eyes almost breaks my resolve. "Dawson, no."

"You already said you'd play," he counters. The light from the gold pendant hanging over our heads reflects off both the lenses of his glasses and his eyes. The expression in their smoldering depths dances across my face, enticing and inviting me to trust him. A shiver ripples across my skin.

Planting my elbow on the bartop, I rest my cheek in my hand and stare at him, allowing my brain a moment to consider. Finally, I find the words. "Look, I appreciate that you care, but there's just . . ."

I blow out a sharp exhale and lean back, nerves prickling in my gut. I smooth my hands over the skirt of my new cotton dress, studying the fabric. Without looking at him, I say, "There are things about myself that I don't exactly know how to share and things that I don't . . . Well, to be honest, I'm kind of ashamed of them."

At his silence, my heart sinks. Already, I feel like I've said too much and let him in too far. I don't want to continue this conversation.

"Like what?" Dawson asks.

"My Diet Coke habit, for starters," I reply quickly.

"Ava, come on."

"I'm serious. I drink at least two a day right now, and I know they're terrible for me."

"Your addiction to processed sugar and caffeine is the least of my concerns at the moment."

"I'm just dealing with . . . a lot of things, Dawson."

"You've changed."

His quiet observation catches me off guard. "Yeah, that's what people do," I say with a little too much snark.

"No, I mean—correct me if I'm wrong—but the Ava I used to know didn't care so much about what people thought of her. She had random worries like the rest of us, for sure, and she always was a perfectionist, but she was also carefree and silly and confident. And when she smiled, it was *always* genuine."

He's too observant. I shift on the barstool uncomfortably. "You think my smile isn't genuine now?" I give him a goofy smile.

His grin is almost sad. "It doesn't quite reach your eyes like it used to."

I manage a shrug, but I'm at a loss for words, feeling wounded and exposed. I don't know exactly how and when I changed, but when my family fell apart, I did too. My mind, my heart, and my ability to trust have never been quite the same.

Since the day our family split, I've never felt carefree. I've had seasons of good and seasons of renewed pain, but today was the closest I've felt to the carefree, old version of me in a long time. An emotional expert would probably explain what I feel as my mind and heart insulating themselves, preventing me from letting anyone in, safeguarding the most vulnerable places of my heart so that I never experience the hurt and loss I've witnessed in others.

For years, something within urged me to pretend that everything in my life was perfect when, in fact, it was nothing but a painful mess. But how can I share any of the pain and loneliness of the past seven years with Dawson? I didn't just lose my family. I lost him.

I settle for pushing it all away yet again. "It's complicated. Can we just leave it at that for now? Please."

"For now, or forever?" There's hurt in his eyes, and I know what he is thinking. He knows as well as I do how capable I am of blocking him out completely. I've done it before, and I wonder if he pushes me too far, if I'll be tempted to do it again.

"There's nothing about you that I won't—" he continues.

The bartender interrupts him and sets a chilled glass of chardonnay in front of each of us. I reach for mine, my fingers playing with the stem, but I don't take a sip.

"I just can't," I reply quietly.

"Alright, I'm sorry for pushing," Dawson says. "I'll drop it." He lifts his glass toward mine in a cheers motion.

"To . . .?" I ask and wait, wondering how he'll finish the statement.

He pauses, his face thoughtful. After a moment, his lips twist into a grin. "To Billy Joel."

I sit up straight and look behind me, scanning the restaurant. I'm disappointed when I don't see anyone faintly resembling Billy Joel, but then my ears catch the song playing in the background underneath all the noise of the building. I can barely make out the tune and strain to listen.

Suddenly, the lyrics are not so faint, and to my horror, I

whip around in the chair to find Dawson singing them gustily beside me, his glass still lifted.

"I took the good times, I'll take the bad times . . ."

The man on the other side of Dawson gives him a funny look and shakes his head, turning away as if to distance himself.

"Dawson," I say through gritted teeth. "This isn't karaoke."

"I'll take you just the way you are."

My cheeks burn with embarrassment as his voice rises another decibel.

"Dawson Hayes," I whisper, ducking my head slightly as if doing so will prevent anyone in the restaurant from seeing me. "You're going to get us kicked out of here."

To my chagrin, a woman at a nearby table joins in and sings the next lines with him.

When the song fades to a close, Dawson lifts his glass again. "To Billy Joel and you being just the way you are."

My eyes lock with his, a mist suddenly causing his face to grow hazy and faint.

When his hand crosses the distance between us and cradles mine, I grasp onto it like a lifeline. His voice rasps in my ear, just loud enough for the two of us. "Ava, whatever you have going on, it doesn't take away from the fact that you are still the loveliest person I've ever met. And I know that God is going to work it all out so that, one day, the light in your eyes knows it is safe to return."

His words make my heart pound. I know his comment is meant to unravel the stiff, cold parts of me, the ones I'm hiding away, but I feel the ice wall that has protected me for so long begin to rise again. It isn't lost on me that this man—

this selfless and caring man—still loves me. I still love him too. How could I not? But here I am, stuck spinning my wheels in the muck of my life, unable to shake off the painful grip of the past. I can't be who he needs me to be, and I don't have the strength to try.

As if in response to my unspoken thoughts, Dawson's eyes squint behind his frames, shadowy under the dim lights. I feel another flutter in my chest, but there is an undeniable new spark of hope. This has simultaneously been the most confusing day and best day of my life. I must hold onto that.

I gulp down the lump in my throat and lift my untouched glass. "To you, Dawson, for being the greatest friend I've ever known."

As the words fill the silence between us, I clink my glass to his.

20

Dawson

Ouch.

Friend zoned again.

Is it me? Am I the problem?

Ava glances up at me expectantly as if I'm just supposed to echo her feelings that she is a great *friend*, as well.

A mushroom cloud of frustration implodes outward from my chest as we finish our drinks and nibble from the charcuterie board, making small talk that feels unimportant and trite. There's so much I want to say to her, yet when I try to express any of it, she shuts me down. I thought our chapter was closed for good. I never anticipated getting a second chance with her when I moved back to the city. I'm still in shock that our friendship has blossomed again, but she feels just as far away as ever.

I want to tell her how I feel, but I won't because being honest with Ava comes with the risk that I'll lose her again entirely.

Dusk has fallen when we exit the restaurant and wander down the sidewalk again. My hands itch as I hold myself back from slipping my arms around her waist and pulling her to me so I can bury my face in her hair. I just want one more hug before the day is over. The white cotton dress sways around her figure with the same allure it held when she first stepped out of the dressing room. Today has felt just like the days we used to spend exploring the city as students—when everything was right with the world because she was by my side.

And yet, despite our camaraderie and the progress we've made, I can feel her walls going back up. I've tried to be content with what we have. The ease and familiarity of our friendship are a comfort, but I don't want to be her *friend.*

It's hard not to wonder if the heartache and disappointment will ever cease.

My frustration builds. The potential of what we could be to each other is too palpable, too real, too within my grasp. I want to hold her, fold her up in my arms, and kiss away the strained look of tension I've seen creeping into her eyes all too often since my return to the city. I want to hear her every worry, every doubt, every fear. Nothing is too big for us to solve . . . together.

She just won't let me in. As soon as it starts to feel as if we're connecting the dots between our past and our present, she swoops in with a reality check that she is—indeed—not interested in anything more than friendship.

But why?

The same question has replayed itself in my brain since the day she broke up with me.

We linger in the balmy evening air, the summer heat

241

dissipating as the sun slips below the horizon. Ava is telling me about an author whose debut novel she thinks is going to make a huge splash in the market, but I'm struggling to listen, torn between my own thoughts and her soft, melodic voice.

I may be delusional, but each time our connection seems to deepen, there's a moment when I feel as if she wants there to be more between us. Moments like now, when her hand slips instinctively into mine as if there was never a time when I forgot what this felt like.

Lord, why won't she see what I see? Why do I keep feeling what I'm feeling and having these perfect moments with her, but as we turn every corner, I run smack dab into the walls I thought had finally fallen? Am I really missing Your plan that significantly?

As the prayer goes up silently, I feel a wave of guilt. Maybe it is me. Maybe my stubbornness is the problem in our relationship. Is it time to give up the ship and let Ava go? For the past seven years, I've wondered if we would ever get the chance to rekindle our love story.

But are there some stories that aren't ever meant to be written? Am I holding onto the past and preventing myself from accepting the good things the future holds?

We meander past a small bistro, and the lights on the patio glisten in her eyes. Even the growing shadows of the city can't suppress their luminous depths. My head is bent down to her as she talks—I study her, trying to understand what I keep missing—and I catch what looks like the sparkle of tears under her lashes.

Her voice tumbles around us nervously, and I realize she has changed the subject. "By the way, do you think you'll go out with Megan again? Maybe one of these dates will be the moment Blind Date with a Book Nerd has its first success story. Can you imagine being the first user to find true love through the site?"

I hate to be the one to burst her bubble. "I'm not going out with Megan again, Ava."

"Oh." Her voice is soft. "Well, God has the perfect woman waiting for you, Dawson. I know it."

We reach the stoop of her apartment building. The metal door handle is shockingly cold against the almost feverish heat of my hand. I pull it open and follow her inside. It's a given that I'll see her safely to her door.

Hazily, I walk with her up several flights of stairs until we stop in front of her unit. Unlocking the door, she turns back to me without opening it. Her expression is hesitant and full of doubt. A fresh wave of guilt that I've said all the wrong things in the wrong ways at the wrong times crashes with brutal force into my gut.

The subtle way she flinches as I lift my hand breaks my heart. I almost waver and drop it, but I can't help the urge to touch her. This woman deserves to be treasured, revered, and adored. I want to know what hurt her so deeply so that I can promise her it'll never come near her again.

The hallway is quiet and dimly lit. It's just the two of us. My gaze settles, exploring the beautiful shape of her face, searching for a hint that I'm doing the right thing. My lips press into a straight line as I forcibly hold myself back from spilling out every thought in my head. With the utmost tenderness, I allow my thumb to slide along her delicate jaw, outlining her pretty chin, inching upward toward those full lips that every fiber of my being begs me to kiss.

But I won't do it. I'll never push past her boundaries. I'll never cross that line with her until she gives me the signal. And if that signal never comes, then so be it.

But the pad of my thumb brushes her lower lip. She gives a small exhale of surprise, her lips parting just a little. Ava stares up at me.

And with a flash of clarity, I understand why all of the heartbreak that brought me to this moment was worth it. Whatever happens between Ava and me in the future, I'm content to love her as God loves her. If that is all it ever is, that's enough. She's enough.

As if she knows what I'm thinking, Ava's eyes fill with tears, visible ones this time. "You're too good to me, Daws. You're more than I deserve. I'm so sorry that I've disappointed you. I just wish I could . . ."

On impulse, I close the few inches between us and gently touch my forehead to hers. Without hesitation, her arms slide up and around my neck, pulling me closer. Her breath is sweet against my skin.

I wonder if she can hear the crack in my voice. "Don't cry. You have nothing to be sorry for. Nothing you could ever do would disappoint me. All I want is to know you're happy."

If anyone walks down the carpeted hallway, it will look like we are locked in a passionate kiss. I slide my arms around her waist, holding her close. Her slender figure is pliable in my arms, her face buried in my shoulder. After a few minutes, Ava chokes back her tears with a little half-laugh, half-sob. Sensing that she is ready, I reluctantly pull away and put distance between us, forcing down the ache I feel for her. She regains her composure, and her sparkle seems to return, a smile flashing across her face.

"Thank you for this perfectly perfect Nancy Meyers' day." In contrast to her cool tone, her hands scramble behind her. With frantic haste, she pushes open her apartment door, and I catch a glimpse of the cozy, welcoming interior. "Will I see you soon?"

I raise two fingers to my forehead in a mock salute. "Of course. Besides, we'll have book club again before you know it. You'd better get to reading. And no cheating by being on the publishing team this time. I'll be watching you, missy."

She smirks. "I make no promises."

As she turns to enter her apartment, my voice halts her in her tracks. "Oh, and Ava . . ." She glances back over her shoulder, the fabric of her dress swaying around her legs with the movement. I lock eyes with her. "I know God has the perfect man out there for you too."

Something crosses her face, but I don't stop to analyze it. With brisk strides, I make my way out of the building and back onto the sidewalk, welcoming the distraction of the still-noisy city as I set my steps toward home.

I've almost arrived at my apartment building when I feel a buzz in my pocket. An expectant burst of joy flares out of my chest. I almost allow myself to dare to hope as I stuff my hand into my pocket and pull out my phone. With an eager glance at the screen, a message from "Never Met a Classic I Didn't Like" flashes into view. The timing of the message catches me off guard, and I almost put the phone away, my thoughts occupied with the beautiful woman I just left for the night.

But the chance for a distraction from my troubled thoughts is too appealing to ignore. Instead, I tap the notification button and allow the message to open:

I guess I ghosted you. Thank you for your help. I'm new to sci-fi, so your book recommendations are helping tremendously. I finally finished 20,000 Leagues *last night. What a voyage! Life has been a lot lately. Do you have any other recommendations? I need something that can distract me from the world for a while if you know what I mean.*

The perfect science fiction recommendation pops into my head immediately. My fingers tap the screen, typing out a message. But I'm interrupted by another notification, this time a text.

MOM: Guess what! Anne and I just finalized the last details for your launch party. Is everything settled with Andrew for the special project you two are working on?

21

Ava

Moving quickly, I scoop up a folder and notebook from my desk and head for my ten o'clock meeting. Technically, I'm already late because my eight-thirty phone call with none other than James Wolfe himself ran long. And before that, my assistant, Kristi, and I spent an hour working through emails and task lists to prioritize throughout the week. I arrived at the office at seven-thirty, and already, I feel as if I've lived a full day.

As I speed walk toward the elevator, I feel a vibration in my hand. Juggling everything I'm holding, I bring the phone up to the top of the pile to glance at the screen. Amongst the emails, texts, and news alerts on my phone, a new notification from Blind Date with a Book Nerd catches my attention right away.

The speed of my heartbeat intensifies. It's unsettling, but I ignore it. I can't let myself think about the way I feel when

I'm near the app's owner. But I also can't help the number of times per day that I wonder how he is doing and wish I could text him to tell him about something dramatic that happened at work.

During the short elevator ride upstairs, I speed-read the notification, trying to absorb it before turning my attention to the other alerts waiting for me. From my cursory glance, I see an early invitation for an app launch party Dawson mentioned briefly the other day. I think I was distracted by counting the gold flecks in his hazel eyes because I remember him mentioning that his mom and sister have appointed themselves his official party planning committee and that CityLight is sponsoring the event, but I realize I'm hazy on the rest of the details.

When I'm about to close out the app, I realize there's another message in my inbox. It'll have to wait until later. Making a mental note to double-check the date of Dawson's launch party and add it to my calendar, I tuck away my phone and steel my nerves for this morning's meeting with my boss.

As I walk through CityLight's upper floor toward the conference room, the hum of male voices drifts out from Gary Ketner's office. In the conference room, I discover a few members of one of our production teams seated inside. With a wave at my fellow employees, I peek across the mahogany-strewn space. It looks like our CEO is running late, so I don't feel as guilty.

While I'm standing in the conference doorway, Gary steps through the door of his office to briefly say something to his secretary. He leaves the door open, allowing me to catch a quick view of the room's inhabitants. Within my line of sight, Andrew occupies one of the chairs in front of his dad's desk. Repeatedly, he tosses a hacky sack in the air and is chuckling loudly about something. In the chair next to him, I can see the edges of another man, but the chair is angled in such a way that I can only catch a glimpse of the back of his head.

But the dark, curly hair is familiar. My heart leaps.

It looks just like . . .

Gary turns away from Joyce to reenter his office. With a jump, I rush forward as the door begins to close. My feet protest since my heels are not conducive to sprinting, but I push past the pain. I strain my neck to catch a glimpse of . . .

Click.

Too late.

Feeling foolish, I take two steps backward toward the conference room, but curiosity gets the better of me. Back to the receptionist's desk, I go.

"Hi, Joyce. Will Gary be joining us for our team meeting after all? Just wondering if we should wait or get started without him."

She smiles sweetly and nods. "He is just finishing up this one and will be over shortly. Do you need me to deliver a message to him in the meantime?"

"No." Unsteadily, I rock on my heels and narrow my eyes at the door. If Dawson is here meeting with Gary and Andrew, why do I care so much? It sounds like CityLight is sponsoring the Blind Date with a Book Nerd app launch event in some way, after all. Of course he is going to have meetings with the head honchos.

"No, I'll speak with him when he joins us," I resolve, telling myself to stay in my own lane. "Thanks, Joyce."

I walk back to the conference room and deliberately take a seat with my back to the windows. Gary enters fifteen minutes later.

The next hour drags by as the production team presents their new plan for our next James Wolfe thriller. The pompous and demanding hotshot is insisting on making changes to a book that has already been sent into production. He's been threatening to wrongfully pull the plug on the contract for months, and of course, just as we finalize the print galley, he has submitted a series of *major* edits that will transform the entire story.

For all I can tell, Mr. Wolfe is insisting on the changes simply because he got a wild hair and thinks he has the right to do so, regardless of how colossally it will set back our production schedule.

Everyone is frustrated, including me. And, though he is trying to hide it behind a professional demeanor, I can tell that Gary is too. Everything is topsy-turvy, and the fault lies with one man.

Usually, changes of this magnitude wouldn't even be a consideration. But this is James Wolfe.

The man has a million followers on social media, his new releases consistently hit the top of bestseller lists and stay there for months on end, and he has so many book-to-movie adaptations that I haven't had time to watch them all.

He's old-Hollywood handsome, snarky, with a controversial and well-known temper, and is all the things that the public on social media would consider entertaining. And worst of all, after we publish his latest release, we don't have him on contract to publish any future work.

It's no secret that he has the upper hand here and can throw as big of a fit as he wants. If we give in to his demands—which means throwing a wrench into our production schedule and practically starting over at the beginning—he says he'll be happy to sign his name on the dotted line come contract renewal time. And if we stick to our guns, he'll take his business and reputation elsewhere.

He has already fired the independent marketing team that faithfully promoted his work for years, citing irreconcilable differences. It's like he's on a tirade, ready to demolish anyone in his way like an angry toddler who has never been told "no" before.

I'm at the whiteboard presenting my notes on all the logistical parts that need to move to cater to Wolfe's demands when movement out of the conference room windows catches my eye. Striding down the main corridor, engrossed in a lively conversation, are Andrew and Dawson. They've just walked from the direction of Gary's office.

"I knew it!"

"Knew what, Ava?"

I blink twice and startle when I realize I'm still in the conference room. *Did I really say that out loud?* Slowly, I turn with fiery red cheeks to the group of people around the table staring at me like I've suddenly grown a second head. CityLight's production assistant, Imani, eyes me curiously, her eyes darting to follow the direction I was looking. One of her shapely, dark eyebrows arches pointedly toward her hairline.

"Um, the . . . What I was saying about . . ." I clear my throat and take one daring glance through the window again, but all I see are the retreating backs of my two friends.

"Never mind. I'm sorry. Where was I?"

"The new editing timeline?" Imani answers with a knowing tilt of her head.

Yeah . . . I try to shake the image of Dawson out of my mind and sigh. *Back to James.*

———

The meeting went as well as the rest of my life has been going lately: chaotic with a pretense of orderliness. Finally seated back at my desk with my lunch spread before me, I can't resist and decide to shoot Dawson a text.

ME: Did I see you in the office this morning?

DAWSON: Time to call up the eye doctor.

I shovel a forkful of salad into my mouth and frown. Is he . . . kidding? Before I can send back a snarky reply, another message *pings* through.

DAWSON: Just kidding. Yeah, that was me. I didn't see you though. Where were you hiding?

ME: Meetings all morning. I saw you when you were walking out with Andrew.

My thumbs hover over the screen. Dawson and I haven't spoken much since our dreamy Nancy Meyers' day together. As the days pass, I feel more and more discombobulated. Why the sudden silence? Did Dawson stop by my office this morning and find it empty? Or was he all business today, focusing on his personal ventures, feeling no need to say hello to the woman he almost kissed in front of her apartment door after the most perfect day ever?

Why didn't he kiss me that night? Why didn't I kiss him first?

Without any right to, my heart feels bruised. I wish I

understood why.

DAWSON: You ninja. Yeah, we grabbed some lunch after our meeting.

ME: Going over sponsorship and app launch details?

DAWSON: Something like that.

I realize I want the conversation to continue. I want Dawson to ask me about my day, to make me laugh, to tell me something about his week. But when he doesn't text again, a nagging feeling also tells me this conversation is over. Maybe it's me. Maybe I'm reading too much into absolutely nothing. Or maybe Dawson is finally doing what I told him to do: moving on.

Closing out his text thread, my instinct is to blindly scroll through social media as a distraction while I finish my lunch. Connecting with my bookish community always cheers me up. I'm behind on responding to comments and messages, but I tell myself I'll get caught up after work, even if keeping up with it all makes me want to pull out my hair. I feel as if I'm failing people I've never even met in person.

The first thing I see when I open the app is my mother's account. She has posted a throwback picture of her and Natasha with a gushing caption that reads: *One of my favorite memories. Time spent with Tashi is always the best. She knows how to spoil her mama! Shopping! Lunch! Manicures! Let's do it again soon, sweetie.*

I remember the day clearly. Originally, I tried to arrange a girls' day between the three of us, but my schedule didn't work with Tashi's. So, the two decided to go on a mother-daughter date together and exclude me.

Since the day of the big blowup at her house, my mother and I haven't spoken. It isn't that I don't want to. But no matter how many times I attempt to call her, I always get sent to voicemail. But even though Mom and I haven't exchanged words, this still feels like communication.

Well, message received, Mom. Loud and clear.

Filled with a sense of defeat and disgust, I toss my phone into a drawer and push away my lunch altogether, my appetite suddenly gone. Am I reading too much into Mom's words now? Am I losing touch with reality here? Is she just hurting, too, unable to move on with her life after Dad left? Maybe I should cut her some slack?

Why didn't Dawson stop by to say hello?

Everything feels so wrong, and yet, when was the last time it felt right?

Knock it off, Ava. You have a great life.

Even my subconscious is getting sick of me.

Propping my elbows on my desk, I let my head sink into my hands. A fresh wave of guilt gnaws at me. I know I have a good life. There are so many blessings and privileges all around me that I don't have the right to be sad for even one day. My mind drifts back to Pastor's message from a couple of weeks ago, and his words echo in my memory.

"We can't control what other people do or think or say about us. But we can give control of our emotions, thoughts, beliefs, hopes, and dreams to God and depend on Him to see us through the tough days."

Even though I recognize my need to turn it all over to God, why does the truth still feel impossible to embrace? Where's the peace I'm supposed to have? Why do I feel like I'm running in slow motion toward an ever-moving goalpost?

Kristi pops her head through my doorway. "James Wolfe

on line one for you, Ava. He said he couldn't reach you on your cell." She gives me a puzzled look as if I've somehow dropped the ball and forced her to talk to the resident dragon of CityLight Press.

I sigh and reach for the landline on my desk. "Thanks, Kristi. Put him through, please. And hold all my other calls until I'm done."

22

Dawson

"Are you already headed out, Hayes?" The voice in my doorway forces me to pause in the act of shutting down the trio of screens on my desk.

"Yeah, boss." I look toward one of the senior partners at the firm, an older man named Ben, who is generally kind but also hard to read. I know his question isn't an accusation since he has been one of my key mentors in the software development field. But it still feels odd to admit the truth to him, especially because I'm leaving work before seven in the middle of the week.

Lately, I've been spending more and more time at the office. His surprise makes me wonder if it's been too much time.

I keep my voice low so the rest of the office doesn't overhear. "I have a date tonight, actually."

Surprise registers on his face. "Well, that's . . . I'm glad to hear it. Is this date because of your little love connection app?"

While I respect his software prowess, Ben is of a generation that simply found his wife in his local community and didn't go searching all over the world for love through the power of the internet. When I explained the concept of my app design to him and asked for his blessing, he gave it readily, but sometimes, I can tell he is still a bit vague on the details of how it works.

I laugh. "Yes, sir. It's with a woman I matched with on the site. I've been using myself as a test dummy as we countdown to launch."

"Well, get to it then." He slaps the doorframe and turns to walk away. "Maybe this girl will cheer you up so you can stop moping around the office."

I look away from my screens in surprise, but Ben is already halfway down the hallway. His words linger as I grab my laptop bag and take the elevator down to the street.

I'm beginning to wonder why I let Ava talk me into being a test dummy for Blind Date with a Book Nerd in the first place. So far, the experiment has gone the way I predicted. The score has been dating app zero and flame-I'm-still-holding-for-my-ex-girlfriend one thousand. I realize that even the moments in which I have to pretend I'm content with being Ava's platonic friend are one thousand times better than any of the matches my algorithm has arranged so far. I truly believe Blind Date with a Book Nerd will help other people find love . . . It's just not for me.

Two more dates, and I'm done.

I'll be the dating app designer who doesn't date.

But I'm a man of my word. Dutifully, I hurry home,

shower, change into fresh slacks and a button-down shirt, put on uncomfortable shoes, polish my glasses, and take several flights of stairs down to the street to hail a cab to take me uptown. I'd rather stay home and pick a random science fiction book off my shelf to reread, but hey, who cares what Dawson Hayes wants out of life?

As I slide into the backseat of the cab, I have a nagging sense that I'm forgetting something, but my mind is too preoccupied to linger long enough on the subject to remember what it is.

One of my matches, "Bend It Like Bennet," confirmed that she wanted to set up a date this week, and we're meeting for dinner at a new bistro in the heart of the city in forty minutes.

I find myself refreshing my messages for the fifth time in three minutes on the off chance that I missed a new text from Ava. Nothing. I try to tell myself that, at the very least, these dates are keeping me from falling into complete hermitville while I wait for the next opportunity to see Ava. Having a social life is a good thing, or so they say.

Save for a few measly texts the day I went to CityLight to finalize some details with Gary and Andrew, it's been over a week since Ava and I have spoken . . . or texted . . . or direct messaged . . . or sent a letter by carrier pigeon. I have no right to expect anything else from her. We said what we said that night after book club, filling in the blanks with both the spoken and unspoken words.

It's my own fault that I can't stop thinking about the way she looked when she stepped out of the dressing room in that white dress or the joy on her face when she waxed poetic about a book she wasn't supposed to have read at book club or the spearmint scent of her breath when I pulled her into my arms in the dimly lit hallway of her apartment building.

I should have kissed her then and there and kept kissing her until she remembered all the reasons we should be together, but, of course, my mother had to go and raise a gentleman.

I'm beginning to think the only thing that has kept me sane this week is the unlikely friendship I seem to be building through my random conversations with "Never Met a Classic I Didn't Like" on the Blind Date with a Book Nerd forum. Somehow, one forum message about space operas has turned into an ongoing private argument about whether the space opera subgenre could ever produce something that fits within the classic novel genre. I've been tempted to pull rank on all the reasons I'm the expert in this field but reading her wildly speculative arguments has provided much-needed amusement when my thoughts get too heavy lately.

I don't know anything about the account other than that she is a fairly new member of my app. I've been sorely tempted to peek into the backend of things and check the registration form the account submitted when she first signed up for the site, but my commitment to testing my dating app as a regular user has kept me from cheating the system. It feels like I'm keeping my promise to Ava to avoid abusing my administrative privileges, too, so I know next to nothing about my new pen pal. All I know is that she has some amusing ideas about literature, and neither of us seems interested in anything beyond casual conversation.

Which is just fine with me.

I should have canceled this date. The words seem to be my

usual refrain anytime I show up to one of these things. The cab driver pulls up to the drop-off zone in front of a swanky new restaurant. I tip the driver and force myself out of the car.

I can imagine the forum headlines on Blind Date with a Book Nerd if anyone gets wind of how I really feel about going on these dates: *Tech startup whiz kid creates book-themed dating app so book nerds can find love, but he dreads every dating opportunity it creates for him.*

"Pathetic," I mutter to myself as I pull open the etched glass door and stride into the elegant bistro. It's cozy and intimate and dimly lit . . . and the perfect place for a first date if you are one of those people interested in such a thing. Immediately, I also recognize that it's the type of place that serves tiny portions and hefty bills.

My date is supposed to have blonde hair, be wearing a turquoise dress, and have a pink dahlia tucked into her ear. I'm supposed to be wearing a turquoise button-down and have a pink dahlia tucked into my chest pocket. I look down and realize what I forgot on my way out the door.

There's only one woman in the restaurant wearing a pink dahlia tucked into her gleaming golden hair. When I spot the pretty woman at one of two tables placed in a quiet corner, I know that I'm here to meet her. I let the hostess know and head to the table.

Her locks cascade around her shoulders in perfectly styled waves, no doubt the halo effect made more intense by the soft, aesthetic lighting that glows above her head. The woman is pretty . . . very pretty . . . in a way that reminds me of lake days and bright blue summer skies. She looks about my age, too, which is a good place to start.

My mouth goes dry. *I'm not in the space for this,* says my heart, but my head tells me to put one foot in front of the other.

I approach the table, and the woman lifts her head, a smile painting itself across her full lips. But it drops a little when her gaze flits to my shirt pocket and doesn't see a dahlia there.

"Bend It Like Bennet?" I ask.

The light in her eyes returns, and that smile blossoms on her face again. "Lord of the Book Nerds?" she replies. "I was looking for the flower and . . ."

When she trails off, I feel a flicker of guilt at my lack of foresight. "I am so sorry I forgot it. Work was crazy . . . I was running late . . ." I realize all I'm doing is making excuses, so I stop.

She nods and motions to the seat. "Well, please sit. I'm pleased to meet you. My name is Dahlia. I thought the flowers were a charming touch, but . . . It was silly."

I extend my hand to her, and when she places her slender fingers in mine, I shake them gently. "Dahlia, I'm Dawson. It wasn't silly at all. It is quite charming," I say, motioning to the one in her hair. "And now, I am even more upset with myself for forgetting."

"That's quite alright. I'm sure you're a busy man with many things on your mind." She looks at me with a question and a look of hesitation in her eyes, which I now realize are a deep shade of green. The teal dress she is wearing brings out their color. "I'm not very good at this online blind date thing," she laughs. "I want to ask you a million questions, but I'm not sure where to start."

Her awkwardness sets me at ease. Having dinner with a

stranger doesn't seem like it's going to be the worst thing after all. I find myself grinning in return. "I'm a software developer. I am a junior partner at a tech company based overseas, but I now live here and facilitate the management of our New York City branch after quite a few years of living abroad. I'm also developing an app that is just about to officially launch called—" I'm just about to tell her that I designed the app that paired us up tonight, but I'm interrupted by the waiter taking our drink order.

When he leaves, she says, "Whew. Your story's not so bad. I love the Blind Date with a Book Nerd dating app, but I wasn't sure how many out-of-work playwrights or aspiring content creators I might get paired up with. I've been on a couple of dates, but our life goals haven't quite aligned."

The casual statement feels like a sticky piece of tape that I can't get off my hand, but I tuck it away to think about later as Dahlia continues without pause, "I am a restaurant designer. Actually, I helped launch this one."

With a wave of her hand to include the elegant restaurant we're seated in, Dahlia launches into an enthusiastic description of everything she loves about her job.

We pass questions and stories back and forth for the next few minutes, and I feel myself relaxing in her easy presence. It turns out that she has had a hand in designing several of my favorite eateries around the city. We order an appetizer of Oysters Rockefeller—which I don't like but which seems like the classy choice—and a refill of sparkling water as we discuss the rise of mid-century modern influences on interior and commercial design as well as architecture.

I quickly discover that Dahlia is intelligent, witty, and well-traveled. I find her both easy to talk to and not unpleasant to look at.

The lights dim as the restaurant fills up with patrons. It's a small space, designed for dark, intimate corners. I barely notice the newcomers until, without warning, the back of my chair is jostled as a couple scoots by to get to the other table in the corner.

Startled by the disruption, I glance over my shoulder as they get settled in.

"Ava?" I blurt out her name. My throat croaks as if I've had a frog in it for weeks. Dahlia's stream of words halts abruptly, and she looks toward the woman and her well-dressed male companion seated at the table next to us.

Ava's head pops up, her golden hair falling over her shoulders like a silken waterfall. The shock on her face is unmistakable. There's another look in her expression too—one I don't have time to analyze. The man seated across from her turns to look at me.

"Dawson?" she exclaims. "What are you doing here?" Her eyes dart toward Dahlia, and a new wave of shock emerges.

I sense, rather than see, Dahlia lift her water glass to her lips. She clears her throat. Ava's date stares me down. He's tall, stocky, and good-looking in a conventional sense, with dark hair and piercing eyes that make me instantly uncomfortable. I remove my glasses, which have suddenly fogged over with steam, and rub them on my shirt.

"We're book nerds on a blind date," I say, waving my glasses somewhere in the direction of Dahlia. I set my glasses back on my face and try to pull my eyes away from Ava, but I haven't succeeded yet. She's wearing a ruffled, light-blue dress with puffy sleeves, and the fabric is the exact color of her eyes.

A look flashes across her face. "We're book nerds on a blind date too," she laughs awkwardly, pointing to her handsome dinner companion.

Her date tries to flash me a friendly smile, but I catch the annoyance in his expression. I've interrupted their date, and he isn't happy about it.

"Do you two know each other?" Dahlia's pleasant voice speaks from across the table, and I finally pull myself together enough to turn back to her.

"Yes! Dahlia, I'm sorry. This is my friend, Ava Fox. Ava, this is my date, Dahlia."

Dahlia and Ava do a demure little wave since they are too far away to shake hands. Dahlia leans forward, studying Ava with interest. "I know you from somewhere . . . wait, you're on social media. 'Foxy Book Lady.' That's you, isn't it?"

Ava laughs. "Guilty as charged."

"Your account is so aesthetic. True book-lover goals!" Dahlia declares. "It's how I heard about the Book Nerd dating app. I saw your post looking for volunteers to test it out, and I couldn't resist."

Ava motions toward me, a playful smile dancing across her lips, which she has painted with the prettiest pink color I've ever seen. "Anything for my friend, Dawson Hayes, here. Did he tell you he's the brilliant mind behind the concept?"

"We hadn't gotten around to that detail," I mumble as Dahlia turns toward me with a curious expression.

"Really?" she remarks.

I give her a humble wave and duck my head.

"Well, your username makes perfect sense. 'Lord of the Book Nerds.' How clever." She laughs.

Ava lifts her hand to gesture across the table toward her

date. The man is still eyeballing me with a great deal of distrust. "Dawson and Dahlia, this is Owen. We were matched on the site when I first signed up a few weeks ago based on our love for C.S. Lewis' *Till We Have Faces.*" She's pointing to Owen, but her eyes, wide and bright, are on me. For the first time, I catch sight of the well-loved books on the table between them. The one closest to Ava is worn and faded, the dust jacket all but torn away.

"That's just lovely," Dahlia says.

"Can't go wrong with Lewis," Owen speaks for the first time. His voice has a pleasant timbre.

"You still have that old thing," I say.

Ava looks at the book on the tablecloth. A short laugh chortles out of her. A dark pink color flushes her cheeks. "Oh, well, yes, of course. I guess it is getting rather tattered. What can I say? My books are old friends, and I don't know how to give them up. You gave this one to me, what? Years ago, after that Bible study class, right?"

The scrape of Dahlia's fork on the plate as she spears an oyster breaks the brief silence. "Wait, you two really do know each other?"

Ava glances toward her, the flush only deepening. "Dawson and I are old friends. Actually, we even dated." Her eyes flash to mine, an unspoken question in their blue depths.

"It was a long time ago," I hasten to clarify. I'm not sure why she just brought this up in front of Dahlia, and I wonder what kind of impression it gives. What man is friends with his ex-girlfriend?

Oh, that's right. A man who is still in love with her.

"How long ago?" Owen interjects.

"Oh, so long ago," Ava says.

"Feels like yesterday, to be honest," I hear myself say before I bite the words back.

The maitre d' appears next to us, his face friendly and open. "Are you all friends? Would you like me to move your tables together?"

A sudden and loud hush falls over our group. I pull myself together enough to shake my head. "That won't be necessary, thank you."

The man fades into the background, and I refocus my attention on Dahlia, feeling as though I want to yank off the tie I put on for the occasion, jump up from the table, and run outdoors for some air. The color on her cheeks is high, and there's a sharp glitter in her eyes that wasn't there just a few minutes ago.

"Now, where were we?" I attempt to smile at her, but I can't feel any emotion behind the expression.

"Where were we?" she says. "Oh yes, I was telling you about . . ."

Ava and Owen bend over their menus. Laughter sparkles over from their table. I try not to be acutely aware of the pair as Dahlia picks up our conversation from earlier. It's hard not to tune out her voice as I listen to the conversation at the table next to us. Ava and her date appear to be having a pleasant time getting to know each other, which makes me want to scowl, but it shouldn't.

"Perhaps we should start with the Oysters Rockefeller?" Owen says, his deep tones resonating across the short distance. From the quick impression I made of him, the man is a classy fellow, so I'm glad my choice of the questionable appetizer has now been validated.

"I can't remember if I've ever tried . . ."

"You won't like those," I blurt out. My head swings toward their table, and Owen throws me a death stare.

Startled, Ava lifts her head to look at me, her hair swaying across her shoulders. "Oh, are they like the ones we had in Atlantic City?"

An involuntary smile crosses my lips as that day flashes across my memory. "Just like that. And we don't need a repeat of that catastrophe."

She matches my grin with one of her own, a smile spreading from ear to ear, lighting up her face as if she has captured the sun and it is shining from within. "I can go without repeating that day as long as I live—"

23

Ava

"Would you two like to be on a date?"

My playful grin fades as I look away from Dawson and back to my date. Annoyance paints Owen's face, his lips twisted into a grimace. And why wouldn't he be upset? My gut sinks. He has every right to be. Dawson and I have completely derailed both of our dates, focusing on one another instead of the people who took their time to come out for a blind date with us. We've flirted and shamelessly rubbed our history in their faces.

Owen and Dahlia didn't sign up for this, and I feel horrible. A wave of guilt crashes into me, so crushing I feel as if I can't breathe. How could I be so selfish?

"Yes, it certainly seems like you two make a good match," Dahlia replies tightly, tucking a stray golden curl behind her ear.

It strikes me how much she and I resemble each other.

We could almost be sisters. I wonder if Dawson thinks she is pretty. A sense of being replaceable eats away at my gut.

"Nah, Ava isn't interested in a guy like me," Dawson quips with a sudden intensity, his tone laced with a tinge of bitterness.

An anvil drops in my stomach as the summer sky darkens beyond the restaurant's floor-to-ceiling windows. In a *whoosh*, all the fun has been sucked from the room. My chest constricts. It's as though a windup toy is inside, but the lever is jammed, and all that kinetic energy is building up and ready to spill out but has nowhere to go. Anxious and jittery, my eyes dart to Dawson.

Words won't come. I can't even muster a fake smile. Instead, I chew the insides of my cheeks to keep from crying. Why can't I conjure up an air of levity to get me through this awkward encounter? It's as though my very will to continue existing within my fake bubble has popped, and there is simply nothing left.

Owen flags the waiter down and asks for the check to be delivered as soon as possible. Our table dissolves into an uncomfortable silence as we wait. My cheeks turn raw as I chew on them, and a sweaty flush creeps up my back. When the waiter returns, Owen kindly pays for me even though I certainly don't deserve it. His movements are hasty, and the few words he says are terse. I can tell he wants to leave as soon as possible.

I do, too, if I'm being honest.

I feel terrible because he seems like a really nice guy, and I hate the fact that I've ruined his evening.

As soon as the bill is paid, he rises and leaves without saying a word to me. In short order, Dahlia follows suit, leaving just Dawson and me alone, quiet and awkward at our respective tables. I want to flee, to disappear, to somehow undo this entire night. My spine burns with heat.

Dawson signs his bill and tosses it onto the table. He rises. Tentatively, I follow suit, unsure of what I'm supposed to do but not wanting to be left alone just yet.

"Why did you say that?" I ask softly across the narrow distance between us.

Dawson tilts his head and stares at me. "Because it's true," he finally replies.

Why does he feel so far away? So unreachable? He is standing right in front of me, and yet it feels as if he is a thousand miles away.

"No, it's not," I protest lamely. I don't want to make a scene in the restaurant, but for the first time since he has been back in New York, I feel a pressing need for him to know that our breakup had nothing to do with my level of interest in him. I was very interested in him. But I also loved him too much not to protect him from the chaos of my family tree.

His lips press into a thin line, and an expression I can't quite understand pulls on his face. A moment passes, and it seems as if he is preparing to say something very profound. But then, the moment slips away, and he releases a small breath instead.

Shaking his head, he turns and walks through the restaurant, weaving around tables filled with happy people, and heads for the door. I'm left standing next to the table, and at that moment, I feel more purely and utterly alone than I've ever felt in my life.

His retreating form blurs in my vision for a moment. I

blink a few times, trying to get him back into focus. Within a few more blinks, he's through the door, and I can't see him anymore.

My feet move of their own volition, and I make for the exit. When I reach the sidewalk, the air smells heavy with rain, pungent and humid and musty. The sky is dark and splotchy with gray clouds. An unexpected summer rainstorm seems about to hit the city. I spot Dawson just down the street and hurry to catch up to him, my long legs doing their job. When I reach him, I fall into step at his side. If he's bothered by my presence, he doesn't let on or tell me to leave him alone. My heart pounds. Side by side, we walk a whole block before I manage to speak.

"Please tell me what you meant back there."

Without warning, Dawson stops short and faces me. My feet grind to a halt. He looks like a man who has nothing left to lose. "Oh, I don't know, Ava. If I wasn't good enough for you seven years ago, why would anything have changed now?"

I gape at him. "What are you talking about?"

"You shut me out, Ava. For no reason at all. Do you know what it does to a guy to be cut out of the life of the woman he loves? For the past seven years, I've wasted countless hours questioning 'why?' Why, when I thought everything was going so well, did the woman I loved dump me? The only rational answer: I didn't fit into her perfect world, so you got rid of me at the first opportunity."

"What does that even mean?" My voice is edgy, my senses sharpened to an intensity that is painful. I'm numb as a raindrop hits my hand, then my scalp, then my face. The rainstorm hits with a wild force, but neither of us moves.

Pedestrians scurry around us in the deluge, seeking shelter from the storm.

But not us.

Dawson runs his hand through his hair. Rain covers the lenses of his glasses, and he has to keep using his shirt sleeve to wipe it away. "Come on, Aves," he says. "Don't play dumb. Look at you. Look at your life. Every tiny detail is curated to fit this unattainable and unreal aesthetic. I can admit it. I don't fit in with that. Sci-fi-loving, glasses-wearing, tech-nerd Dawson is not the type of guy who ends up with Daisy Buchanan on his arm."

His words stun me. I'm frozen, rooted to the sidewalk as the rain soaks my dress and hair. So this is what Dawson has been thinking all this time? I'm powerless to move, to speak. All I can do is stare into the eyes of the man whose heart I utterly shattered when I ended our relationship.

The downpour of rain increases every passing second. Despite the lingering summertime warmth, I shiver as it soaks me through. Finally, I manage to make my tongue work again.

"You thought I was ashamed of you?" I whisper. "Of *you*?"

"It's the only thing that makes sense." He shrugs as if he has resigned himself to it. His eyebrows pinch together; his glistening eyes are full of pain, and it wrecks me.

I feel the weight of the earth's tears. Though it feels as though even this colossal downpour is unmatched in comparison to the one threatening to fall from my eyes. "Dawson, I have never been ashamed of you. Our breakup . . . it was me. It's always been my issue."

"Yeah, the whole 'it's not you, it's me' gimmick," he

replies. "I get it. If you can't be honest, how do you expect us to be friends?"

When he throws his hands into the air and turns to walk away from me, I grab his rain-soaked shoulder and squeeze in a silent plea for him to turn around. To stay.

"It's *true*," I plead, aching for him to understand.

He lets me pull him around and faces me.

Bravely, I continue, all my fears and worries spilling from me, no longer inhibited. "I loved you, Dawson. I truly did. You were—and are—the most incredible man. But right after graduation . . ." I shove a strand of wet hair from my cheek. "Everything at home—it became more confusing and difficult than ever. After you left for London, my parents—they got a divorce, and it just . . . it felt like the rug was pulled out from beneath me. Suddenly, I realized how broken and burdensome I was. And what if my parents' toxic relationship traits were passed down to me?"

The floodgates of my words are finally open. I've been waiting to tell him this for so long, and nothing is going to stop me now.

"I'm broken, Dawson," I repeat. "I put on this persona now to convince everyone that I've got it all together, but I'm a mess. You deserve someone better, someone you can trust."

He opens his mouth to speak, but I cut him off.

"I couldn't put you through that," I continue. "Not knowing that one day you would wake up and see the real me—the one impossibly flawed by my toxic family—and you'd realize you should have run long ago."

Dawson's eyes are dark. He licks his wet lips, the effort useless as the deluge continues to soak us. His voice is raspy when he finally speaks, a husky whisper that goes straight to my soul. "That was your first mistake. Assuming I'd ever leave you."

I clamp my mouth shut and turn away. I walk beneath the overhang of a nearby shop to get out of the rain, the urge to hide away swelling in my chest. Dawson follows me, and we stand under the shelter, staring at each other, our chests rising and falling rapidly, our breath labored. I want to quench the burning in my belly and brush my emotions under the rug. If only I could carry on as though this isn't a moment marked with my deepest regrets and most devastating heartbreak. If only there were a way to heal what is broken between us.

I straighten my shoulders and tighten my core like I'm bracing for a sucker punch to the gut.

"Daws," I say, thinking that this conversation only confirms how dysfunctional I really am. "I left you because I was afraid you would leave me. And I couldn't bear that kind of pain."

I open my mouth again, but he speaks first.

"Why didn't you ever tell me your parents divorced?"

His question sends a wave of uncertainty coursing through me. Looking back, I can see now that Dawson would have understood. He would have comforted me and been my safe place. But hindsight is twenty-twenty.

"I guess . . . it felt easier to hide than to show you the cracks in my life," I reply. "You come from this perfectly imperfect family that offers everything I've never had: love, safety, acceptance. You deserve to be with someone who won't ruin that."

I take a breath and steady myself. "When my dad left, it rattled me to my core, Daws. He didn't just leave my mom.

He left me and my sister too. And I was left to clean up the mess. If it was that easy for him to leave, why wouldn't it be easy for you to leave too? I mean, you were in London. How was I supposed to know if I was worth coming back to?"

A frown tugs at the corners of Dawson's mouth as he studies me. His eyes glimmer with worry. He takes a step closer, narrowing the distance between us until we are standing toe to toe. His hands come up to cup my elbows as the rain pours over the edge of the overhang, thundering on the concrete. He holds me steady as I feel the winds of my emotions trying to blow me away.

"Ava," he leans in and asks, "how do you see yourself?"

The question catches me off guard. "What?"

He repeats himself.

I blink a few times and attempt to wipe at the mascara that is assuredly streaming below my eyes. "Not quite," I finally answer.

"Not quite what?"

I take a moment to process my racing thoughts and answer slowly. "I'm not quite *anything*. I always feel so close, but a nagging in my ear says I'm not quite enough."

"Enough for who?"

"For *whom*."

"If nothing else, you're smart enough to be captain of the grammar police." He smiles and adjusts his glasses. "You don't have to prove yourself to anyone, Ava. Why don't you try seeing yourself through Jesus' eyes?"

"That only makes me feel worse," I mumble, the familiar guilt threatening to swallow me up again.

His face reflects his inner pain. "How so?"

I swallow hard. "I want to be a good Christian, but

275

sometimes . . . I feel so far from God as if I don't know how to fully embrace His grace. There is a whole cycle: I'm doing well, reading my Bible, going to church, spending time with friends, succeeding at work . . . and then, it all becomes too much. I feel myself spiraling out of control even as I'm trying to regain control—of my image, my career, the things I can tangibly touch. But then I end up feeling even farther from Him, and it crushes me."

Strangely, admitting these burdens out loud lifts a weight from my chest. My voice doesn't shake as I press on. "I can easily give grace and understanding to others, but it feels impossible to do so for myself. And that makes me even more ashamed of myself than I already am."

Dawson leans in until all I can see is him. He cups my jaw with a warm hand. "Ava, we aren't called to be perfect. We can't be; only He is. All He asks of us is to have faith and to bear His likeness well."

Dawson's words swirl around me. I hold my breath as he continues, "He didn't die for you because you have it all together or look a certain way. No." He shakes his head, leaning closer. "If you trust in Him, you can walk forward in life, not looking for the approval of others, but looking for the approval of God alone. Who cares if you have baggage or a dysfunctional family? We can sort through that later. Together."

Finally, I pull in a sharp breath, my breathing hitching at the word. *Together.*

Dawson's voice is sure, his eyes steady. "Part of the whole wild wonder of Jesus offering His unconditional love is freedom from our burdens. He makes us new, Ava. You aren't your shame and fear. You're His daughter."

I can't speak, only nod.

"And Ava?" His hand caresses my cheek, and I've never felt so safe and understood.

I blink a tear away and try to see his eyes through his rain-splattered glasses. In my summer wedges, we're almost the same height. As we've inched closer together, there is now only a narrow space between our lips.

"Having it all together doesn't make you enough. Perfect hair, perfect makeup"—dropping his hand from my cheek, he twirls a lock of my sopping golden hair between his fingers—"isn't where beauty is found. You're stunning and always have been. But I've always seen beyond the surface level of your beauty and found what is invisible on the outside. That's where your real beauty lies."

My heart lurches. I want to believe him so badly.

"Your eyes light up when you discuss things you're passionate about: an old book, a beloved song, to-do lists, the Bermuda Triangle."

Despite my churning emotions, a giggle escapes me.

"And I think that's beautiful," he concludes, his voice husky.

My heart seizes.

"You care so *deeply* about the well-being of others. I can't tell you the number of times I've seen you slap a smile on your face and bless someone else even though you were hurting inside. You're beautiful, Ava, but for far deeper reasons than you think. And I think just the very fact you care enough to be self-aware of the dysfunctions that could carry over from your family says you are nothing like them at all."

Dawson pulls off his glasses, which are starting to fog as the rain slows and the humid summer air returns. He tucks them into his pocket. "I know what you're thinking. This is the part of the movie when I take off my glasses and am suddenly transformed into this irresistibly attractive man. But slow your roll. I just want to look at you without rainwater and clouds blurring my vision."

I can't help but laugh. The urge to fall into his arms swells in my core. Dawson is my safe place—I am beginning to see it now—the closest thing to home that I've ever really had. The thought of what he has done for me and all I lost by letting him go is more bitter than sweet. The urge to cry presses in on me stronger than ever.

Suddenly, the evening sun pierces through the gray sky, the summer shower driven out by its rays.

Dawson takes a step back, and the space between us feels like a canyon I don't know how to cross. "I think that one day you'll learn to love yourself and see yourself how I see you and how Jesus sees you. But until then, I'll keep finding ways to remind you." He stares at me, a sad smile playing across his face. "Maybe you and I aren't meant to be. Maybe I was put into your life to remind you of who you are in Christ. That is a calling I would be proud to carry."

I'm not sure what to feel, what to think. A cacophony of emotions screams from within, but I have no time to sort any of them out.

"The rain has stopped." Dawson holds out his hand. "I'll walk you home."

24

Dawson

The moment I leave Ava at her door and emerge again on the wet street feels like the moment in *The Great Gatsby* when Jay realizes he really did lose Daisy all those years ago.

For the first time since moving back from London, I don't see any hope for reconciliation, and no amount of wealth, status, or success will bring my Daisy back to me. She may not be with anyone else, but she certainly isn't with me. The situation feels hopeless, just like Fitzgerald's masterpiece.

I used to despise Ava's favorite classic novel for its grim perspective, but the similarities between our stories aren't lost on me. When Ava broke up with me, I nearly drove myself mad with grief. I respected and loved her too much to argue against a decision she made, but now I wonder if I should have dropped everything and come home to fight for her.

Instead, I assumed Ava had realized my social status, financially humble background, and ordinary dreams for the future couldn't provide the life she expected. My silent protest was to throw myself full force into making a name for myself in the software development world. I might not have been able to change certain things about myself, but I knew there would come a day when I could give her the life, wealth, and social standing she always deserved.

If our paths ever crossed again.

Like Jay Gatsby, I dove headfirst into the battlefield of business. I rose through the ranks after my internship turned into a full-time job offer. I scrimped and saved and put every extra penny into strategic investments. It took years for it to pay off. When I decided to launch Blind Date with a Book Nerd, money wasn't an issue anymore. I could have hired a firm to create the app, but it was too important to leave its development in the hands of someone else.

Now, I can afford a luxurious apartment in a swanky neighborhood in my old city. I'm a junior partner in my firm, my financial investments are paying off, and I am finalizing the dating app I always knew would delight Ava's book-and-romance-loving soul.

Because of God's graciousness, I'm a self-made man, just like that all-American hero of the Roaring Twenties.

And just like him, I've returned home and am still unable to win back the hand of the fair maiden I lost long ago.

Except, unlike Jay, I'm far from disillusioned and jaded. Ava's insecurities and doubts don't make her any less wonderful of a person in my eyes. She has made mistakes, but she is still a valued child of God.

As I process everything that happened tonight, I'm

beginning to see that my priorities have been selfish. I've put them all in the wrong place. Rather than try to win Ava back for my own happiness, I should have made sure she understood how adored she is by her Creator first.

Love shouldn't stop our witness, no matter how much our hearts hunger for it. True love is sharing Christ, praying for our loved ones, and laying our desires at the foot of the Cross for our Savior to use as He wills.

My heart feels as if it is numb. I'm still damp from the earlier rain shower, the evening humidity setting in and making me feel sticky and uncomfortable. Cars drive slowly along the streets, their tires splashing up mini-waves of leftover rainwater onto the sidewalk. Since I was lost in thought, I passed my own neighborhood block, so I double back and make my way home.

Two truths are becoming clear: It's time to let go of my hope that Ava will find me worthy again and focus instead on showing her the love of Jesus with no strings attached. Though I want to take this as an opportunity to prove myself to her, I realize that isn't what she needs. Ava needs to discover the love God has for her. I will be her friend and point her to Christ with no selfish agenda as I should have done all along. And it's time to give my own heart the freedom to heal. Maybe I really was only put into her life to direct her closer to the Lord. And maybe it really is time for me to move on. I don't know exactly what that will look like yet, but I think I know what I need to do.

When I walk into my apartment, the atmosphere feels cold. Not for the first time, I wonder if city life is right for me.

A faint hope of something different sparks up in my

heart. New York City, with all its exciting possibilities, is a far cry from the small and quaint upstate town I grew up in. I've been running from that small-town life for almost a decade, pretending the warmth, home, and family it promises weren't enough for me.

I move about the space aimlessly, staring out of the windows, my mind running through a hundred new possibilities. Technically, I can work from anywhere. Maybe it's time that I take myself home for good. There are still a few things I need to wrap up in the city—like the launch party of my own app—but maybe the future can look far different than I imagined.

The brown leather Bible I've had since right after high school catches my eye from its permanent spot on my coffee table after I exit the shower a half hour later. The book has seen better days and is about due for retirement, but it's been with me since Dad slipped it onto the passenger seat as I packed up my belongings to move to the city for college.

Pushing my glasses up on my nose, I fall onto the sofa, grabbing the book on my way down. It falls open, as it often does, to one of the many places where the spine has permanently widened, acting as a bookmark of sorts. Reaching up, I adjust the overhead lamp until it illuminates the pages and the promises contained inside.

There is nothing like the Word of God to soothe your aching heart, sharpen your convictions, and strengthen your resolve to live in a way that reflects the goodness of your Savior.

"God takes great delight in you . . . He will rejoice over you with singing." My voice breaks the heavy silence as I read the words aloud.

The verse in Zephaniah seems to stare back at me. It's an often-overlooked book, but I spent some time in it during an online Bible study last year, and my Bible falls open to it naturally now.

The verse must have impressed me deeply because it is underlined in three colors of ink and highlighted as well. I think of the many times I've faced God with sorrow, regret, and shame filling me because of some grievance I've committed or some failure that has been eating away at my conscience. And yet, here were these words all along, reassuring me that God not only delights in my existence, but I also bring Him joy.

And because I'm a flawed human in need of redemption, I know He isn't waiting for me to be perfect to take joy in me. I am made perfect in Him, but He loves me in the present tense as well, never wavering in His unconditional love because I belong to Him.

Ava belongs to Him, too, but I'm not sure she's had that revelation yet. Feeling a deep need to share the truth with her, I grab a pen from the basket on the table and begin to write in the margins of the Bible. A hunger gnaws at my stomach, an urgency setting in that I can't ignore.

The drizzle begins again outside, and I listen to the drops as I flip through the familiar pages. I've flung the balcony doors open to invite in some relief from the stifling summer humidity of the city, and the scent of rain on concrete and asphalt fills my apartment. With the Bible on my lap, I flip back and forth as snippets of verses float through my brain. A highlighter makes its way into my hands, joining my arsenal as I search the Scriptures, writing in the margins every time I find a verse I want to highlight.

I don't pause until my phone begins to buzz on the sofa cushion next to me. "Hi, Mom," I answer on the third buzz.

"Hi, honey. Are you okay? You were on my heart tonight, and I just thought I'd call to check in."

Her motherly instincts never miss, but I don't feel ready to share the events of the night. "Doing just fine. Just finishing up a project."

"You work too hard." She always says this, even though I learned by the example she and Dad set. "But I called for another reason too," she continues. "The caterer confirmed the hors d'ouevres for the launch party. And the DJ says he can be there at five o'clock."

"Thanks, Mom," I reply, setting the open Bible on the coffee table. "Putting you and Anne in charge of this event was one of my best ideas yet."

"Well, you did give me carte blanche to design the evening. I've had a blast racking up the bill and reliving my college literature class days," she replies. "The theme was such a clever idea, Dawson. What made you think of it?" I can hear the wry smile in her tone.

"Thanks, Mom. I was due for a good idea. And I'm sure I'll have a blast paying the bills when they come through." I laugh. We chat for a few more minutes, and I consider it a success that I manage to steer her away from prying any deeper.

When the call ends, I turn my attention back to my Bible. A verse about forgiveness pricks my heart. For whatever reason, I think of Dahlia and how rude she must think I am. I never even apologized to her about my behavior at the restaurant. What kind of a witness, let alone gentleman, am I? I stare at my phone and slump against the seat, feeling an overwhelming struggle not to be utterly crushed and defeated.

But there is no doubt in my mind that this is the right thing to do. I have to try to heal this wound before it tears even more and leaves an ugly scar in its wake.

Resolutely, I open the private message board on the Blind Date with a Book Nerd app and locate her profile. My message is brief and to the point. There's no point in sugarcoating it when I was so clearly the one in the wrong. Sending it off, I release a deep exhale, stand up, and walk toward the bedroom as the summer drizzle turns into a full-on thunderstorm beyond the balcony.

As I try to quiet my racing mind enough to fall asleep, I tell myself there is no reason to sit and worry over it. What's done is done, and I'll just have to see where the road takes me.

—

Two days later, there isn't even a hint of the rainstorm that soaked the streets a couple of nights ago. Instead, the afternoon sun blazes down on the city as I walk to my coffee date, the concrete, asphalt, and metal buildings trapping its heat and turning the streets into a sauna.

The only place I've found relief from the muggy heat the last couple of days is walking the miles of tree-shaded pathways in Central Park. I've been there so often that I'm beginning to think I need a dog. Andrew and Charlie certainly seem to enjoy their two canines. I've run into them a couple of times so far in the Park, and I'm getting pretty good at throwing balls for the two energetic dogs.

Chasing after a rambunctious Labrador would keep my mind off my problems.

The thought takes serious root in my mind as I spot the elegant and modern storefront of my destination. Despite my resolve, my nerves spike, my mouth goes dry, and my muscles are suddenly stiff. Adjusting the strap of the leather messenger bag flung over my neck, I reach into it one more time to make sure the contents are still safely inside before I grasp the door handle and step into the coffee shop.

Her golden head is turned away from the window when I walk into The Drip, but she seems to sense my presence and turns toward me as I approach the small marble and wrought iron table. The scent of freshly ground coffee beans and gourmet pastries permeating the shop try their best to soothe my warring emotions.

Dahlia's soft smile is kind but tentative as she greets me. She isn't wearing teal today, but the vibrant green hue of her eyes is just as striking. As she nods toward the seat across from her and I pull it out to sit, I silently acknowledge again what a disservice I did to her the other night.

There is a beautiful, book-loving, clearly generous woman in front of me who actually wants to be here. How did I miss this realization the other night on our blind date?

Her shy smile morphs into a genuine one as I lay the small bouquet of pink and yellow dahlias on the marble tabletop between us.

"Are these to make up for the fact that you forgot to wear one the other night?" She picks up the bouquet and brings it to her nose. I have to admit she makes an adorable picture with her eyes peeking at me over the top of the flowers.

"They are," I reply. "And they are a tiny gesture of penance. I apologize for the way things went the other night. I hope you can forgive my lack of manners."

She stares at me with a curious expression. Her head is tilted, and her hand lowers the dahlias to the table. "Was there truly anything to forgive, though? It's not like you stood me up."

My chest rises and falls with a sigh. "I was distracted and impolite. That wasn't fair to you."

"When you messaged me the other night asking if we could meet up again, I wasn't sure if I would say yes until this morning. You and Ava have history," she says, and we both understand that it isn't a question.

My lips press together. I nod. "A lot of history. Some good, but mostly sad. At least to me."

"I think it saddens her too," Dahlia replies, her voice soft. "Why aren't you two together? Honestly, Dawson, even from my vantage, it seems as if you still have feelings for her."

I'm startled by her bluntness, pausing to collect myself before I respond. "Miscommunication. Distance. The falsehoods we tell ourselves to protect our hearts."

The corners of her lips lift. "The usual suspects, then?"

I smile despite the twinge of pain. "Pretty much."

"And you don't want to try to get her back?"

I shake my head. There isn't any reason to go into the details of all I've done to win Ava's heart. Clearly, it wasn't enough.

"We're not meant for each other. I think I see that now. It might take me some time to fully heal, but I'm ready and willing to try. It's time to move on."

She nods slowly, biting her bottom lip. "Thank you for your honesty, Dawson. I think it's safe to say that you're a great guy. Ava is missing out."

She looks at me thoughtfully.

"I'll admit that I'm a little wary of dating a guy who still has feelings for another woman," she continues, "but if you'd like to make a new friend, I'd love to go out for coffee sometime."

"I'd like that," I admit. "I'm not looking for anything more than a friend."

When I sat pouring over Scripture the other night, I knew that connecting with Dahlia again to apologize was the right decision, even though I didn't expect anything to come from it. True to what I thought, she is the kind of person worth getting to know.

Lifting my head, I take in the coffee shop for the first time. The pastries in the case catch my eye, and I realize I could go for a strong cup of something caffeinated right now. I turn back to her and grin. "How about right now? May I buy you a cup of coffee, Dahlia?"

A smile overtakes her face. "Why not? I could use some fuel before heading to my next meeting. But I'm going to make you buy me one of those gigantic chocolate muffins too."

An hour later, she drives away in a cab, and I pause to watch it before turning and walking up the street toward the high-rise building looming a block in the distance. When I step into the building and pass the security guard station, exchanging a nod with the dark-haired man who was on guard the first time I visited the offices of CityLight Press, I don't need to check the directory to know where I am going.

The ride in the elevator ticks by with agonizing slowness. The messenger bag is heavy against my hip. When I step out of the metal box, I walk with purpose past the bank of cubicles that congregate in the center of the spacious building. I don't glance inside the small offices that line the exterior wall. Instead, I make a beeline for the one office I have been in before.

I'm sure Andrew is around somewhere, and I do need to talk to him about some changes to the special project I've got him working on, but he's not who I am here to visit today.

I don't know if I am disappointed or relieved when Ava's office door is closed and the windows dark. A small plaque on the glass reads: Ava Fox, Senior Editor.

A woman—I'm guessing her assistant—is sitting in front of a large computer in a cubicle a short distance away.

"Excuse me?" I approach her and lean over the divider. She barely glances up, her focus on the red-marked document on the screen in front of her. "Would you happen to know when Ava Fox will be back in her office?"

She adjusts her reading glasses and looks up at me curiously. "She has only been gone a few minutes. She had a meeting on her schedule this morning."

The fact that I just missed her feels strangely like Divine Providence. While Ava and I didn't part on angry terms, I don't know exactly how we are supposed to move forward after she poured out her heart to me—and I subsequently told her that I'm not sure if we were ever meant to be together. Can we move forward as friends or even anything else after that?

But I came here on a mission, and I am determined to follow through with it.

"I brought something for her. I was hoping to leave it on her desk. Would you be able to give it to her for me when she returns?" I hoist the messenger bag up to reach inside, but the woman holds up her hand, pointer finger directed toward Ava's door.

"She doesn't always lock her office when she leaves. Why don't you just try the door and leave it on her desk yourself?" She shrugs and turns back to her work, clearly not suspicious of my intentions.

Although, what could I really steal? I think, turning back toward Ava's office with amusement. *The advance cover reveal for an upcoming novel? A release date that is still a month away from going public? The blurb for a popular author's next book? Or maybe, like Andrew, the manuscript to CityLight's next big seller?*

Trying to prove my ability to keep secrets to absolutely no one, I keep my eyes front and center as I try Ava's door. To my surprise—but also, I'm not surprised because it's Ava, and she has always been forgetful—it swings open. The desk sits at the other end of the room in front of a large and inviting window. Leafy, potted plants, walls lined with bookish art, shelves stuffed with bestsellers, as well as an essential oil diffuser that is still on, its hazy mist puffing out something minty, have turned a boring office space into something cozy and welcoming.

Without lingering, I stride across the floor toward the desk, the messenger bag lightening significantly as I pull out the heavy book I stashed inside before my coffee date this afternoon.

Carefully, I place the well-worn leather Bible on Ava's desk. It's falling apart, with the spine cracked in so many places it would either warm or break a book lover's heart. While I thought it was about time for the copy to retire, it turns out that it is still needed.

Over the past two nights, I've spent hours in this book, underlining and highlighting countless verses, filling the margins with my cramped handwriting. Every verse I poured over spoke in some way of God's heart for Ava, of the love He carries for her. It's a flame that will never go out, a love that will never fade.

I hope that by the time she finds the last note I wrote in the margins for her, she'll look at the judgment she is harboring toward herself and the insecurities that plague her mind a little bit differently.

Pulling out the small notecard I tucked into the first flap, I place it on top of the Bible where she'll see it first. Then, I take one last look around, walk out of the office, and shut the door quietly behind me.

25

Ava

My lips twitch into a smile as I spot the gift on my desk. Charlie has a habit of stopping by my office on her way to have lunch with Andrew, and she always brings some sweet, little offering to leave for me. Sometimes, it's a new book she wants me to read. Sometimes, it's a coffee or a pastry. My heart fills with gratitude that I have been blessed with such an amazing friend in her.

But the smile quickly fades as I walk forward and notice the scrawl of my name on a notecard placed on top of a Bible in the center of my desk. The note is in Dawson's handwriting. I pause mid-reach and glance over my shoulder through my open office door.

When was he here? Is he still here? Did he not want to speak to me?

The troublesome thoughts race through my mind. Before I even read the card or peruse the pages of what appears to be a well-loved Bible beneath it, I walk out of my office and scan the floor. No sign of Dawson. I march straight to Andrew's office, sure that if Dawson is still on the premises, he'll be in there visiting his friend. We have offices on the same floor now, so I don't have to go far.

But I find Andrew alone at his computer when I pop my head through the doorway, and I can't help but recognize the sense of instant disappointment that fills me.

He leans back in his chair when I enter. "Have you tamed the Wolfe yet?" he asks with a half-grin, half-grimace. "I heard he has been terrorizing you all week."

With a groan and a roll of my eyes, I sink into one of the chairs in front of his desk. "James Wolfe is the bane of my existence. If he wasn't one of CityLight's biggest authors, I'd burn all his books out of spite."

"Burn his books?" Andrew's eyebrows shoot up in surprise. "That's a little harsh, especially for you, Fox."

"Yeah, well, the way he's burning through my every last nerve is a little harsh."

A chuckle escapes him. "Come on, he's not that bad, is he? My interactions with him have been alright."

"That's because your last name runs this company, not to mention the fact that he's not exactly interested in your type. No offense."

"Has he made a pass at you?" Andrew leans forward and places his elbow on the desk.

I shrug. "I think he genuinely believes that all women will drool over even the remote chance of being in the same room as him."

"You're a fortunate woman, then."

I pick up the wood and gold nameplate sitting on the

desk and chuck it at his head. He snatches it out of the air before it smacks him in the face. "Woah, there. Someone fetch this hangry lady a snack ASAP!" he bellows in the direction of the open door.

Without missing a beat, I grab the nearest thing to me—a porcelain lamp sitting on top of his desk—and lift it. "Don't test me, Drew," I grumble, my voice irritable.

Slowly, he rolls the desk chair away a few inches and pretends to wave a white flag. I set the lamp back on his desk, carefully watching his next move. When he lets out a deep chuckle, I laugh, too, knowing that my threats haven't offended him. I would never allow myself to tease another office coworker with such ease, but Andrew Ketner is like a brother. I'm so glad to have a friend in this office like him to take the edge off the hard days.

"I'm guessing you didn't come in here to blow literal dragon smoke about James Wolfe. Ava Fox is too calm, cool, and collected for that," he says, rolling back up to his desk. "What's up?"

A sudden flush crawls over my cheeks. He's right. I've worked with all types of authors and agents over the years, and there is usually little that can get me this flustered. But I wasn't prepared to explain that I came in here looking for Dawson.

"Um, I was . . ." It occurs to me a few awkward seconds too late that I could easily have claimed I actually did come in here to let off steam about CityLight's arguably most famous (and conceited) author. After my momentary hesitation, though, there's no way Andrew will believe that excuse. "I was coming to check on, um . . ."

My friend folds his arms across his chest, obviously

amused at my squirming. "To check on . . . the status of a manuscript I'm working on? My progress with that charity fundraising idea we discussed a few weeks ago? How Charlie feels after regrettably giving herself bangs? Or maybe the fact that a certain handsome man in very sophisticated glasses was in the office earlier today?"

I level him with a glare, and in true Andrew fashion, his laughter fills the room as if he knows he caught me. I stand and shake my head. "Why I even come to visit you is a mystery to me."

"Come on, Ava. You can talk to me."

"You have an editing deadline in two days, don't you? Better get back to work, Ketner." My smirk reflects more amusement than I feel as I stride out of his office.

He calls after me. "I still think you need a snack!"

Though I shake my head as I walk away, he's not wrong. Making a quick detour to the breakroom, I linger there before I venture back into my office and assess the gift on my desk. But before I can open the Bible and find out why Dawson left it for me, my cell phone rings.

The caller is James Wolfe, of course. I regret the day he got ahold of my personal cell phone number. I sigh and make sure my voice is cheery and fresh, as though I haven't already spoken with him and the team for almost two hours earlier today.

By the time we end the call, most of my coworkers in the office have called it a day. Andrew stopped by on his way out to invite me to grab dinner with him and Charlie, but I waved him off, pointing to the phone pressed against my ear.

I'm entirely drained and physically grimace as I enter the

details for the dinner date I somehow agreed to go on with James into my calendar. It was the only way I could get off the call as he insisted that we needed to meet face-to-face to finalize the book.

Often, dining with clients on the company's dime is a blissful and rewarding experience. I mean, who wouldn't love having dinner with famous authors? Unless that author is James Wolfe, that is. He is out of town at the moment, or I'm sure I would have had to deal with him at the office. At least I have until next week to mentally prepare for the occasion.

As spent as I feel, I don't have the heart to open my gift now. I just want to get home. Gently, I put the Bible into my bag along with Dawson's card and head out for the day.

On the commute back to my apartment, I check my notifications for the first time all day. I scroll past the social media alerts, news articles, and random text messages I can answer later until I find something that captures my interest. I make a mental note to go in and read the new messages that have popped up on my Blind Date with a Book Nerd app over the course of the day. The NYC singles scene must be popping because there is no lack of book-loving matches I seem to be getting paired with.

While I know I could ignore them completely, I still feel a sense of obligation to Dawson to at least go in and confirm or deny a match. If someone has messaged me, my sense of politeness forces me to write a reply. In the short time his app has been open for beta testers, a lively forum has also popped up, and I find quite a bit of enjoyment from perusing its latest topics. I've even joined in a few discussions myself and posted a question or two.

I don't feel like responding to anything at the moment, my finger whisking past the line of messages with disinterest. It isn't until I scroll to the bottom of the list that I find an official notification from the Blind Date with a Book Nerd app that went out this morning. I tap on it, and an elegant invitation for the app's official launch party pops up.

My heart softens for a moment. I've been so preoccupied with life and my own troubles that I haven't had a chance to connect with him about it. Though I don't even know if we are on speaking terms after all the ugly truths I poured out to him in the rain the other evening, a deep sense of pride and admiration for him takes root.

At long last, Dawson Hayes is about to fully launch his first official app, and I know his business is going to thrive.

Look at you go, Dawson.

Briefly, I wonder if the gift in my hands has something to do with the launch party, though I can't imagine how it would. I scroll down to the details to refresh my memory with the date. My stomach drops. Of course, Dawson's launch party would be the same night as the dinner I just scheduled with James Wolfe.

Ignoring the messages waiting for me on the app, I sigh and click out to check my texts. There's nothing from Dawson, but I suddenly see a slew of new texts from Natasha, all of which make my jaw hit the floor of the cab.

NATASHA: Can you just apologize to Mom already? I'm tired of hearing about what you did to her.

NATASHA: By the way, she's really hurt to find out that you are talking to Dad so much when you hardly ever call her.

I've had approximately three calls with Dad in about as

many months, so I'm not sure where she is getting this information.

NATASHA: Anyway, thoughts on this? I plan to wear it to a wedding this weekend but don't know if it's too extra.

I'm not sure if it will ever stop amazing me how visceral of a reaction my family can elicit from me. My eyes prick with tears, and my stomach boils with anger.

Before I type back a response, I look at the attached photo she sent. My eyes widen. Is my sister being serious? The dress she sent looks like it is straight out of a prom in the eighties. Maybe this particular retro style is having an epic fashion comeback I'm not aware of, but the thing is hideous. I'm not sure how anyone can mistake it for "fashion," and any good sister would tell her as much.

I pause for a moment and reread her messages. They flare a fire within me, stoking an anger that has festered for a long time. It's time I stand up for myself and take back the autonomy Mom has taken from me for years. With a steely resolve I'm not used to, I type out a furious response.

ME: Hi, sis. I did nothing to warrant an apology. In fact, I feel like I'm owed one myself. I know you've only heard Mom's side of the story, so you couldn't know that. However, I don't expect an actual apology from her as humility isn't a trait she possesses.

I hit send and hate how good the words feel. I find that I have more to say. My fingers fly.

ME: Mom has wounded me without remorse for years, and you have only perpetuated the hurt. I have no idea what you're talking about with Dad. I barely speak to him, only when he tries to throw money at me to make up for everything in the past. Mom is most likely making up a story to get you on her side. It makes me sad that you can't see through her manipulative games at this point, or perhaps you love the drama so much that you allow yourself to be sucked into it.

ME: Anyway, the dress is adorable. I hope you bought it.

The last message is petty, but I hit send anyway, pushing away the nagging feeling of guilt. I'm sure before long, I'll reach out and apologize for misleading her fashion sense. By the time I walk through my apartment door, my body feels like radio static, a buzz of rage coursing through me.

I drop my bag onto the dining table, and as it clunks a little harder against the surface than usual, I realize I've forgotten about Dawson's gift. My heart both soars and sinks. The buzzing anger in my body shifts into nervous energy, and I'm not sure why.

Reaching in, I carefully extract the heavy Bible and fish out the card. My couch is a refuge as I sink among the many throw pillows and situate this unexpected gift on my lap. I'm sure it's simply a thoughtful gift of appreciation for the feedback I've given him regarding his app. I can't believe Blind Date with a Book Nerd is officially launching. And I might not even be able to attend his party to celebrate him.

My stomach drops again. Stupid James Wolfe.

I try to shake the thought of the author's smug face from my mind and focus on this gift from Dawson. Slipping my nail under the seal of the envelope, I break it. An unexpected sense of dread suddenly winds around my heart, cinching it tight. Do I really want to face what could be inside?

With a few slow breaths to steady myself, I open the card and begin to read:

Ava,

For a long time, I convinced myself that Fitzgerald lacked a true understanding of the human experience. You know that I've always felt that he highlighted only the dark side of humanity and bypassed all the light. But after living under a false hope of a reunion with you, I realize now that the character I despised is not so unlike myself after all. Jay's grasp onto a similar hope for his love story with Daisy reminds me of how I have always felt about you. It's a familiar heartbreak.

While Fitzgerald knew more about the human condition than I gave him credit for, I still hold to my conviction that he greatly missed a key aspect of the human heart: the chance for redemption. I no longer view the idea of redemption as reconciling a lost romantic love but rather the regaining of a true love that was never realized.

Unlike Jay Gatsby, my goals are not elusive. I live firmly in reality, not with my heart guiding my path, but with Christ as my Light. My chase for your affection ends here, Ava. I turn from the green light and instead hope to direct you to the only Light through which true happiness and peace can ever come.

I've highlighted and annotated this Bible, which was once gifted to me. Now, I pass it on to you. You will always have my love, but even more so, the love of our great and wonderful God who made you.

Always,
Dawson.

If it wasn't for the loud, incessant ticking of the vintage clock on my wall as a testament that time keeps moving forward, I might wonder if I am still alive at all. Everything in me has gone still. I'm too stunned to even move. With a few false starts, my brain attempts to make sense of what I just read but goes blank every time.

I don't understand what's happening.

I blink a few times at the Bible in my lap and impulsively open it. Dawson wasn't lying. As I flip through, I find highlights and notes in the margins, all added just for me. Annotation tabs point to specific verses, and instructions lead me from one verse to the next. My eyes hungrily devour every single one. Hours slip by as I move between passages, the theme of Dawson's gift planting itself deep in my core—themes of walking as a new creation in Christ, being secure in His love, giving Him my burdens, and experiencing freedom from the incessant need for validation, either from the world or my own family.

My eyes sting from the intensity of my concentration. Have I even blinked this whole time? I come to, realizing that the evening has slipped away. It's time to take a break. With great care, I gently set the Bible aside and ignore the storm of emotion building in my chest.

I go to find eye drops in the bathroom. My reflection in the mirror startles me. I blink at myself. My eyes are red and tired. My makeup has worn off, and my skin is freckled with hormonal blemishes today. My hair is dull under the lights. Staring back at me is the face of a woman I feel ashamed of, an imperfect creature I want to hide away—both out of protection and embarrassment.

I don't love her, I realize with shocking clarity.

My eyes prick with tears, the Bible verses fresh in my mind. I should have turned to it when I felt unworthy rather than living as if I alone could earn my worth.

The woman in the mirror stares back at me—imperfect,

yes—but, as I suddenly realize, also worthy of love. Worth the love denied by family and denied by even herself. But that love I'm missing is what I'm now also discovering is in constant flow from Jesus.

She is loved, I realize.

Tears pour from a deep well inside of me. I watch myself cry and see the pouring out of hidden darkness being replaced by a light in my eyes that I thought was lost long ago.

26

Dawson

"Welcome to our humble abode." Charlie's sweet voice and beaming smile greet me first as the apartment door swings open to reveal the newlyweds. A caramelized scent that I recognize as butterscotch wafts out to me in the hall.

The Ketner's dinner invitation couldn't have come at a better time. When Andrew called me just as I was about to give up and order Indian takeout from down the street, I accepted his invitation to share a meal with him and his bride eagerly.

There is something about the newlywed couple that is like a balm on a burn or a sheltered port in a storm. I'm always in a better mood when Andrew is around, doubly so when it's the two of them.

Now, Charlie's spunky yet gentle demeanor instantly soothes the agitation gnawing at me for days. As I step into their penthouse apartment in the residential building

Andrew inherited from his mother years ago, the first thing I see is a fluffy rocket of golden fur launching itself at me. The rocket is closely followed by a second fluffy ball of black and brown.

The two dogs jump around my knees, bouncing up, tongues out, eagerly begging for pets. Kneeling, I welcome their affectionate greetings as their tongues find my face.

Charlie flutters around, gently scolding the dogs. "Sergio and Hank, that isn't the greeting we practiced for visitors."

I pull her into a side hug. "Haven't you taught your kids manners yet?"

Andrew's exuberant laugh booms out as I tease her. He steps toward me, pulling me into a bear hug and slapping me on the back. "Don't get her started, bro. She'll put these boys through their paces just to prove to you how well trained they are, and we'll never get to eat dinner."

Charlie's cheeks turn a pretty shade of pink as she tosses her hair over her shoulder and walks toward the kitchen, from which delicious, fragrant smells emanate. "You're not wrong. Andrew, my love, will you please give our guest a tour of our home while I put the finishing touches on dinner and pull the cookies out of the oven? I hope you're ready for my world-famous butterscotch cookies for dessert, Dawson."

"Oh, you betcha, I am," I call after her as she disappears into the butler's pantry.

Andrew's hand claps me on the shoulder. "As you wish, darlin'," he says. He leads me toward the open doors leading out to the balcony. "Dawson, you have to get a look at the view of the city from up here."

Sergio trots happily after us while Hank pauses in the center of the living room, his head swiveling back and forth between following his rambunctious brother or staying close to his mistress's side. As if anticipating his dilemma, Charlie shoos him toward us when she emerges from the pantry.

When we step onto the balcony, Andrew pulls the doors shut. He is correct. The city stretches before us, highlighting all the glory of the beginnings of a magnificent sunset above the dark and shadowy reach of the skyscrapers. Leaning my elbows on the railing, I breathe in the fresh air deeply, trying to enjoy the moment and allow my brain to shake off its heaviness.

"How are you? How is the app?" Andrew asks, joining me at the railing.

"The app is everything I hoped it would be. Or mostly, I guess. I've worked out all the kinks I can and turned it over to my firm for a final inspection. This has been a labor of love from the beginning, and it should be ready to release to the public on schedule." I shrug, already wondering what comes next now that I've finalized the project I set out to create.

My idea for a dating app meant for book lovers has been a success, even on its soft launch. It has grown exponentially over the past few weeks. We already have several thousand members on the waiting list for our official launch day. And I have Ava to thank for all of it. If she hadn't taken to her social media platforms to encourage her followers to sign up to get matched with their very own book nerd, it might have taken years to get where we're projected to be on launch day.

The honorary members we invited to be part of the beta testing team are loving it. Matches are being made, and blind dates are being scheduled. A lot of people are going to end up very happy when they find their bookish soulmates. I'm still in shock that the app is the result of my brain and a bunch of lines of code.

But I have to admit, the victory feels lackluster. Lately, I feel detached. At this point, I'm just going through the motions to officially launch the site, and then I'm turning it over to my software firm. I've already made arrangements with them to manage it day-to-day. After the disappointment and heartbreak of the last few weeks, I just don't know if I can be part of it anymore.

Andrew eyes me. "And how are you personally holding up?"

I grip the railing, processing the best words for my response. "I'm okay. You know, I've been really seeing lately that when we reach the end of our rope, God is right there, holding out His hand. And when you finally take hold of it, you realize He was right there with you all along." I clear my throat. "He's been showing me a lot of things in the last couple of weeks, things that don't feel so great. I tried to control the outcome of a situation I thought I knew the best answer to, and all I've done is hurt someone I really care about in the process. It's hard not to let the guilt of not fully trusting in Him win."

My friend is quiet for a minute. The evening is filled with the resounding echoes of city life, carrying up to us from the street below. The balcony is an oasis from the chaotic hustle and bustle below, strewn with comfortable chairs and plants.

As the silence lingers, I think about the wealth and privilege Andrew grew up in. His mother and maternal grandfather were members of the old money crowd. Perhaps if I'd had the same upbringing, I wouldn't have left New York to make my fortune in London. Perhaps I would have gone straight over to Ava's apartment when her life came crashing down, pulled her into my arms, and kissed her until she never wanted to let go. Perhaps our lives would have turned out very differently.

But I wasn't raised the way Andrew and Ava were. I had to make my own fortune, and along the way, my future was shaped for better or for worse.

And yet, I can't help but remember that Andrew lost his mother some time ago. I imagine he would give it all up just to have her with them again. My loving, crazy, wonderful family is still whole. I can't regret too much of the way my life has turned out with so much to be grateful for.

Finally, he breaks the silence, and there is a new depth of wisdom in his normally lighthearted voice that is welcome. "Mistakes are part of our life here on earth, Dawson. We're going to keep making them despite our best intentions. But God is the faithful one, not us. I should know. Look how He redeemed my life from the mediocrity and self-destruction I was headed down after I lost my mom."

He glances over his shoulder, and I follow his gaze through the wide picture windows. Charlie walks back and forth from the kitchen, carrying plates and trays to the dining table. When she sees him watching her, a smile beams out on her face. She motions to her wrist, then holds up all the fingers on her right hand, mouthing "Five minutes." Her husband nods, his face pure sunshine in response.

Andrew's voice is full of emotion when he speaks again. "Tell me how it is that God would be so merciful, taking the biggest mistake I've ever made and turning it into the greatest blessing I've ever imagined. I could never live so perfectly as to deserve what I have now, yet He's given it to me along with so much more."

I've learned a lot about their history together in the months since I moved back. I know he is referring to the circumstances in which he plagiarized—albeit accidentally—Charlie's debut novel. She came storming into New York to set things right, and they ended up meeting on pure chance. He pretended not to know anything about the situation—trying to rectify it behind the scenes and protect his dad's reputation—until the truth came out a couple of weeks later.

And the rest, as they say, is history.

With eyes full of the purest joy I've ever seen, he looks at me, his hand landing heavily on my shoulder. "But God," he says.

"But God," I murmur in reply, emotion working within my chest.

"Give Him time to work without you getting in the way," my friend concludes.

I nod, the words hitting me with deep conviction.

Something has shifted in my prayer life since I wrote the note telling Ava I am well and truly letting her go. I left the Bible on her desk and walked away, knowing it was the right thing to do.

Despite the nerves accompanying the launch of my dating app, I have been filled lately with a sense of unshakable peace and a deep hunger for the Word of God that I haven't felt in months. I've spent countless hours in prayer. As a result, I made the decision to hire my own software firm to manage most of the site from here on out. I don't want anything on this earth to get between me and God ever again.

Not even the woman I have loved for close to a decade.

"Dinner's ready if you boys are," Charlie says softly from the doorway.

Andrew looks at me. "Are you ready?"

With a slow and deliberate nod, I reply. "I think I finally am."

—

"Looks like we'll need to add another hundred to the head count for the launch party, Mom. Another round of RSVPs came back from the invite." I direct the words toward my speakerphone. The device is propped up on my bathroom counter. I look into the mirror and brush my hands through my hair, attempting to give myself any style other than "curly-haired software nerd." But it is no use.

I sigh and let the hair flop over and do its thing. I am who I am, and at long last, it feels like enough.

Besides, my date for tonight has already seen me twice, and I didn't scare her away.

"The caterer might not be able to handle the extra volume at such short notice, honey," Mom replies, the sound of running water and the *clink* of dishes punctuating her words. "I might have to whip up a few appetizers myself just to have enough."

In addition to hosting a speed dating event to launch the app officially, the party will also feature book-inspired games and appetizers and drinks inspired by the Roaring Twenties. A live band will play period-inspired music. It could have been a basic mixer, but I was convinced by my mother and sister to do it with flair. *The Great Gatsby* seemed like the perfect theme at the time.

Mom handled the refreshments, scheduling, and decorations. Anne volunteered to be in charge of the games and speed dating setup. There is no way I could have designed such a creative event without their help.

"Don't add anything extra to your plate," I hasten to reply to my mother's words. "You've already done too much for me, and the event hasn't even happened."

"I don't get to plan enough parties," she laughs. "Besides, Annie and I have bonded so much over this. I don't think I realized how far apart we've drifted since she's been so preoccupied with college."

I catch the tail end of a sigh and stop fastening the clasp of my watch to pick up the phone. "Everything okay with you two?"

Her voice brightens. "Oh, yes! You know how it is, though. You grow up and start to take on your own life responsibilities, and the next thing you know, it's harder and harder to connect on the same level."

I do know. All too well. It's part of the reason I hastened my move back to the States. So much time was passing while I pursued a career in tech, and meanwhile, I was shocked each time I returned home for a visit and didn't recognize my siblings.

"I'm sure Anne misses you too."

"She does." My sister's serious, smooth tone fills the speaker. "Thanks for ditching all your responsibilities for this party, Daws, and dumping it on us. Mom and I have had a blast planning it."

"Aw, you're welcome, sis," I reply with snark.

I glance at the time on my watch and hasten my steps. The apartment door slams behind me as I pull a light sports jacket over my t-shirt. No stuffy button-downs and slacks for me tonight. My favorite khaki pants, a simple t-shirt, and tennis shoes suit me far better.

Our banter continues as I emerge into the open air, cross the street with my phone in my hand, and walk the next few blocks to my destination.

I see her waiting for me outside the coffee shop and use my free hand to wave.

"Hey, ladies, I have to go. Love you both."

A few days ago, Dahlia reached out with an invitation to accompany her on a bookstore hop around the city. I was unsure at first. Even now, it feels a little odd to be toying with the idea of getting to know anyone other than the woman I have been stuck on for years upon years. But Dahlia and I are only friends. We clearly established those boundaries. I need time and space to breathe and heal. Romance is not on my radar.

But as part of my commitment to moving forward in life, grabbing an afternoon coffee and perusing a few bookstores with a new friend doesn't seem like a bad way to begin.

I pocket the cell phone as I close the distance between us. She is wearing a flowy lavender dress and sandals. A book bag hangs over her shoulder. She looks up at me with a smile as I approach.

"You found it," she says.

I glance up at the sign on the doorway above us, which declares the coffee inside the best in the city. I lift an eyebrow, a skeptical expression crossing my face. "I don't know if I believe them. I'm a pretty harsh coffee critic."

Her laugh sparkles out. "Well, I hope my favorite coffee shop doesn't disappoint you. We sampled your favorite the other day, so I thought we'd try out mine today."

"Oh, that isn't my favorite coffee shop," I hasten to

correct her, though it really doesn't matter. I conclude awkwardly, "I just had . . . something important that needed to be done nearby that day."

She gives me a funny look—as if wondering why in the world I'm still rambling on—and I pull myself together so I stop sounding like an idiot. Reaching out, I grasp the door handle and hold it open for her to enter ahead of me.

"So, what do you recommend here?" I ask. It's a comfort that almost every shop will inevitably smell like coffee beans and baked goods. At least that much in life is dependable.

"Iced shaken espresso with vanilla cream," she replies without hesitation. "Try it. I promise your life will be forever changed." Her dancing eyes glance back at me.

I nod, twisting my lips into a smile. "I'm not opposed to shaking things up a little in life. Two iced shaken espressos to go it is."

27

Ava

My phone vibrates loudly across the surface of my desk. I glance down to see a message from Charlie pop onto the screen. Still no word from Mom, and Natasha ghosted me after my last series of texts.

CHARLIE: Hey! You're going to the Book Nerd launch party tonight, right?

Why is it that everything seems to happen all at once?

I turn my phone screen off, make a mental note to text Charlie back in a minute, and finish typing the email I am writing.

I'm not quite sure what to say to her. The Blind Date with a Book Nerd launch event has hung like a sad cloud over me all week. Tonight is a big deal—no, a huge deal—for Dawson. He has worked hard to bring this app to fruition, and I want nothing more than to cheer him on and be there to celebrate his accomplishment.

If he wants me there, that is. It's still radio silence between us, and I'm unsure what to make of it.

And, of course, tonight just has to be my dinner with James Wolfe. I asked to reschedule, but he insisted that his itinerary for this trip into the city only allows for tonight.

Losing him would crush the publishing house's financial projections for the entire year. I'll make it work somehow. I resolve to cut the dinner short if need be. Despite his over-the-top demands, hopefully, James will understand. And if my other social obligations infuriate him (which may very well happen), then Gary will just have to realize that I have a life outside of CityLight Press too.

Clicking the send button with a little too much vigor, I pull my tortoiseshell blue-light reading glasses from the bridge of my nose. The email is one more thing off my to-do list for the day, though if I'm honest, it doesn't feel as if it is getting any shorter.

I drop my head into my hand and take a deep breath, my mind drifting to Dawson again. I think about him a lot lately, even though we haven't spoken since I texted him a "thank you" for the gift of the Bible.

The Bible is perhaps the most thoughtful gift I have ever received. I've spent the past week ruminating on the truth in the passages he highlighted. When I pour over them, the answer seems so simple—too simple even. It's clear I overcomplicated my life all this time when, really, all I ever needed was Jesus.

I'm enough in Him. He's enough for me.

Even when I can't or won't believe it.

The simple truth turns slightly into tangled spaghetti when I think too hard about it—again with the overcomplicating—so I just let it take root in the soil of my heart.

My phone buzzes again, and I lift my head. A knife twists in my stomach at the name on my screen.

MOM: I'm in the emergency room.

ME: What? Why? Are you okay?

Immediately, I dial her number, but she doesn't pick up. I try my sister. Nothing. I shoot Natasha a text.

ME: Have you heard from Mom? Is she okay? She just texted me that she's in the ER.

A hole forms in the pit of my stomach as I wait for either woman to answer me. Nervously, I tinker with the book-themed figurines and decorations on my desk, eager for a return text. A minute ticks by, then another, and another. I try to call them both again and get only their voicemails.

Which hospital would Mom be in? I can start calling around. Before I begin my search, I first make another call to someone I haven't spoken with in far too long.

"Hi, Dad."

"Hey, Nugget. How've you been?" There's a heavy sound in the background, a rush of wind, and a stir of voices. It's hard to hear him.

"I'm . . ." My voice falters as my walls rise. *Funny you should ask,* I wish I could say. *You've been too preoccupied with your life in California to find out how your daughter is faring.* Does he really care? Does it matter to him how I am? The annoyance and hurt fester.

Dad continues, "I'm about to go for an afternoon sail with a few friends. They're waiting for me. What's up? Are you good?"

A lump appears in my throat. I can almost imagine him,

cold drink in hand, leaning against the portside railing of a fancy sailboat, wind in his hair, and a smile on his face. I love the knowledge that there is a smile in his voice now. It breaks my heart that he chose to leave us all, and a swell of bitterness nips at my heart, but truly I'm happy that he's finally happy. I know all too well what hardships he endured for years on end.

Yet another thing that feels overcomplicated and confusing in my life. In a rush, I'm hit with a reminder that stops the negative thoughts in their tracks as they start to swirl through my brain: *Jesus is enough. In Him, I am enough. He's enough for me.*

In this weak moment, Jesus really must be enough for me because I can't do any of this without His guidance. I steady myself and choose to believe.

Without asking, it's obvious that Dad doesn't know anything about Mom. I don't bring it up. "Yeah, Dad. I'll talk to you later. Have fun today."

He says that he loves me and then hangs up the phone. Clearly, he knew nothing regarding Mom being in the hospital, which leaves me feeling slightly better. But maybe I should have told him about her. Then again, what would be the point? They're divorced. He's on the other side of the country. She'd choose to die before ever looking at him again.

My phone buzzes, and I grab it eagerly.

NATASHA: I just called. She's at Montefiore. I don't know what's going on.

ME: I just tried calling too. Is she okay? Are you heading over?

NATASHA: I don't know. She said she had to go and

will call me back. No, I'm in Austin for a friend's bachelorette.

I stare at Tashi's text for a moment. She is away from the city, which shouldn't be a surprise, but it leaves me to deal with this potential crisis alone. I try to call Mom again, but it goes to her voicemail.

ME: I'll head there now.

I send a quick email to my team about my emergency absence for the afternoon and rush for the train station so I can head to New Rochelle without delay. My fingers tap on my knees the whole ride. When the automatic doors to the emergency department *whoosh* open, I make a beeline to the front desk.

There are three people ahead of me, all patients waiting to be seen. When they've been triaged, I stand at the desk, waiting to be acknowledged for what feels like five minutes. Finally, the nurse sends me a look. I tell her my name and that I'm here to see Helena Fox.

She checks my mother's chart on the computer and shakes her head. "I'm sorry, but you're not on the approved list of visitors."

I frown. "I'm her daughter, the only local family she has right now."

The nurse stares at her computer screen. For a moment, I don't know if she heard me. Did I forget to speak out loud? Just as I open my mouth to repeat myself, she says, "I can check with her and see. What did you say your name was again?"

"Ava. Ava Fox."

The nurse disappears. I wait awkwardly in front of the desk, a little too afraid to enter the waiting area where a man

317

is about to hack up a lung. Finally, she returns with another shake of her head.

"I'm sorry. You are not on the approved list."

My mouth falls open. "Well . . . But I . . . Can I at least speak with her doctor? I'd like to know what's going on."

"That would be a violation of patient privacy." She plops back into her desk chair and waves the next waiting patient forward to check them in.

I'm shocked, embarrassed, and a bit humiliated. The man in the waiting area coughs harder, and I swear I feel the floor shake. I make a mad dash for the exit and pull out my phone. Another phone call to my mom goes immediately to voicemail.

I pace for minutes on end in the stuffy heat and practically wear a path into the pavement outside the hospital's entrance. I try calling my mom again. I try Natasha, too, and she is next to no help. After another round of pacing, a sneaking suspicion crawls up my spine. On my phone, I open the only form of social media my mother has and navigate to her profile.

Sure enough, posted thirty minutes ago, is a selfie photo of my mom propped up in her hospital bed, a mask pulled over her mouth and nose, an IV in her arm, and visible anguish knitted upon her brow. The caption reads: *Emergency room. All alone. Life is so unfair sometimes.*

Suddenly, I feel sick. My skin prickles with sweat. My vision blurs. There are a handful of comments from distant relatives under the photo:

Oh no, Helena! Are you okay?

Alone? In the ER? Where are your girls?

Praying for you! Let us know how we can help.

I taste bile in my mouth as I read my mother's reply to the second comment, which, according to the app, was left one minute ago: *It is in moments of trial that we learn who really cares and who doesn't. I know if Tashi were in town, she'd be here in a heartbeat, though. Thanks for caring. Scary day, but I pray I'll be okay.*

My blood boils. She's punishing me. She knows I'm here, purposely blocked me from seeing her, and is now intentionally leading people to believe that I am a horrible daughter who doesn't care to be at my own mother's side.

Is this whole thing a ruse? It wouldn't be the first time she has made false claims about her health or overexaggerated something in order to get attention. I don't want to accuse her of such an atrocity, but . . .

Staring at the post, I type out a comment: *I'm here at the hospital, Mom. They won't let me in because they say you didn't list me on the approved visitors. I've tried calling you multiple times. Can you tell them they made a mistake so I can come in and see you?*

The comment posts. I try calling another time. I send one more text. When she doesn't answer or respond, I refresh Mom's social media post and see that my comment is now gone. Deleted.

I take one long look at the emergency room sign over the door. Something settles in my gut, and I take a step backward. If she doesn't want me here, it's time to leave.

—

By the time I arrive back in the city, it's too late to get any more work done for the day. I'm racing against time to even make it to dinner with James without being embarrassingly late. At this point, my tardiness is borderline rude.

It's inevitable that I'm going to look like a mess at dinner. In the back of a cab, I comb my hair with my fingers and fix my makeup the best I can. It's far too late to stop at home and change into something other than office attire for the evening. My fitted slacks, sleeveless mock-neck, and flats will have to suffice, even if I manage to make it to Dawson's party later.

My heart thuds. Will James understand when I tell him I have to leave early this evening after being so late to dinner in the first place?

Traffic does me no favors, and I have to talk myself down from a proverbial ledge when it finally comes to a complete standstill. I am left with no choice but to call James. He answers on the third ring. Something blares in the background as we exchange greetings.

"I apologize, James," I begin. "A family emergency took me away for the afternoon, and I'm now the victim of New York City traffic. I'm trying to make it to the restaurant, I promise."

He smacks his lips. "Well, that's reassuring to hear. I was just about to send off an email to Rudy Hibarger and let him know I've accepted his terms."

He's bluffing. Right? He had better be bluffing. If not, and I lose this author for CityLight, I may very well lose my job as well. I take a breath.

"I'm glad I caught you in time. James?" I bite my tongue, hesitating to grovel and kiss up to him. A sudden idea occurs to me. "Since dinner at this point is shot, how would you like to accompany me to an event that CityLight is sponsoring tonight instead?"

The thought of James being next to me as I enter

Dawson's event makes me want to throw up, but it's the only way I can guarantee I'll even make an appearance there at all at this point. I spill a few details to James, making the party sound as enticing as I can, though I realize I know next to nothing about it. I cover the receiver to release a small squeal when he agrees to meet me there. I give the cabbie the address to the party and breathe with a bit more ease. I'll still be late—and late with an annoying, egotistical curmudgeon on my arm—but at least I'll be there.

There's still no update from Mom or Natasha. When I check for new texts, I realize I never responded to Charlie earlier. I send a quick text letting her know I'll be there but late, and then settle into my seat and watch the city crawl by through the backseat window.

After today, I feel like a failure, and I list all the ways in my head. I'm a bad enough daughter that my mother would go to great lengths to prove how terrible I am. I'm unimportant enough that my father couldn't stay close enough to see me—let alone call me more often than once a month. I'm an employee incompetent enough to nearly lose the company's most lucrative author. I'm a friend poor enough to almost miss a party celebrating the one person who has selflessly loved me for years. And I'm a woman stupid enough to lose that same man for good.

Among the beautiful truths carried within Dawson's gift, one message overshadowed them all: Dawson is letting me go . . . for good.

And how could I blame him? This is what I want, isn't it? I want him to leave me and move on. The way I feel right now reassures me that he's dodging a bullet. What a joke I am.

As soon as the ugly thought enters my mind, I can almost hear Dawson in my head reminding me that isn't how Jesus sees me. *"You are beloved, accepted, new, redeemed, a friend of God . . .* He'd written the words across the top of one of the pages.

I close my eyes and let the words sink deeper as I focus on not crying and smearing my freshly applied mascara. When I finally open them again, the cab is pulling up to the curb in front of a gorgeous building, its exterior reflecting the opulence and glamour of the Art Deco period. Immediately, I recognize the iconic Ziegfeld Ballroom on 54th Street. My eyes catch on James lingering near the entrance.

How did he beat me here?

I pay the driver and straighten my shoulders, feigning a false sense of confidence as I stride over to James. He watches me approach. The usual smugness in his demeanor is present and accounted for, but beneath it, I suddenly catch a spark of something new. Curiosity, maybe? Interest in me?

Please, no, don't let it be.

He extends his arm and flashes me a sultry smile. "Not the party attire I was envisioning, but you always are a vision, Ava Fox."

I let my smile stretch across my face pleasantly, despite the way my insides want to curl into a ball at his words. Now is not the time to offend James even further. Instead, I loop my arm with his and let the usher at the door scan the code on my phone for entry.

When I walk through the front door, I'm completely caught off guard. My breath hitches, and I turn in a wide circle. It's as if I've stepped back in time. *The Great Gatsby* theme takes my breath away. Nothing is as I expected it to be, and yet I understand exactly why Dawson chose this theme. I half expect Jay and Daisy to come around the corner any second.

Every inch of the building is dripping with the 1920s elegance of a lavish estate in West Egg. Crystal chandeliers hang from the ceiling. There must be a thousand tropical plants in here. Glittering coupe glasses catch the light and sparkle. Even the furniture that populates the lounge space in the lobby looks as if it was taken from the pages of a magazine in days long gone. Ahead and to my right is a tall poster display with CityLight's name splashed across the top. My heart pounds as I read the sign and realize just what it means. I am not sure if I'll be able to take another breath.

Beneath the flyer is an advertisement for a reprint of *The Great Gatsby* itself. My eyes dart over to the table next to the poster, and I see stacks and stacks of the featured book. Grabbing his arm, I tug James closer. With each step toward the table, my heart puts itself back together a little bit more. When we stop, I stare at the hardcover books, thinking that I've never imagined anything so beautiful.

The edition is stunning, with a design featured on its cover like nothing I've ever seen. I pick up a copy, and James does as well. I flip to the copyright page. It's CityLight's reprinting signature, sure enough. But why haven't I been privy to this special project?

Is this what Dawson was doing the times he visited CityLight's offices? Was he planning this surprise for me?

When I glance up and look around, a figure across the room catches the edge of my vision. We lock eyes at the same moment.

"Ava. You came."

At the sound of his voice, my heart flutters, and I watch as Dawson crosses the floor, making a beeline straight for me. With each step, the butterflies in my stomach increase because it's as though I'm suddenly looking into the face of Jay Gatsby himself.

28

Dawson

As the evening progresses, I am reminded of why I wanted to keep my role in the creation of Blind Date with a Book Nerd as low-key as possible.

Many pairs of bright, curious eyes follow me with interest around the event hall. Everywhere I go, heads swing my way and track my steps. The men in attendance give me a friendly nod of respect and admiration. The women smile and try to catch my eye.

According to the consensus I'm hearing from my guests, my app design is brilliant and is going to become a smashing success. Voices call out to me as I move around the hall, making excuses as yet another group of people reaches for me to congratulate me on my success.

"Epic event, Hayes! A real winner."

"Such a clever concept!"

"Why hasn't someone created an app like this for book

lovers before?"

It's already taking the internet by storm, that's for sure.

I wave them off with a smile and indicate that I've got duties as host to attend to. By the number of people coming up to me tonight to congratulate me or comment their praise on the official launch of the Blind Date with a Book Nerd app, I am one introvert who has about filled his quota for human interactions for the entire month.

Ava is noticeably absent, and I push my disappointment down a little farther with each moment that passes. It's just as well. Despite my best intentions to think of her as only a friend, having her here at an event inspired by our book-centered romance years ago would just be a painful distraction.

Without her here, I'm probably the only one who gets the significance of the emphasis on the Art Deco theme, but my guests seem to be loving it. The invitation that went out to their accounts invited them to experience the grandeur of the Roaring Twenties by participating in a masked "blind date" introduction to the evening consisting of a cleverly designed speed dating event, which is to be followed by an unmasked mixer where they can spend time getting to know each other with food, drink, and book-themed games. Guests were invited to dress in their favorite twenties-themed costumes. Anyone who arrives without a masquerade-style mask is offered one at the door if they want to participate.

The Ziegfeld Ballroom was a brilliant choice, the building a relic of days long past. Extravagant ostrich feather vases placed here and there rise above the crowd, and the space is filled with tinsel, geometric patterns, and glittering towers of delicate glass. A live jazz band, sparkling drinks served in elegant coupe glasses, and a plentiful flow of twenties-themed hors d'oeuvres are the finishing touches on an evening I think would have made Jay Gatsby himself proud.

The pièce de résistance to the evening is the magnificently reprinted edition of *The Great Gatsby*, sponsored by CityLight Press. Each guest will walk away with a gifted copy to commemorate the evening. It was an extravagant expense that was completely unnecessary, but one which I couldn't live without.

When the reprint idea had come to me years ago, I had it in my head that the book would make Ava happy. It would show her why I'm her Jay Gatsby, only better.

A sharp stab of regret and chagrin pains my chest as our third round of speed daters take their seats. Jay never got the girl, and neither, it seems, will I.

Anne is coordinating, and I watch as she runs around, calling out directions and orders with a grin on her face. Mom and Anne designed a launch event that has fully exceeded my expectations. I was right to turn it over into their capable hands when the idea of finding the right venue, decorations, catering, entertainment, and communicating with vendors made my forehead break out in a sweat.

On par with tonight's theme, each RSVP filled out an online questionnaire in which they were asked to list their own qualities, favorite things, and personality quirks as if they were describing a book. Painstakingly, Mom, Anne, and I transcribed each guest's answers to a piece of brown craft paper over the past few weeks. That paper was then numbered and wrapped around a copy of our *Gatsby* reprint, with a note inside the dust cover that read: *True love means never having to pretend to be more than you are. May your future romance bring out the best in you (and end more happily than this book).*

The whole effect at the entrance to the speed dating room is like walking into a bookstore to embrace the unknown, choosing a book not based on its cover but on the clues written across the inconspicuous wrapping.

Tonight, everyone who signed up was assigned a number, which is pinned to their clothing on arrival. They get to browse the shelves of wrapped, numbered books set up by the decorations team. They choose a date based on the qualities listed on the outside of each wrapped book, pair off, and have a chance to sit down one-on-one with each other. If they hit it off, they will remove their masks and go for the full date experience in the ballroom. If not, their books get returned to the selection table, and they are able to go another round.

Not every guest has chosen to play the speed dating game. Many are simply mingling in the ballroom, drinks in hand, enjoying the music, and striking up conversations at one of the many bookish game and trivia stations we've set up around the venue.

It's a fun and playful event, and the plentiful smiles and laughter tell me that we're a success.

When Anne darts past me, I reach out for her arm. "Anne with an E, you've outdone yourself with these game designs. Maybe you have a calling as a party planner?"

She tosses her long hair over her shoulder and smirks at me. "You're just saying that because you've heard everyone oohing and ahhing over the theme of this party, and you want me to coordinate more events for you."

It's not a bad idea. I hold up my palms, feigning innocence. "Me? Why, whatever do you mean?" I follow it up with a wink.

She laughs, calling over her shoulder as she dashes away. "You know my dream is to be an editor at a big publishing house like Ava."

The casual mention of her name guts me a little as Anne goes back to her duties as speed dating host. She isn't aware of the events that have transpired in the months between Ava and I since I've been back in the city. I try to shake it off and move on as I stride toward the lobby. I need a little break from mingling, so I'll take up door duties and welcome new guests through the front doors of the ballroom for a while. I reserved the entire event hall for the evening, so it feels a little like I'm welcoming partygoers to my mansion in West Egg.

Ava's conspicuous absence tonight is beginning to sting, and it's just as well. The space and the silence between us have been good for me. Maybe one day we can truly be just friends. For now, I'll have to rely on time and trust in God to soothe the hurt of it all.

With a sudden rush, Dahlia appears at my side, her face bright and grinning ear to ear. She's dressed in a flapper costume that looks like she pulled it off a vintage 1920s clothing rack. Feathers are in her hair, and long, beaded pearls drape off her neck.

"This event, Dawson," she exclaims. "It's amazing! What a fun and clever way to kick off the launch of your app."

"I had some talented helpers," I reply, with a grin that splits my face from ear to ear.

While the friendship between Dahlia and I has not developed beyond our bookstore hopping date, I'm glad to see her tonight. She's a welcome anchor in a sea of strangers.

She recognizes a friend in the crowd and hurries away, her hand lifted in greeting. I watch her in amusement, her vivacious enthusiasm clear evidence of her social butterfly personality. I survey the rest of the crowd for a moment, thinking that, at some point tonight, I'll need to give the speech I prepared. I'm not looking forward to my public-speaking debut, so for now, I'll just continue my duties as a door attendant. I swing back toward the lobby, and it's as if all the air in my lungs dissipates as a weight drops heavily into my stomach.

The sight of Ava standing at the welcome table with a copy of the newly reprinted edition of *The Great Gatsby* clutched to her chest undoes me to my core. She's staring straight at me, her expression unreadable. My stomach lurches again as I see the sophisticated man standing next to her.

Are they together? Did she bring a date to my launch event? Did she match with this guy on my app?

I'm unsure if I'm hurt, relieved, upset, or a combination of the three. Instead of getting worked up, I try to focus on the fact that she cared enough to show up tonight. I have no doubt Ava came to show her support. That counts for something, right?

Resolutely, I walk forward, forcing a welcoming smile I don't feel. "Ava. You came." The obvious statement is the only thing I can choke out as I struggle to breathe.

Ava's full lips part. She looks startled and shocked and almost stricken. Perhaps she didn't expect to see me right as she walked through the door.

The man at her side steps forward, his hand outstretched.

He is taller than me, with a presence so gallant that it seems to take up most of the space. His grip is firm.

"James Wolfe," he announces, with an inflection that makes me think I'm supposed to know who he is, and the name does sound vaguely familiar.

I can't take my eyes off Ava, though. She looks a little frazzled, her blonde waves ruffled by the outdoors. She is still in her typical office clothes, but there's a light gleaming in her blue eyes that I can't seem to look away from. In a flash, I recognize the brilliance of unadulterated joy shining in her expression. It's a look I've rarely seen on Ava since I moved back to New York. My heart drops again as I realize it must be because of him.

Whoever James Wolfe is, he must make Ava happy.

And I want Ava to be happy. That's all I've ever wanted for her. I just didn't expect to face it tonight.

She's saying something, but her voice is hazy. "James . . . author . . . CityLight . . . meeting . . ."

I don't want to hear any more about how they met. Whether it was through my app or CityLight, it doesn't matter. Ava isn't mine. I have no right to expect anything more, but I'm splintering into a thousand pieces, nonetheless. There is only one thing I can do, and a silent prayer for help bubbles through my brain with desperation.

It gives me enough composure to pull it together for a minute longer. I need to focus on running my event. I've got book lovers waiting to open a new chapter on their own love stories.

"It's great to meet you, old sport," I reply to James' greeting with my best Jay Gatsby impression. My gaze shifts to Ava. "Thanks for coming tonight. I couldn't have gotten to this point without you, Ava. I hope you know that."

There is a bright sheen of moisture in her eyes that wasn't there before. She's murmuring something again, but I don't trust myself to wait to hear it.

All my resolve to move on with my life flew out the window at the sight of her. I'm the Jay Gatsby in this story once again, sacrificing everything to prove he is worthy of Daisy, yet in the end, he still doesn't get the girl. I wave my hands grandly around my head as if I'm the man himself, welcoming my carefree guests to another opulent party.

"Go on in, enjoy some refreshments, play some games. And please, help yourself to a book." I gesture wildly toward the table stacked with the elegant hardcovers. "They are a gift to all our guests tonight."

I finish by mumbling something about attending to my duties as host, spin on my heel, and walk away as fast as I can. Trying not to bump into any of my well-dressed guests, I make a beeline for a side door. Everyone in the ballroom seems to know me, their bright eyes and sparkling smiles turned my way.

Dahlia spots me and waves, but her attention catches on something behind me, her expression washing over with curiosity. Voices call out to me, but I keep moving. Eventually, I'm going to need to attend to my duties as host, but right now, I need a few minutes to gather my composure.

The kitchen is bustling with the caterer's staff. The scent of salmon en croute and crab cakes fill the air. I sidestep the servers as they pass into the ballroom, trays piled with savory hors d'oeuvres and sparkling drinks balanced expertly on their shoulders. I see the door I'm searching for straight ahead. A few more steps, then I can pull myself together enough to get back to the launch of the app I've worked tirelessly to bring to life.

A dating app designed by a man who couldn't let go of one woman long enough to make room for anyone else.

The irony of what I have created and what I can't do isn't lost on me.

I reach the door, my fingers itching for the handle. Shoving the door open, I step into the calming balm of the evening.

I stop short in the middle of the open space, my hands in fists at my side, my head thrown back so I can see the sky above the buildings. The door clicks, and then I hear her soft voice behind me.

"Dawson, can we talk?"

29

Ava

As my eyes dart around the magnificent space and take in the stunning Art Deco details that Dawson has incorporated to create the party of my dreams, I realize how much I missed when I didn't read the invitation thoroughly. That's what I get for obsessively working and forgetting to actually live my life.

I remember now that the invitation did say something about the theme being the Roaring Twenties, but that fact was tossed in the waves of my overloaded brain. I only vaguely remember tapping the RSVP link. It doesn't matter now as I look into Dawson's eyes and attempt to explain why I'm late, why I'm not at all dressed for the occasion, and why James Wolfe is standing beside me.

But the words come out disjointed, and I'm honestly not sure what I'm mumbling because Dawson's shadowed eyes are boring into mine and distracting me so much that I don't know which way is up anymore. He isn't wearing his glasses tonight. He's dressed in an elegant tuxedo suit with a soft pink shirt under the jacket, and it makes me happy because he looks like he just stepped out of a magazine fashion plate from decades ago. There's a question in his eyes somewhere beyond the hazel sea. Desperately, I wonder what's going on in his brain.

As if a veil is being stripped away piece by piece, the truth begins to click into place. What have I missed? Our history is years in the past, though it feels like we were just in love yesterday. When Dawson created the Blind Date with a Book Nerd app, planned this Gatsby-themed party, and commissioned a reprint of my favorite book—the book he has always despised—was it all for me? What did the note he left on the Bible—the greatest gift I've ever received—mean?

The air leaves my lungs. Before I can speak or ask any of the questions rattling in my mind, I hear Dawson making an excuse to leave. He turns on the heel of his vintage leather brogues and speed walks away. I grip the beautiful reprint of *The Great Gatsby* to my chest and run after him, calling out excuses to James as I leave him standing alone.

Dawson walks through the ballroom with a determined clip in his walk. I follow him at a slightly slower pace, trying not to make a scene, and another piece of the puzzle falls into place.

All this time—just as he'd hinted in his letter to me—Dawson has been trying to prove that he is worthy of my love. He is my modern-day Jay Gatsby. He'd go to the highest lengths for me—his Daisy Buchanan—but I've only hurt and destroyed our relationship because I've been too much of a fool to see how safe I am with the person filled with so much goodness and light right in front of me.

I didn't have to push him away. I could have waited for him all those years ago when he went to London. We could have built a lovely life together. I'm well aware that Dawson isn't just like Jay Gatsby in every way, but neither am I exactly like Daisy. Our stories aren't the same. But we are enough alike that I certainly have been the cause of messing everything up between us. And now, unlike Gatsby's character in the timeless tale of a man who loves a woman, Dawson has given up the chase.

My inward protest is immediate and marked by a fierceness foreign to me. *Not if I have anything to do with it. Our story will not end like theirs.*

My flats tap against the floor as I go after him. For a moment, I lose sight of him as the crowd of people dressed in flapper dresses and vintage suits eddy and sway around him. I catch sight of his tuxedo jacket as he steps through a door leading outside. Dodging the servers carrying trays of hors d'oeuvres high on their shoulders, I spill onto the street after him.

"Dawson, can we talk?" My voice is ragged and strained, and my breath hitches as I watch him stiffen.

Slowly, he brings his hands to his sides and turns around to look at me with a painful expression. He is so handsome and sophisticated, but I've long missed the old Dawson, the handsome but nerdy techie who wore glasses that made him so cute I could barely stand it, his curly hair always mussed, his voice a little too loud and too excited as he spoke about something that intrigued him.

Adorkable.

That's the Dawson I once fell in love with. His pursuit of me has driven that version of him away, and now, I'm just afraid it's too late to rekindle things with the man I'm still in love with.

Because I never fell out of love with him.

We stand in silence for a few moments. The evening air stretches quietly around us, the sky painted a beautiful mixture of purple and orange as the sun sets this summer night.

I hold up the copy of *The Great Gatsby*, its cornflower blue cover a bright contrast to the shadows of the evening. "You always hated this book."

He shrugs. "Yeah, well, it grows on you when you realize how much you resemble the book's hero."

My heart sinks. I search Dawson's eyes for a sign of hope, but the light in them has been extinguished.

"It's a lesson to us all, I guess," Dawson continues. "When God closes a chapter, don't try to reopen it. There's nothing but heartbreak between those pages."

Confusion swirls in my brain. "But like you said . . . in your note the other day . . ."

He grumbles. A flicker of pain passes over his features.

"Explain all of this." I gesture to the closed door behind me and back toward the party inside.

"Do I really need to?" His voice cracks. His eyes drift away from me and fixate on a splash of graffiti on the exterior of the building. He clears his throat. "When I began to design this app years ago, I thought I could win you back by impressing you with the one thing I'm good at: coding. I thought we'd reconnect again at some point, and you would learn what I'd been up to. Maybe you'd see we were meant to be. But that day never came, and designing the app turned into more than just a flex. It grew to be so much more.

"Fast forward to this year when our lives suddenly intersected again, and I wondered if God was maybe giving me the chance to win you back. Finally."

My heart lifts. I sense there's more, so I wait.

"I worked with Andrew on designing a reprint of *Gatsby*. It doubled as a fun launch gift for my guests, and yet another way to impress you. In a way, I wanted to show you that reality is far better than fiction. But the joke is on me." He laughs and shakes his head.

My heart hurts.

"Unknowingly, I'd stepped right into the pages myself. Maybe that's why I thought I despised the story all those years. Fitzgerald probed too far into my subconscious and shined a light on all the ways I wasn't honoring the plan God has for me, which apparently doesn't include—"

He stops short. The pain in his eyes is evident, but he holds my gaze steadily. The strength of his faith in God, even when the outcome disappointed him again and again, takes my breath away.

"Me." I finish the broken sentence for him. Everything seems to narrow, as though the buildings are crowding together. My throat constricts tightly. Heat prickles my skin. "No, Dawson . . ." I falter, trying to find the right words.

Dawson licks his lips. His eyebrows pinch together. A sickly feeling washes over me.

"We're not fictional characters," I finally manage to say. I lift the book in my hand. "You're right: Reality *is* better than fiction, especially when you have the very thing Fitzgerald's characters were missing—God. And I think I forgot how powerful and freeing trusting in Him is until you came along to remind me. Please forgive me for the

338

hurt I've caused you."

My heart beats painfully, but I breathe out the emotion, the words catching on the tightness of my throat. "I'm the one who has been the fool. There was a time when I thought if I could just create the perfect façade of a life—if I could just have all my t's crossed and my i's dotted—then I would be worthy of love and commitment. I thought if I could control my life, it wouldn't turn out like it did for my parents. I would be worthy. I would be enough." I bow my head, my hair falling over my face. "I took control away from God and look what a mess I made. For that, I'm especially sorry because it affected you too."

When I gather the courage to look up again, his eyes are soft and full of kindness. "It looks like you and I aren't so different," he says softly. "I thought if I could reinvent myself and be the type of guy you wanted—since obviously, something wasn't working before—"

"And I told you that had nothing to do with you."

"I know that now, Ava." A light laugh escapes him. "Showing up tonight on the arm of a handsome man doesn't help though. But that's my own jealousy talking. If he makes you happy, Ava, then—"

"Wait, what?" I don't hide my startled reaction. "James is not my date, Dawson. He's just an author I work with. He's globally renowned . . ." I trail off, seeing how it would have appeared that way to him.

"You know what, it doesn't even matter." He lets out an exasperated sigh. His eyes flicker up toward the sky briefly. "I mean it when I say I want you to be happy, Ava. That's all I've ever wanted. I'm just finally getting out of the way."

"Please stay," I step toward him. "I don't want to lose you."

"I'll always be here if you need anything."

"No." I close the space between us and reach up to rest a hand on his shoulder. "Stay in the way, Daws. I'm done making messes, hiding away, and fighting for control. I know I still have things to figure out, but I want to make this work. Triple prom. Please."

As my voice breaks, the threat of tears just under the surface, Dawson steps forward. His arms wrap around me, and it's like I've always belonged in their strong embrace. Pressing my face into the space between his neck and shoulder, I breathe in the familiar scent of him, memorizing the firm contours of his frame and remembering the way he used to hold me like this, back when I knew I never wanted it to end.

The truth is right in front of me. This is where I was always destined to be. This is the man God designed for me. But I've been so wrapped up in my own pain and struggle for control against the things that hurt me that I was too blind to recognize what a gracious gift he is.

When Dawson releases me, I deflate. A rift grows wider and wider in the small space between us. In the letdown of my emotions, I hear the whisper of new yet familiar words in the quiet recesses of my heart: *Jesus is enough. He is enough.*

The question is: Do I believe it? Is He really enough for me? If everything is stripped away—even more than it already has been—*is* He enough?

If I am entirely wiped away from my father's memory as he continues to revel in the freedom of his life far away, will I be okay? If something happens to my mother, or if she cuts me out of her life completely, will I be okay? If I lose my hard-earned identity as a book editor at CityLight Press and lose all the followers I've amassed across my social media community, will I be okay?

And if Dawson decides to let me go for good, will I be okay?

My heart pounds. Dawson lets a soft exhale slip from his lips. Another piece of the puzzle slides into place, settling in with a harsh finality that guts me.

"I'm too late, aren't I?" I whisper.

His face reflects the war of emotions inside. He doesn't answer right away. I want to speak, to plead my case, but I don't know what to say. The silence is punctured by the door swinging open. We both turn toward it. Onto the street steps a beautiful woman, dressed to the nines as a stunning flapper in a black and gold dress. The golden sheen of her hair, styled into a faux short bob, catches the light inside. I recognize her instantly as the woman on the blind date with Dawson when we inadvertently showed up at the same restaurant. Dahlia gives me a once-over, then looks at Dawson.

"Your sister is looking for you," she says brightly. "I think it's speech time."

"Right," he mumbles. I glance at him and see his posture stiffening. His eyes flick to mine. The unspoken words between us hang in the air with an awkwardness so intense it could rival the way Dawson is suddenly acting. Dahlia doesn't retreat to give us space but stays in the doorway, waiting for him. After a moment, he steps away and follows her through the door without another word.

I wipe the tears away as quickly as they fall.

Okay, Lord, my heart whispers. *You're all I have.*

Somehow, I don't quite fall apart. My chin quivers as I draw in a breath, but I feel . . . okay.

I feel held.

I lift my chin and walk back inside. In the ballroom, I find all the guests gathering in front of the stage, where a rattled-looking Dawson stands. He wrings his hands and blinks a few times as he squints at the crowd. Public speaking was never his strong suit. Even when we were in college, he was always the guy behind the scenes. But watching him from my place along the wall, I see how the years have shaped his growth and maturity. He has the courage to try new things, even if they feel difficult or unnatural.

Despite the ache in my heart, the sight brings a smile to my face.

Warm fingers close around my wrist from the side, and before I can turn my head, I am yanked into an embrace.

"I found you! Finally!" Charlie squeals. "And you are . . .?" Moving to the front of me, she places her hands on my shoulders and pushes me away from her enough to assess my outfit. "Dressed as a time traveler? Where is your twenties attire? I figured you'd be all over this party! Wait." Her rush of words pauses. She cocks her head to the side, her chocolate brown eyes studying me. "And you're sad. What's wrong?"

Beside her, Andrew clears his throat. "Is it unfair of me to place the blame on . . . *that?*" He points across the room where James Wolfe is currently making a fool of himself.

Raising my hand, I let my forehead fall into my open palm. "Andrew, please, with all your public relations and management skills, can you take care of that man for a little bit?"

"On it." He nods briskly and gives his wife's shoulder a quick squeeze as he walks toward James.

Immediately, Charlie turns back to me. I take a moment

to admire her outfit. She's dressed in a vintage, gold, floor-length cocktail dress. Its sequins catch brilliantly in the lights. Her long dark hair is twisted on her head, a band of pearls wrapping around the strands to finish the look. She is stunning, as usual.

"I can help dress you up?" she offers. "You can take my pearl necklaces, and there are masks all around. I'm certain I also saw a few extra costume pieces in the back."

I look down at my stuffy, professional office clothes and shake my head. "It's fine. I'm not sure how long I'll be staying anyway. I have a lot I need to take care of." I always have a lot to take care of, but I know Charlie knows I'm making excuses because something has happened to upset me. The events of the day swirl in my mind. Guilt nibbles at my stomach as I think of my mother.

"Isn't this technically a work party?" Charlie tilts her head and studies me.

"CityLight only sponsored it. We're not required to be here."

Her eyebrows cinch together. "Are you okay, Ava? Is something else going on? Andrew said you weren't at the office today."

I try to pin on a smile that doesn't look fake. "It's been quite the day. But I'll be okay."

My eyes dart to the stage where Dawson is calling for the room's attention. A bittersweet calm sinks over me. My reply to Charlie's concern is part truth, part I'm-not-sure-yet. Despite the heaviness that I suspect is going to weigh on my heart for a long time, something deep inside whispers that somehow, finally, I'm beginning to think that I'm going to be okay.

30

Dawson

"You need to fix whatever you did to ruin things with that woman."

My hand freezes over the open box of extra *Gatsby* hardcovers I'm packing to take home. Lifting my eyes to Dahlia's face, I stare at her in disbelief. She is staring back at me with an earnest expression in her deep, pretty eyes. Approaching the table, she leans over it.

"Dawson, you are a great guy. I saw that as soon as we met. But I'm beginning to suspect that you are also quite the numbskull."

My lower jaw drops a little. "Did I miss the start of this conversation somewhere?"

Dahlia shakes her head. Her blonde curls loosened during the evening, slipping out of the flapper bob she'd styled them in. It's late. We're almost alone. Only the catering staff remain, cleaning up in the kitchen. The guests have departed. Every face I saw throughout the night wore a smile, and I noticed quite a few single attendees turned into pairings as the partygoers left. I wonder how many book lovers will pinpoint this night as the start of their love story.

I've barely had a chance to glance at the reports my team sent over a few minutes ago. It looks as if not only was the meet and greet mixer a successful launch event for the app, but our downloads have tripled, and our memberships have also increased exponentially in the last four hours. And we've just officially launched and opened to the public. Inviting several well-known local influencers to the event was a smart move, and I have Ava to thank for the introductions. The future is already looking bright for Blind Date with a Book Nerd.

I sent Mom and Anne back to my apartment while I finished packing up at the event hall. They worked all day getting set up, and I wanted them to rest while I mulled over the party. It was a great night on all accounts, though my troubled heart hasn't caught up enough to feel the satisfaction. I didn't speak to Ava the rest of the evening after she poured her heart out to me outside, partially because so many guests asked for my attention, and also partially because I don't know what else is left to say.

I was grateful when Dahlia lingered behind the rest of the guests, helping me to gather banners, tablecloths, and masquerade masks that were left behind. I'll have them delivered back to my apartment tomorrow. The lighting and decorations company will pick up their things tomorrow too. Dahlia and I worked in silence for the most part, right up until she just walked into the foyer and began to blurt out her thoughts.

She puts her hands on her hips and shakes her head. "I'm serious. When Ava and her date crashed our first blind date, I was annoyed. She's stunning, she's elegant, and she's clearly successful. Before I recognized her from social media, I thought she had to be some uppity Manhattan socialite you were hung up on."

When she pauses, I swallow past the discomfort in my throat, searching my brain for what to say. Dahlia continues before I can get any words out of my mouth.

"But now, I'm realizing that while you may be hung up on her alright, Ava is just as much hung up on you. She's crazy about you, and I'm starting to wonder if you are too dense to see how deeply in love with you that woman is." She stares at me as if I've grown two heads.

"Ava and I—" My voice cracks incredulously. Ava's plea with me outside earlier tonight completely blindsided me. She asked me to give us another chance, which is exactly what I've always wanted. And yet, I can't fully believe or trust her words. My heart simply won't allow me. The glitz of the night probably sparked her emotions. Once the glamour of the evening fades away . . .

"We can't go back down that road," I say. "She'll realize I'm not enough for her, and I can't go through that heartbreak again. History always finds a way to repeat itself."

She pushes off the table and waves her hands around her head. "History-schmistery. I know what love looks like. Believe me, I've been keeping my eyes open for it for a long time. She couldn't keep her eyes off you all night, Dawson. Neither of you could keep your eyes off each other. You didn't need to say a word, and your conversation was still the loudest in the room."

A hot flush creeps along my skin. I'd thought my glances toward Ava throughout the event had been discreet. Apparently not.

Dahlia's expression is full of disapproval. "I think it's time to take a leap of faith, Dawson, and do what it takes to make it work with her."

Bitterly, I tuck my chin and shrug, shaking my head. "I've tried."

"Then you need to stick by her side until she releases whatever is preventing her from admitting how much she needs you." Dahlia comes close, her soft hand alighting on my shoulder. "You're meant for each other. I believe that."

I try to deflect her attention away from the wave of emotion I feel threatening to crash over me by fixing a playful smirk on my face. "So, you and me . . .?"

She returns my smirk with a gentle gaze, her reply soft but filled with a touch of sadness. "I wish it could be different, but I think you and I know it will always be Ava for you. I could never get between two people's destinies." She brightens. "Hopefully, your brilliant dating site will bring love my way. I'd be happy forever if I could belong to a man as good and kind as yourself."

My heart stirs toward her. "Give all your worries and cares to God because He cares for you. He has your perfect man for the perfect time. I believe that."

She laughs softly, but the sound suddenly has a ring of joy in it. "Do you think so? You should try following that same advice yourself." She looks around the event hall. "Your launch party was so much fun. Have you thought about making these meet and greets a regular thing? It would be the perfect place for blind date matches to meet in a casual and engaging environment."

"After tonight's success, I've been mulling it over," I admit.

Dahlia rests her hand on my forearm. "Well, if you do make them a regular thing, call me. I'll connect you with some of my favorite event planners, so the whole thing is easy-breezy. Believe me, the book lovers of New York City need what you are offering."

"Thank you, Dahlia."

Smiling, she stretches up onto her toes to plant a soft kiss on my cheek. Then, she smacks my bicep with a little more force than I would think necessary to make her point. "Now, go tell that woman you love her."

"Ow," I call after her as she prances gracefully away. "There's no need to get violent. I get your point. Wait . . . let me call you a cab."

Her only answer is a wave over her shoulder as she disappears through the front doors and into the night.

—

Weeks pass, and surprisingly, I've found a new sense of hope that hasn't existed since the fateful letter in which Ava broke up with me all those years ago. A part of me died that day, but I feel the stirrings of life again.

It isn't lost on me how wide the chasm between Ava and me is. Our foundation cracked long ago. While we've been gingerly dancing along the crevice since I moved back to the city, the space has been gradually widening to the point I now don't know how to get across it.

I don't know what to do, so I don't do anything at all.

My life is incredibly and satisfyingly full. As summer wanes, it brings new projects and responsibilities to my role as a junior partner in my software firm. The senior partners were more than impressed with the design of my matchmaking algorithm, and it gave them even more confidence in my abilities to lead the East Coast division of our company in the right direction. They haven't had any issue with me launching my own business, especially since I've hired the firm to manage the day-to-day tasks. When I'm not at the office or spearheading some new app development for one of our clients, I'm overseeing the management of the constant influx of new Blind Date with a Book Nerd members or troubleshooting issues and coordinating with my team to ensure the software does its job well.

I've also been praying and studying the Bible with a renewed zest. In the mornings and evenings, when I'm not glued to my bank of computers or laptop, my latest habit is to take long walks in Central Park, escaping the heat of the summery days. The woodsy setting soothes my soul while I talk to God. It feels as if He is the only One who truly knows me as I set about the enormous task of getting to know myself outside of my relentless pursuit of Ava.

It's clear to me now how much I put the idea of proving myself worthy of her love over my love for God, my family, and even above my love for Ava herself. The unofficial breakup of our friendship—because we haven't spoken since the launch party several weeks ago—feels like a chance to get to know myself all over again.

It's better this way. While I miss Ava's presence, this is the distance I need to move on. Above all, I want her to be happy, and I'm not sure if keeping myself in her life accomplishes that.

I've even taken a step back at church. I'm still in faithful attendance. But rather than plant myself boldly near Ava in the front rows, I'm slipping in during worship, sitting in the back row, and slipping back out after service ends.

I've seen the back of Ava's head bowed in prayer, and that's about it. It feels appropriate to put space between us now. Perhaps it won't always be this way, but for now, I see no reason to rip the scabs off old wounds that are trying to heal.

Because I am healing. I feel it a little more each day. The world feels bright to me again. I'm noticing details that weren't there before. And while part of me will always love Ava, my hope in God's plan for my life is growing.

And honestly, my conversations with "Never Met a Classic I Didn't Like" through my "Classic Book Hero Guy" account have punctuated the hectic days with moments that feel singularly calming in the midst of the media frenzy that quickly descends after my app's official launch.

Once word got out that "Lord of the Book Nerds" is the creator of the dating app taking the internet by storm, my inbox was instantly flooded with messages from curious women, all hoping to match up with the "cute, hotshot, software nerd who reads" (that's what the influencers on Bookstagram and BookTok are saying, not me), in addition to influencers and journalists wanting to interview me. Suddenly, my quiet and private world isn't so quiet anymore. I've stopped trying to keep up with the messages because I sent the same response every time: *Thank you for your interest, but I'm on a hiatus from dating at this time.*

It's true, but I reserve the right to change my mind. Because if I do choose to date again, I'll be using my "Classic Book Hero Guy" account to do it, the account where no one knows who I am, and I feel as if I can still be myself.

That secret profile is set to "Waiting to Turn the Page" so that I don't inadvertently match with anyone, but the possibility of toggling it to "Ready for a New Chapter" plays in the back of my mind now and then. Eventually, I'm going to need to set aside the past and open myself up to whatever God has for my future.

For now, I'm content to observe the online world I created from the privacy of my anonymous account. Every day, I peruse the forums, engaging in lively conversations with other book nerds. I run across "Never Met a Classic I Didn't Like" in the forums quite often, and we've continued our science fiction chat on the side. Most recently, we got into a heated debate about which classic or science fiction book-to-movie adaptations are actually decent.

I've been able to provide reading recommendations to her in spades. It's nice to ruminate on the books I've always loved but which have often taken a backseat as I prioritized other genres of reading that seemed more conventionally acceptable.

Through it all, I'm also discovering that it's okay to be different. I don't have to read what the world tells me are the most scholarly or the most popular genres to peruse. There is a comfort in not having to pretend to be anyone other than who I am: a tech nerd who reads more science fiction than classics and would rather design an app than play sports.

My anonymous pen pal and I have never spoken about meeting up, and I'm content with that. It's just nice to have someone who doesn't know me to talk to now and then.

Especially since I'm in the middle of packing up my entire apartment to move.

The epiphany struck me in the middle of a troubleshooting session that lasted well into a Sunday night after a BookTok video went viral, and Blind Date with a Book Nerd had several thousand new users sign up in the span of a couple of hours. I'd been stuck at my desk with barely enough spare time to order a pizza. My cell phone had been *pinging* all night with updates from Anne and Grayson, who were keeping me up-to-date on the family game night score.

A game night that I was missing yet again.

"I need to move home," I said aloud in my empty, lonely apartment.

Instantly, it made sense. With the summer drawing to a close, Andrew and Charlie are relocating to her Vermont country home while she and Andrew finish drafting the book they are writing together. Besides the newlyweds and Ava, I don't have many friends in New York City, or at least not many I'd want to stick around for. And the city can be a cold and lonely place without a community.

I'm done playing the lone wolf on a mission to prove he belongs to the pack.

My own warm and welcoming family is just a few hours away. With nothing to keep me in NYC, finding a small house in Aurora would be an easy way to transition back into my hometown. I can commute to the office when I need to and work remotely most of the time.

I didn't waste any time in turning in my notice for my current lease and looking for a house.

Only a few weeks after the launch party, the moving truck is scheduled to arrive bright and early tomorrow morning. Since it's my last Friday in the city, I treat myself to a break from work and take the day off to finalize all the last-minute moving tasks.

Rather than sleep in, I'm up early for my last walk in Central Park. I grab a coffee from the man at the donut and coffee cart. Leaving the temptation of his apple cider cinnamon donuts behind will probably prove a good thing. Though summer is still in full swing, it's unusually cool, and the scent of the air carries a hint of fall. The breezy morning has me thinking of my first autumn in New York City as a college freshman.

I stop and pause in the middle of the Park, feeling the hum of the city, even from the wooded oasis of the walking trail.

It's undeniable that New York City is full of life. Even in its chaotic energy, this city has been part of my history for over a decade now, and in so many ways, it's been good to me. I've made friends, I've jump-started my career, I've loved and lost and loved again. And through it all, the city is ever present, rarely changing, a constant force in my life.

It has its faults, but there is no place like The Big Apple.

Suddenly, a wave of nostalgia hits me. I take a sip of coffee to steady myself and discover that the to-go cup is regrettably empty. My stomach growls with an urgent force, and I'm struck with an idea.

There is no better way to say goodbye to the city than spending the day visiting my favorite places. Perhaps I'll end up grabbing a slice of New York's finest pizza or a hot dog. Perhaps I'll visit the Empire State Building or take a ferry ride to the Statue of Liberty. But first, breakfast. There is no doubt in my mind where I'm going to go.

The line out the door of the bagel place on the Lower East Side is as long as last time. I groan internally as my stomach protests the delay, but I'm committed. A double chocolate chunk bagel and a fresh cup of coffee are calling my name, and I'm going to answer.

I join the line of devoted bagel-seekers, relishing the cooling breeze and the feeling of the sunshine on my skin. Its pleasant warmth lulls me into a peaceful reflection, and if the line didn't move occasionally toward the entrance to the shop, I'd probably have fallen asleep standing up.

The sweetness of her soft voice would bring me back to consciousness anywhere, though.

"Dawson?"

I jolt upright, a zing running along my skin. When I turn to look at her, Ava's blue eyes are the color of a summer sky after a thunderstorm. She's looking at me with a smile that is both tentative and shy playing across her pink lips. A casual workout set drapes across her graceful frame.

It's a rare, relaxed look for Ava Fox, and I instantly decide it suits her perfectly.

"I guess great minds think alike?" she begins again when I don't speak. The bag in her hand rustles, and I peer inside when she holds it open toward me.

"Did you get a double chocolate chunk bagel?" I can't help but laugh. "What happened to being a cinnamon raisin girl?"

Her polite smile turns into an adorable grin, and I have to put a tight rein on myself when it causes my stomach to do somersaults against my will.

"What can I say? A girl needs chocolate in her life."

"Ah! What's a girl without her chocolate?" I reply, scrambling for something clever to say and feeling like a bumbling idiot.

Ava rolls the top of the paper bag closed again. Her sneakers scrape the sidewalk as she half turns away, then swings back to me. "Hey, can we talk for a few minutes?"

Awkwardly, I glance toward the open door of the bagel shop and then scan the line. From the grim looks stamped on the faces of everyone in the procession, there is no way I'm reclaiming my spot if I leave. Ava reads my mind and holds up the paper bag. It rustles again as she gives it a little shake.

"Fortunately, I ordered two bagels, so I have one to share."

"Well, if it'll save me from standing here for the next thirty minutes . . ." I joke, stepping out of the line. Immediately, it closes the empty space as if I was never there.

Ava leads us to a small outdoor table on the patio. When we sit, she immediately hands over a bagel and a small container of sweet cream cheese as if to prove that giving up my place in line was worth it.

We don't speak at first. Instead, both of us smear an inappropriate amount of cream cheese on our bagels. I painstakingly ensure that the full, rounded edge of my bagel is covered before looking up to find Ava staring at me. I place the bagel down on the paper wrapper it came in, suddenly not interested in it anymore.

"Ava—"

She holds up her long, delicate fingers. "Dawson, please, if I may speak first . . ."

I nod.

Her palm descends on the patio tabletop, fingers reaching toward me. I wish I could hold her hand. Her eyelids flutter closed.

"How can I ever thank you for what you did for me?"

It isn't what I'm expecting her to say, so it takes me a minute to process the words.

While I catch up, she continues, "I owe you so much. For so long, I've been struggling with myself, believing that because my mother and father went through such a bitter divorce, it somehow defined my worth in the world. I've borne the burden of my mother's toxic behavior, and it's crushed me."

Her voice cracks, and my heart cracks with it. I'm not sure if I could speak if I tried.

"For years, nothing I have done has felt like it measures up to the impossibly perfect standard I've held myself to. I've obsessed over every detail and tried to control every outcome . . . all to still feel as if I am a failure. It has led me to believe that the last thing I deserved was a good and loving relationship because I thought that my struggles proved that, just like my family, I couldn't even manage the relationships I had.

"Until you placed that Bible on my desk." Her voice fades. Ava's eyes rise and capture mine, their crystalline depths glassy with unshed tears. "Within those pages, I found more hope than I've ever felt. Things are still a struggle, but I know I'm beginning to see them differently . . . and to see myself and what I deserve differently. My faith and relationship with God are expanding in ways I never dreamed possible. And I have you to thank, Dawson."

I can't hold back any longer. Lightly, I place my palm over her warm hand, squeezing it with gentle pressure. My heart feels as if it is beating outside of my chest.

"Ava, thank you for sharing this with me," I begin, the

words choking me a little. "Gifting that Bible to you . . . writing those words . . . this is everything I hoped for. It's even brought new life to my own walk with God. Something was missing from my faith walk for a long time, and I think I'm finally returning to the heart of Jesus and who I am in Him too. So, it's me who should be grateful."

The morning sunlight catches the tears running down her cheeks. It sparkles as she laughs and uses her free hand to dash at them. "It's just a thank-you-fest over here, isn't it?"

I squeeze her hand again. My thumb runs across the soft skin on her wrist. "It's not a bad place to be."

"Not a bad place at all."

I stare into her eyes, and she doesn't flinch or look away as I memorize every shade of blue in their depths until I know that it's time to leave.

"I've got to go now," I whisper into the space between us.

She presses her lips together, and I wish I had the right to take her in my arms and kiss her until the chasm between us closes as if it never existed.

But I know now that our chapter is closed for good.

"I know," she whispers back.

Slowly, I lift her hand from the table. Bringing it up, I press my lips to her delicate knuckles, listening to her sharp intake of breath as I graze her flesh tenderly. Releasing her, I rise from the seat. Her gaze rises with me. My heart is too full to speak again. Turning away without another word, I step toward the sidewalk. I take a few steps and then freeze. I look over my shoulder, my voice husky as the words float across the short distance between us. She's watching me with a mournful expression.

"Ava, I'm moving back to Aurora tomorrow. It's time I go home." The thought of leaving her behind again crushes my soul, but I know that it's time for our paths to part for good.

She fumbles for words, her hands lifting to wipe away the tears rolling down her cheeks. "Will you be back?"

We both know I won't, but I can't leave things like that between us. Not with all the history existing in the gorge of our broken relationship. "Of course I will," I reply cheerily. "I've got to come back for Shelly's book club, after all." I wink behind my glasses and grin at her with a lightheartedness I don't feel.

"Good," she replies, pretending to match my cheerful tone, even as another tear trails along the path of the others. "I'll be there too."

I don't stay because if I do, I don't think I'll be able to leave tomorrow. I flash her another smile and turn away, forcing my unwilling feet to follow the sidewalk. My heart is ripping in two, but I remind myself it's for the best. I've surrendered my future to God, and I can't go back on my word.

My mission to explore the city now abandoned, I'm nearly back at my apartment before I pull my phone from my pocket and open the Blind Date with a Book Nerd app.

Locating the message thread, I type out a quick message and send it off: *Hey, this is random, and we've never officially been matched since we connected through the forum, but I'd like to put a face to the name. Would you be up for a blind date tonight?*

A sensation of peace mixed with trepidation comes over me. It's time to let go. I'm ready to accept that the future I wanted isn't the path God has for me. Lifting my head, I straighten my shoulders and smile at the next person I see.

It's all going to be okay.

My phone alerts me to a new message: *I'd like that. Today has been a rough one, and I could use a friend tonight.*

31

Ava

Dawson blurs in my vision as he walks away. He's . . . moving? Just as quickly as he reentered my life, he's leaving. Just like that.

After breaking up with him years ago, I never expected to see him again, let alone spend copious amounts of time together over the last few months. Saying goodbye to him because I thought it was for the best was hard, but this? To put into words the intensity of the wave of emotion his announcement sparks would be impossible. If I had to try, I would say that all at once, it's devastating, and yet I feel a sense of hope. It's understandable and yet completely bewildering.

Could it be that Dawson was only ever meant to teach me the truths he has? Was that his divinely appointed role in my life? Was he brought into my path to point me to Jesus' love without a romance in our future? Surely, this can't be the end?

The sun washes over me as I close my eyes to keep my composure. I stay in my seat on the patio outside of the bagel shop. I need a few minutes to gather my thoughts before I attempt to walk home. I just wanted a bagel to celebrate the fact that I took a Friday off for the first time in over a year.

I thought that when I told Dawson I wanted to make us work, he would pull me into his arms and kiss me and keep kissing me until we made up for all the years we missed. I thought my profession of love was a chance for us to start again. But the ball has been in his court since, and I don't see Dawson picking it up anytime soon.

Especially since I've now discovered that we won't be living in the same city anymore.

It's hard not to feel desperate. I feel my future slipping out of my fingers, and I want to beg and plead with him to risk loving me again.

I breathe, willing back the tears, and remind myself that when I feel out of control, that's a moment when I can practice surrendering to the Lord and accepting His perfect plan for me. Acceptance has been the theme of my life lately, and this feels no different. I'm learning to accept what comes and what goes while remembering that my worth isn't defined by either. And I'm learning with acceptance comes trust. The trust that God is holding everything together, even (and especially) when it feels like it's all falling apart. At least with that trust comes comfort.

Even now, I remind myself that in the ups and downs and in-betweens, Jesus is enough.

Tears abated, my eyes flutter open. I don't know how long I've been sitting with a now-unappetizing chocolate bagel in front of me. Dawson is entirely gone from view.

Will I ever see him again?

My phone *dings* with a notification and brings my focus back to the present. I stare down at the message on my screen.

After the launch party, when everything seemed to come to a screeching halt between us, I didn't delete the Blind Date with a Book Nerd app. Checking it daily and browsing the forums for interesting conversations between book lovers has been a comfort, and hanging out in a space that Dawson created is nostalgic and wistful. Plus, I've had some great conversations with its lovely members, all of whom are passionate and knowledgeable about books.

Though I see new match suggestions popping up daily, I ignore them all, keeping my profile toggled over to "Waiting to Turn the Page." But a part of me feels as if I haven't quite fulfilled my duty to my friend. I was supposed to give him feedback on five blind dates.

Those Super-Blind-Date-With-A-Book-Nerd-Improvement-Team-Sessions. The memory of Dawson's ridiculous name for them makes me laugh despite myself. Sharing my thoughts on the workings of the app was special to me. It was our deal, and I realize now it was just a way we contrived to spend more time together.

After our falling out, I didn't get around to going out on my fifth and final date. I don't know if Dawson has gone on any since we haven't spoken in weeks.

I stare at the invitation to go on a blind date tonight, wondering if it's time.

"I don't know, Lord," I whisper the prayer. "I don't want to make the wrong decision here, but I also don't want to ignore something You are trying to show me."

I wait, my fingers hesitating over the keys. Finally, I type my reply.

There's something deeply satisfying in knowing that at least I'll be able to fulfill my promise to him. Not that Dawson is exactly desperate for my feedback at this point. The app is blowing up and going viral from what I can see, which thrills me for him.

But it's time to close this final chapter of ours. And I feel at peace because I know it's all going to be okay.

—

Hours later, I slip a bookmark into my current read and rifle through my closet for something to wear on tonight's date.

All I can hope is that whoever this guy is, he won't be in a Gollum costume.

After trying on three different outfits and finding all of them to be terrible, the pull toward my Nancy Meyers' day dress can no longer be ignored. The white cotton frock hangs delicately in my closet, reminding me poignantly of Dawson and our day for the memory books. The dress also reminds me of hope and unconditional love.

I slip it over my head and look in the mirror. A smile tugs at my lips. It drapes over me with just as much grace as the first time I wore it. Though the earliest parts of the day are beginning to feel as if they are transitioning into fall, it's still a warm summer night, so something flowy and cool will be just the thing to keep me comfortable. This time, though, I'll switch out the sneakers for a cute pair of chunky sandals just to dress it up.

I check my phone for any updates, but my date still hasn't sent the location he wants to meet. All I know is that we're meeting around seven. While I'm at it, I glance at my texts too. Still nothing from my mom. Her trip to the ER proved to be nothing serious, according to my sister. The doctors had found nothing wrong.

The last few weeks have been turmoil, trying to make things right with her but realizing there's no fixing what I never broke. The ball is in her court now. I let her know how much I'd love for us to have a healthy relationship. I also insisted that it is time for boundaries, honesty, and respect to be essential foundations of our relationship. My message was read, but she never responded. My phone calls are sent to voicemail.

I don't know what else to do, but even within that lost feeling, I'm able to recognize the small victories. I've started therapy. My mother's control over my emotions has lessened. What used to send me into a tailspin, physically making me feel ill with shame and guilt for days, no longer does. I feel a bit lighter, a bit more hopeful, and a bit like I'm taking a deep breath for the first time in a long time.

And boy, does it feel good to breathe.

I blast a playlist of uplifting music as I fix my hair and makeup. Just as I finish the look, I snap a bloom from the bouquet on my dressing table and tuck a daisy behind my ear. It feels appropriate, somehow, like a wink to my former self.

By the time I'm ready, my date has finally messaged me back with instructions: *Meet me at the Battery Maritime Building at seven p.m.? How does a ferry ride and dinner on Governor's Island sound? I've never been and have always wanted to explore over there.*

The idea sounds next to perfect. I type a response: *I've never been there, either, which is shocking after having lived here for so many years. See you soon.*

We send a few more messages, hashing out the details of the evening. I've insisted upon at least paying for my own ferry ticket while he insists on picking up the dinner tab. Not exactly a fair trade-off, but he was bent on paying for everything, so at least I'll be contributing a measly few dollars.

Still amused by the exchange, I pick out a jacket for when the evening chill creeps in and head out the door.

—

The historic Battery Maritime Building looms before me, and for a moment, I feel like a tourist in my own city. There's an underlying thrill to that feeling, and I walk with a bounce in my step, as though I'm about to fall in love for the first time. Not necessarily with a person, but with possibility and history and something new I've never seen.

The sign for the Governor's Island Ferry directs me to the correct building. A line slowly shuffles through the entrance of slip seven. With my ticket displayed, I hold up my phone screen and show the ticket monitor, who waves me through.

On the dock, I let the other passengers pass me and watch as they scurry onto the awaiting ferry. A waterfront breeze tickles my face and blows loose strands of hair from my braid. I check my phone again. It's five until seven, and I don't see anyone who looks as if he is waiting to meet someone. Everyone around is either already in a pair or a group. Maybe I missed a message, and my date is already on board?

But there isn't a new message waiting for me. I sigh. If I'm ghosted tonight, then so be it. Tonight will be a journey just for me.

Confidently, I take a few strides toward the boat. My heart is more buoyant than it has been in ages. Perhaps this is what true freedom feels like. Being out by yourself with the wind in your hair and the open harbor stretching before you as it leads out to sea.

"Thank you, Jesus," I murmur.

"Ava?"

My steps toward the boat falter on the wooden ramp. I glance up toward the sky. "Jesus?" I say it aloud, half-expecting a deep and tender voice to answer me from beyond the blue.

But instead of a voice, a gentle hand lands on my shoulder and spins me around.

And my heart splits open as everything around me stills.

Dawson stares at me in disbelief. He is dressed casually, in a pair of khakis cuffed at the ankle, a white t-shirt, and white tennis shoes. The look reminds me of his college style, and I instantly approve. Yanking his glasses off his face, he uses the bottom of his t-shirt to polish the lenses before he slides them back on and peers at me.

If he is feeling anything remotely similar to what I'm feeling right now, we're both going to need a minute to pick our jaws off the floor.

Ferry passengers scoot past us, their expressions reflecting their annoyance that we are blocking the ramp, but I can't bring myself to care.

Finally, I manage to choke out a few words. "What are you doing here?"

I watch him blink a few times. "I . . . um . . . I'm meeting a friend," he replies hesitantly. "Actually, I guess it's technically a blind date because I've been chatting with her on my app. Since I'm moving tomorrow, I figured I could spend my last night in the city exploring with a friend."

My heart thuds with a painful beat. So he is dating. I can't help the crushing sense of disappointment upon realizing that Dawson is well and truly moving on. I refuse to let myself cry on this ferry dock. What else could I expect, though? It's not like we're together.

"Why are you here?" Dawson continues in a wary tone when words fail me again.

"I don't know really." I shrug, realizing the words are true. "I just got to thinking about this summer and our deal to go out on five dates." A rueful smile spreads over my lips as I see the humor in the situation. "We never quite finished those dates, so here I am. Chalk it up to not quite being ready to let go," I conclude softly.

"So . . . you're here on a blind date?" By the twist of his lips and the pulling together of his eyebrows, I don't think he is happy at the thought.

I stare at him, hoping he'll say something to stop me, anything to tell me he still cares. And then my heart falls again because I remember he is here on a date too. She's probably going to show up any minute, and I'll have to live with the sight of them together, just like my nightmarish vision weeks ago.

"Yeah, I guess I am." My shoulders fall, and the only thing that stops me from collapsing on the floor is a sudden, funny thought. A small puff of air escapes me. The accidental double-date debacle when we both showed up to the same restaurant runs through my mind. "Wait. Don't tell me we've done it again. I mean, running into you on a date once was a fluke. But twice? Come on. We're a little too in sync,

Hayes." I don't want him to know how much it hurts, so I keep my voice light and my smile wide.

"Ava, what is the name of your date?" Dawson blurts the question out suddenly, catching me off guard.

"Uh, I don't know. I assume I'll find that out when he gets here. We never actually matched on the site, but just got to talking about books." I look over my shoulder, searching the onboarding passengers for anyone who could remotely be the person I've been chatting with. I would even take Gollum at this point, just to escape this uncomfortable encounter with some of my dignity intact.

Is this how it's going to be when we run into each other from now on? He's with someone, I'm with someone, but we're never with each other.

"That is the point of a blind date, after all." I make one more attempt to save myself with humor because if Dawson keeps looking at me like that with those gorgeous hazel eyes behind those adorkable glasses, I'm going to lose it.

"Ava, is *Dune* military or space opera science fiction?"

"Space opera, Daws. Why does it matter?" I reply with a sudden bloom of annoyance in my chest. I scan the crowd again, desperately hoping a pair of eyes will connect with mine.

"Ava, what's the name of the science fiction trilogy written by C.S. Lewis?"

"*The Space Trilogy.*" My gaze cuts to him sharply. There's a distant call from the deck for final boarding, but suddenly, nothing seems to exist outside of the man standing in front of me. He moves a step closer, closing the distance between us. Dawson's gold-flecked eyes dance in the evening light, and as I memorize their magic, something triggers a deep well of understanding in me.

"Ava, what's my favorite classic science fiction book of all time?" He whispers the question in a husky tone as if he, too, is afraid of the answer.

Tears spark in my eyes, overflowing immediately onto my cheeks. Only a few inches remain between us now.

"*20,000 Leagues Under the Sea*," my whisper matches his. The words are whipped away by the wind off the harbor, but he hears them, and a light clicks on in his face.

"Dawson, are you—" I can't even say it.

"'Classic Book Hero Guy?'" His head dips, his expression sheepish yet full of hope.

When I throw myself into his arms, he catches me . . . He has always caught me, even when I didn't know I was falling. As he wraps his arms tightly around my waist, I don't think he'll ever let go.

"How can it . . . Wait." I pull back, confused. "Did you know? Did you know the whole time?"

"Of course not." He shakes his head in vehement protest.

"But your whole algorithm, the matchmaking software . . . this whole thing started with you manipulating our answers to match. I thought you were . . . you're Lord of the Book Nerds. I don't understand why you'd be—"

"I made a second account to test the matches made on my first account after I altered all of my initial contrived account parameters."

"Oh. Wow." I can't take my eyes off his lips.

"And how does it happen to be that you started posting chats under a brand-new account?"

I dip my head toward him, chagrin on my face. "I made a new account after our first blind date. I wanted to experience the site's design without wondering if you were spying on me on the backend.

"And then I stumbled across the forums, and I had this idea . . . I wanted to read the science fiction novels you love so that I could understand why you loved them, the way you read *Gatsby* so you could understand my love for it. I thought if I read those sci-fi books, we could talk about them when we met up about the app, and I'd get more time with you. And the account who answered me was so kind and knowledgeable . . ."

Dawson watches me carefully. I continue, "With you telling me you're moving and then receiving the date invite only a short while later, I thought maybe it was a sign . . ."

He stares at me with a look that I can't read.

"But you had to know it was me. You have access to all that information."

He shakes his head, and I watch his gaze dart down to my mouth, then back up again. His voice is a raspy whisper, and I have to lean in to hear it before the wind whips it away. "I never knew. I just answered a random forum post asking for recommendations for the best classic science fiction books. I promise that is all."

His face is serious, filled with an earnest fervor. A mist covers his eyes. He pushes a hand through his hair, mussing it up in the most adorable way. "I promised you, remember? I kept my word. I would never break a promise to you because . . ."

"I love you."

"I love you."

We say the words in unison just as a foghorn blows in the distance and a call for last boarding fills the air. But nothing can hide the loud and wild ticking of my heart.

"I love you," I whisper again. "I mean it, Daws. Triple prom. I really do."

His arms grow tighter around me. My hands clasp the back of his neck. My words are a passionate murmur straight from my heart.

"You can't deny that life and technology—or more to the point, God—keeps throwing us together. I don't want our chapter to close. I want to open to a blank page and keep writing and writing and writing until we've filled enough pages to last a lifetime."

He leans over me, his voice sending shivers dancing across my skin. "I've never wanted anything more than to be with you, Ava Fox. Triple prom."

I shake my head, clinging tighter to him. "I'm so sorry it took me so long to see it. I was too scared to take a leap of faith on us. But I trust God, and I trust you. And honestly, that's more than enough for me."

His lips twist into a question, and he squints at me behind his glasses. "I guess, maybe my app—"

"Really is a success." I interrupt and can't help the grin that spreads over my face.

Our tangled words end in matching smiles, beams of golden light as the sun narrows the space between earth and sky. Everything around us seems to fade, and all I can see is him. When he draws me closer, our breath mingles in the balmy summer air. And when our lips finally meet, it's as if a silent symphony is being written in our hearts, like "a tuning fork that had been struck upon a star," as the scribe eloquently wrote. When his lips press against mine, their touch is passionate yet tender, brand-new yet familiar, and I know, without a shadow of a doubt, that I want to spend the rest of my life writing a love story with this man.

When he finally pulls away, Dawson rests his forehead against mine. Our chests rise and fall with the urgency of our breath. Excitement, anticipation, and the sweet relief of peace dance within my heart. I want to laugh. I want to sing. I want to dance across the water like a shooting star.

He's my home, and I'm never leaving it again.

"You two lovebirds can do that on deck, can't you?" The captain calls from the boat. "Final chance to climb aboard!"

Pulling away, a grin spread from ear to ear, Dawson weaves his fingers with mine and looks at me with a question on his face. "Ava," he says gravely, "will you go on a date with me?"

"Yes, yes, a thousand times, yes," I reply.

As the foghorn sounds a final time, we sprint together toward what I know is the start of our forever.

Epilogue

Dawson

"Dawson, she's not here. We can't find her anywhere."

My sister rushes into the foyer of my childhood church with the hem of her blue silk dress gathered in her hand. Anne's usually collected demeanor is frazzled, her mahogany waves tumbling haphazardly around her shoulders. Frantically, she approaches Andrew and me, where we stand waiting for the signal that it is time to proceed down the aisle.

"What do you mean you can't find her?" I demand, stepping forward. My nerves are already frayed, and her announcement only sparks greater urgency in the pit of my stomach.

Anne pauses, the clatter of her heels loud on the wooden floor. "I mean, after Mom prayed over her with all of us, she went to put the finishing touches on her dress, and the next thing we knew, she wasn't in the dressing room. Or anywhere, for that matter. Charlie, Mom, Josephine, Lucy, and I have been running all over for the last fifteen minutes looking for her."

She pauses to catch her breath before continuing, "They didn't want to tell you yet, but I thought you should know. You know . . . just in case . . ."

Her sentence breaks off unfinished. Andrew looks at me, his expression simultaneously worried and pretending to be unconcerned.

"I'm sure it's nothing, bro." He claps me on the shoulder. "She probably just stepped out for some fresh air before the ceremony."

His voice is nonchalant, but all three of us know exactly what thoughts are running through my brain. I'm supposed to be marrying the woman of my dreams within the next ten minutes.

If she shows up, that is.

"We have time," I say, falsely confident.

As a trio, we glance up at the large wooden clock on the far wall. Five minutes to go.

Inside the small sanctuary of the tiny Aurora church that my family has called their church home for nearly two decades are a few people we love, my childhood pastor, our church organist, and so many colorful, blooming flowers it looks like the room has been turned into a flower market. Their sweet scent wafts out to the small foyer.

Ava and I are getting married today. I feel as if I've been walking on a cloud for two weeks, and I often have to stop and shake myself to see if I'm only just dreaming. It turns out that real life can feel like a dream too.

I'll never forget the moment that I realized "Never Met a Classic I Didn't Like" was somehow—through a twist that I can only attribute to the Lord Himself—my very own Ava. It was no wonder the conversations that started as merely classic science fiction book talk on the Blind Date with a Book Nerd forum felt so natural and . . . right. Discovering that she posted the question that initiated the two of us connecting specifically to be able to read the books she knew I loved warms my heart every time I think of it.

That moment on the tour boat dock when we realized we both showed up on the same blind date with each other *again* changed us forever. After that moment, there was no way I was letting her out of my sight. It was obvious to both of us that letting each other walk away again would be the worst mistake of our lives. When we simultaneously blurted out our desire to marry each other as the sun set over the water, it took all we could do not to run to the justice of the peace first thing in the morning to tie the knot.

For the sake of our families and closest friends, we delayed and planned this small ceremony for only a couple of weeks later.

Unless Ava has changed her mind.

I turn to Andrew with a helpless expression, a jarring sense of déjà vu taking hold. The moment in London years ago when I realized Ava wasn't coming, and instead, I held a devastating letter in place of the woman I loved, comes roaring back with painful clarity.

I refuse to let the memory play through my mind, refuse to even let the feelings of regret, disappointment, and inadequacy take hold. Andrew and Anne linger with awkward expressions, waiting for feedback from me on our next move.

Lord, please be with Ava right now, wherever she is. The

silent prayer is instinctive, a brief call for help to the only One who knows all that we've been through together. *If she is struggling right now, please comfort her and lift her up with the knowledge that she is a beloved daughter of God, chosen, redeemed, and sanctified. In the name of Jesus, thank you. Amen.*

Just as I'm about to speak, Lucy comes rushing in, her eyes wide. "Ava is in the garden," she yells, the newly formed empty space in her front row of teeth giving her a pronounced lisp. "She's crying!"

"Is she okay?"

Lucy shrugs and lifts her hands. "She said she can't right now."

"Can't what?"

Lucy shrugs again.

Anne starts forward. "I'll go—"

"No." Stretching out a hand, I stop my sister. "I'll go."

She stares at me with a distressed expression written across her freckled cheeks. "But you're not supposed to see—"

My tone is firm. "It's going to be okay, Anne. This is more important. I've got this."

When I glance at Andrew for validation, he gives me a single nod and motions me toward the door. "I'll go in and let everyone know it'll be a little while."

When I step into the sunshine, the soft warmth of the early autumn day plays across my face. Turning my steps toward the prayer garden and small community orchard that the congregation maintains to provide fruit and vegetables for anyone in need, each stride emphasizes the prayer for wisdom that swirls around my heart as I make my way toward my bride-to-be.

When I get closer, Ava's tall, willowy form is visible,

moving slowly through the trees. I catch a glimpse of white fabric draped around her. Even from afar, I admire the graceful way she walks. It's as if each step reflects the buoyancy of walking on a fluffy cloud. It's the same way she has always walked through life, with grace, dignity, and unwavering gentleness.

I'm so proud of her. She has grown leaps and bounds in a short matter of time. But I know that old habits die hard, and as I walk down the row of apple trees in pursuit of her, I can only hope that the woman I love isn't struggling again.

If she is, though, I know what to do now. I'll hold her and whisper words of life and love into her ear until the light of God's truth banishes the darkness from her heart and mind.

She doesn't turn around at my approach, so I speak softly to avoid startling her. "Hey, beautiful, whatcha doin' out here?"

Ava spins to face me, and her features light up with a smile as those crystalline blue eyes lock with mine. There's a cell phone pressed to her ear, but I barely register it as my breath catches sharply in my throat at the sight of her. Swallowing hard, I take in every detail of the woman I asked to marry me only a couple of weeks ago but who has owned my heart for nearly a decade.

The only word to describe her is breathtaking. When I told her to spare no expense in planning the wedding of her dreams, she told me that she only wanted a quiet day to celebrate our love with our families and closest friends. No extravagant or glamorous wedding details will be broadcast to the world. Instead, we're having the ceremony at my childhood church and a quiet reception back at my parents' house.

It's the opposite of what I always imagined the posh and elegant Ava Fox would want, the opposite of the life I thought I had to earn for her to be worthy of her love. And I love this version of Ava even more deeply than I ever imagined possible. I don't have to strive and struggle to fit into her world. Instead, we're just two people in love who want more than anything to finally belong to each other.

I take in every detail of my bride-to-be. A simple white silk dress adorns her frame, draping to the ground like a silken waterfall over her willowy curves. Her golden hair is gathered into a voluminous braid and drawn over her shoulder. Tiny pearls have been woven through the thick plaits of her hair, and tucked behind her ear is a single daisy, which matches the simple bouquet of the same flower in her hand.

My Daisy.

I stop and stare at her with my jaw on the floor, aware that my eyes must look like saucers behind my glasses, but not caring in the slightest. Seeing her before me and knowing that in just a few minutes, I'll claim the woman I never thought would be mine again takes my breath away.

Her soft voice speaks smoothly into the phone, and I fade out of my mesmerized admiration long enough to register what she is saying.

"Well, I'm sorry to hear that she's upset, Tashi, but I'm not going to leave my wedding to rush to the hospital just to find out that I'm not even on Mom's visitor list."

Ava listens, one hand twirling the end of her braid absently. I watch carefully for any signs that this phone call is causing her distress. I've only recently become aware of the toxicity of her relationship with her mother and the burden that taking much of the responsibility for her emotional care had placed on Ava's shoulders.

I'm still finding out so much that happened just before the end of our relationship and through all our years apart, and things are coming to light that I know will need the healing hand of our loving Heavenly Father to fully repair. But one thing I've made clear to Ava in no uncertain terms is the fact that she no longer has to face her mother alone. If I see that she or any of her other family members are attempting to make her their punching bag again, I'll be the one to step in.

Because that's what husbands do.

"I have to go, Tashi. I'm sorry you and Mom can't make it today. Yes, Dad is here. He flew in this morning, and I think he said he'd like to catch dinner with you before he heads back. I'll tell him you said hello. Take care."

Ava ends the phone call, and less than a second later, she is in my arms. Her face is buried in my shoulder, and we're laughing, but I don't think either of us knows exactly why. Joy, I suppose.

When she pulls back to stare up at me, I look down regretfully at her full, pink lips. "I want to kiss you right now, but I don't want to mess up your makeup," I admit.

Without hesitation, she rises slightly on her toes to press her lips to mine with a shy and delicate softness. It's a kiss filled with all the wonder and exploration of something that is still almost brand-new, yet there's also the feeling that our hearts never let us forget what the gentle swell of her lips felt like against mine, and only time and distance have made us out of practice.

"If you want to kiss me, I don't think a bit of lipstick should stop you," she laughs softly against me. "After all, we are going to be married in just a few short minutes."

"The wedding is still on, then?" I ask, letting a teasing lilt slip through my tone but watching her carefully for any signs of stress. "You aren't out here planning your escape?"

"Goodness, no." The humor fades from her face, replaced by an earnest expression. "Dawson, is that what you thought? Is that why you came out here? My sister just called, and it's easier to process it all in private. She and Mom won't be able to make it today. Mom needed to get checked out by her doctor."

"Do you need to go see her?" My eyebrow lifts. "Is there an emergency?"

"No." She shakes her head. "I told Natasha that I'll check on Mom later. Probably after the honeymoon if I'm being honest . . ."

I study her face to see if the disappointment of her mom's absence from her wedding is present, but it doesn't seem like she is sad. Rather, she seems lighter than I've ever seen her. Recently, the heaviness that sometimes seemed to linger over her like a dark cloud has disappeared. There is a new spring in her step that I can only think is the result of her happiness.

Ava grins up at me. "You know, you really weren't supposed to see me in my dress before the ceremony."

She smacks my shoulder playfully, but I only tighten my arms around her waist, pulling her closer, my expression instantly going somber.

"You mean this stunning ensemble? I don't think I would have made it a single minute more anyway," I murmur in a deadpan tone. "Have I told you yet that this is my favorite outfit you've ever worn?"

She throws back her head and laughs, the curve of her creamy throat begging to be kissed. "I'm pretty sure you've said that about everything I've ever worn."

I don't break. "And it's been the truth every time. You are stunning. Though, I don't think it's the clothes I love so much."

Her eyes glisten with sudden tears, and her face grows serious. "Dawson Hayes, you are the missing piece my heart was seeking for so long."

The words are a whisper for my ears only. Their hum reverberates in my chest, swelling it with gratitude.

"Well, you *and* Jesus." She smiles through the tears. "I won't do life without either of you."

"Ditto to that, darling," is the only response I can muster.

"Shall we stop keeping the good people waiting and go get married?" she asks, smiling as she turns her face up, seeking another kiss. "Oh, wait, before I forget. One more thing."

She presses herself into my chest, pulling my arms tighter around her. Turning toward the church, she lifts her phone up to eye height, and I realize the camera is on.

"Before we go in . . . I was planning on sending out a message for all my bookish followers before I walked down the aisle to share something on my heart, but it's even better now that you are here! Will you make a pre-wedding video with me?"

As if I could ever refuse her. Her enthusiasm is contagious, and I'm grinning like a fool when she starts recording. Her sweet voice fills the orchard.

"Hey, Foxy Book Family, meet my husband! In T-minus

ten minutes, anyway. We just wanted to commemorate this moment because real life really does have love stories that are just like the books. For so long, I searched for happiness in a world filled with shallow glitz and glamour. I wanted my bookish knight in shining armor to come along and scoop me up, but I thought that a relationship like the ones I've read about in books would always elude me.

"Little did I know that my own hero was waiting just on the other side of the Blind Date with a Book Nerd app. Except our story has a far happier ending than any book I've ever read because it is rooted and grounded in something that has stood the test of time and goes beyond the pale of this shallow world.

"If parts of your story make you doubt your worthiness for a fairy-tale ending, don't stop fighting for the truth. And that truth is this: You are a beloved child of God, made worthy by the Hero of the greatest love story ever told. Love you, bookish family! We'll see you on the other side of the sunset."

She ends the video and holds out her hand to me. The simple diamond ring I presented to her as an engagement ring sparkles on her finger. Joy, hope, and anticipation play across her face as I take her slender hand in my own.

"Well, Miss Fox, are you finally ready to become Mrs. Hayes?" I lift her hand to my lips and press a tender kiss to her knuckles.

Her eyes shine with tears that I am sure will be shed many times throughout this night together. "I think I was born ready. Who would have thought a book lovers' dating app would create this much happiness? I'm so grateful."

"Not as grateful as I am that you chose to be a part of it.

How can I ever thank God enough for what He has done for us?"

She lifts her face to mine for a last, lingering kiss before we become man and wife. "That I don't know. But what I do know is: I'm more than ready to walk by your side on this journey He has written for us."

With that, we run toward the soft, hazy sunlight that is just beginning to dip toward the spire of the old church rising in the distance.

Acknowledgments

As the second book we've co-authored together, *Blind Date with a Book Nerd* was an incredible delight to write. It allowed us the space to truly marvel at what it means to be free in Christ and how deeply cared for we are as God's beloved creation.

If you, dear reader, have ever felt the crushing weight of the enemy's lie that you are valueless, unworthy, or unlovable, we hope that you close these pages with the reminder that YOU matter and that the burdens you carry can be laid at the foot of the Cross. No matter your social status, wardrobe, looks, job title, or follower count, your worth doesn't change—regardless of what the world says. Jesus is enough in every circumstance, and we pray that you know your true identity resides in Him and His love for you.

To Kim Griffin and Victoria Dixon, thank you for the valuable feedback you provided as our alpha-readers. We're so grateful for both of you! To our incredible community of book lovers, our promotional team, and our ARC readers, once again, thank you. Your support and enthusiasm for our work brings us immense joy.

Erica and Britt

Britt's Acknowledgments

When my fellow author and dearest friend, Erica Dansereau, and I set about writing a series celebrating our love for books and romance, I don't think we knew what a marvelous adventure was about to take place. Erica, I couldn't ask for a better co-author. Writing with you is such a joy and a privilege. You keep me both grounded and inspired. Creating *Blind Date with a Book Nerd* with you was so much fun. I can't wait to see where our literary adventures take us next!

To the most encouraging, supportive, and uplifting community of readers an author could ask for: Thank you! Writers are often told that writing a book is a lonely and solitary endeavor, but I've never found it so. I know that anytime I need the encouragement and strength to move forward, I always have a community of the most lovely, insightful readers to cheer me on, book lovers who will discuss every detail of a story with me and obsess over the characters we love.

To Joe, the sweetest and most supportive husband anyone could ask for. I could never write a love story that wasn't influenced by your witty humor, selfless generosity, faith-filled wisdom, and love that feels like sunshine. Thank you for being my best friend. I love you.

Erica's Acknowledgments

We did it again, Britt! Writing with you is such a blessing. This co-authoring endeavor is something I will forever treasure. Thank you for laboring with love alongside me to bring this story to life, for your talented writing, editing, and cover design skills, and for always being willing to "pivot" when needed. You are a gem. Here's to the next book(s) in The Bookish Romance Series!

To my friends and family, you are irreplaceable lights in my life. What a gift your presence is to me. Thank you for your love and support. I love you all so much.

To my bookish community of fellow readers and writers, I thank you for inspiring me to fall more in love with books every day. Words are powerful tools, carrying the strength to change lives and touch hearts, and we are all privileged to have access to so many incredible works of literature. I will never take this ability to write and publish for granted.

To Patrick, the best husband I could ever ask for, you remind me daily that my worth and identity is found in Christ alone. The way you love me and our children is the greatest blessing in my life. Thanks for loving us like Jesus. I love you.

To my children, may you always remember that you are loved beyond measure. May you always walk with confidence in who God created you to be. May you always press forward and shine the love of Jesus to those around you. Mommy loves you.

Also available in The Bookish Romance Series
by Erica Dansereau and Britt Howard

The Bookish Bandit (TBR Book One)

To stay up to date with Britt:
Website: www.britthoward.com
Instagram: @britthowardauthor

Also available from Britt Howard

Song of the Valley, a Christian contemporary Western
romance and the first book in the *McCade Family Series*

To stay up to date with Erica:
Website: www.ericadansereau.com
Instagram: @ericadansereauauthor

Also available from Erica Dansereau

Come Forth As Gold, a Christian historical fiction romance
and the first book in *The Gold Series*

After the Water Brooks, a Christian historical women's fiction
and the second book in *The Gold Series*

About the Authors

Britt Howard's goal as a writer is to create a thrilling tale that merges all the best parts of literature with a story that ultimately leads readers to a deeper relationship with God. She makes her home in Idaho with her husband and a very cute dog. Whenever she is not editing books for other authors or writing (or reading) new love stories, she heads to the mountains to recharge in nature.

Erica Dansereau is an award-winning author known for her compelling storytelling and deep exploration of faith. She currently resides in Idaho with her husband and children. Aside from reading and writing books, Erica loves spending quality time with her family and friends, embarking on new adventures, and savoring a nice cup of coffee or tea.

Made in United States
Troutdale, OR
09/25/2024

23100490R00235